DARK BADGER

SAVAGE LAW: BOOK 7

DARK BADGER

SAVAGE LAW: BOOK 7

KIRBY JONAS

Cover design by Clay Jonas

Howling Wolf Publishing
Pocatello, Idaho

Howling Wolf Publishing
1611 City Creek Road
Pocatello ID 83204

For more information about Kirby's books, check out:

Facebook, at: www.facebook.com/kirbyjonasauthor/

Or email Kirby at: **pocatellocowboy@gmail.com**

Manufactured in the United States of America—*One nation, under God*

Publication date in electronic format for this edition: April 2023
Jonas, Kirby, 1965—
Savage Law 7: Dark Badger / by Kirby Jonas.

ISBN: 978-1-891423-45-1
Library of Congress Control Number:

To learn more about this book or any other Kirby Jonas book, email Kirby at **www.facebook.com/kirbyjonasauthor/**

To my friend, William Hardisty "Ioway"
"SASS 214"

You've been with me longer than
almost any of my readers.
Thank heavens for that trip to Iowa!

CHAPTER ONE

♦ *14 February 1973* ♦
The night of Valentine's Day

The ebony eyes of Hunter Jack, known by the elders of the Northwest Shoshone tribe and anyone who followed the old ways as Dark Badger, could bore right through a man's skull and snip his brain loose at the stem.

In place of a normal nose, the center—more or less—of Hunter Jack's face had been fitted with the rusty blade of a Bowie knife after the same knife was used to carve out all the other features of his deep red-brown face, from the creases in his wide forehead to his heavy cheekbones and powerful jaw. But always, always, it was those ebony eyes a person would remember in waking dreams, or the nightmares that brought them out of their sleep in a cold sweat. Those eyes cast a spell; those eyes sized up an enemy like a frightened fox; those eyes seemed capable of bringing death without any assistance of the hands.

In the upper body, Jack was a wall of human flesh melded with red sandstone. His sloping shoulders had the breadth of a horse trough, and his arms the circumference of a mountain lion's forelegs. His gigantic hands were the fodder of legend. It was those bare hands that had won Hunter Jack an eight-year stint for manslaughter in the penitentiary in Boise, after he killed a man he had caught trying to rape his younger sister some twenty years earlier, two days after his eighteenth birthday. It was the height of irony that he had committed that crime with his bare hands and could easily do the same again, and yet Hunter Jack, like all other felons since the passage of the Gun Control Act of 1968, was not allowed to own a firearm.

Below his ribcage Hunter Jack was a wasp, with a waist like Scarlett O'Hara and thighs like red licorice whips. His feet were so small the word had gone about town like a fire creeping in the underbrush that the reason he only wore hand-made moccasins was to keep from having to shop for footwear in the women's or children's sections of McPherson's, in downtown Salmon.

Jack dressed in the old way—too traditionally in fact, in the eyes of many. Even some of his own people scoffed at him and laughed—always behind his back, because no one ever laughed in Hunter Jack's face, at least not when they were sober. In summer he wore hand-stitched calico shirts, and buckskin leggings with a wool breechclout, letting enough of his gluteus maximus show to push the indecent exposure law to its utmost limit. But no one seemed particularly interested in bringing it up with him.

In winter, he wore full buckskins, and on the coldest of days, if he ventured out, he wore a coat made from the hide of a cinnamon black bear, a luxurious coat that must weigh ten pounds, with the reddish-brown hair at its prime.

In all seasons he wore his beaded moccasins, and, in an elk skin sheath with porcupine quill work on it, a knife with a six-inch blade and a deer antler handle. He had used the antler of a mule deer buck he claimed to have jumped out of a tree onto the back of one December and stabbed to death with a knife—the very same blade that was now supported by the five-inch butt section of the buck's right antler.

Hunter Jack—Dark Badger—stood six-foot-two and came in around two hundred fifty pounds. He was an eighth of a ton of fury to handle sober and a rabid bear to try controlling when drinking anything with alcohol in its ingredients.

Jack started walking toward downtown from the Indian village on Highway 93, at the edge of town. With the ugly, bent tin thermometer outside his log cabin telling him the temperature stood right at zero degrees, it was one of his bearskin coat nights. And this time, over his slick black hair that hung a foot and a half down his back in a tightly braided ponytail, he also wore a hat constructed of the hide of a skunk. He had made the hat one time when he was sober out of a skunk he had killed when he wasn't. The story was that he had been jacked up on Thunderbird and Mad Dog 20/20, and while his friend Joe Teton drove his old pickup out through a harvested hay field in the middle of one late autumn night when skunks were putting on lots of sleek, heavy hair for winter, Hunter Jack was riding in the bed with a spotlight. They had spotted a huge skunk, exactly what they had been searching for, and Jack jumped out of the back of the pickup right onto the middle of its back and killed it, but at the cost of filling the air all around them with a noxious spray like garlic juice concentrate.

He insisted on riding back to the village inside the warm cab, and Joe Teton, who had to roll down his window and put his head out to drive, swore his truck when it was dry smelled like a skunk for three years, and when it got moisture inside the cab it still smelled like one to this day, six years later.

Somehow Hunter Jack hung onto his Shoshone traditional name of Dark Badger, while Joe Teton, even in his innocence in the whole incident, was known as Skunk Teton from that time on. This seemed a great shame to the citizenry of Salmon who were in the know about the incident, because while "Skunk Jack" didn't sound all that smooth, "Skunk Hunter" would have been poetic perfection.

With his full, beaded buckskin regalia and moccasins, his bearskin coat that reached to the middle of his thighs, beaver skin mittens, skunk hat, and his nose that looked like the blade of a fighting knife sticking out from the general middle of his wide-boned face, Hunter Jack looked like someone's myth of a blood-thirsty warrior . . . a Shoshone on the hunt for trouble that didn't always come in the form of a hapless skunk.

Mysterious truth is sometimes the mother of myths . . .

When Coal Savage returned home the night of Valentine's Day with little Sissy, it was only to try and leave her behind. He wanted to go by himself down to the river, him alone with the dark gray Old West gunfighter-style hat Maura PlentyWounds had personally crafted for him, and give that hat a burial at sea—or at least as close to the sea as he was likely to get any time soon.

He did finally manage to leave Sissy with his mother, who to no avail loudly protested Coal's leaving. Sam Browning and Alex Martinez were still in town until tomorrow—they were staying at the Stagecoach Inn—and after sending the hat to sea, what Coal needed was some good company—someone who didn't love Maura PlentyWounds almost as much as he did. And that cut out his entire family.

Ironically, when Coal pulled into the parking lot at the Stagecoach, the dark gray, flat-brimmed hat not only had not been sent off to sea in the River of No Return, but he was wearing it, and he wouldn't admit why—even to himself.

Coal knocked on Sam and Martinez's door at the Stagecoach. It was Martinez who pulled it open. He stared at Coal quizzically. "Well, hey, Coal. Nice hat! You look like you just walked out of the Old West."

"Thanks—I guess. Can I come in?"

Martinez got a concerned expression at Coal's blunt reply and stepped aside, waving him in. "Sure. Come be bored with us."

Sam Browning sat on one of the queen-size beds staring up at Coal. "What are you doin', Coal? It's freaking Valentine's Day. I won't say I don't want to be your valentine, but what about that chick you keep pining about?"

Coal drew a deep breath. "You boys want to go down to the most famous bar in the county? Shoot some pool?"

Sam and Martinez glanced at each other. Sam shrugged. Martinez shook his head at Sam and turned his eyes back to Coal. "Coal, you don't wanna do that. Sam isn't allowed to drink in public."

Sam giggled and lifted his muscular frame off the bed. "Oh, get off it. Coal wants to party." The big man turned his pale blue eyes on Coal, his short-cropped, frizzy pale blond hair sticking up like a dandelion backlit by the sun. Tall and bulging with vascular muscle, light of skin and blond of hair, Sam could have passed for Hitler's ideal example of what a man should look like.

Coal shook his head, and with his eyes he made the statement plain: *Don't even ask me about Maura.*

Sam made an understanding face and turned his eyes to Martinez. "All right, Q, so it seems Coal an' me are going out for a drink. You coming or you wanna stay here like an old woman an' suck your gums?"

One side of Martinez's mouth came up, more of a disgusted expression than one of humor. "I can already see how this night's gonna end. Let me get my jacket."

Annie Price lay on her couch with the television buzzing in her ears, but none of its drivel registered on her. Lying on her back in the dim light, she held Coal's note above her at arm's length and stared at it, an untouched half-full glass of Wild Turkey bourbon forgotten on the carpet by her side. She had read this hand-scrawled note from Coal fifty times, she was sure, but somehow she couldn't keep herself from reading it again. And again.

I'm just checking on you, Annie. I wanted to make sure you're doing okay. Coal

Was she trying to read between the lines? Did she simply want there to be something more in the note than there really was? Was she a desperate woman? It didn't even say *love, Coal.* Just *Coal.* Perhaps she really was that pathetic. But at least she hadn't succumbed to her yearning to call him. Mandy, the receptionist at the hospital, had told her Coal stopped by to see her. And thanks to this note she knew he had been here as well, not only *to* her house, but inside. That thought touched her almost more than anything, the fact that he had entered unlawfully to leave her this note. Who would do that if they didn't have at least some kind of feelings for another person?

Yet she knew, just like pretty much everyone else in this petty little town, that Coal had taken a fairly extensive road trip with the EMT Maura PlentyWounds, and that Maura had even been staying at the Savages' house. She also knew, from the rumors that ran like whirlwinds through Salmon, that Coal had slept at Maura's house—the two of them, alone. So why call him? Hadn't he made it plain where his heart lay? A man didn't simply go waltzing off on a cross-country trip with some woman he didn't have eyes for, and maybe even his cap set on. And he most certainly didn't invite her to come live at his house, or sleep over at hers.

So Annie lay there on the couch, now reading Coal's note for the fifty-first time, wishing she were drunk, or stoned. Or even dead. Why did she even care anymore?

Then she made the mistake of reading the note for the fifty-second time. After that was when she reached for the phone, spilling her Wild Turkey on the carpet and cursing her own clumsiness. While the bourbon was soaking into the pretty blue carpet, Annie was holding the phone in her left hand and using her middle finger to spin the dial.

All the while she kept cursing herself for knowing this phone number by heart, and thinking she should probably be using her middle finger to send a clear message to Coal instead of for dialing his number.

CHAPTER TWO

Joe Teton lay on a sofa—or at least what he, perhaps somewhat arrogantly, referred to as a sofa—with a Michelob in his right hand and a big, raw, red steak over his right eye. He had been whacked there good, and he had learned from an episode of *The Big Valley* that red meat would take down the swelling and possibly the discoloration as well. It might not really work, but whatever was good enough for fighting Nick Barkley, on *The Big Valley*, was good enough for Joe Teton.

The sofa Joe Teton lay on he had made himself, with pride. It consisted of two plywood boxes he had tacked together, to the top of which he had then glued three dung-yellow sofa cushions he had dug out of the city dump. A fat pillow tacked by the fabric at its edges to one end with four fencing staples completed this most showy piece of furniture in Joe's entire ramshackle abode.

The television was droning, but it wasn't *The Big Valley* or even *Gunsmoke,* so Joe didn't really care. He had on his mind only one thing, and that was the red-bearded little fool who was living up by the cemetery in a travel trailer, shacked up with a used-up little Bannock girl named Irene Boyer, whom he had collected at one of the local bars. The guy's name, as far as Joe knew, was Everett Sherman, and he made up for all his diminutive size and gauntness with a streak of mean at least one yard and two and a half inches wide.

Joe, who had lost all expectation of the use of his name the fateful night he allowed his best friend Hunter Jack to ride in his truck cab after getting potpourried by a skunk, sipped his beer, spilling some down both sides of his neck and knowing he would wish later he had that mouthful back. Lying on one's back isn't conducive to beer-drinking, he supposed, but he didn't have the energy or desire to sit up.

His dark, deep-set eyes ratcheted toward the TV. There sat his two little boys, Pete and Nathan, on their lower legs as if getting ready to pray. Their eyes were glued to the TV. He loved those little guys. Since his wife had succumbed to the nasty liver disease, they were all he had—unless of course he included a few other family members scattered loosely throughout the village or his friend Hunter Jack, who quite often wasn't much to lay claim to. There was also a striped gray cat the weight and shape of a bowling ball, a cat he called Cannon, and which occasionally wouldn't bite him—if he fed it enough soft food. Sometimes he thought idly of tossing Cannon in the Salmon River threaded onto a big iron hook to see what kind of monster steelhead he might drag out of the river's deepest holes. Other times, he thought of doing the same with Hunter Jack, but out in the ocean. He always gave up on the idea when he pictured trying to thread Hunter Jack onto a hook, though; he suspected Hunter might object.

Sometimes when Joe found himself looking at Pete and Nathan he wondered what he was going to do if he lost them. Even the thought that someday they would grow up and drift on made his stomach knot up tight enough to give him cramps. He liked to pretend he was one damn big tough Injun, but it was a sad lie; he would die the day his boys left home.

That was why he had lost his temper so bad earlier when that Everett guy came tearing through the Indian village in his pickup, with no regard for anyone else around, adult, child, or even wandering dogs, of which there were quite a few. And he didn't even have the common courtesy of running over Cannon.

He had then narrowly missed the boys as they were running across the street, then driven over the stretch of dirt Joe generously called his lawn, drunk as could be for certain. He momentarily got stuck on a stump Joe meant one day to soak with diesel and burn if he ever got bored with Westerns on TV. It was just enough time for Joe to run out and smash a big rock into Everett's driver's door.

Joe had to admit, for all Everett's minuscule size, he barreled out of that truck like a man twice his size. And he hit Joe in the eye with a balled-up fist way before Joe saw it coming, then kicked him square in the groin with his sharp-toed cowboy boot. He could probably really have done some damage then, since Joe could hardly see at that point. But he must have seen the crowd of tribal members building up around him and decided the better part of valor was to take his little Injun girl and flee to fight another day.

The thing was Everett couldn't flee far, or at least he wouldn't. Everyone around there knew he had moved in up by the cemetery and had gone so far as to pull the wheels off his travel trailer, which would take him a while to put back on. He had made himself at home up there.

So Joe Teton lay on his sofa watching his little boys stare at the TV and brooding about red-bearded Everett and Irene, and his blackening eye and aching crotch. That Everett was becoming a worse and worse nuisance. He was going to kill somebody before he was through. Joe felt it with all that was in him, and he prayed it wouldn't be Pete or Nathan.

Someday somebody was going to have to stop him. As Joe pulled the steak off his eye and touched the hurt place with soft fingertips, he winced. Someone was going to have to put a stop to red-bearded Everett's wild, drunken trips through the Indian village. And the honest-Injun truth was Joe really wished he could be the one . . .

* * *

Coal drove his friends and former partners downtown, where another pickup happened to be pulling away from the front of the Owl Club bar as he got there, and he sneaked into their parking spot, one of the few still available near the bar. He wasn't lucky in many things, but apparently when it came to finding parking places close to the bar he was about to go into to send his pathetic life plummeting toward certain destruction, Lady Luck adored him.

Before Coal could open his door, Martinez looked over at him. "Coal, are you sure you wanna do this? I'm not kidding. It's your last chance to back out." Sam had already thrown open his door, and he grunted at what he would consider his babysitter's stupidity, but to his credit, he didn't say anything.

"I'm a grown boy."

Martinez chuckled. "I never knew you to be a drinker. Are you sure you're all right?"

Tonight Coal wasn't anything that resembled all right, but he could never admit that to two tough guys like Martinez and Sam. Since losing Laura, he had fought as long and as hard as he could not to let himself fall for a woman. He knew better! He knew the heartache the first time had brought him—and was still bringing him. And then, when he finally succumbed and fell in love, and worse, was stupid enough to admit it to the object of that love, he found himself cut and bleeding, and the woman gone. No, for a fact he wasn't all right. He wasn't going to be all right for some time to come—or at least until he was sloppy drunk and lying in the bed of his pickup, while someone else drove his pointless carcass home like a sack of soured wheat.

"I'm good. I just want to celebrate feeling safe again."

Martinez grunted, ignoring some stupid comment Sam made from the other side. "Yeah. Safe. Funny. We're going out drinking alcoholic beverages with Vike Browning. I wouldn't exactly consider that safe."

Coal heard Sam giggling clear from the other side of the pickup as he got out and slammed his door. The sound echoed between the frozen canyon of the brick and wood buildings of Main Street.

Then, from out of the shadows, he saw a bear. Only it really wasn't a bear. It was but an old Shoshone acquaintance by the name of Dark Badger.

Annie Price cursed herself for reading Coal's note. She should have wadded it up and thrown it away. Of course she had no doubt Coal really cared about her. He had come that darkest of dark nights to check on her, and when he found her in a bad way he had stayed with her the entire night to comfort her and make sure she was safe. He had also gone out of his way to leave her this note, and he had stopped in at the hospital especially to see her. But caring for someone and loving them were two different things. And she didn't like feeling like anyone's charity case.

Yet here she was, driving toward town like an imbecile, looking for a man she had been ignoring now for some time to prove to him how independent she could be. He was going to know what a fool she was. And she did care—but she didn't.

Connie had told Annie Coal went to town to see some of his friends. Annie realized she didn't know Coal well enough even to know what friends he might have in town, but it didn't matter. Connie said they were staying at the Stagecoach Inn, so it was friends she wouldn't have known anyway.

And what did she plan on saying, or doing, when she got to the hotel and found Coal with his friends? He had obviously gone there to be with them because he had no reason to be with her. Why poke her nose in where it didn't belong? Why force herself on him simply because he cared enough to leave her a note, a note which, in all honesty, could have been written to his third-grade teacher, as far as any kind of romantic semblance went.

So why was she driving to town? Maybe because tonight of all nights, when she was feeling mentally healthy, when she was feeling whole again, she wanted to *be* with someone, not spend another heartbreaking night alone with her television and her empty, pathetic life. Besides, she had been too ready to turn to Wild Turkey tonight. It was a road she had been down long ago, she had conquered it, and she had no desire to be there again, not if she could find a true friend . . . a lover would be icing on the cake.

In and of itself, driving her glacier blue 1962 Buick LeSabre convertible sedan was therapeutic, even if it was zero degrees outside and dark. Perhaps that was all she needed: a good drive. Nighttime, daytime—what did it matter? It was the smooth feel of the wheel, the comfort of these seats, the hypnotic hum of the tires on the road. That was all she needed. She fondly recalled driving along the river road during the middle of the autumn before, a spectacular, incredible autumn of golden cottonwoods and fresh breezes and deep blue water, blissfully before she had ever heard of Coal Savage. The top was down, her hair blowing in the wind, and the world was her own heaven. She—

Annie swore. There was Coal's turquoise green GMC pickup, centered exactly in front of the Owl Club. If she had wondered how she could find him, if she had thought him unreachable tonight, she was wrong. And then she realized it was even worse. It wasn't only the pickup.

At first she didn't even know him, because he wore a different hat than normal. But there was Coal, in a group of men on the far side of the pickup, standing on the sidewalk between it and the front door of the Owl Club. "Damn you, Annie Price," she said, and she took the next left turn.

If she drove fast enough, maybe she could get back around the block before Coal vanished. And then she surely could find some spectacular way to make a royal fool of herself, not only in front of Coal, but in front of his friends as well.

Because love was blind, and no one was more blind than Annie Price in love.

It was local bar legend that Hunter Jack never smiled—unless he was eating someone's liver or jumping out of the back of a pickup onto a skunk or a deer. But Coal never put much store in legends, and especially not the one about Jack's smile. Although it was a little crooked, and hidden within the thatch of many scars, Hunter Jack always had a smile for Coal Savage.

And so he did tonight.

"Hey! Savage!" Jack's face lit up, and his stride swiftened. He came close to Coal and threw both hands out as if describing the last big fish he had caught. He looked Coal up and down. "Brother, I ain't seen you since the dinosaurs went extinct! What's up?"

"Hello there, Badger." For years, Coal had never called the Shoshone anything but that. "How are you?"

Jack threw out his right hand as Sam and Martinez eyeballed him with utter amazement, and when Coal shook it Jack cupped his right shoulder in that gargantuan left hand. "I'm great, bud. Spectac'lar, even! You like my hat?"

Coal laughed. "That's a real dandy. I wish I had one." He didn't tell Jack, but he had shown the hat to him last time he was home on vacation, and it had led into quite a long discussion about it, and about the lingering potpourri of skunk, which Jack claimed he had an unexplained affinity for. If Coal recalled correctly, it had been decided that the skunk's real-life superpower of stink was matched only by the fictional powers of Superman.

Jack grinned again, which looked more like a wolven leer. "I like yours too, man! Old Western style! They could put us in a movie together."

Coal had to laugh. Apparently, Maura's gift was going to be a real conversation starter every time he put it on.

Catching the curious concern of his friends over this wild-looking apparition coming out of the dark, Coal introduced the three of them. "Alex and Sam, this is an old friend of mine, Hunter Jack. His Shoshone name is Dark Badger, and I just call him Badger."

Because the two men were friends of Coal's, and that had always been good enough for Jack, he shook their hands. Coal knew Jack could likely have put even Sam on the ground, for sheer grip strength, but as always he refrained—luckily for him, since Sam had far more fighting skill than the simple rough and tumble brute strength tactics employed by Hunter Jack. Even so, Coal couldn't help but notice that even Sam's hand looked almost like a normal-sized person's when compared to Jack's.

Coal's mind went into a brief whirl. Martinez was trying to convince him, he hoped somewhat jokingly, that it was dangerous to let Sam drink in public. There might have been some truth to that, although Coal had never been with them when they went out. But he knew the same was true for Hunter Jack, and not in any joking way. It wasn't that he and Jack were carousing pals, bosom buddies, or long-lost brothers, but he really did have a soft spot for this big Shoshone, and in spite of how badly he wanted to soothe his pain tonight with the boys, he felt a sudden responsibility for Jack that overrode whatever needs he had for himself. Did he let him waltz into a bar without doing one thing to stop it?

His train of thought was shocked off the track by the sound of a female voice calling his name from the street. He spun to look past the front of his pickup cab and saw a familiar blue Buick stopped in the street, too far into the oncoming lane of traffic. Annie Price was standing on one leg outside the open door looking his way and waving.

"Hey, Annie! What the—"

"Don't go anywhere, okay?" she cut him off. "There's a parking spot right around the corner!"

Coal glanced around, reminded how crowded the curbs were. He didn't even have time to reply before an oncoming car started honking its horn at her and she jumped back in and sped up the road, turning left at the next street, Center.

"Hey, man! That's a damn perty girl," said Hunter Jack, drawing Coal's attention back to him. "You better grab onto that when it comes around again, uh?"

Coal chuckled, but his mind was scrambling. He couldn't just leave now, because of Annie, but what about Jack? He envisioned his plans for the evening, of getting sloshed with the boys and forgetting all his woes, lying in a pile of embers on the sidewalk before he even got to build a good bonfire. Maybe God was stepping in to save his sorry carcass from his sorrier plans.

Then Coal saw Annie, practically running up the sidewalk from Center Street. He had sudden cause to wonder, was it God pulling him away from his evening's plans with Sam and Martinez . . . or was it the devil?

CHAPTER THREE

Coal had never seen Annie Price looking more beautiful than she was tonight, and that was saying something. She didn't appear to have much if any makeup on, and her hair was a little tousled, as if she had been driving with her window down. He wasn't sure that wasn't part of her appeal—that natural look. But it was as always the somewhat haunted look in her sparkling eyes that gave him the urge to hold her and tell her everything would be all right. He never stopped to think the gentle lighting of the night, mingled with the multi-colored neons and incandescents glimmering out of the business windows might have been acting as a kind of makeup and concealer of the lines of stress and worry harbored in Annie's face. Maybe that was a big reason so many people enjoyed the nightlife, and maybe, again, it was why so many people fell in love out on the night scene—or something remotely like love.

With his heart hurting like it was, and with the cursed neons acting as cupids even before he got any alcohol in his system, Coal saw the warmly questioning look in Annie's eyes as a rescue beacon. She opened her arms to him, and he grabbed on tight and held her to the point that Sam Browning finally cleared his throat.

As Coal looked over, his big blond friend in the Huskers ball cap said, "You know, buddy, me and Q are still here. Maybe you should get a room."

Coal busted up laughing, and Annie did too, in spite of her obvious embarrassment. Coal thought the slap on his back was from Sam, but when he glanced over, he and Martinez were standing too far off. Coal looked around and saw Hunter Jack grinning at him. The wolfish look again.

"I didn't know you was gonna take my advice so fast, Savage," Jack said.

Coal laughed again and turned his eyes to Sam and Martinez. In a flash of inspiration, he started introducing Annie to everyone, and them to her.

"Some of us like to call him Badger," he said when he got to Hunter Jack. "His Indian name is Dark Badger."

"Ooh. I like how that sounds," Annie said, and like a champ, she thrust out her hand to the Shoshone with the intimidating look of the wild warrior about him.

Jack's huge paw could have closed over both of Annie's at the same time. She couldn't help her eyes dropping down to it, because like most anyone she had to check and see if it was real. "It's nice to meet you. Do you prefer Hunter, or Badger?"

Jack's eyes narrowed a little in thought, and he glanced over at Coal. "Remember—always make sure an' listen to your buck when he gives you some advice. He says Badger, so I'm Badger. An' you're Annie? Good to meet you, Annie."

Annie smiled. "You too. And okay—it's Badger; I'll listen to my buck," she said, her smile metamorphosing into a grin. Jack nodded and finally let go of her hand.

"You coming in this world-renowned bar Coal's been telling us about?" asked Sam, turning to Annie and hooking his thumbs in his pockets. Coal saw Martinez give a little eye roll.

Annie looked up at Coal, her eyes danced over to the wild man, past Sam and Martinez again, and back to Coal, looking somewhat overwhelmed. The question was there in her eyes for Coal alone to answer.

"We'll step in for one round of pool and one drink," Coal said. Somehow he felt empowered by the look in Annie's face to make decisions in her behalf. His glance switched to Hunter Jack. "You coming in?"

"You know it, man. I ain't lettin' you boys have all the drinks in this town."

Full-blooded Bannock Alma Vance and his wife Ruby, who had a gnat's whisker of Bannock blood but at least five quarts of Shoshone, loved to fight. When Alma wasn't down at the mines working—a place where he had to refrain from fighting, but only if he wanted to keep his job—he could often be found at home going the rounds with Ruby. When they got bored of that or couldn't find any unbruised or uncut places left to hurt on each other they would get in Alma's old white and rust and red lead-primered 1949 Dodge Wayfarer and wander into town to see if they could find anyone else who wanted a brawl. If they couldn't raise a scuffle, they would rely solely on drinking for their entertainment, but generally they found plenty of both.

Rumor had it that Ruby Vance, in the old days when she was Ruby Timbimboo, and a maiden of the Shoshone-Bannock Nation, had been a sightly young woman, narrow in the waist, with muscular thighs she used to lock herself onto the wild mustangs from the Challis herd, which she and her family used to round up and bring in to break for riding stock. But somewhere between then and now she had to have been dragged behind one or more of those mustangs for several miles, dropped into a deserted mine shaft full of filthy water and urinated whisky, and left to fester for a few weeks. Anything comely about Ruby Vance had long since worn off, sloughed off, aged off, or been beaten off her. Many other things, from an extra hundred pounds of not-so-delicious weight on her five-foot-two frame to an oft-broken nose and a swollen brow and cauliflower ears, had been added on, much of it from her loving husband Alma.

Alma himself still had the looks of a man who might yet be considered handsome, to those who favored a rugged-looking specimen. Like his wife, he was considerably battered, but like the iron-gray streaks laced at random through his hair, as common wisdom would have it, the scars and blemishes that dotted, dashed, and basically made constellations all over his galaxy of a scraggly-mustached face only made him look more dashing—more of a man. Oh to be male, where most of the things a woman fretted and frowned about supposedly made him look more rugged, rather than used up, worn out, and beaten down.

Alma Vance, who wore his pepper and salt hair down to his collar and his sparse mustache only slightly past the corners of his lips, was a cowboy at heart. He wore tight Wrangler jeans whose thirty-two-inch waist actually fit him, brown Justin boots, a big black cowboy hat whose brim, like Coal's silver-belly one, started to curl up right in the very center, and a purple snap-front shirt—because that's what Casey Tibbs wore, and anything that was good enough for that famous rodeo champion was good enough for Alma Vance.

He also wore a fantastically large brass buckle that said simply, "Jack Daniels Old No. 7 Brand", but which Alma Vance most likely wished with all his heart proclaimed him the saddle bronc riding champion of some rodeo, somewhere.

The Vances were drinking in the Owl Club because apparently it had been long enough since bartender Red Levine had kicked them out that his memory had grown foggy or else he simply didn't have the energy to evict them yet tonight—which usually took an act of Congress, an iron will, and a shotgun or billy club to accomplish.

Aspiring young scientists can attest that when a portion of potassium permanganate is placed in a pile, and the plain-old drugstore variety of glycerin is poured into it, in a few seconds it will create a bright flame and a certain amount of pleasant-smelling smoke, of the same odor produced by fireworks. That is a different kind of chemical reaction than any foolhardy danger junkie has observed upon throwing the smallest piece of the soft alkaline metal known as cesium into a glass jar of water. The instant explosion thereby created results in shards of glass going everywhere, and only an extremely fortunate perpetrator who isn't blinded or badly injured in the explosion.

The addition of Hunter Jack to a bar that already contained Alma and Ruby Vance was nothing like the first benign chemical reaction, and almost everything like the second—usually including the shards of glass.

Red Levine had made the mistake of allowing the Vances back in the bar. But when he also let Hunter Jack in he was throwing the cesium into the jar of water, and anyone who knew the shared history of Alma and Ruby Vance and Hunter Jack would have seen it.

Red Levine was begging—either for a night of excitement or one of woe.

CHAPTER FOUR

Coal and his compatriots, along with Annie and Jack, bellied up to the bar. Coal's senses were alert on the instant, even more so than they had been before walking through the front door. But even scanning the big crowd already present, and listening to the din of conversation over the jaunty "Mr. Bojangles" being sung by the Nitty Gritty Dirt Band, he failed to pick out Alma and Ruby Vance. And if he had he would have known nothing about the animosity they and Hunter Jack had toward each other.

Coal attributed the sense of danger he felt at the moment to the mere fact that he was in a barroom, among people he might have arrested, helped arrest, or who simply knew him now as the local law; he was with Sam Browning, a man pretty famous among certain circles for his righteous indignation toward wrong-doers and his tendency to act upon this indignation in various physical fashions; and he was standing beside Annie Price, after recently having been forsaken, apparently forever, by the woman he thought he loved. If he had stopped to ponder it he could have come up with any number of bad scenarios and reasons why he should have turned and slunk out of this room.

Coal ordered a glass of Imperial whisky and water, simply because an Imperial whisky magazine ad was the last one he had seen and the girl drinking it made him remember her—and of course her drink of choice. It said, if he recalled correctly, "Make a splash with an imp," and somehow it seemed fitting at the moment. Annie copied him, he guessed because the only thing she was otherwise familiar with was the now very aged bottle of Wild Turkey she kept but never seemed interested in emptying. Martinez ordered a Miller beer—Coal couldn't guess why—and Sam ordered a Jack Daniels.

"With water?" asked Red Levine.

Sam gave him a confused look. "What's water?"

Everyone laughed except Martinez, who gave Coal "the look". Then Coal really started feeling guilty for asking Sam to come here, because Martinez seemed genuinely worried. And that compounded his feeling of guilt for being in here with Annie when he knew he was on the rebound from Maura. He was starting to question a lot of his motives tonight as he put the whiskey glass to his lips and had his first taste of alcohol in he didn't remember how long. He was pretty certain that last occasion had also involved Annie Price and her bottle of Wild Turkey.

With their drinks in hand, the five of them wandered closer to the billiard tables, looking for that one game of pool Coal had mentioned. They watched for a while at the first table they came to, which only had three stripes and a solid on the green when they stopped. That game ended quickly, and although there were a few people waiting, when they recognized Coal, after greeting him, they waved him on in.

"We're gonna be here till the place shuts down," one of them said, then looked leeringly at Annie. "Looks like you better git to it, 'cause you got more important things waitin'." The speaker and his crowd laughed, and Coal chuckled politely. Annie, on the other hand, made some comment back to them that made them laugh even harder, delightedly, and made Coal blush.

Annie declined to play, choosing instead to stand sipping her Imperial and water, making sour faces as if she were drinking something that would melt paint off a car. That was fine with Coal, who didn't want to hang out with a lush anyway. Martinez also stood back, and Hunter Jack told them his hands were too big to be good with a pool cue. That left Coal and Sam.

It didn't take long into the game before Coal remembered why he was a rifle and pistol shooter, not a pool shark. And it was painfully obvious that Sam Browning was both. He sank all his stripes while Coal still had four solids on the table.

Sam looked around when the game was over. "Anybody else?"

Coal didn't hear him. He had let his guard down foolishly during the game, but it was back up now, and he saw Alma and Ruby Vance leering like an alpha wolf and its mate over another smoky billiard table at the far back of the room. And Hunter Jack was meeting them eye for eye. Between Jack and the Vances, tonight it seemed indeed like a night for wolves to howl.

Coal laid a soft hand on Jack's left arm, ready to duck out of the way if his touch caused a bad reaction. "Badger. You okay?"

Jack nodded, slowly, but his eyes never left Alma Vance. "Sure, bro. I'm always okay. You?"

With a chuckle, Coal gave the Shoshone's arm a friendly squeeze. "Of course. You sure you don't want to play a game? Maybe Sam will agree to tie an arm behind his back."

He realized that Merle "the Hag" Haggard was coming over the speakers crooning, "You're Walkin' on the Fightin' Side of Me," and he thought how ironic the title was considering the look in Jack's eyes.

"You know those guys?" Coal asked casually.

"Uh . . . yeah. I know 'em."

Coal gave a cautious glance to the Indian couple again. The woman had finally looked away. She was chalking a pool cue, but by the look of her pudgy, scarred face, she was well aware Jack's eyes were still on her.

"Who are they?"

Jack apparently didn't hear him this time. Coal felt obliged to step in between the ire he could see building wordlessly in the room. "Hey. Jack."

The barrel-chested Shoshone finally turned, raising his chin to acknowledge him.

"You want to go find a different bar? There are plenty more as good as this one."

"You think? No Jack never run from no fight."

Coal's eyes flickered back to the other couple, and by now there were several more people looking this way, and all of Coal's crowd had caught the mood and were standing about cautiously.

"I don't see any fight to run from, brother," said Coal. "That's why it's a good time to leave. How about the Lantern? They tell me the barmaid down there is really something. Her name's Elisa."

Jack's eyes returned to the couple. Coal looked at them, and now their hands were both full of pool cues, and they were watching, waiting. At this smoky distance, neither of them appeared to be overly inebriated, but in Coal's experience there were a lot of people around Salmon who could be far over the legal limit without showing much effect from it. That didn't mean their judgment would be sound.

Suddenly, Hunter Jack drew a deep breath. "Yeah. All right, Savage. Let's go down to the Lantern 'n' see this bar girl of yours. Air stinks in here anyway."

Coal had to agree with that last statement, but he doubted the air in the Lantern would be any better, even though he knew Jack was referring to another kind of air.

Leading his group, Coal wandered to the front door, feeling eyes on his back all the way, and when Jack tried to turn one last time to look back into the shadows of the bar Coal took his arm and gently guided him out into the cold. They went down to the Lantern, and by the time they arrived there the icy temperature had cooled Hunter Jack enough that he was once more telling Coal the story of how he had jumped on his future hat that one dark autumn night.

Going into the Lantern, Coal found his arm slipping naturally around Annie's waist and guiding her inside. She looked up at him, and her eyes glowed in the lights of the barroom. They had a nice warm glitter, like Christmas tree lights reflecting in a blue glass ornament. Like a fool, he squeezed her harder before letting go.

"You want another drink?" he asked.

"Sure, you buyin'?" It was Hunter Jack, not Annie, who replied to him.

Coal laughed. "Sure, Badger. Tell her." He nodded toward the bartender, a brunette in her early thirties or thereabouts with long, flowing hair curled back on the sides and a thin pink, plaid cotton shirt tied in a knot at the bottom to reveal an unsettlingly luring navel. If this was the Elisa he had been hearing about, she was every bit as attractive as he had heard, in spite of a quarter-pound of makeup marring her face.

When the girl smiled, she beamed, her teeth so white they nearly glowed. "Howdy. You're the sheriff, right? Sheriff Savage?"

Coal gave a chuckle. "I'm afraid so. Off duty, of course."

She kept smiling. "I'm Elisa. Elisa Doan. I don't know your first name."

"Sheriff," he replied, smiling back.

"His name's Coal," Sam cut in from the side. "Judas, Savage, you're a charmer. I'm Sam," he said, looking back at Elisa and shoving his hand across the bar to take her much smaller one. "And this is Alex Martinez—who isn't married."

Elisa gave Martinez a coy look. "Well, good to know." Her eyes slid back over to Coal. " 'Sheriff' isn't married either, right?"

"No, but Sheriff is with me," Annie blurted. "Hi. Annie Price. I'm a nurse at Steele Memorial—if you ever find yourself in need of any medical care."

Coal was glad he didn't have a mouthful of whiskey. He might have spewed it across the bar top. If anyone had ever hammered a big stake into the ground to mark her claim, it was Annie Price. If he were reading between the lines, Annie's comment made it sound like if Elisa wandered into Annie's territory, unwittingly or otherwise, she *might* need medical care.

Coal introduced Hunter Jack to Elisa, who gazed at him with curiosity not even thinly veiled. "I've seen you before. Nice to meet you." She didn't hold out her hand to him, but she certainly looked in awe at his when he flopped it out on the bar top, big and raw like a skinned turkey breast.

When Coal tried to order Annie another drink she told him she had had enough, and although she tried to convince him to go ahead and have a second he followed her example and declined, while Martinez had another beer and Sam another whiskey. Jack ambled toward the first empty pool table with a full glass of Johnny Walker Black Label Scotch engulfed in his fist, and when he got there he turned to Sam.

"Still want a match? Think I changed my mind."

Sam gave him his impish look and sipped his whiskey. "Sure, if you're game."

Hunter Jack was game. Game to lose. And he was amenable to that loss, too. Old Hunter Jack had already located the person—or persons—he wanted a fight with tonight, back at the Owl Club, and Sam Browning was neither of those people.

Half an hour after walking into the Lantern, Coal finished his third game with Sam, another dreadful loss because apparently he wasn't a beginner and didn't deserve beginner's luck. He just stunk at pool. Annie nudged him hard with her hip. He looked down at her, and when she got up on her tiptoes and raised her face toward him it was an obvious signal that she had something she didn't want everyone else to hear.

Her breath was warm in Coal's ear, yet it sent chills all over his body. She whispered, "Aren't you ready to get out of this place? You don't seem any more comfortable in here than I am."

Coal straightened up, chuckling. He sighed, and after making sure the guys had all averted their eyes he nodded at her. He was trying to figure out a polite way to excuse himself and Annie when Sam, busy chalking his pool cue, quartered away from Coal, turned and looked over his shoulder. "Hey, why don't you two duck out of here? Don't you have anything better to do?"

Coal laughed outright while Annie was giggling. "Don't have a problem being blunt, do you? All right, I'm ready. You boys want a ride back?"

Sam frowned and looked at Martinez. "Do we?"

"Damn right we do. We haven't been in a fight yet, and that's a good sign."

Coal turned to Hunter Jack. "You want a ride home? It's pretty cold out there."

"Nah. I gotta stay and stoke up the jukebox some more." It was one of the rare moments since their arrival when nothing was playing, and the mournful notes of the last song played, Glen Campbell's "Galveston", still hung like country music magic in the smoke and warmth of the barroom. There must have been at least five or ten more songs as magical as that one waiting only for the poke of Jack's finger to choose them.

"You sure?"

"Sure, Savage. Hey, good seein' ya, uh? We should go out shootin' sometime."

Coal smiled and shook Hunter Jack's hand, amazed once more at the size of it. He was glad not to be on the "fightin' side" of Hunter Jack, that was for certain. He was wondering if Jack was baiting him, since they both knew he couldn't own any guns, but he decided not to take the bait.

"All right, then I'll see you around. Take it easy now."

On the ride back to the Stagecoach Inn, Annie had to sit on Martinez's lap, which Coal was pretty certain didn't bother Q any. When Coal stopped in front and Sam disembarked, Martinez crawled out reluctantly from under Annie so she could plop back down next to Coal. "Hey, I got a notebook in the room if you want to have me write you up a bill of sale for the Mustang."

Coal stared at him for a moment. "You're serious about that?"

"I'm dead serious. I think I'm gonna go home and buy a newer one. A Mach One. You still want it, right?"

Coal shrugged. "Of course! But I didn't bring a checkbook. Why don't you just go write down all your information and I'll either wire you the money or send you a check."

When Martinez left, Sam stood awkwardly outside the pickup, allowing frozen air to flood inside, and Annie turned to Coal. "You're seriously buying a Mustang?"

"Yep. Proud owner." He jingled the keys at her, for emphasis.

"You're going to have your own car lot out there on Savage Lane."

He laughed. "And only the nicest cars in it."

When Martinez returned, he handed a piece of paper across to Coal. "I'll mail you the title. So hey. You even gonna get out to say goodbye?"

Coal sat there for a second. "When are you leaving?"

"First thing in the morning. We're gonna fly out of this airport to Idaho Falls and head home from there."

It was the first time the idea had hit Coal that his friends were actually not going to be in Salmon anymore. His heart began to thud strangely as he climbed out of the cab and went around where they both stood.

"I don't know how to thank you guys." He felt awkward. He was talking to a lifetime Marine brother and an Army Green Beret, both tough as nails, and both former agents of the Bureau. What was the proper etiquette for saying goodbye to two macho men who were the biggest reasons—if not the only ones—he was still alive?

Sam stepped close and held out his hand. "Buddy, I know you'd have done the same for me. I'm proud you called on us."

Coal shook his friend's hand. A handshake and a box of Russell Stover's chocolates, Sam's only request for payment, seemed like such pathetic ways to pay him, and to say goodbye for what would most likely be the last time.

"Hey," said Sam while still grasping Coal's hand, and he leaned forward and gave him a quick embrace. When he pulled away, he was obviously embarrassed that Martinez was looking at him. "Hey! Men can hug!"

Martinez gave him the mere hint of a grin and shrugged. "What? I never said anything." He turned back to Coal and held out his hand. "I'm glad you made it, man. It was pretty nip and tuck. I hope you have better luck with that Mustang than I did, huh? It's a good car. That 289 will whip any car in town—for the first block."

Coal grinned and shook his friend's hand firmly. "I guess I may never know."

"Right. I guess you better not—Sheriff. See you around, Marine. *Semper fi.*"

Alex Martinez and Sam Browning turned and walked to the front door of the hotel. Coal couldn't stand to watch them disappear, so he got in the truck and pulled away, feeling Annie's hand warm on his leg. He felt guilty that in the back of his mind, if he wasn't looking, it felt like Maura was beside him.

Her voice broke the quiet. "I didn't get a chance to say anything earlier, but I sure love your new hat. It totally changes you into another person, somebody straight out of the Wild West." Other than the word "wild" replacing "old", her words seemed to be the general consensus. Thinking of the words before that, however, he knew he could tell her something that would make sure she no longer loved his new hat.

Annie had no idea it had been crafted and given to him as a gift by Maura. And if he was smart, and lucky, she never would know.

CHAPTER FIVE

Coal woke up in the middle of the night on the couch beside Annie, the television quietly playing its clash of black and white dots and creating the only light in the otherwise stygian darkness of the single-wide's semi-cool living room. Who knew how much time had passed since the network's playing of the "National Anthem", signaling the end of another broadcasting day.

Annie was snuggled up warm against him, and he could smell the fragrance of her shampoo. With her face against his chest, he could feel her soft breath, warm and moist against his skin. She had been in that position long enough for the moisture to penetrate his flannel shirt and undershirt.

When he tried to move his right arm he realized that not only was it trapped, but it had a complete absence of feeling. He wondered what time it was and hoped his mother hadn't decided to stay up and worry about him. But he knew better. Even if it was three in the morning—and maybe especially then—she might be in bed, but she would be staring at the clock.

He filled his lungs, relishing Annie's warm scent. He pondered their evening together. She had been a good girl and avoided any talk about what he had been going through since they saw each other last. He knew probably the hardest part for her would have been not mentioning his trip out of town with Maura. Or perhaps she didn't even know. But that would be more than he could hope for in this small town, where if Ryan and Emily Capson's daughter got an A in math it was just as likely to make it into the *Recorder-Herald* as a stabbing death down on Main Street. In Salmon, any personal news was big news, and fodder for the rumor mill if nothing else.

Annie knew about the trip with Maura. As sure as God made little brown horse apples, she knew.

"You're thinking about leaving, aren't you?"

Coal wasn't sure why Annie's unexpected voice didn't startle him. Maybe he simply wasn't scared of her—although any sane man would have been.

"No, not really."

She kept her head on his chest, her right hand warm on his abdomen. "What then? What are you thinking about?"

"Salmon. This valley. This place has chewed me up and spat me out since I came back here. I don't know what to think anymore."

She was quiet for a long time. She gave his side three pats, and those solid thumps were the only sounds for a while, beyond their quiet breathing. But inside his own head Coal's thoughts were like thunder, and Annie's wheels were spinning almost as loud.

After some time, she got up and went to turn on the lamp on a little round table at the end of the couch. She then returned and snuggled back into her exact previous position. Another half-minute passed before she spoke again.

"Do you wish you didn't come home?"

It took him a while to answer that. He thought about Katie Leigh and all her drug and boy problems in Virginia. He thought of his boys living out there on a wonderful farm, but with no mother figure anywhere on their horizon. He thought how strangled he had started to feel in and by the big city, and how cynical he had started to get, and how it felt like everyone but other members of the Bureau was his enemy.

"No. I had to come. But why did I walk into this hornets' nest? Salmon never used to be like this. I think we have a worse crime rate than Washington since I moved here."

"I guess you brought it with you."

Coal tried to find that funny. He even chuckled, but it was forced.

"I was kidding, Coal. I'm sorry." Putting her hand on his thigh, Annie pushed herself up straight and looked at him. "I want to say something that I hope you'll think about. It's crazy, in all our time together I don't think we've ever talked about how we feel about spiritual things, so I'm not sure where you stand, but . . . What if this was the time you had to be here? What if God knew you were the only one that could handle all this?"

The thought struck some deep emotions in him. He could have spoken, but again he waited for a while, not trusting himself to have the right words, and seeking to find them.

"I guess I probably don't feel very spiritual to you, do I?" He thought back on the drink he had had at the Owl Club, and the glass of Wild Turkey she had offered him when they got here, and which he had polished off to the drop—without water in it. She must think he was a weakling. Maybe even a latent alcoholic.

She reached out and took the fingers of his left hand, squeezing them. "No, I feel the opposite. I think you are stronger than most men, and certainly more virtuous. Maybe more than any man I've ever known."

Inside, Coal cringed, thinking of the night he had caved in to Maura. He didn't reply.

"Coal, do you find me attractive?"

Coal stared at her as if he had been kicked in the solar plexus. He felt like a crowd of people had been gathered around a wonderful-looking pot of simmering stew, watching it with anticipation, and then someone had walked up without warning or explanation and dropped a turd into it. *Do you find me attractive?* What kind of a person asks a question like that!

Annie stared at him, her face surprisingly calm. She wasn't going to giggle and say she was kidding and that he didn't have to answer. She wasn't going to hide in embarrassment and bring up another subject. She wasn't going to let him off the hook at all. She had obviously taken a while to get the courage to ask her question, and now it was there before them, a piece of cake she had made that he could nibble at, gobble down with an expression of ecstasy, or pick up and rub in her face. The choice was his.

"Of course I find you attractive! You should never have to ask a thing like that. Annie, you are without a doubt one of the most gorgeous women I've ever seen. You seem like everything a man could want."

She almost smiled. But not quite. Her eyes searched his, and the sparkle in them told him she found the truth she was looking for. "Okay then. So that's why I can say you are stronger than any man I've ever known. I don't know how many times I've thrown myself at you. You've spent a whole night with me, and some partial ones. I've given you whiskey, kissed you with everything I had. Pretty much tried to do every unlady-like thing in the book. And you have always been a gentleman. I've never known that kind of thing before you, Coal. Every man I ever dated, if he had the chance, was all over me. I don't know how many men I've had to ask to leave my house, here and where I lived before."

"You've never told me where that was." He jumped at the chance for a new subject.

"Ha-a-a-h. You're not getting out of the conversation that easy, Mr. Slick."

He laughed, seeing he had been caught. "Well, I didn't want you to ask me to leave."

She gazed into his eyes. “You know I wouldn’t have. I wanted you then, and I always will if you ever change your mind. But I know from those times how strong you are, and how good you are. God was preparing you to come back here to this valley. I really believe that. I think he knew you were the only one who could handle all the things that were coming.”

Looking at her, feeling her admiration for him, he tried for all he was worth to push Maura out of his mind. “I hope you’re right, because sometimes I want to crawl into a hole and bury myself over.”

“You too, huh?”

He didn’t take her bait by asking her to clarify. “Yeah. Me too.”

“Can I kiss you, Coal?”

“Innocent?”

“Innocent.”

Before she could make the first move, he leaned forward, and his lips touched hers. They were soft, and they tasted, he had to admit, like honey. He didn’t care how cliché it sounded.

It was deep in the throes of passion ten minutes later when the God Annie seemed to think he was so close to decided to rescue Coal from himself. The phone rang, and it startled them both. To Coal’s credit, it was Annie who swore this time, not him. He saw her face pinken with embarrassment. “Sorry! Oh, I hope they aren’t calling me in to work.”

“Don’t answer it.” He was breathless. The alcohol was still working in him. He wanted her, wanted to throw caution to the wind and not care if she respected him later.

“Oh, Coal. How I love that you said that! But I have to. If they’re calling, it means something bad enough has happened they’re desperate.”

That was certainly something he could understand, and he respected her for her sense of duty. He let out a long sigh and sat up, nodding and running his hand back through his hair. He took a deep breath to try and slow his breathing down.

Annie jumped up and ran to pick up the phone. "Hello? Uhh . . . Hi." Seconds passed, and by now he was watching her, trying to read her expression. Was she leaving, or wasn't she? "Yes, he is, actually. I'm so sorry we didn't call you earlier. I . . . Well, hang on. Here he is."

Covering the receiver, she made an apologetic face. "Sorry, Coal. It's your mom."

"What the hell?" He instantly regretted saying that. But a mixture of anger and embarrassment made him not even apologize. He was a grown man! Why was his mother tracking him down? He got up and snatched the phone. "Hi, Mom." Part of him wished he could have sounded nicer.

Son! I'm so glad I found you. They've been trying to get you, and I had no idea where you were.

"Wait! Mom, what's going on? Who's they?"

Dispatch. Son, there was a big fight down at the Lantern, and Officer Lacey was stabbed.

"Lace— Tim Lacey? How bad is it?"

I'm not sure. I just told them I'd try to find you. I'm sorry I had to call Annie's. When you weren't down at the fight Annie was the only person I could think of.

"It's okay, Mom. It's really okay. Thanks for tracking me down. I should have let someone know where I was anyway. Do you know if anybody else got hurt?"

Yes, I think that Indian man, the strange one who wears the furs.

Coal didn't curse out loud, but he did in his head. Hunter Jack! This had something to do with Alma and Ruby Vance. They had followed Jack down to the Lantern!

CHAPTER SIX

After hanging up with Connie, Coal turned to Annie, giving her a quick rundown of the news. "The hospital's going to be busy, all right. But maybe they won't call you."

Annie nodded. Coal caught a look of moistness in her eyes beyond the normal.

"Hey, you all right?"

She nodded again, not speaking. He stepped close and took her shoulders. "Annie. I'm serious: Are you going to be okay?"

She smiled, a sad smile, and the tears came into her eyes. She wiped at them angrily. "I'll be okay. It's just . . . It's always something."

He grabbed her and pulled her close. "I'm sorry. Maybe it was God talking to us."

She laughed, a bitter sound. "Sure." Then, pulling away from him, she said, "Maybe I should get my shoes on and go with you. Luckily I didn't get any more undressed than this." She laughed again, and it didn't sound so bitter, but still rueful.

"If you want to, I wouldn't mind the company. But what if I'm in there for a while?"

"It's all right. I just want to be with you." With that, she was already rounding up her shoes.

He went to the hooks by the door and got her coat, then waited patiently. When she had tied her shoes but was still dressed in wide-legged, high-waisted blue jeans, a pink long-sleeved shirt and a white sweater, he said, "You don't look much like Nurse Annie."

"It's all right," she replied with a giggle. "I have uniforms in my locker at work if they need me."

Flying down the road a few minutes later, Coal was questioning his ability to drive responsibly. Well, if one and a half drinks put him under the table he would be surprised. And besides, who was going to arrest him for driving while intoxicated? All the other officers would be in town at the fight scene, and he was the sheriff!

Coal parked in the south lane of traffic in front of the Lantern, feeling pretty safe because that was where all the other police cars were parked as well, their red lights filling up Main like a Christmas parade. He told Annie to stay in the pickup, but she proved to be a little more like Maura than he knew when she simply waited until he got out and slammed his door, then jumped out her own side and ran after him.

He had heard her door slam, but now he turned when he heard her feet pattering up beside him. "Kind of a defiant little thing, aren't you?"

She gave him a feigned look of shock, then giggled. "Well I'm not staying in there by myself. It could be dangerous out here!"

Swiveling his head to study the rough-looking, mostly inebriated bar crowd that had regurgitated out onto the sidewalk in front of the Lantern, Coal could only shake his head. "Fine, well stay close then."

He found Jordan Peterson in the crowd first, because Jordan was usually the biggest man around next to Coal. When he called to him, Jordan excused himself from a citizen he had been talking to and hurried over. "Hey, boss! Sorry they had to track you down. The chief was hoping for all hands on deck."

Coal's eyes swept the vehicles on the street. "Looks like he got them too. Was the fight that bad?"

Jordan shrugged as Coal spied Grant Fairbourne and Bob Wilson striding toward him. "It was the worst one I've seen, but that doesn't mean much. I guess everyone's pretty up in arms, though, because Tim Lacey got stabbed."

"How bad?" He didn't dare ask who had done the stabbing. He was afraid he already knew.

"I don't think it was terrible, but bad enough. Got him in the gun arm."

Coal cringed. "Oh hell. As if we aren't short-handed enough around here already."

"Yeah."

"Hey, Coal." He turned to Bob Wilson, who had spoken. "Glad you could make it down here. Sorry to ruin your night off."

"That's okay. Where's Badger?"

"Oh, don't even— That son of a—"

Bob cut himself short, so Jordan finished his sentence, then said, "I've already got him up at the jail."

"What about the others? I'm guessing the Vances were in the middle of all this."

"The who?" Jordan looked confused. This time it was Bob's turn to answer in Jordan's place.

"No, the Vances weren't here."

Coal stared at Bob, processing what he had said. "Wait. The Vances . . . Alma and Ruby? They weren't involved in the fight?"

"No, I haven't seen them all night," Bob replied. "This was some guy that's been living up toward the cemetery in a travel trailer."

Coal couldn't hide his surprise. "This time of year?"

"Yeah, I know. I don't know how he does it. But yeah. White guy, scruffy red beard. Name's Everett Sherman. Forty-ish, thin as a scarecrow. He's pretty much a punk. I've dealt with him off and on since he moved here. War vet, but not the good kind. I think Nam messed him up in the head—or maybe he always was."

"So what about the fight? What happened?"

The fight had played out about as Coal would have expected. Witnesses said Everett Sherman and some of his friends came in being loud and obnoxious, apparently already pre-intoxicated so as to have a head start on the rest of the crowd. Sherman started making fun of Hunter Jack's outfit, as men often did, but almost never to his face. It was obvious to onlookers that there was going to be a fight, but they all swore Jack kept his cool for a while, maybe because he could see the odds stacked against him. Everett Sherman had five or six guys rallied around laughing at his stupid jokes. It wasn't until Sherman decided to up the ante and rip Jack's skunk hat off his head that Jack struck him. It was said, and Coal knew it to be truth, that his fist was centered on the other man's nose but still covered most of his face.

Everett Sherman at that point was down and out, but his friends had enough alcohol in them to carry the fight, and by then Hunter Jack didn't seem to care about the odds anymore. He liked to fight, and these white boys had brought it to him.

They had torn the bar up pretty good, broken four or five chairs and a table, before witnesses said they heard someone yelling something and saw that Everett Sherman had come to and had a knife out. Standing there with blood smeared all over his face and still running, he was holding Jack's skunk hat by the tail, and as he laughed crazily and taunted Jack he punctured the hat near the tail, then ran the blade all the way down and out the front, making the hat into halves.

It was only then, seeing his pride and joy ruined, that Jack drew his knife, but it was also when the cavalry showed up, and Tim Lacey was the first unfortunate through the front door. When he yelled, *Halt, police!*, Jack whirled and thrust.

No one could say whether Jack was coherent enough to realize it was a police officer confronting him or not. They only knew it appeared that he saw Lacey and then stabbed him, the blade going in on the inside of Lacey's arm and narrowly missing his brachial artery as it went all the way out the other side.

Then there were cops and citizens swarming everywhere, and before they could take Hunter Jack down, Everett Sherman laid a pool cue hard across the side of his head. The second time he did it, it broke, and Jack slumped to the floor.

"So I thought you said Jack is in jail," said Coal, looking around at the others.

"He is!" retorted Bob.

"What about— You said that guy broke a pool cue on his head? Come on, guys. He went unconscious after getting a pool cue broken on his head, and you didn't take him to Steele?"

"Nothing could hurt that s.o.b.," said Bob.

Coal looked at his friend, trying to hide his disappointment. "Sure. Well, I once saw a guy in Korea, a big tough guy like Hunter Jack, and everyone thought the same thing about him too. Somebody broke a cue over his head in a club one night, and he didn't even go unconscious. He turned around and made short work of the guy. Then he went back to his hooch, and the next morning the other guys found him cold as a stone."

"He died?" asked Jordan.

"Dead as they come."

Jordan and Grant looked at each other, then at Bob. Bob remained stoic. "Nobody's killing Hunter Jack that easy."

"Well, I'm going to go get him and take him to Steele. He's not going to die in my jail."

"Coal! Just friggin' leave him," said Bob angrily, as Coal turned to his truck, then spun back around.

"Or what?"

"Or . . . Come on, man. He tried to kill Tim."

Coal frowned. "We don't know that. I know Jack doesn't run from a fight, but I've never heard of him fighting cops. And I've also never seen him being the killer kind."

"Ha! You forgetting he did time in Boise for manslaughter?"

Shaking his head, Coal said, "That was a long time ago, and there was a good reason for that fight if you remember. Besides, it's a moot point. He dies in our jail when we could have done something about it, we're going to have an internal investigation here. You don't want to be any part of that, and neither do I." Coal took a deep, calming breath. "You guys need anything else here before I go?"

"No, go take your buddy down to the hospital. Waste some more county money. I guess we don't need you here after all." Bob turned away and stalked off through the crowd toward the Lantern.

Jordan and Grant looked after him, then turned nervously to Coal. He saw a lot of questions and concerns in their eyes. He tried to hide the disappointment in his face over the way Bob was acting.

"It's not something we have a choice in, guys. This is the 1970's, not the 1870's. If there's ever another question like this in the future, I'll have a piece of your hides if you take an injured prisoner up to the jail without having him checked out by a doctor or at least the EMT's first."

They both nodded, and Coal headed for his pickup. At the last second, he turned back. "Hey! Jordan. I hope they didn't put Sherman and the others up there with Jack, did they?"

Jordan looked sheepish. "Well, uh . . ." His glance darted over to Grant, then back. "They didn't arrest them at all."

CHAPTER SEVEN

All the lights were out in the jail but the lamp on Coal's desk. The only other light illuminating their path was the dim yellow one shining on the concrete steps that went down to the beat-up metal door leading into the sheriff's office. Coal let Annie out his door this time, then took her elbow because there was still a little ice on the lot. He was going to have to chew somebody out over that. All the county needed was for some old lady to come to the courthouse and break a hip.

Before they started down the steps Coal looked at Annie. Against her little white coat, her golden-brown hair looked a tad darker, and her eyes, even in the semi-darkness, seemed to take on more sparkle.

"You look kind of cute tonight, you know it?" Coal didn't even know where that came from and instantly realized he should have regretted saying it, but he didn't.

"Cute? Hmm . . . Well, I guess if that's the best I can get. So do you."

Coal laughed. "Cute! I don't think I've been called that since I was in high school—at least not by anyone who was being serious."

As their laughter was dying down, they stepped into the dim-lit office, smelling coffee on the brew. "I think that's some java left over that Sam brought with him from Nebraska."

"Sam? Oh! Yes, Sam. Really? It smells good."

"You want some?"

"No, I'm not really a coffee fan."

He turned fully to her, frowning in fun. He was going to say something more, take a good jab at her, but then he remembered Hunter Jack. "I guess I'd better get in there. Listen, I'm not sure who-all is back there or what state that place is in. You'll probably want to wait for me in here."

"Do I have a choice?"

Now, with the keys in his hand and shutting his desk drawer, he turned fully to her again. "You serious? Well, I guess you do. You can go back there if you want, but it's usually on the scary side."

"I'll pretend it's part of the next movie we're going to."

He grinned. "Okay. Come on."

He went to the cell block door, unlocked it, and stepped inside, flipping on the light. True to Jordan's story, all the cells were empty except the one at the far end. They heard a groan from there, and Coal walked down cautiously, with Annie stuck to him like a bur in a horse's tail. "Badger? It's Savage."

Another groan. A rustle. "What? Who's there?"

"It's me, Badger. Coal Savage."

A long, low groan came out of Hunter Jack's throat, and when Coal stopped in front of his cell door, the man's big arm flopped down from covering his eyes. Blinking at the bright light, he turned his head, trying to focus on Coal.

"How are you feeling?"

"Like dung. Warm wet dung." A drunken laugh escaped Jack. "How are *you*?"

"A step above that. Cold dry dung. Hey, buddy, just so you know, I've got a woman in here with me. It's Annie—the nurse you met down on Main earlier tonight."

Jack struggled to sit up on his bunk, wiping his hand back over his sleek hair as if to straighten it. It didn't need that; the braids held it in place like molded plastic. "Hey, lady. Man, Savage, you really took my advice and grabbed onto her, didn't you? You two needin' a bunk back here?"

For a few seconds, Coal couldn't respond. Annie fixed the problem. "I'm working on that, Badger. I'll let you know if I have any success."

Hunter Jack started cackling with glee, and just when Coal, in his embarrassment, was starting to think Bob Wilson was right that Jack didn't need any medical care, the man put his big paw up to the side of his head and groaned. "Man, that Viking guy sure whacked me good. That was him that hit me, huh? That red-bearded prick? Oops— Sorry, lady."

Annie laughed. "It would take worse than that to bother me."

"Hey, Badger, I'm going to come in there and look at your head," said Coal. "You all right with that?"

"Sure, I guess. But . . . Well, didn't you say your friend's a nurse?"

Coal stopped. He blinked. Then he frowned, feeling the fool. "Uh, yes, as a matter of fact . . ." He turned to see Annie standing there with her hands on her hips looking up at him, her eyebrows raised.

"Well, I know you're off duty. You . . . Okay, so do you feel like helping out?"

"Of course I'll help. No point in getting all worked up yet and going down to the hospital for no reason."

Coal shrugged. "All right, Badger. Then we're coming in. Best behavior, my friend. Best behavior."

He opened the door and went inside, then let Annie come in after him. Jack sat on the edge of the bunk quietly, and when Annie reached him he gave a ginger tap on the side of his head. "It's right there. I think he mighta hit me twice."

"That's what I was told," said Coal.

While Annie began feathering her fingers around above Jack's right ear, Coal decided it was a good time to talk to him. "Badger, they told me you stabbed Officer Lacey. Do you remember that?"

Jack cringed, closing his eyes hard. Because of the timing, Coal wasn't sure if it was because of the memory of the stabbing or if Annie had touched a sore spot. Annie stopped probing, so apparently she wasn't sure either. The Shoshone looked up. "You find somethin'?"

"Uh, no. I thought I hurt you."

"No, no. No, lady, I was thinkin' about that cop. Hey, Savage, I wasn't in my right mind. That Viking guy was messin' with me so bad, man. Bad! I didn't even want a fight t'night. I swore I was goin' downtown, get me a drink, maybe find some lady to dance with a couple times, an' then I was gonna head home. I didn't . . . Savage, I swear I didn't know who that was. He was just yellin' at me, an' there was so many of 'em, and then . . . Man, I'm real sorry. Is that cop gonna be okay? I'm real sorry." They were drunken words, but they seemed sincere.

Coal nodded, glancing over at Annie and indicating with a tilt of his chin for her to continue her adventure of discovery along the Indian's scalp. "I didn't think you really meant to do it."

"So what's gonna happen then? It was an accident, right?"

"Well, I wouldn't exactly call it that. I hope they take everything into consideration. But I still think you're in a lot of trouble. You pulled a knife in a fight."

"Yeah. An' so did that Viking guy. I had to defend myself."

Coal was amused that Jack kept calling Everett Sherman "that Viking guy". Sherman must look like quite a character, and according to the description they had given Coal, it must all be in the man's hair, beard, and perhaps his face. He had never thought of Vikings being skinny punks, the impression Bob Wilson had given Coal of Sherman.

"You're right. And we're going to see about all that, Badger. It sounds like there was some injustice done tonight."

"Yeah. They arrested the wrong guy."

Coal shrugged with one shoulder. "Buddy, you stabbed a cop. Believe me, they arrested the guy they wanted to arrest."

"'Cause I'm a Injun," said Jack sullenly.

"No, because you stabbed a cop. It didn't have anything to do with your skin color. Bob and his dad both have a lot of good friends in the tribe."

"Yeah. Whatever."

Coal sighed. Maybe everything would make more sense to Jack when he was sober. He looked at Annie. "Well, what do you think?"

"I think that's one heck of a goose egg under his hair. It should have gone down by now."

"Think he should go get some X-rays?"

Annie made a cringing face. "If I were in your place I'd sure feel better about things. Honestly, just the fact that it made him lose consciousness should have been enough to make them take him in for observation."

"Then that's what we're doing. All right, my friend, why don't you get up and we'll go get your clothes."

He waited as the stout Shoshone got up, half expecting him to get dizzy and fall, and knowing full well the task he was going to have of catching him if he did. Jack did indeed appear to get dizzy, and he put out a hand to rest on Coal's shoulder, supporting himself. He and Jack thought of the same thing at the same time.

"How much you wanna bet I could clout you with one hand and knock you out right now, Savage? Then grab your woman an' take off outta here." He paused, and Coal waited in silence. "How much you bet?" Jack repeated.

CHAPTER EIGHT

Coal braced his legs, but he kept his knees loose. He was studying Jack's eyes, and as close together as they stood, with Hunter Jack's huge hand resting on his shoulder, it seemed like he could see clear into his soul.

"You know what I bet, buddy? I bet I'm about your only friend around here tonight, and it would be a sorry day when you did that." In his head, he had thought the words more like, "a sorry day the day you *tried* that." But he didn't want to sound like a braggart and maybe give Hunter Jack the feeling he had to prove something. Coal knew he could take Jack. But in reality, it could be one heck of an ugly fight, and he certainly wouldn't come out of it without battle scars to show.

Jack chuckled. "I wouldn't do it anyhow. You always been square with me, Savage. I know a ally when I see one."

"Good. Let's get you down to Steele and see what they have to say."

They got out to the truck, and while Annie scooted to the middle where he was sure she preferred to be anyway, Hunter Jack got in on the passenger side. At the height of everyone's hips, it was an easy fit, since Coal had a waist of thirty-four inches, Hunter Jack's was probably thirty-three, and Annie's was a number Coal wasn't fool enough to try and guess. But upper body-wise, because both Coal and Hunter were well above average size, it was an entirely different story, and Annie had to turn a little sideways and crowd into Coal not to feel claustrophobic. Somehow Coal found he didn't mind.

When they got down to the Lantern, the crowd was getting sparser, and Jordan was making his way to his pickup. Coal stopped and motioned him over. "Do me a favor and follow us down to the hospital. I'm going to have you stay with Badger while they get some X-rays and make sure he's all right to be up in the jail."

It was obvious from Jordan's expression that he felt picked on, but he quietly followed them to Steele Memorial all the same. So far, Coal had never seen Jordan be anything but a model employee.

At the hospital, they all trooped inside although Coal was wishing Annie would have stayed in the truck. He needed a moment alone with Jordan, and he guessed he was going to have to flat-out ask for it.

A nurse took Hunter Jack into an examination room before running him down for X-rays, and Coal looked over at Annie. "Hey, can you excuse me and Jordan for a minute?"

Annie nodded and walked away. He guessed she was probably thinking he was going to chastise Jordan a little more over not taking Hunter Jack for medical care, and that was a good alibi. When she was out of earshot he turned to Jordan, who from his nervous expression might have been thinking the same thing.

"Hey, buddy, I'm sorry I have to tell you this right now, but I didn't see a better time."

"What's that?"

"Well . . . And this just happened, so . . ." He knew he was stalling. He was bearing news he didn't like being the bearer of. "All right, so Maura's gone."

Jordan stared at him blankly. Coal could tell he was on the verge of smiling, like maybe he thought Coal was playing with him. When Coal didn't smile or laugh, Jordan's brow furrowed, causing two vertical wrinkles to form between his eyebrows. "What do you mean gone?"

"She's gone, bud. Gone. I tried to stop her, but she packed up her dogs and her truck, and she moved to Idaho Falls. She said it was to be close to her boys. And . . . and I guess because she didn't like wondering how long it was going to be before she heard I got killed."

Jordan searched Coal's eyes. At last, it appeared as if he sank back on his heels, and a gust of breath escaped him. "You aren't kidding, are you?"

"Huh. Man, I sure wish I was. I'm sorry you had to find out this way." Although he wasn't so sure the way he himself had found out wasn't quite a bit worse.

After finishing the chore he had dreaded, Coal left Jordan there with Hunter Jack, and he and Annie walked down the hall looking for Tim Lacey's room. It wasn't hard to find since there were only three patients in the ER.

Coal knocked lightly on the frame of the slightly open door, and when he heard a man's muffled voice, he eased the door open. A doctor Coal wasn't familiar with was leaned over his patient, with a nurse Coal had seen a couple of times before but never officially met standing by to wait on him when he needed something. The patient was sedated, but he wasn't out. Judging by his eyes, though, Coal was going to have to wait to interview him. Whatever the doctor had him on—Coal would have guessed morphine—had put him in another world, a soft, fluffy one all his own.

The doctor, a slender man in his mid-thirties or so with curly black hair and a perfectly trimmed mustache, looked over and saw Coal. He paused with his needle all the way out of Lacey's arm now and hovering in mid-air with the clear nylon thread hanging off the back of it attached to the line of stitches he had begun.

"Oh, hi, Sheriff. Rough night downtown, huh?"

"Yeah, sounds like it. Listen, I won't take much of your time. I was thinking about asking Tim some questions, but it doesn't look like he's in much of a state for it."

From the corner of his eye he saw Lacey move his head, and when Coal shifted his eyes he had a strange grin on his face. Coal couldn't tell if the officer was looking at him or Annie, who stood beside him.

"No, I wouldn't bother if I were you," the doctor said. "I'll be done sewing this up in twenty minutes or so, but I'm going to guess he'll be pretty gone by then. If you could come back tomorrow morning he'll probably be fine to talk. As deep and nasty as this wound is we're going to hang onto him at least until ten o'clock or so tomorrow. By the way, I'm Doctor Kozlowski. Jacek, if you want to be more casual."

Coal turned his head a little bit as if to put his ear in a better position for hearing. "I'm sorry—what's that again? Yak-sik?"

Doctor Kozlowski smiled. "Yes. My first name. I know, I know. Strange, huh? My parents were very much straight over from Poland and highly traditional. It's actually spelled J-a-c-e-k, and most of my friends call me Jace. Any other time I'd shake hands." He held up his bloody needle and thread by way of apology.

"That's all right—Jace. I'm sure I'll be back, the way things are going in this town."

Koslowski grinned. "Yes, I'm sure you will."

After leaving the hospital with Annie, Coal returned to the Lantern. Bob Wilson was still there at the bar talking with Elisa Doan. When the girl turned and saw Coal, who was walking with Annie, her face lit up. "Hey! Imagine seeing you two times in one night." It was conspicuous to Coal that Elisa avoided letting her eyes touch Annie after the first glimpse.

"Yeah. Imagine," said Coal with a rueful grin.

Bob turned fully to him. "Hey, buddy, I'm sorry about earlier. I know you're right about the medical examination. But man, I really just wanted to knock that guy's block off."

"I know. I understand. Well, he's being checked out now, and Jordan's with him. Can I talk with you for a bit?"

"Sure." He turned to the bar maid. "I'll see you later, Elisa."

Bob and Coal walked off while Annie went up to the bar. For some reason that made Coal nervous, and when he looked over there he wasn't sure he was comfortable with the way Elisa and Annie were looking at each other as they spoke in tones far too quiet to hear.

"Hey, Bob, is it true nobody else got arrested from the fight?"

"True."

"Why?"

"It was just a fight. Can you imagine how full our jails would be if we threw every guy in there that got in a fight?"

"They'd be full for sure. But . . . Okay. All right, never mind." He could feel himself getting too personally involved in tonight's altercation, merely because he knew Hunter Jack and he didn't know the others who had been in the middle of it.

"I'm gonna put that guy away, Coal," Bob said. "I swear I am. He stabbed my partner. Nothing personal, but it seems like you're a little too attached to that nut."

"I just don't think he would have stabbed him if he knew he was a cop, that's all. He's not the same man he was twenty years ago."

"Sure. They all say that."

"Hey, Bob, do you remember why he killed that guy he went to the pen for?"

Bob shrugged. "I'm not sure, no."

"He caught him with his sister's shirt off and her face all bloody. He was trying to rape her. And to be fair, they decided he only hit that guy twice. So before you condemn him, you ought to think what you might have done if that had been your sister."

Bob's face sobered. "Yeah. Okay. I guess I didn't know that. But he still stabbed Tim. He shouldn't have had that knife out if he's that volatile."

"He had four or five guys swarming him, from what I heard, and that Sherman guy already had a knife. I'm not so sure I wouldn't have done the same thing Badger did. And I'm pretty sure you would have too."

"I wouldn't have stabbed a cop."

"Yeah, that's if you knew he was a cop."

"All right. All right! No point in us gettin' all worked up about it. I just wanted you to know where I'm gonna stand."

"Okay, I'm fine with that. Just know that I like Tim, from what I know of him, but unless I find out something different I'm going to have to back Badger in this. I just want to make sure it doesn't change our friendship."

"Oh hell, Coal. Nothing could ever change that!"

Coal turned and started back toward Annie, banking on Bob Wilson's promise.

CHAPTER NINE

When Coal reached Annie, he cleared his throat to let her know he had returned. But his eyes were drawn to Elisa Doan, behind the bar. Her face looked harder than he would have imagined it, a little more jaded, and full of controlled anger.

"Well, Annie, it sure was nice talking to you." And it was plain by the smoky look in her eyes that Elisa Doan meant every word of none of that.

Annie smiled like a dragon with a toothache. "Same to you—Elisa. Keep in touch."

Coal wasn't the brightest male specimen who ever walked the planet, but from Annie's voice and the look in her eyes he was fairly certain the translation was something more like, *I can't stand the sight of your face, Elisa. Stay out of my way or I'll bury you.*

Elisa's face changed when her eyes pivoted over to Coal. "It was nice to meet you—Coal. Your name isn't 'Sheriff' at all, is it?" She smiled at him, and it was genuine, but it had that guarded, still half-angry look from knowing Annie was watching her, and trying to gut her with her eyes.

"Nope. Coal. I was saving that for later."

Wrong thing to say—not for Elisa, but certainly for Annie.

"I'll see you again," said Elisa, and she lifted a hand and gave him a wave with wiggling fingers. He was pretty sure that kind of wave was supposed to mean something deeper than only goodbye. Of course probably *all* waves had some kind of meaning behind them. Annie likely had a one-finger wave that if he weren't there she might have given to Elisa Doan.

Even as they were passing through the front door, Annie started. "I never knew you were such a flirt." She was trying to sound fun-loving, and she succeeded about like a hydrophobic dog thrown without warning into a creek.

"Flirt? What are you talking about?" He was opening the pickup door for her as he said it. And he honestly had no idea what her question referred to, but she was a woman, and he was a man. So she didn't believe him. Women always seem to assume men instantly know what they're talking about, when in reality they're lucky if men are listening in the first place.

Annie laughed though it was obvious she didn't want to. "Oh, come on. 'I was saving that for later'?"

As Annie climbed in, Coal noticed immediately that she left a few inches between her and the door, but she definitely didn't scoot all the way to the middle. He came around and got in. He set both hands on the steering wheel, let his shoulders sag and sighed, looking over at Annie. "Okay, you got me. What's wrong with saying I was saving that for later?"

She skewered him with her eyes. "Really? You don't think she took it that you plan on coming in there to see her again?"

Coal laughed, but like Annie he wasn't feeling any humor. The laugh was part reflex, part self-defense, and a third part, *Oh hell, here we go again.*

"Annie, I think we should change the subject. I promise you I wasn't flirting. I have enough trouble already."

"What's that supposed to mean?"

Coal stared at her. Out of the blue he was seeing another side of Annie Price that gave him pause. "My hell. Really? It didn't mean anything. Hey, I think I should probably take you home."

"So you can come back and interview some more witnesses?"

"Annie, stop." Coal let out a long sigh. "I think we're both getting a little cranky. I wasn't planning on coming back to town at all."

He started the truck down the street to the hollow, lonesome, deadly sound of gravel crackling under the tires. He could hear it because there was such an overpoweringly loud silence inside the cab. A full minute passed, and the lights of civilization died to a sporadic sprinkling as they rolled out of city limits.

"I'm not cranky."

Coal took a deep breath after the long silence and looked over at her. Several comments and some questions raced around inside his skull, but luckily they found no outlet. None of them would have been endearing.

"Well, let's forget it. If I said something wrong, I didn't mean to. And I wasn't flirting."

Annie fell silent, and for another mile or so she remained that way. She must have been thinking of how close they were getting to her house, however, for eventually she scooted nonchalantly over in the seat until her thigh touched his.

"I'm being stupid, Coal. I'm sorry."

She spoke with such sincerity he felt his guts immediately begin to unwind. "It's all right. I know we're both stressed out right now. Do you want me to drop you off at your house?"

Annie shrugged. After half a minute of silence she said, "I really am sorry I acted that way. That isn't me."

He had started to wonder, but then it was the first time he had seen her act that way, so maybe it really was a freak thing. Either way, it wasn't worth brooding about.

"Let's pretend it never happened."

"Okay. Coal?"

"Yeah?"

"To answer your question, I don't want you to drop me off at my house."

“What’s that?” Being a man, he had to say something stupid, and those were the two fastest stupid words he could come up with.

“I still want you to stay with me tonight.”

He thought back to Jordan, sitting at the hospital babysitting Hunter Jack, having his hands pretty much tied when it came to being able to respond to any calls. “You know it’s almost two o’clock, right?”

She nodded. “Is that bad? I kind of like two o’clock.”

At least that made him laugh. “Well, it’s not exactly conducive to getting up and going to work the next day.”

Again, a little nod, and Annie’s eyes dulled almost imperceptibly. “Okay. Yeah, you’re right. Maybe this weekend then? Maybe we could catch a movie?”

His mind was whirling. For one thing, Maura PlentyWounds was in it way too much. He should have taken a week after the Maura fiasco and kept to himself, maybe hidden somewhere in a cave trying not to paint images of Maura on the rock wall. He shouldn’t have been with Annie tonight in the first place, the night of Valentine’s Day, of all nights.

“Sure, I guess we could do that. I haven’t had much time with the kids lately, but maybe we could take some of them with us, huh? We could make a family thing of it.”

“Yeah. Yeah, that would be fun.” Said her words. Her tone belted out something else entirely, at the top of her imaginary voice. And those were the last words she spoke until Coal pulled up in front of her house.

Before he could get out, Annie threw open her door. “Hey! Not even going to let me open the door for you?”

She looked at him across the cab and tried to smile. “Oh, it’s okay. I know you have things to do.”

By “things” he knew what she really meant. Her dark thoughts had slunk back to bartender Elisa Doan. And he wasn’t going to give her the satisfaction of getting into that topic again.

He slammed his door and went around to her side, hearing her shut her own door before he got there. But at least she didn't run away. Now that he was standing there with her in front of him, he didn't know what to say or how to act. He only knew he didn't like the way she was making him feel right now. This was shades of Laura, or at least the Laura he had known during her last several years of life.

"I enjoyed tonight, Coal," she said softly. "Honestly, I did. Thanks for staying with me for a while. I hope I didn't ruin anything for us by being an idiot."

He smiled, feeling kind toward her, even if he was still a little cautious. "You didn't ruin anything."

"Are you sure?"

"Annie. I'm sure. You didn't ruin anything. Please, let's just start over. We'll do a movie—when, Friday?"

"Sure. No—Saturday. I work Friday."

"Okay. Saturday. And I won't bring anyone. Just me."

"No, it's okay. You can bring the kids."

Coal had thought better of that stupid idea. "No, this will be just us. I'll have Friday with the kids and Mom. Okay?"

"Okay." She put out her arms, and he took her and held her close. When she stepped away, she raised her face, so he lowered his to her. She kissed him, but other than the fact that it was on his lips it wasn't much different from the kind of kiss a mother would give her child. Then she turned and went up her stairs into her house and didn't look back. The shutting of the door seemed somehow like the ominous sound made by an old drawbridge in front of a stone castle.

Coal pulled out of Annie's yard back onto dark, lonely Highway 28 wondering if, in his entire life, he would ever begin to understand the mind of the female beast. Spending the rest of his adult life with dogs and horses was starting to seem like a viable option to any other choices he could think of at the moment.

He only hoped Annie had watched him out her window long enough to notice he was driving east toward home, not back toward town.

Coal blinked his eyes open to a still-dark world. He had been in bed by 2:20, but he recalled a lot of tossing and turning, especially after he had to get up an hour later to let Shadow and Dobe out of Virgil's room, and then they of course migrated to his when he let them back in from outside, almost as cold as the icy road itself. Dobe got up on Coal's bed, where he always slept if anyone let him, and then he began to practice his typical find-a-new-sleeping-position-every-five-minutes routine, and every time he moved, Coal did too.

But it wasn't only Dobe's moving around, and Shadow's snoring. A lot of Coal's lack of sleep he owed to Annie Price's poor behavior during the night, and his thoughts of Hunter Jack being stuck in a jail cell. That was not the kind of man who should be locked up.

Rolling over to the edge of the bed, Coal reached out and fumbled his hand around on his nightstand until he found a little four-inch pocket torch flashlight and shined it toward his flip clock, whose letters had long since lost their neon glow. It was 4:35, if his blurred vision could be trusted. Hardly a restful night of sleep.

But there was nothing for it. He might be able to find sleep later in the day if he looked for it, but no more sleep was going to find him tonight.

Getting up, he got dressed in the chilly dark, pulling on his brown Dickey's carpenter pants and a gray flannel shirt. He wandered downstairs, hating how his eyes felt but feeling lucky the dogs didn't knock him down the stairs and break any of his bones in their pell-mell descent. After sitting with his eyes half shut to down a breakfast of most of a carton of scrambled eggs with hot pepper sauce that seemed almost instantly to start digesting his gullet, he went out and fed the horses, letting the dogs run around again although they had just been out two hours previous. To a dog, any minute outside with their favorite master is like going to a favorite vacation spot after a year of hard labor.

He found himself missing the excited sounds of Maura's dogs, Chewy and Dart, when they would charge out of the barn upon someone's opening the door and run around the yard like their stubby tails were on fire. So many things reminded him of Maura. He wondered if he would ever have any relief from that.

After going back in and stoking up the fire, he sat in his mom's chair and tried to read her new *Time Magazine,* which was some feat, with his eyes unable to focus. They did, however, focus briefly while he was reading about the war in Vietnam. The supposed ceasefire had turned out to be a joke, as expected. Both sides kept fighting, and the North Vietnamese bases in Cambodia, which apparently weren't part of the ceasefire agreement, were getting hit especially hard.

But it warmed Coal's heart and moistened his eyes when he read about how they were going to release close to six hundred prisoners in what was being called Operation Homecoming. He could only imagine what those brave boys had been through. He had seen how the Viet Cong treated American fighters, and it was ugly and vicious. His thoughts returned unbidden to Slugger Janx, another casualty of a war that seemed to have no end.

It wouldn't be light for quite a while, but Coal was getting nervous. He would have driven into town right then to interview Tim Lacey, but he was pretty sure the hospital staff would advocate having him thrown out if he showed up at 5:40 in the morning. So for a few minutes he closed his eyes.

He woke to Connie coming down the hall to the coat tree and slipping into her coat, and with his eyes still half shut he told her he had already fed the horses. Taking her coat back off, she thanked him and asked what he wanted to eat, and he was so tired he almost forgot he had already eaten.

"What time is it, Mom?"

"Six."

So his "few minutes" had become forty. He stumbled up and went over to get his coat, suddenly realizing that in his state of exhaustion he hadn't made coffee. And the funniest part was he hadn't even missed it—maybe because he dreaded tasting name-brand coffee now after the delicious mix Sam Browning had brought with him from Nebraska.

"You must be out of it, Son," said Connie as he fumbled with his coat. "No coffee?"

He grinned. As always, she was reading his mind. "Maybe later."

"Why off so early?"

"I'll tell you later. It's about all that crap they called me in for last night."

"Oh, yes, I was going to—" She stopped, apparently changing her mind about whatever she had intended to say. "Sorry. Yes, you can tell me all about it later. So . . . how's Annie?"

Coal cringed. "Hey, Mom, I'm really sorry about that. I should have called. Just so you know, nothing happened. I didn't even get drunk last night. I wanted to, but I didn't."

Connie raised an eyebrow and smirked. "I don't know what you mean. What would have happened?"

With a grin, Coal walked over and squeezed his mom's shoulders, then kissed her on the forehead. "I wish I could stay longer and see the kids off. But hey—let's do something nice with the family Friday, all right? A movie or something."

Connie smiled, making her eyes almost disappear behind their mask of sleep that had yet to fade. "That would be real nice, Coal. The kids would love it—and so would I."

CHAPTER TEN

The warm thought of an upcoming movie night with the entire family gave Coal something to ponder while driving in the ice-cold cab toward Salmon. On a whim, he had loaded Shadow up with him, and she sat on the seat beside him, staring out the front window with bright eyes, headed out on a big new adventure. She was with Daddy, and that was probably her biggest adventure of all.

Coal stopped first at the hospital and got the expected reaction from the receptionist, whom like the nurse and doctor the night before, he didn't know. She wasn't keen on letting him go into Tim Lacey's room, but the badge on his coat seemed persuasive.

The doctor Coal had met the night before, Jacek Koslowski, met him in the hall outside Lacey's room, looking about the way Coal felt.

"Early bird gets the worm, huh?" the doctor said, blinking to clear his tired eyes.

"Something like that."

The doctor thrust out his hand, a much stronger hand than that of Doctor Bent, his colleague. "And you're Coal, right? I had to ask Jordan."

"Yes, Coal. Jace, right? Sorry I wasn't so sociable last night. So is Officer Lacey coming around at all?"

"Well, at this time of day . . ."

Coal nodded. "I know. I'm sorry. I just need to get some questions answered if at all possible before the judge gets to the courthouse this morning."

Doctor Koslowski shrugged. “Well, you can only try, right? Just don’t shake him too much if he doesn’t wake up easy. Deal?”

“Sure. I know it’s hard to guess from my looks, but I’m not quite that much of a barbarian.”

They laughed, and Coal stepped into Tim Lacey’s room. His bed was the only one of two that was occupied. Lacey appeared to be sleeping soundly, and it pained Coal to wake him, but he felt like what he had to do was pretty important.

“Tim. Lacey.”

He spoke quietly, hopefully.

“Lacey?”

The sleeping man’s eyes fluttered then finally came open. They shut again for a few seconds, fluttered once more, and then opened on Coal.

“Hey, Sheriff. What time is it?”

Coal hated to tell him. “Too early.” At least he didn’t have to lie. Lacey could take the reply however he wanted.

“What’re you doin’ here?”

“I don’t want to bother you, but I really need to ask you something.”

“Shoot. I’m feelin’ like I need some more morphine anyway, so I doubt I’ll go back to sleep.”

Coal decided to play the nice guy and went to tell the doctor Lacey was hurting. When he came back, figuring they would administer morphine soon and render the patient unable to talk, he jumped right into why he was here.

“Hey, Tim, what I’m here about is Hunter Jack, the guy that stabbed you.”

One side of Lacey’s mouth came up slowly in what resembled a sardonic smile. “Oh yeah, I know Jack well. What about him?”

“Well, I need to know your impression of him last night.”

“Painful.”

That made Coal laugh. "Sorry, bad question. I meant . . . Well, I know that kind of crap always happens fast, but do you think he recognized you? Or did it seem like he was acting by reflex?"

Lacey shrugged with his good arm. "You know, Sheriff, I've seen that guy be a real ass sometimes. I'm not gonna deny that. But I think he was in a bad spot, and he just whirled around when he heard me and stuck me. That's all. He had so much alcohol in his system by then, I doubt my words registered on him. Bein' that close was really stupid on my part. I'm only gonna blame myself for getting hurt."

"You sure?"

"Well, I'm going by past experience with him and the expression on his face. He was pretty surrounded, and I think he was sure he'd have to fight his way out of there."

"Okay. Thanks, Tim. I had a gut feeling about that."

"So why are you asking?"

"Well, I need to go talk to him now that he's sober and see what he says. Then I'm thinking about going up to his hearing when the judge comes in and see if I can get him out of that cell. It's like having a wolf locked in a bathroom with no windows."

Lacey nodded, seeming noncommittal.

"What do you think? I hope that doesn't offend you."

"Oh hell no. No, let 'im out. Overall he's always been pretty decent to me. Reminds me of a line in *True Grit.*" He grinned. "He never played me false until he killed me."

Coal laughed, remembering that line delivered by Moon, a character played by Dennis Hopper. "Well, let's hope he doesn't do that. Hey, thanks for being understanding." He stepped forward and thrust out his right hand to shake, then felt sheepish and changed hands. Lacey wasn't going to be using his right hand for much of anything for some time.

When Coal got to the courthouse it was every bit as quiet as he would have expected. There was no longer a night jailer, of course, until he could find someone to replace Victor Yancey, but Jordan's pickup was in the lot, and he saw a flash of movement go past the window in the door.

Going down the stairs, he peeked in and saw Jordan at his desk, nursing a cup of coffee and staring into space. He eased open the door, but even as quiet as he came in Jordan jumped up and sloshed his coffee.

"Hey, bud, it's just me. You okay?"

Jordan nodded. "Sure. Just tired."

Coal liked the smell of the coffee, and he wondered if it wasn't residual still from what Sam Browning had brought. Walking to the pot, he poured himself a mug full, more out of habit than because it sounded good. In spite of the smell, for some reason the thought of its taste didn't seem appealing. He took a sip, thought it tasted fine and was definitely Sam's mix. But it had lost something, and it was almost overnight. Maybe it was the same way that Maura seemed to have lost her love for him overnight—assuming she had ever loved him at all. And that last was a stark thought that had never come to him until now.

While Coal sipped the coffee he had lost his taste for, Shadow had gone back to her puppy days and was happy to run around the room sniffing at everything but the coffee, probably to make sure she was doing her job of keeping Coal safe. Or looking for scraps of food, whichever came first.

"How's the prisoner?"

Jordan stopped scratching Shadow behind the ears in one of her slow passes and looked up from his reverie. He was sitting in Coal's chair again. "Huh? Oh. He's good, I think. The doctor told me to check on him every now and then and make sure he's breathing."

Coal chuckled. "Yeah, like that's going to do any good. He could stop breathing thirty seconds after you walk out of there."

Jordan gave a tired grin. "Yeah, I thought about that. Hey, Coal? What do you think about that guy? You really think he's cool?"

"You mean Badger? I don't know what you mean by 'cool', but he's always been pretty good around me. Why?"

"I don't know. I don't know, it's just . . . Man, he sure did a number on Lacey, huh? That's a nasty one."

"Yeah. That's what alcohol does to a man. Especially in a tight spot like he was in last night."

"So do you think he knew what he was doing? Knew it was a cop?"

Coal shrugged. "Tim doesn't think so." He told Jordan about his visit to the hospital that morning, and Jordan sat in silence for a time, sipping his coffee.

"He sure looks mean as hell," he said, breaking an extended quiet so profound it had started to seem almost peaceful. The only noise before Jordan's voice was the clicking of Shadow's toenails on the pale-yellow concrete floor.

"He does that. So when's the last time you went in there?"

"Twenty minutes. He's sacked out good."

With a nod, Coal scanned the room, trying to think of something to kill time. Even though he had gone to the hospital and bothered Tim Lacey, it really hadn't been necessary. The judge didn't come in until just before nine anyway. Maybe he'd let Badger sleep some more. At least *someone* could benefit.

"Hey!" Jack's voice from the cell block made Coal and Jordan jump, as well as Shadow. Jordan swore.

Coal looked at him mildly. "Watch it. You're stealing my lines." Shadow, with ears pricked sharply up, looked from one to the other of them, the bright look in her eyes seeming to indicate she could actually understand them. She looked at the cellblock door, tilting her head to one side.

When Coal heard Jack holler again he walked to the door and looked in, then came back to the desk and with a brief thanks took the key Jordan had extended toward him.

He went back into the cell block, where Jack was still alone, but now standing up with his meat hooks curled around the bars. "Hey, Savage. I gotta get outta here, man. I gotta get out!"

"What'll you do if you get out?"

"I'll maybe go down the river and do some trapping and not come back for a month."

"It's iced-over."

"I don't care. Savage, I never begged nobody for nothin', but you gotta listen. I'd kill t' get outta this place."

CHAPTER ELEVEN

Coal stayed with Hunter Jack for a while, interviewing him in depth. Unfortunately, Jack had been quite inebriated during the night, so his memory wasn't crystal-clear, but one thing he maintained adamantly was that he didn't recognize Tim Lacey as an officer, he didn't see his badge, and he was certain he was about to have great bodily harm done to him if he didn't act on the instant. He knew the moment his knife sank home that he had made a big mistake, and for him the fight was over then.

"That knife you had, it was on your hip in plain sight, right?"

"Of course. Like always. I ain't lookin' for no concealed weapons charge."

"All right. Well, I already went in and talked to Officer Lacey at the hospital, and he says he agrees that you didn't seem to recognize he was a cop. I don't know how much it'll help, but I think it'll be worth something. At least maybe we can get you out of here until your arraignment."

"Okay. Man, Savage, I really owe you. This place is bringin' back bad memories. I swore I'd never do anything to get me back in a place like this again. That's why I don't ever drive when I go down to the bars."

After Coal left, he went out into the office again where Jordan was getting ready to pack it in for his shift. The deputy was still sitting at the desk, now with his gun belt off, and he was looking at a photograph he had pinned between thumb and forefinger.

"Makes you wonder if I should keep somethin' like that, huh?" So saying, he flipped the picture out on the desk toward Coal like he was dealing him a card. Coal picked it up, and a wave of unbidden heartache rushed through him.

The picture was of Jordan standing with his arm around Maura's shoulders, the icy Salmon as a backdrop. The pangs in his heart at seeing this picture of Maura looking so beautiful could not be denied. One thing he noticed that made him feel a little better was that although Jordan's arm was around Maura, hers were folded across her chest. Maybe it was only his pride that made him believe it, but he was pretty sure had that been him in the photo she would have reciprocated with an arm around him. All in all, and in spite of her sudden, heart-breaking departure, it felt like he really had meant something to her. He just didn't know how she could drive out of the valley, away from him, and worse, make it look so easy.

Coal flipped the photo face down and slid it back to Jordan. He couldn't look at it anymore. "Yeah, I don't know, buddy. That could be a tough decision, I guess."

Leaving the photo upside-down on the desk, Jordan went over and changed out of his shirt, pulling on a sweatshirt and hanging the shirt he had been wearing for his uniform from a hook on the wall, the badge still attached to it. Coal watched him, wondering what that was all about, because in this little county a deputy was technically always on duty, or at least on call. It simply had to be that way. A strange thought came to him, and he took a long swallow of coffee, studying his deputy and hoping not to be caught. Jordan wasn't planning on anything rash, was he? Like walking out and leaving him even more short-handed?

It made Coal feel better when Jordan stepped over and slipped his gun belt back around his hips, buckling it tight. Then he quietly unfastened the badge and slipped it into a front pocket of his pants, and Coal knew he was staying.

Jordan went to the front door, looking lost in thought, and picked his coat off the hook, pulling it on as he leaned down and looked out the little square window in the door.

"I'd keep it." The sound of Coal's voice was the first loud noise in the room in some time, since Shadow had decided the room was secure and had sacked out by the radiator.

With his hand on the doorknob, Jordan turned toward him, eyebrows raised. "What's that?"

Walking over to the desk, his coffee cup in his left hand, Coal slid the photograph of Jordan and Maura off the desk with the fingers of his right hand and stepped to where Jordan was waiting, holding it out to him with the face of it showing. "If you don't keep this you're going to wish you had."

Coal knew that for a fact. He didn't have any such photo, and he would always wish he did.

After Jordan was gone, Coal sat alone and thumbed through some issues of *Outdoor Life* and *Sports Afield* that he always kept around for boring times. He really couldn't go out and do much with it being so close to the judge's time to come in, and in truth he didn't want to anyway. He had knocked himself out since first arriving in Salmon back in November, and a few quiet moments stolen for himself were not going to make him feel the slightest bit guilty.

Keeping an eye on the parking lot, he finally saw the judge's black Lincoln Mark IV pull into the lot and park, and taking the bull by the horns, he vaulted up and went outside, meeting Sinclair as he stepped up out of his car.

"Good morning, Judge."

Sinclair smiled. "Good morning, Coal. Say, I thought we discussed calling me Wiley. As long as no one else is around."

Coal returned the man's smile, once more amazed at how much he had come to like and admire this man after they had had such a sour start. He reached out and shook his hand.

"That's right—Wiley. So I was hoping I could have a word with you this morning real quick."

"Sure thing. We can go inside though, right? It's a little nippy out here for my old bones. How cold is it supposed to be, anyway?"

"About two or three degrees, I think."

The judge rubbed his hands together, affecting a shiver. "Yes, let's go inside and talk."

They walked side by side to the door that led to the upper floors of the courthouse—where the more important people worked—and Coal yanked the door open to allow the more important person to go in first.

They went up to the office, and Wilma Frank, the judge's receptionist, was already at her desk, dressed in a red blazer and white shirt. Wilma, who was in her late fifties, with thick-framed glasses and short, curly brown hair that had soaked up its fair share of dye, was by no means anyone's beauty queen, but she had a good heart. "Good morning, Wilma. You look very nice today." And Coal wasn't lying, because she did: *nice.*

"Why thank you, Coal! Flattery will get you a bowl full of Tootsie Rolls if you aren't careful." She reached out and nudged such a crystal bowl toward him across the top of her cherry wood desk.

"Thanks anyway, but I'm watching my figure." They laughed, and Coal followed the judge into his office, where the judge took off his black wool overcoat and hung it from a coat tree.

He waved Coal toward a chair in front of his desk. "Want to sit?"

Coal had sat enough today. "No, thank you. I won't take long."

"All right then. So what's on your mind so early in the morning?"

"Well, there was a fight down at the Lantern last night."

Judge Sinclair smiled, and Coal thought he held back a laugh. "I'm sure that wasn't what you wanted to talk about; you'd be up here every morning!"

Coal had to grin. "That's true. No, this was worse than normal. Officer Lacey got stabbed."

The judge's face became all business. "Oh no. Was he hurt bad?"

"Well, bad enough to put him off the streets for a while. It was in his right arm and just missed the artery."

"Heavens. I'm glad he's all right."

"Me too. But what I specifically wanted to talk about is the man who did the stabbing. You might already know him." Coal hoped he didn't. It generally wasn't a good thing when the local judge knew you, unless he knew you because you were a member of his church. "His name is Hunter Jack. Some people call him Dark Badger. He's a Shoshone."

"I see." Coal could tell the judge was flipping through his mental files, and after a moment he shook his head. "I don't think that name sounds familiar."

"Well, that's good."

"Yes, very good. So you say he's the man who did the stabbing? Is he a local? From the village?"

"Yes. He's been here for years."

"He must keep his nose pretty clean then."

"He does. And he's always treated me with complete respect, and any other officer I've seen him talking to. Even when he's drunk he never challenges the law."

"So what led to this stabbing then?"

"Well, it sounds like a bunch of guys were giving him a bad time, making fun of him because he likes to dress . . . Well, sort of what you might call "traditional". Anyway, to make a long story short, these guys were harassing him, knocked his hat off, and one of them cut it in half. He hit that guy, the guy pulled a knife on him, and about when it looked its worst Tim Lacey came in behind Jack and challenged him. That's when Jack turned around and stabbed him. And that's the gist of it."

The judge mused on the story for a moment, his brow knitted. "Coal, would you like a cigar?"

"No thank you. They don't agree with me much."

"Oh. I didn't know." By the look in the judge's eyes Coal wondered if he was remembering back to the time just before Christmas when he gave him two of his prize cigars. "You don't mind if I smoke, though." He said it more like a statement than as a question.

"No, not at all."

The judge took a cigar out of the case he kept in his desk drawer, along with a match. Snipping the end of the cigar off with a guillotine cutter, he struck the match on the inside of the drawer, then pushed it shut and held the light to the tip of his cigar. After a couple of deep puffs, he blew the smoke toward the ceiling. Coal caught the somewhat-pleasant, bittersweet scent.

"From Cuba," said the judge, around his cigar. "Hard to get."

"Oh, yeah, I bet." Illegal to get, too, thought Coal, but he would do nothing with that information beyond filing it away in his mental cabinet as an interesting tidbit about the local administrator of law.

"Let me ask you, when did this Hunter Jack fellow pull his knife?"

"According to all witnesses, only after the other guy confronted him with a knife."

The judge nodded, thoughtful. That revelation seemed to please him. "So Coal, what exactly is it that you would like to see happen? I have a feeling you have some personal interest in this affair. Is this Hunter Jack a friend of yours?"

"I wouldn't call him a friend, exactly, but a friendly acquaintance. Really just a guy I don't think belongs in a cell. Before you get looking into it much, I should tell you that he did eight years in the Boise pen, but it was because he struck a man a couple of times who was trying to rape his younger sister, and the guy ended up dying."

"You don't say! Struck him? With a fist? That's some punch!"

"You'll understand when you see the size of his hands."

The judge puffed on his cigar again and gave a close-mouthed smile and a shrug. "I don't know, I always thought getting hit with a bigger fist would feel easier—sort of spread the pressure out."

Coal laughed at that. "I guess there's some truth to that. But Jack's got enough pressure in his fists to go around. Oh! And Wiley, one other thing: I went down to Steele Memorial to visit with Tim, and he said he feels like Badger didn't realize who he was when he stabbed him."

"No?"

Coal shrugged. "That's what he told me this morning."

"Okay. Well, that's promising. So back to my question, I guess I'd like to know what your interest in the case is. You're not friends, you just don't think he belongs in a cell. But he stabbed an officer. What if he had hit his artery? Or maybe put that knife in his chest? He sounds like a dangerous man."

"I sure can't deny that, but I don't think I've ever seen him in a fight. Well, at least not any that he started. I just hate to see him caged up for very long. And I don't really care to feed him either, to tell you the truth."

The judge chuckled. "No doubt. It sounds like he would take a lot of nourishment just to feed his fists. So Coal, if I let this fellow out at his hearing, can you assure me he'll be back for arraignment? And trial?"

"I think so. I'm pretty sure he has relations in the Indian village, and quite a collection of historical Indian artifacts he wouldn't want to lose. Strong ties here. I don't think he'll leave."

Looking down at his desk, the judge put the fingers of one hand up to start massaging his forehead as he brooded in silence for a moment. At last, he looked up at Coal. "All right. I trust you. Let's give him a chance. With the one consideration that he seems like a good fellow when he appears before me. Any sign of contempt, I might change my mind."

"I understand, sir. I mean Wiley, sorry. I would feel the same way."

"Good." The judge flipped his hand over to look at his wristwatch. "It looks like we'll have preliminary hearings in about half an hour. Bring him up and we'll see how things go."

"Thanks. I appreciate it."

The judge almost smiled as he studied Coal. "Thank you, Coal. I appreciate *you.*" He put out his hand to shake.

CHAPTER TWELVE

Inmate Hunter Jack, beside his shack under a tin roof which was held up by a four-by-four on each corner, kept an incredibly beautiful 1955 Buick Special, deep burgundy with an immaculate white top, flawless chrome all around, and perfect white wall tires. It was a vehicle that when brand-new would have run close to thirty-five hundred dollars on the showroom floor, and because of its condition and the low mileage of 22,000 miles it was likely the car had retained much of that value.

Coal had only seen Jack out driving that Buick four or five times, but on one of those occasions he remembered Jack telling him he won it in Elko gambling with some rich old lady who seemed like she had nothing better to do in life than give her car away. He had found out later it belonged to the woman's husband, who at seventy-two years old had found some twenty-five-year-old woman who apparently loved him more than his faithful wife did and had run away on her. She was dumping everything of value he had left behind and squirreling the money away as fast as she could so if he ever returned to his senses there wouldn't be anything worth coming back for—except of course for his wife, and she would no longer be available.

Coal chuckled every time he thought about that feisty old lady. But he didn't chuckle when he thought about that incredible car, which Jack had carefully draped in sheets and then covered in tarps, almost never letting it see daylight, for any reason. Even in spite of all his antique Indian artifacts, that Buick was Jack's most prized possession. It was almost as beautiful a car as anything Coal had ever seen, and unfortunately the only thing Jack could put up for his bail.

The judge set bail at one thousand dollars, and Jack had to find a hundred in cash or a check to pay the bondsman, who would put up the rest. The alternative was to find something else of value, and in Jack's case that was going to be the title of the Buick.

Coal had taken it upon himself to get Jack out and take him back to his house, where they picked up the car and caravanned back to the jail with Coal in his pickup and Jack in the Buick, although Coal was sort of wishing it could have been the other way around.

The bondsman, in Jack's case, was a bonds*woman*—and Coal had no doubt after their meeting that he would be laughing long after she left his office. He had called down to Cherry Bail Bonds and got a curt-sounding woman on thc phonc who cut him off mid-sentence and told him she would come right down to arrange things for Jack to get out of jail.

Seven minutes later, almost to the second, into Coal's office without knocking strode a dark-haired woman in a cherry-red corduroy blazer, a pink blouse with ruffles all the way down the front, and a pleated red skirt made of the same corduroy as the blazer. She couldn't have stood much over five feet tall, and her face was pinched and wizened, in spite of Coal's guess that she probably wasn't much older than he was. In a day when most women were wearing semi-square or round-lens glasses big enough to cover the faces of two cats sitting side by side—perhaps the ultimate *Siamese* twins—this woman's horn-rimmed glasses, which had gone out of style in the sixties, seemed far out of place. But then, in Salmon, Idaho, the woman seemed far out of place as well.

"Hi. You the sheriff?" she said in a decided northeastern accent that instantly grated on Coal's ears.

He had already stood up, and he nodded. “Yes, ma’am. Sheriff Savage.”

The little woman marched over to him, her high heels clickety-clacking on the concrete. She seemed to get smaller and smaller as she got close, rather than larger. Reaching Coal, she thrust her hand out in front of her like a spear. “Cherry Bales, Sheriff. Pleased ta meet ya. Oh—I own Cherry Bail Bonds.”

A smile tried to break over Coal’s face, but the little woman seemed so serious he held his humor back. “Your name is Bales?”

She almost smiled. Reaching up to adjust her grossly outdated glasses, she said, “Yeah, ain’t that funny? Back when I was a kid my name was Cah-pent-a.” Coal assumed in Idaho that would translate to “Carpenter”. “But I never knew nothin’ about workin’ with wood. I stah-ted datin’ a guy named Cook, but I didn’t know how ta cook nothin’ neither, so I thought that wouldn’t work. Then my next boyfriend was named Messer—no kiddin’! For real! Nasty. Couldn’t do it—even though he was my favorite of ’em all. Finally I hooked up with this old dolt named Bales. Not a bad sort, ya know? Just dumb. Had lots o’ money, though. So I decided ta take all his money an’ start us a business, an’ here I am ta-day. Now don’t bother askin’ how I ended up here in Salmon, because that’s a whole othuh story, an’ I’m not into talkin’ that much.”

Coal had tried so hard not to laugh, but now he had to. Cherry Bales wasn’t laughing. She wasn’t even smiling. But there was no way anyone could have convinced him she wasn’t messing around with him. Messer might not have been such a bad name for her at that.

“Well, Mrs. Bales, that’s a pretty fitting name for someone in your business.”

“Thanks. Oh, so ya know, I prefer *Miz* Bales. Ya know, that dirty rat ran out on me? Yeah, he did. Clod. Found another woman, an’ she wasn’t even younger or prettier, and she worked at a McDonald’s. See? No accountin’ for taste, huh?”

Coal laughed again. This wizened-looking little lady was a laugh a minute. “Nope, no accounting.”

“So ya know what I thought would be funny? If I coulda found some paht-nas for this business—some guy named Jump, and then another one named Dye. It woulda been great. We woulda had a great big billboard up, ya know? A bunch o’ business cahds. An’ they would all say, ‘Jump, Bales, an’ Dye’.”

This time little Cherry Bales actually smiled, slyly, but Coal didn’t know if she was entertained more by her own joke or by the fits of laughter she was giving him. Cherry Bales was one little firecracker.

It had been a while since Coal was able to really laugh. It felt so good that when he was through he had to wipe his eyes. “Well, Ms. Bales.”

“Hey. Can ya just call me Cherry? That’s what all my friends know me by, an’ then if I find some other schmuck an’ get married again you won’t have ta learn anothuh name.”

Grinning, Coal said, “All right. Cherry it is. And I’m Coal. It’s good to meet you. I needed some humor right now.”

She stared up at him—*way* up. Her expression never changed. “You think I was tryin’ ta be funny?”

Again, Coal laughed. “Well, Cherry, I sure hope so, or we’re both in a lot of trouble.”

“Hey, Coal—you mind if I smoke a cigarette? Jeez, this Idaho air is cold an’ dry.”

“No, go ahead.”

While Cherry Bales took care of the business of preparing to drive another nail into her coffin—a process which Coal wasn’t sure would cure the cold, dry air—he thought about Hunter Jack. It was going to be interesting to see how that big Shoshone and Cherry Bales got along. It was a pretty sure bet he had never met such a woman before. But how many Idahoans had?

“So what we got, Coal? Some really bad guy? A killa?”

Coal laughed again. “No, luckily not something quite *that* bad. Just a guy who got worked up while he was drinkin’ and went after the wrong guy—a cop.”

“Ahh. Okay. Well, his honuh says it’s a thousand bucks, right? This guy in your jail—what’s his name, now?”

“Hunter Jack.”

“This Huntuh Jack, do you think he can pay the ten percent? Or what?”

“Did you see that burgundy car in the lot? The shiny one with the white top? Hunter owns the title to that.”

“Huh. Well, I didn’t pay attention ta no cah. But your eyes are lightin’ up so much talkin’ about it I gotta think it must be some beauty, huh?”

“It is. And I’m guessing it’s probably between twenty-five hundred and three thousand dollars’ worth of car.” *Cah,* he felt like saying.

She dipped her head. “All right then. I think we can get this gentleman outta here with that—assuming’ he brought the title up heah with him too.”

When Coal brought Jack out of the cellblock to sign paperwork and be released, *Miz* Cherry Bales started in again with her dry humor. A confused look engraved semi-permanently on his face, Jack kept looking from the woman to Coal. Coal wasn’t sure if he was more confused or simply amazed.

After Cherry stopped at the door, turned and wiggled her fingers at Coal and said, “Ta ta,” then flounced out the door and up the stairs, her hips swaying as she tried not to slip on the ice, Jack turned to stare at Coal. “Hey, man. Now I know *she’s* in town . . . I ain’t so sure it’s safe goin’ outside no more.”

Coal laughed again, still enjoying all the good humor in his office today. “I’m sure you can handle it. So. You want a ride home, or do you plan to walk?”

“I’m gonna walk.”

"That's what I thought. Remember, you have to be back here at nine o'clock next Tuesday—the twentieth. It would've been Monday, but that's President's Day. You got that? Where's your paperwork?"

"Pocket."

"Okay, Badger. Well, you're free to go. Stay safe out there, all right? And do me a favor, would you? Stay out of trouble. I'd be sick if Cherry Bales got that great car from you."

"So I got a question: She said she gets ten percent when it's all done, right? So what is that . . . fifty bucks?" Hunter Jack was no mathematician, drunk *or* sober.

"No, that's one hundred." The number sounded huge when Coal said it out loud.

"Where am I gonna get a hundred bucks, Savage? Supposed to sell my Buick, or what?"

"We'll figure something out, all right? It really isn't that much, in exchange for getting out of that cell. Try to enjoy your freedom and not think about it. You have enough to worry about."

"That judge said I'd prob'ly get a public . . . what was it?"

"Defender."

"Yeah. He said I'd get that, right? When do I get that guy?"

"I'm not sure. But I have a friend here in town I might go talk to for you. His name's Keith Perkins, and I think he's a crack lawyer. Best of all, though, he's an honest, good guy. I think he might help us. It'd probably be worth talking to him."

"The public . . . *guy,* he ain't enough? He's free, right?"

Coal's face went serious. "Badger, I think we need to get something straight. We haven't talked about it a lot because I didn't want to worry you, but you're in a really bad spot, I'm afraid. This isn't some little misdemeanor. Honestly, if this were a different town I don't even know if you'd be getting out right now. You could go to the pen again. Do you understand that?"

Hunter Jack stared at him. "I can't go to the pen, Savage. You know that. I won't go back there."

Coal shrugged. "Then we need to go see Keith Perkins. That *free* public defender might be worth exactly what you're going to pay for him. Even if you had to sell that Buick, it's better than being in the pen again isn't it?"

A film seemed to come over Hunter Jack's eyes. Coal knew the look. It was a true film—a film *reel*—showing all Jack's bad memories of the Idaho Penitentiary in Boise. Then his dark eyes cleared again, and they didn't look misty or far away. They looked cold—and deadly.

"I ain't goin' back to the pen."

CHAPTER THIRTEEN

Coal couldn't think of any way to help Hunter Jack out of his predicament other than to talk to attorney Keith Perkins, a man he admittedly wasn't extremely familiar with. But from the little he did know about Perkins, he had seemed an honest man and a caring one. So Coal finally convinced Hunter Jack they needed to go see him. Jack went reluctantly, and leaving Shadow in the truck, they headed for Perkins's place of business.

Perkins fortunately was in his office and not with anyone when Coal and Hunter Jack slipped in. At an oak desk ten feet or so inside the front door of Perkins's law office sat a middle-aged woman with medium-length red hair who gave an overly friendly smile but whose wrinkle-lined face and nervous blue eyes gave off a somewhat different aura. Although it could be a huge help in his line of work, Coal sometimes hated his intuition about people, but he couldn't deny it.

"Good morning!" The woman was beaming, her teeth well cared-for and shiny white, her voice on the verge of annoying because of its put-on cheer. "I'm Kelly. Can I help you?" She was directing her attention to Coal, probably in part, or perhaps fully, due to his badge. Her eyes skipped over to the rough-looking Shoshone and immediately back to Coal.

"I hope so. I wanted to see if my friend Hunter and I could visit with Mr. Perkins for a little bit, if he isn't busy. I'm Coal Savage, by the way."

He didn't offer his hand, having come from the old school where a woman must offer hers first, but Kelly did. Her arm shot straight out across the desk, her fingers curving down to point at the desktop. She was too eager to shake, and her arm and hand too stiff. But when Coal took it, it was likc holding a banana pccl—thc same limp, cool, moist feeling—and he was thankful she dropped her hand almost right away.

"It's so nice to meet you," she said in her pretend happy voice. "And I think Mr. Perkins—my cousin, actually—is free at the moment. If you'll wait here a second I'll go check."

Kelly got up, revealing a slim figure dressed in wide-legged white slacks to go with her pale-yellow sweater, which he guessed was what made her dark makeup seem almost overpowering. She knocked lightly on an open door off the lobby, and Coal heard her speak in a low tone. Then he heard Keith Perkins's big, booming voice and the sound of his huge personality shining through with it.

Perkins erupted with a big smile on his face, a smile that could not have been faked. "Sheriff Savage, how the heck are ya? Man, I haven't seen you in a coon's age."

"A young coon, I guess," Coal replied, thrusting out his hand to meet that of Perkins.

Perkins laughed in his warm baritone voice, and his eyes twinkled. "You got me there. I guess it would be one of those younger ones. My friend, what the heck can I do for ya?"

"Well Keith, I came to introduce you to a friend of mine, Hunter Jack."

Warmly and genuinely, Perkins offered his hand to the Shoshone. "It's good to meet you, Mr. Jack. Or can I call you Hunter? I'm kind of partial to that name."

Jack shrugged. "Whatever you want, I guess." He took the outstretched hand, and his swallowed it whole.

"Sheesh! Man, I hope you played football, with hands like that!"

With another shrug, Jack looked over at Coal. Coal was unable to read whether the Shoshone liked Perkins or found him too personal. Perhaps he wasn't as good at reading people as he liked to think.

"I played a little. Mostly not. Fought in Nam, though."

Perkins nodded. "Well, thank you for your service to the country, Hunter. So hey" —he stopped talking long enough to wave the two of them into his office— "why don't you step into my little domain here, and we'll chat."

Coal and Jack preceded Perkins into his office and paused at the chairs he offered them as he walked around to the other side of his desk. Coal's eyes scanned the room, jumping from a full-sized taxidermy mount of a mountain lion stalking the wall behind the desk to a massive full curl bighorn ram which appeared to be of the desert bighorn subspecies. He wasn't going to broach the subject of hunting because it didn't seem like the time, but Jack took care of that matter for him. And now, from what Coal could see and hear in Jack's voice, he had suddenly decided Perkins was perhaps okay.

"Nice ram, man! Is that a desert one?"

"It is! It sure is," said Perkins, nodding. "Yeah, I get a little crazy with the hunting thing. You hunt?"

Jack's eyes crinkled up, bounced over to Coal, then back to Keith. "A little bit."

"Don't let him fool you, Keith. This guy's a legend out in the woods." It was common knowledge to Coal and to anyone else around town that one hundred percent of Hunter Jack's hunting was done with a bow since the passage of the Gun Control Act, but he didn't mention that. With a rifle or with a bow, either way Jack's legend could not be denied.

"I don't doubt that a bit," said Keith. "Not one bit. Heck, I'm betting with those hands you don't even need a gun—just get close enough to bat 'em upside the head." He looked down at the meat hooks on the ends of Jack's arms again with real admiration in his eyes. "So . . . You guys wanna have a seat? Or we can stand for a while too."

"No, we'll sit," Coal replied for himself and Jack, and he nodded Jack toward the chair in front of him.

When they were comfortably seated, Perkins scooted his chair back a little and leaned forward to put his elbows on his knees, doing his best to share his gaze equally between both of them. "So what can I help you gentlemen with this morning?"

"Well, Keith, Hunter got himself into a little bit of trouble." He went on at Perkins's urging to tell the entire story, including how Tim Lacey, the proposed victim, didn't believe the stabbing was intentional on Jack's part. Then, before Perkins could say anything about whether he would be able to take on the case or not, Coal threw in the monkey wrench. "I can't let you go any further on this whole thing without knowing Jack doesn't have a lot of money to pay you. I wanted you to know that right up front. I know you aren't in business to work for free, but any kind of break you might be able to offer would sure be appreciated. The judge already said he would appoint a public defender, but I just feel a little nervous about leaving something this big to . . . Well, no offense to public defenders, but . . .”

“Well, you know, actually most public defenders can hold their own with the best of us.” Perkins interlaced his fingers and steepled his index fingers up to his chin, nodding slowly. “Why don’t you boys let me give this some thought, all right? Let me look over my schedule, what I’ve got going on . . . But yeah, I think there’s definitely some wiggle room. I’ve been in tough places before myself.” He directed his gaze at Hunter Jack.

“Sounds good, man.”

“We’ll need to know fairly soon,” Coal interjected. “Not to rush you, of course. But his arraignment will be on Tuesday morning.”

“Oh, sure, sure. Yeah.” He bunched his lips and seemed to be pondering some intriguing thought, then took a deep breath and looked at them both as if he had had a big revelation. “Hey. You know what? I’m just gonna jump in with both feet and say I think I can help you.”

“You can?” asked Coal.

“Sure. Let me tell you something. Confidentially. I’m actually what you call a panel attorney, on top of my regular cases. That means I’m basically a pinch hitter for the judges if something goes wrong with the PD—the public defender. You know, some conflict of interest or something. So I think I can go have a chat with Judge Sinclair and get myself appointed to the case. Just don’t spread that around.”

Coal and Jack stared him down until Coal finally said, “You’re kidding. You’d do that?”

“Sure! Sure, I would. One hunter to another, man. I’d be happy to.”

Now Jack was grinning, and Coal clapped him on the shoulder. “There you go, Badger. The Lord works in mysterious ways, doesn’t he?”

Perkins slapped his desk with both hands and gave them his huge grin. "He sure does. He sure does. All right. We're in business. Let's meet back here at . . . On second thought, you know what? I'm positive I can get appointed your case. Can we talk right now?"

Jack nodded. "Sure, I ain't got nothin' goin'."

Coal stood up. "All right, I'll just leave you two on your own."

Jack's voice stopped him as he was standing up. "Hey, Savage . . . I don't suppose there's any way you c'd stay is there? I'd kinda like it if you did, you bein' a brother Marine an' all."

A list of things that needed doing flashed across Coal's mind. But the Marine slogan *Semper fi* flitted across his mind as well: *Always faithful*. In the Corps, you stood by a brother, and you came running when he called. Everything else was going to have to wait. He only hoped that staying here and hearing everything didn't create some kind of conflict of interest later.

By the time Perkins had filled a few pages with notes and got a good start on a case worked up, with a few short breaks mixed in to talk about hunting and the outdoors, two interests that the three of them shared, it was eleven-thirty. Coal invited both of them to dinner with him, but Perkins had previous plans and Jack politely declined.

So Coal decided to try and keep a posthumous promise he had made his best friend Larry MacAtee: to keep an eye on Kathy, his widow, and help her any way he could.

As he drove the pickup through town, with Shadow sitting contentedly beside him and gazing out at the sights, he realized it was probably a big faux-pas not to call Kathy first, but at this point he didn't want to take the time and find a place to stop. So he kept on driving. If she wasn't home, or she was busy, that would be fine. It would be a nice drive anyway, and maybe he would continue on to Leadore and have lunch out there, since they were part of his bailiwick too and he hadn't spent much time out there lately. He hadn't even taken time to meet their town marshal, and that was something he truly needed to take a day out for, since that man could be his backup one day on some serious call.

He was mid-way through the drive when one of those strange realizations came to him that almost always come to women but seldom to men. Today would have been Luke MacAtee's eighteenth birthday. Luke, who had died not long after getting his driver's license, had been a godsend of a son, one of the kindest-hearted, smartest, and best-looking young men Coal had ever known—none of which were a surprise, considering who his parents were. Now he knew his idea to come out and see Kathy was inspired. With Larry gone and the girls all in school, this would be a hard day for Kathy. She was going to need him.

He pulled off 28 into Kathy's drive, and the first thing that greeted his sight wasn't Kathy's blue station wagon but a pickup he didn't recognize. For some reason that caused his heart to do a disturbing little jump. Well, she obviously had company, probably some girlfriend who had come over to console her, so he wasn't about to horn in. He got into the yard and went to swing around, seeing Kathy's blue station wagon parked beyond the blue and white Dodge pickup. Before he could make his escape, however, Shadow snapped to rigid attention, drawing Coal's eyes over to the right. The first thing he saw was King, Kathy's golden retriever, who came to a stop to stare toward his truck.

"Easy, girl," Coal soothed Shadow. "Keep quiet."

King's mouth had been open, but it clamped shut as he fought with the obvious decision in his eyes of whether or not he should sound a warning about the intruder. Coal guessed he probably hadn't spotted Shadow yet, only the arrival of the pickup.

Before the dog could choose whether to bark or not, Coal saw more movement beyond the straw stack that brought back so many painful memories from the investigation of Larry's murder. When he shifted his attention there, what he saw made him ease the pickup all the way to a stop: a thick-set man of medium height, dressed in a thick coat and gray cowboy hat, walking beside Kathy toward the house. Kathy smiled and waved at Coal, and he was sunk: It was too late to make his escape.

Drawing a deep breath and chiding himself for being silly, he drove up to the house and parked on the other side of the station wagon, using it as a kind of psychological barrier between his GMC and the stranger's Dodge.

For fifteen seconds or so, he watched Kathy and the stranger in his rearview mirror. The first thing his eye went to, instinctively, was their hands. They both had them stuck deep into their coat pockets. Then he looked at the expressions on their faces.

One thing he noticed from this distance of fifty feet was that the man was a decent-looking sort, around Coal and Kathy's age or perhaps younger. Beyond that, Coal wouldn't allow himself any judgments, and he forbade himself thoughts about things that weren't any of his business.

When Kathy and the stranger were close, Coal threw open his door and got out, mechanically adjusting his gun on his hip without thinking what it might look like to the stranger. He caught a hesitation in the man's step, but Kathy came on without a pause. However, in spite of the smile on her face, her overall aura didn't reflect the kind of smiles, the expressions, or the delighted eyes she had had for him in the recent past.

Coal cleared his throat quietly and waited.

"Hi, Coal. Wow, what a surprise! What brings you all the way out here?"

"Oh, I was just taking Shadow out for a drive and thought I'd stop and see if you needed anything." He saw no obvious opening to mention Luke's birthday, not with the stranger there.

She looked surprised, maybe even confused. "Oh! Umm . . . Well, no, not really, but thank you for stopping." She looked beyond Coal at his pickup cab. "Oh, yeah, there she is! She looks good, Coal."

He turned and followed Kathy's eyes over to Shadow. She was right: Shadow had on her young dog face, and it lifted his heart a little. Anymore, it seemed he caught sight of Shadow's face of an older dog more and more often.

Kathy cleared her throat, making him return his eyes to her. "Hey, Coal, I'd like you to meet a friend of mine, Gunnar Westerlind. He has a ranch a few miles down the road."

Up close, Coal saw that his first impression of Gunnar Westerlind was, if anything, a little shy of the mark. He was a remarkably handsome man with hair a little lighter than Coal's that was graying around his heavy sideburns and over his ears, and a well-trimmed mustache somewhat smaller and less full than Coal's, a man with a good, straight bearing and a stout but not fat build.

"Hi, Coal. Sheriff Savage, right? My friends mostly call me Gunn."

Coal shook the strong hand the man offered. It was a firm, slightly drawn-out handshake, the kind a man gives a good friend he hasn't seen in a long while, is taking leave of for an extended time, or to a stranger he wants to take the measure of.

"Good to meet you, Mr. Westerlind." He purposely made his greeting formal, since Westerlind himself had said his 'friends' called him Gunn, and Coal most definitely hadn't earned that status. "I won't keep you two. I just wanted to say hi."

Wishing he could at least have acknowledged Luke's birthday, but more than half-embarrassed, and some eighty-five percent uncomfortable, Coal looked over and searched Kathy's eyes, knowing Gunnar Westerlind would be studying him, and hating the feeling. He wanted some kind of sign that Kathy still missed him, maybe a hint that she still cared to have him come around. He saw no such sign. "So . . . everything's going all right? I see you still have King."

Kathy smiled. With her rosy cheeks and the sparkle in her deep brown eyes, she looked stunning, but the look was because she was thinking about King. Coal knew it wasn't for him. "Oh, of course! You know those girls wouldn't let me get rid of that dog!"

"Yeah, those girls. How are they?"

"They're doing great, Coal. Thank you for asking. Do you want to come in for a minute?"

He hung on that "for a minute" part. If ever there was a sure sign that someone needed to move along, that was it.

"Oh, no! No, I'm good. I was just heading down to Leadore." *Please don't ask me why,* he said in his head. He was still too shocked about handsome Gunnar Westerlind's being here to think up any reasonable-sounding story.

"Okay, I'll let you go then. But it sure was nice of you to stop."

She pulled her right hand out of her pocket and put it out toward him. Coal's eyes flittered down to it and back to her face. He was momentarily at a loss, but he recovered in time to avoid making a scene by not taking that hand in farewell. And farewell was exactly what this seemed to be. A handshake? They were parting with a handshake? If anything ever said *It's been nice knowing you,* that was certainly it.

With a suddenly blue feeling, he took Kathy MacAtee's outstretched hand. It was cold, the way her hands often were. But it was also stiff, the way they *never* were.

Like a fool pretending he was in some old Western, Coal dropped his hand, dipped the front of his hat brim at her, then turned and nodded at Westerlind, the good-looking rancher.

"Well, again—it was good to meet you, Mister Westerlind. We'll see you around. Tell the girls I said hi, Kathy." He said that as an afterthought, and he knew she answered him, because he saw her lips moving.

But in his numbness he didn't hear a word. The next thing he heard was the slamming of his own pickup door, then the firing up of his engine, and the crackle of frozen mud and gravel as he pulled around and drove out of the MacAtees' yard, with Shadow turned around and gazing back at the dog they were leaving behind.

Coal hated himself for not saying anything about Luke's birthday, but when all was said and done, maybe it hadn't been that important. Perhaps she would not want to be reminded anyway.

CHAPTER FOURTEEN

When Coal got home from work that night, after dealing with the assault of one big Doberman pinscher jealous of being left behind when Shadow had been privileged to go out with him for the day, and three young children, he forced himself not to do anything before taking time to listen heart to heart to Katie and Cynthia as they told him about their adventures at school, their homework, their grades, and anything else any teenage girl dared share with the adult male of the home—at least if they considered him the "cool dad". He had seen how kids treated their parents if they didn't consider them to be cool, and it was heart-breaking.

Virgil was of course in his room, so Coal went and sat with him for a while, watching him work on a drawing he was doing of old Cody, their big gray horse. The likeness was remarkable, and Coal watched in silence for ten or fifteen minutes, wondering if Virgil minded. Of course he would never have said.

Bringing up the subject of some of the things he and his father used to do together, Coal got Virgil to open up a little, and by the time he left the room it even seemed like his son was somewhat excited at the prospect of going for a ride in the mountains when spring finally came to the valley. He also liked the idea Coal still wasn't relinquishing of starting the cattle operation back up, in spite of the absence of Maura PlentyWounds. At Virgil's age Coal had considered himself to be his father's top hand on the place, and he had a feeling Virgil would be a great top hand too, now that he was in a country place with the opportunity to learn.

The evening had started out to be just the medicine Coal needed after so many days and hard times away from his family. And then Connie had to drop the news in his lap: An hour or two earlier, Kathy MacAtee had called.

Coal took the news with outward casualness as he opened his mother's crockpot to see how the roast inside was coming along.

"You heard me, right? And don't open that—you're letting the heat out."

Coal half-smiled and looked over at her. "Sorry." He started to turn away.

"Coal." Gritting his teeth, he turned back. "You heard I said Kathy called."

"Oh yeah. Thanks. Did she happen to say why?"

"No. That's why I thought maybe it was important."

"Well I was just over there around lunch." He didn't mention how that went.

"Oh. Okay. Well anyway, now you know. Maybe it was nothing."

"Yeah, maybe. Or maybe I left my underwear over there," he said offhandedly, forcing himself to keep a straight face. Then when Connie's expression went from momentary confusion, to shock, then indignation, he dodged the slap of her hand on his shoulder, walking away with a grin. It was always a worthwhile effort when he could get his mother's goat.

Supper that night, like ninety-nine percent of the time his mother cooked, was perfect. The biggest things missing from the family meal were fresh homemade bread and butter and Maura PlentyWounds.

Coal had been doing his best with Sissy on his left leg to eat his food and now and then share a bite with her, but when she looked at him with those big, innocent eyes and spoke her first words of the meal, they brought with them the hardest part of the evening yet—at least the hardest for Coal having to hold back his emotions.

"Pop Coal? When's Maur' comin' home?"

Later, after all the other kids were in bed, Coal lay on Sissy's bed with his feet dangling over the end and Sissy tight against his side, her hand resting on his chest. Once in a while, seemingly almost out of reflex, she would rub a few little circles on his chest through his flannel shirt, and then her hand would go still again. It had taken him a lot of fast talking to get the little girl past wanting to discuss "Maur", and he would have bet money that even now that was the biggest subject on her mind. It was the biggest on his too.

After she finally drifted off to sleep, he slunk away and went to look at the clock. It was ten-thirty. Too late to call Kathy back if he wanted to—which he didn't. His mom was just finishing the nightly news, so he told her good night and went up to his room, finding the dogs had both been kidnapped by the older kids.

In bed, he lay staring up into the dark, thinking about Maura, Kathy, Annie . . . and Laura. He was thankful his children and Sissy and Cynthia had his mother, and he prayed she would hang around until long after all of them were grown. He didn't know if he could do this single father thing, but there was a part of him since Maura's rough departure that was resigned to try. In fact, right now that was the biggest part of him. His reception at Kathy's had sunk the final nail in that coffin.

* * *

The next several days were as idyllic as anything Coal could have imagined—minus Maura. On Friday, he and the whole family packed like sardines into his mom's Newport and drove into town to watch John Wayne and Ben Johnson in *The Train Robbers,* because in Sissy's case a child was never too young to start getting culture in her life. On a whim, Coal went to his friend Ken Parks's house, where Ken kept what amounted to an entire armada of vehicles, and borrowed a station wagon. Then he and Connie drove the whole troop up to Lincoln Street, to the home of Todd Mitchell, his senior deputy, to invite Jan and the boys to come with them. With Todd still in the hospital, he guessed they probably didn't have much reason to get out of the house—if they could even afford to.

Standing on the porch after the invitation, it took Coal an idiot moment to realize that because Jan Mitchell was looking down at the concrete stoop with a hand up to her face it didn't mean she had something in her eye. Jan was crying.

Coal would never get used to the smell of cigarette and wood smoke mixed with the rancid odor of fried food that always seemed to permeate the Mitchell home, and all of their clothing. But he couldn't let that little aversion keep him from taking Jan in his arms and holding her while she wept. He had no idea why she was crying, but since she hadn't called him he figured it wasn't because something bad had happened with Todd.

Finally, sniffling, Jan pulled away from him, wiping at her cheeks and nose in a very un-ladylike way. He jerked a handkerchief out of his pocket that fortunately he hadn't had reason to use yet.

"Here, Jan." She took his offering and blew her nose while he waited. "You all right?"

She gave a brisk nod.

"Is Todd doing okay?"

Another nod was the answer, as she squeezed the handkerchief in her hand like she was trying to ring all its fresh contents out onto the ground. She put her other hand up instinctively on Coal's chest. Again, he waited. Some things simply weren't to be rushed.

"I'm sorry about your hankie," Jan finally managed, and Coal laughed.

"That's what it's for. Now it's something to remember me by."

She let out a little, teary giggle, managing to glance up at him shyly. "Sure you don't want it back?"

Coal grinned and squeezed her shoulders. "Nope, pretty sure."

The boys, Bub, Toby, and little Jerry, finally managed to find their way to the door, probably wondering at last what had become of their mother after the knock on the door. Coal guessed the drone of the TV in the background to be the reason they hadn't come sooner.

Three-year-old Jerry's face exploded in a shy grin when he looked up and saw Coal. After Coal had greeted four-year-old Toby and six-year-old Bub, Jerry walked to him without a sound and put one arm around his leg, leaning his head into him. Coal couldn't help the emotion that move brought up in him. It always did.

"Boys, Coal asked us to go to the movies with him," Jan said after a moment of awkward silence. "There's a John Wayne movie on."

The boys' eyes all got big, and they looked up at Coal as if he were Santa Claus. None of them spoke, but that was par for the course.

"You boys game?" Coal asked.

They all nodded. He found himself wondering if they had ever been to a movie at the theater before.

After the movie, they all ate burgers and fries at Wally's, then shared eight gigantic cinnamon rolls among them for dessert. The hug Jan Mitchell gave Coal that night in front of her house, after the boys had all taken their turn—even Toby, who had always pretended to be too tough before that night—was long and lingering. He found that with the cold, fresh air surrounding them her scent didn't even bother him that much.

Jan stepped away after twenty seconds, obviously having embarrassed herself. She fiddled with her fingers, and he could tell she was searching for words.

"Do you— Can I—" Jan all of a sudden scoffed at herself and laughed, and he saw tears glitter in her eyes.

He put a finger under her chin and lifted her face up. "What is it?"

"Do you mind . . . I mean, can I just hug you for a while more?"

A little laugh escaped Coal. Apparently the other long hug wasn't enough. "Of course you can!"

And so she did.

The next day Coal spent the early morning on the couch holding Sissy, watching highly entertaining cartoons with her and the other children. He wasn't actually entertained by the cartoons, but it certainly warmed his heart to watch his children laughing.

Later, when Annie woke up after a late shift, she called and came over, and they played board games, another on Coal's long list of things he wouldn't normally care to do. But after the way things had been lately, and the times he had wondered if he would even survive the day, suddenly cartoons and board games with his family and Annie Price seemed like heaven. Best of all, he was able to put Maura out of his mind for a while.

In the evening, he and Annie went back to see *The Train Robbers* and once again watch Ann-Margret make a fool of John Wayne's character and every other man on the show. When it was over, he was pretty sure Annie was even angrier at Ann-Margret's character than he had been. Coal was more miffed that the immortal John Wayne had actually let himself be taken in so easily by a woman. He was supposed to be The Duke, not a plain old mortal dope like Coal Savage.

Coal felt foolish eating supper out two nights in a row, but he had sworn to himself to show Annie a good time, so he made the sacrifice to his fitness and took her to the Coffee Shop. Tonight, those eyes of Annie Price's that had always seemed so haunted had something else inside them that danced in the overhead lights. Coal wasn't sure he had ever seen more true happiness in her face. It wasn't until they were halfway through their meal that he had a guess as to why.

"Hey, Coal," said the woman as she was dipping a French fry in ketchup. "I heard Maura moved." She spoke so casually that he knew with every fiber of his being this had probably taken up the majority of her thoughts during the meal—and perhaps even during the movie.

"She did. She went to the Falls to be near her sons."

"Oh." Annie ate her fry in silence, then another. "Are you okay? I mean, you seemed pretty close to her."

Coal put on a mask and gave a little facial shrug. "Yeah, she was a good friend. The kids liked having her around. But I'm fine. It's not like we were permanently attached."

Annie nodded. She carved off a piece of chicken-fried steak and ate it slowly. At one point she looked as if she were about to speak. Then she fought to hold back a little smile as she continued chewing, looking down at her plate and cutting another piece of steak. Coal quietly went from watching the crisp brown breading sluff away from the perfectly cooked meat as she carved it to watching Annie's pretty perfect face.

Annie Price was a contented woman tonight. And for Annie he was happy.

It was the woman's idea after dinner to go back to Connie's instead of going to her own house. Coal's suspicious mind saw it as a blatant move to start trying to win the affection of his children.

And with what Maura had just put Coal and the family through, it might work. As much as Coal fought it, at least on this night which otherwise might have made him feel lonely, it seemed to be working on him as well.

Sunday, they had church, and even Coal went. After church, Connie had the brilliant idea of inviting Kathy and her girls over for dinner, but Coal shot that notion down like a slow-flying goose. He wanted to spend the day with his family. Or at least that was his excuse. The reality was he couldn't stop thinking about his reception the other day at Kathy's, about the new guy, Gunnar Westerlind, and about the possibility that Kathy might turn his mother down cold. It was another rejection he didn't want to face.

Monday was President's Day, and Coal stayed home with the family, starting to feel like they were once more exactly that: a family. They played the card game of *Authors,* then a round of *Life, Clue,* and *Twenty-One*, watched TV, listened to some of his mother's records, and even went out to do some target shooting, although the temperature never got over twenty-eight that day. At least they were finally doing something he actually enjoyed.

In the evening, they ate a wonderful supper, and then the kids begged Coal to get out his guitar and play cowboy music, which he was more than happy to do, especially because almost no one ever requested his music. He sort of wished he had learned "My Horse", the song Maura wrote for him, but he wasn't sure he could get through it right then even if he knew the words and the tune.

Coal went to bed a happy man, still wondering why Kathy had called but putting off making the return phone call to find out until he was back at the office. As Dobe jumped up on the bed, making it shake, and started snuggling down into the covers beside him, Coal thought of his family and smiled. Shadow came over and nosed his hand, and he petted her until she plopped down on the floor where he could no longer reach her.

If there had ever been a heaven on earth, perhaps this was it.

But on the outskirts of Salmon, someone else was going through hell . . .

The phone was clear downstairs, but that didn't stop Coal from jerking when it rang out in the dark depths of the night. Dobe, reacting to Coal's reaction, leaped to his feet and stood there on the bed, invisible in the night, but a tall, strong presence beside him.

There was one more ring, and then it stopped, and Coal waited. Soon, he heard his mother's soft tread on the stairs. That was the beginning of his short notice that his sweet, quiet interlude with his family was coming to an end.

CHAPTER FIFTEEN

Seventeen-year-old Troy was not a happy kid. His mother had run off with a farm implement salesman when he was only nine, and no one knew where they went. She left him with an overbearing father who didn't need to be a drunk to be an ass to his only son. In fact, his father hardly ever drank at all. But he was degrading, condescending, and a slave-driver to boot. And any of the things a teenage boy living in the sticks should have liked to do with his father, Troy hated—*because* of his father.

Troy had often thought his friend Dale Moore was the lucky one between them. Dale's father *was* that infamous slobbering drunk, or at least an alcoholic. But when he wasn't drinking he was a heck of a guy. All Dale had to do was wait out the drunk times and try to block them from his mind and he knew in time his father would pass out drunk and then wake up kind and fun-loving again, at least for another week or two.

Troy didn't have any such relief. His father was *never* fun to be around. Actually, even that wasn't true. What made his father even worse, to Troy, was seeing how he pretended to be when he was around other people. With most people, men *or* women, his father was a real card. A prince, too. Sweet, smiling, handsome to a fault. And sometimes he seemed even generous—although Troy knew better, because the only times his father really did anything for anyone or gave anything to anyone he expected to be paid back double—whether they knew it or not. Most people looked up to and liked his father. But most people didn't know him the way Troy did.

Tonight, Troy was driving his father's pale blue and white Dodge pickup, with Dale Moore against the passenger door, and, crammed up close against Troy's leg, his girlfriend, Dawn Kelly. Dawn didn't have a great life either. For her, it was only her mother at home most of the time, and according to Dawn her old lady got passed back and forth between the rowdy element of Salmon like a soft-stone knife sharpener at deer camp. Her dad was a long-haul truck driver, and Troy was pretty sure he had talked to enough other guys whose dads did the same job to know Dawn's old man was gone on the road far more than any trucking company would have required. Dawn's old man simply didn't want to come home.

Troy didn't blame the old guy, either. But then again he didn't blame Dawn's mom for not wanting to be with the ugly old slovenly weasel, who grew a beard down to his collarbone, had a beer gut bigger than any three men should, and chewed Copenhagen like kids chew Doublemint. He invariably had a collection of dark flecks around in his teeth and gums, and smelled like Copenhagen, Budweiser, garlic, and pickles.

Thanks to a trio of home lives that were nothing to boast about, Troy, Dale, and Dawn spent a lot of time going out if they could, although for Troy it could be pretty brutal when he returned. Most of the time it was worth it. Five, six, even seven hours away from that old piece of work he had to claim as his father, that was paradise.

Troy drove the pickup clear up on the pass, and they turned off the headlights, leaving the parking lights on, and sat in the middle of the lane, because there was so much snow up here there was no shoulder on which to pull off. They sat there and stared at the star-dazzled sky, and Troy wished on every one of the biggest stars. He wished his father was dead. Sometimes he even imagined killing him. He imagined the entire act in vivid detail. And he enjoyed it. In fact, he enjoyed killing, period. At least anything he could get away with killing, anything for which he would not get caught.

Driving back toward Salmon, as they passed the bug drool spot of Carmen, Troy said, "Hey. You guys wanna do somethin' crazy?"

"Like what?" Troy knew Dale was a chicken. He generally didn't dare do any of the really crazy things Troy cooked up.

"It's a secret. You gotta swear in first. Then I'll tell you."

Dale stared at the road ahead. Finally, he looked over at Troy. "You know I hate that crap, man. Come on, just give us a hint."

"Yeah, Troy, give us a hint," echoed Dawn. "Last time you sucked us into something we all got beat—and that's when you got expelled."

"Well, it's nothin' like that. Besides, nobody's ever gonna know this time. They'll never find out."

"I'm not doin' it," Dale said with firm decision.

"Oh, come on, you freakin' coward! Jeez, I'm gonna have to start leavin' you home."

"What're you gonna do?" Dale said, his voice indicating the inevitable weakening of his resolve.

"I'm gonna kill somethin'. With a spear."

Dale and Dawn both stared at Troy. Dawn was first to recover. "A spear! What are you talkin' about?"

"You'll see. You'll see!"

"Where you gonna get a spear?" Dale cut in.

"Don't worry, I know a place. I know a place that has a lot of 'em."

"What're you gonna kill?"

"I told you! You'll see. You in, or aren't you? I guess I might as well drop you both off at your houses if you don't even want to have any fun."

Dale sighed and swore. "Judas priest, man. You get us in trouble again I'm never gonna hear the end of it."

"Don't worry. I told you nobody's ever gonna find out. Or at least nobody'll ever be able to pin it on us."

Dawn shrugged and let her shoulders fall. A little smile came to her face, a smile half of excitement and anticipation, half of worry. "Yeah, let's do it. Come on, Dale!"

Now Dale was alone. And how could he fight against the will of a girl? Especially a girl he was secretly sweet on.

"Okay, fine. I'm in."

Coal drove up Cemetery Lane. He could see the red lights flashing up ahead long before he reached his destination.

The scene up toward the cemetery, which sat on the edge of the city limits southwest of town, past the Shoshone village, was mayhem. There were police vehicles everywhere and citizens, most of them from the Shoshone-Bannock village, clamoring for answers.

Skinny red-bearded Everett Sherman's travel trailer tonight was a crime scene. The kind of crime scene Coal was growing weary of seeing in his jurisdiction.

Because it was outside the city limits, although all the local police, even Chief Dan George, had responded, Coal had no choice but to be there. Coal, thanks to his county jurisdiction, had this case, like a hot potato he would rather have thrown in someone else's lap. It was two o'clock in the morning; tomorrow was going to be another excruciating day.

It took a long time, but the police finally managed to chase off all the spectator crowd, and Coal, state patrolman Lyle Gentry, Chief George, and Kerry Updyke, the coroner, carefully worked the entire crime scene, trying to take the few photos they could get with the aid of headlights, flashlights, or the lights inside the house. Looking around, there were an awful lot more tracks than Coal would have expected. Had an army committed this crime?

At one point, standing beside Officer Gentry, Coal looked toward his deputies. Grant Fairbourne was staring his way. There was something faintly disturbing in the look in his eyes, as if he had something to say but was holding back. Coal turned away. Right now, he had no time for wallflowers.

On the outside of the house, fifteen feet away from the front door, lay the half-clothed body of an Indian woman a witness had identified as Irene Boyer. Apparently, this hard-looking, hard-used woman, standing perhaps five-foot-three, when she had still been able to stand, but weighing in around one hundred eighty pounds, had run from the trailer, and judging by the few tracks they could make out in the hard, crusted snow, someone had chased her down and stabbed her between the shoulder blades several times with a knife no one had managed to locate on the scene. They all tried as hard as they could to give the trail coming from the house a wide berth, but even from a few feet away they could make out pieces of tracks, both from the tennis shoes Irene was wearing and from some bigger ones made by cowboy boots—pieces of tracks that appeared to have been left by someone who was sprinting.

Back in the trailer, it wasn't an extremely bloody scene, but it was more than gruesome enough for the hardest of policemen. The red-bearded, emaciated-looking man Hunter Jack had called "that Viking guy" lay dead on his bunk, apparently where he had been caught in his sleep. A ceremonial-looking spear, replete with beadwork and eagle feathers, protruded from the center of his chest. It appeared to have split his breastbone.

Lyle Gentry shined his flashlight up and down the spear, then looked over at Coal. "What do you think?"

"It's a spear." Coal glanced at Gentry and didn't laugh. What did he expect him to say?

"For sure one of the Shoshones we're looking for, huh?"

Grant Fairbourne had quietly followed the two of them inside, and when Gentry spoke, the younger man cleared his throat into his hand. Glancing over at him, but getting only a puzzling glance back, Coal looked back at Gentry and shrugged. "I'm not willing to jump to that conclusion. Those folks hold their artifacts pretty sacred. I wonder if whoever did the killing would have been so willing to leave it behind."

"Probably didn't have a choice, according to the witnesses."

The story was that two friends of Sherman's, Curlie Burks and Melissa Talty, had been pulling up in Burks's pickup to see if Everett and Irene were already done partying for the night when they saw someone, probably a male, tear off through the dark cottonwoods beyond the travel trailer. They found Irene on the ground, drowning in her own blood. She hadn't been able to make any kind of statement before she was gone.

"Sure, that's something to think about," Coal agreed. "So where are the witnesses? This Curlie Burks and Melissa Talty? Did you cut them loose?"

"No, I think Bob Wilson has them sitting in their pickup until we figure out if we need anything else from them," he said as they were stepping back outside. He pointed toward a beat-up Dodge parked at the edge of headlight beams.

"Are you planning to take them in and get a statement?"

"I wasn't, no. Not tonight anyway."

Again, Grant cleared his throat, and Coal frowned at him. There was that look in his deputy's eyes again. Coal turned back to Gentry. "Say, Lyle, do you mind if I have a word with Grant in private?"

Puzzling, Gentry looked at Grant, then shrugged. "No, of course not. I'll be right back." With that, he walked over to where Police Chief Dan George was standing.

Coal turned his attention to Grant. "What's eating you, Grant?"

Grant blinked. "Oh, I . . ." He paused.

Coal sighed. "All right, out with it. Sorry to sound short, but it's going to be a long night. I can tell something's wrong. What is it? You don't like the idea of turning the witnesses loose, I can tell that much."

Grant matched Coal's sigh, only his seemed much more deflating; it must have emptied him clear down to whatever air was in his boot toes. "I don't want to horn in, Coal, but . . ."

"But what?"

"But . . . Well, I feel pretty stupid saying this. I know I'm the new guy and all, but . . ." Coal stared him down impatiently. "All right. I was pretty much the homicide guy in my last job, you know. I've been to a lot of schools on this stuff, and I've worked homicides all over the western part of the state."

If Coal had given it any thought, he would have realized he probably looked much like a statue right then. His beleaguered mind churned, trying to grasp exactly what Grant's words meant. At last, they struck home like a five-pound rock to the side of a trailer house.

"You're kidding me."

Grant only shook his head.

"Then why the hell haven't you said anything before?"

Grant swallowed, reaching a hand up to rub the back of his neck. "Well, I kind of did, actually. It's in my resume."

The resume Coal had skimmed too quickly. Because he was dealing with his friend Slugger Janx and had many other things on his mind. He swore. "You're kidding me." He didn't realize he had said those words a few moments earlier until he heard them echoing in his brain.

Grant shook his head again. "No."

"Well . . ." A gust of frustrated air came out of Coal's mouth, the cloud of steam vanishing in a second. He swore again. "So . . ." He swore once more. The curse words were like little bursts of carburetor cleaner, as he tried to get the engine of his mind to fire up and run. Flashes of recent memory flitted around Coal's mind, little vignettes of all the murders that had occurred in his county lately. Of course Grant hadn't been around when many of them were happening, but he sure had been for the last three or four. And, looking back, why had Grant seemed so shocked at the sight of county prosecutor Mike Fica all burned up in his van? Was it only because that was what Coal had been expecting to see?

"All right, Grant," he finally said, his mind still churning over all the recent things he might have done that Grant must have thought were pretty stupid. It was a humbling strike to his pride to realize his newest deputy obviously had more experience as a peace officer than anyone else in the department. "So I'm guessing you're going to start telling me all the things that have been done wrong here tonight."

Grant only shrugged, looking sheepish.

"And you didn't stop any of them."

"Well, I used to be a firefighter for the Forest Service. When I changed stations and went to a new place, I got all sorts of grief every time I tried to tell the guys in my new place how we did things on my first crew. I finally learned to keep my mouth shut."

Coal sighed. "All right. I get that. But this is homicide. This isn't the kind of thing to pussyfoot around with. Doing things right could mean someone gets convicted. Doing them wrong . . ."

Grant shrugged, looking out toward the other officers. "That's easy for you to say. Remember, I'm the new kid on the block."

Coal paused and drew in a deep breath. "Well, things are about to change. For starters, why don't we talk about what's going on tonight? Gentry was talking about letting the witnesses go. You didn't seem to like that?"

"Well, no. The first suspects in homicide are always whoever calls it in."

"Sure. That's standard. So . . . Wait. On second thought, I'm just going to let you take over things from here."

"I don't know if the rest of the guys are going to like that much."

"I don't much care what they like. This is my jurisdiction and my case. Come on."

Grant followed Coal with obvious great reluctance to where all the other officers and Kerry Updyke had clustered together not far from the idling Dodge owned by Curlie Burks. Everyone turned to Coal, who by his size generally commanded people's attention.

"Guys, we're having a little change in the program here. Listen up. It's come to my attention that Mr. Bigshot new guy here is a trained homicide detective with a lot of investigations under his belt." Grant stood there looking more discomfited than Coal had ever seen him, or would ever have imagined him. "So I'm turning this scene over to him. If anyone wants to discuss it, we'll talk in private."

He bumped a challenging glance around the group. It was late, he was tired, and he wasn't in any mood to be tactful. Coal was relieved to realize that like a bunch of bystanders at a bad wreck, all the other officers were more than happy to back off and let an expert take over. They all nodded or spoke their approval.

Coal nodded. "Good. So first off, we were discussing letting the witnesses go and not getting a statement tonight. What do you think about that, Grant?"

"It's not a good idea. They should be our first suspects."

Gentry stared at him. "Now what's that?"

"Suspects. How do we know they didn't kill these people themselves? It's kind of the rule to count whoever reported the crime as your first suspect."

After a few more seconds, the state patrolman shrugged. "You know, I guess I never gave that any thought, but sure. You're right."

"I'm only thinking out loud," Grant said. "Trying to cover all my bases. But just because they say they're friends of this dead guy and his girlfriend doesn't mean they really are. It would make a great cover."

"It could. Pretty ingenious one, actually. The only weird thing is you'd think this time of night they would have just run for it. I can see calling it in if it was daytime or if anyone knew they were all together earlier."

Grant shrugged and sighed. "Yeah, I won't deny it sheds a better light on them—if we want to give them any credit for thinking one way or the other. Maybe that's the way they thought it would look too. Was there anyone else around?"

Bob Wilson walked up then, in time to hear Grant's question. "There were some kids up here, Curlie said. He almost ran into their pickup when he was leaving."

"Where are they?" Coal cut in.

"I guess they split."

"So we don't have any idea who they were?"

"Actually, I think we do, or at least one of them. Curlie says he knows the dad of the driver. He's some rancher from east of town. Westerlind?"

Coal stared at Bob for a few seconds, knowing that name should register. When it finally did, he continued to stare. "Wait. Did you say Westerlind? As in Gunnar?"

Bob shrugged. "Could be. It didn't sound familiar to me."

"Well, I'm guessing it's got to be the same guy. How many Westerlinds could there be?"

"Right. Well, anyway, I guess the driver was his kid. Shouldn't be hard to track the other two down if we can find him."

"Okay, I guess that's a place to start." Coal turned back to Grant. "So that could explain why Curlie made the call. Even if he and the woman did the killing, if they didn't want to be identified by those kids later, they might have decided to make the call to make them look legitimate."

"Exactly," agreed Grant.

When he didn't go on, Gentry cut in. "Yeah, I see that point too. Either way, I think you guys are right: One of us should take them down and get some written statements while everything's fresh in their minds."

Grant Fairbourne nodded. By the looks of him, he was starting to loosen up and take to the responsibility of having this case on his shoulders. "Yes, and we'll need to take their clothes and impound their vehicle—at least until we can get any evidence gathered off them."

Coal looked around, liking the looks on everyone's faces. No one appeared to have the slightest problem with Grant's taking charge; this was going to be much easier than he had imagined. "I guess somebody probably needs to go out to Westerlind's place to wake his kid up, too—if he even went home."

"Exactly," Grant said. "We're going to have to get on this while the iron's hot." Coal was hoping Gentry would volunteer. If he didn't, maybe Grant would put Jordan Peterson on it.

Officer Gentry nodded, looking at Coal. "Well, if you want to go bring the kid in, I can run in Curlie and Melissa to get their clothes and some statements."

Coal chuckled. "I was sort of hoping you'd want to go out to Westerlind's. I might have a bit of a conflict of interest." They were going to have to trust his judgment. He had no interest in bringing up how he had met Gunnar Westerlind. "Would you mind swapping?"

"Sure." Gentry looked a little puzzled. "He a friend of yours?"

"No, not at all. I just met him a few days ago. But he seems to be friends with someone I'm pretty close to."

"Ohh . . . I get you." Gentry grinned. "Woman stuff, huh? All right. I'll go see if I can find the kid."

"Thanks, Gentry," said Grant. Then he turned to Coal and Bob. "Let's go talk to this Curlie guy, huh?"

The three of them went over to the Dodge pickup, Bob leading out with his flashlight so they wouldn't trip over anything. When he accidentally let it drift too far up and it hit the pickup driver in the face, the man jerked his hand up to shield his eyes. "Hey! Watch the light, damn it!"

Coal saw the hand and froze. Bob dropped the flashlight to his thigh, and the man's hand came back down. Coal's hand started toward his gun butt, thinking of the appearance of the pickup driver's hand.

"Bob, bring that light up again, would you? Mister . . . Burks, right? Why don't you show me that left hand."

Bob had raised the flashlight once more, and its beam bounced off the top of the door rather than straight into Burks's eyes.

"Why? Watch that friggin' light, would you?"

Coal nudged Bob and Grant a little and sidestepped to his right, putting the man in the pickup at a bad angle of disadvantage as he brought his hand nearer the butt of his gun. "Just put the hand up, sir. Slowly."

His eyes flickering as he tried to crank his head around and see Coal, Curlie Burks inched his hand into the air. Between his fingers and on the backs of them was something unmistakable Coal had seen a thousand times, in a thousand situations.

Dried blood.

CHAPTER SIXTEEN

"What's that on your hand, Mr. Burks?" asked Coal, feeling Grant and Bob on either side of him, both ready to spring.

Burks looked down at his hand and swore. "Blood, I guess. I mean, I think it must be."

"Uh-huh. Do you want to step out of the truck?" Coal's voice was level. "Keep the light on him, would you, Bob?"

Bob didn't reply other than to raise the light a little more, until it hammered like a bolt of lightning straight into Burks's face.

"Hey! Stop doin' that! I didn't do nothin'."

"Well, that's what we're going to talk about," Coal said. "Now I'm going to need you to get out of the pickup—nice and easy."

Looking confused, Burks said, "Why? What's goin' on? Hey, man, I'm the—"

Coal drew his .44, holding it at the ready in both hands, down in front of him with his finger out of the trigger guard. Bob's flashlight beam continued to jet directly into the man's eyes. "Get your hands in sight and get out of the car."

There was apparently enough force in his voice, besides the drawn pistol, that this time Burks complied, easing his door open with his arm once he had unlatched it, and stepping out.

Coal holstered his revolver. He had Bob get the woman out too and bring her around to the driver's side of the pickup. Seeing movement, he glanced over to see Grant patting down his own pockets.

"Lose something?"

Grant grinned. "Uh, no. Would you happen to have a handkerchief?"

Coal's hand started to reach for his pocket before he realized he had given his away to Jan Mitchell and not replaced it. "I don't."

Grant looked over at Bob Wilson. "Hey, Bob, you wouldn't happen to have a handkerchief I could borrow, would you?"

Bob's dark eyes stared at Grant for a few seconds, but then finally he drew a handkerchief out of his back pocket and handed it over. "I don't need it back."

Coal had to hold back a laugh, remembering he had said something almost exactly like that to Jan Mitchell. Grant took the handkerchief and tucked it in a hip pocket, then did a quick pat down of Burks and Melissa Talty. When he found nothing, he took a step back. "So tell me for the record, Mr. Burks. What's that on your hands?" asked Grant.

Curlie Burks looked down at his hands. His eyes widened. "Hey, man, that isn't— Hey, what is this?"

"I need you to calm down, Mr. Burks," Coal cut in. "He's only asking you to repeat what you told me earlier, for clarification. What's on your hands?"

"I told you I guess it's blood."

"Whose is it?" asked Grant.

"I— I guess it's Everett's. But I didn't kill him!"

"Nobody said you did," Coal said.

While he and Bob held onto the detainees, Grant went to his vehicle and came back with a canteen. He sprinkled some onto Bob's handkerchief and came back to stop in front of Burks. "Here, Mr. Burks, you can clean your hands off with that."

Curlie Burks was shaking as he took the handkerchief with a little confusion in his eyes and carefully wiped his hands. Grant quickly took it back from him when he was done and turned to Coal. "You want to go put this in a container? We'll have to remember to set it out to dry later at the office and then put it in a paper bag." That last tidbit was something Coal already knew: You couldn't put wet evidence such as bodily fluids in storage and expect it not to degrade and be ruined, and it always had to be packaged in paper.

As Coal was taking the handkerchief and heading for his pickup, he could hear Grant ask, "Why don't you tell me what happened tonight, Mr. Burks? From the top."

"Hey, man, it's cold! And I already told that other guy everything."

"Why's Everett's blood on your hands?" Grant asked coolly.

Coal turned in time to see Burks's eyes flash back and forth between Grant and Bob. He looked completely disconcerted. "I guess I must've touched him."

"Why?"

Burks whirled to Melissa. "Hey, Liss! Did you see? Did I touch Everett?"

The woman's eyes were wide, and so was her mouth. She started shaking her head, then suddenly stopped. "Uh . . . Yeah. Yeah, man, that's what happened. We went in there, and when we saw Everett with that spear in him Curlie tried to pull it out. I remember now."

Melissa had no particular truth in her eyes that Coal could discern as he came back over to stop before her.

Apparently, Grant felt the same way. "Listen, I don't want to have to put you both under arrest and take you down to the jail. You want to level with me about what really happened?"

Burks stared darts at Melissa, who was looking at him for guidance. That hard stare must have been guidance enough. She returned her eyes to Grant. "I swear that's what happened. God's honest truth!"

"Where do you two live?" Coal asked suddenly. "You have any I.D. on you?"

"Uh, yeah." Burks looked over at Coal and blinked rapidly as he looked down at his pistol grip, then back up. "Can I get it? It's in the glovebox."

"You don't carry a wallet?"

"No, it makes my butt get numb when I'm drivin'."

"Do you want me to look in your glovebox for you?" Grant asked. "I'd have to have your permission."

Coal looked at Grant, thinking of a little legality called exigent circumstances, which meant if there was a danger that evidence might disappear, a person or place could be searched even without a warrant. He didn't want to be a meddler, though, so he would wait and bring it up later. He wasn't completely certain it would apply here anyway, since now they already had the pickup in custody.

Burks froze. His tongue touched his lips. "Hey, you know what? I'm just rememberin' I don't have my license with me today. I think I must have left it home."

Coal wanted to give a grim smile, but he held it back. It was funny how a suggested search of someone's property could make them remember all kinds of things they might not want anyone else to see. He thought again about bringing up exigent circumstances, but before he could decide whether or not to say anything, Bob spoke up from off to the side.

"He lives over on Water Street, Grant. I know the place."

Grant nodded, not removing his eyes from Burks. "You own your house, do you?"

"Yessir. Well, I'm buyin'. Not paid off."

"All right. What about you, ma'am? Miss?"

"It's Miss," confirmed Melissa. "And I live up on the bar. On Fairmont? My license is in my pocket. You want me to get it? Or maybe you could get it," she suggested. The look she gave him would have made anyone watching guess the second option would be her preference.

"Why don't you go ahead?"

Melissa Talty, looking a little disappointed, let out a quick sigh. She reached into her back pocket and withdrew her license, holding it out to Grant. He held it up into Bob's flashlight beam and squinted at it for a few seconds. Coal noticed that Jordan had wandered over now and was closely observing the scene, which made him happy. Jordan was eager to learn.

"It says Des Moines, Iowa, Miss Talty," Grant finally said, looking back up.

"Yeah. Well, I came out here to ride the river—you know, be a river rat. I ended up stayin'. Is that a problem?"

"Not in particular—not for me anyway."

Coal didn't have to be told that Grant was trying hard to decide if these two were flight risks. At this point they were the only people anyone knew for sure had been at the murder scene. Grant simply didn't want to let them go only to have them take off and head for Mexico or somewhere. At least he had picked up a few minor details watching specialized FBI agents work criminal cases in D.C.

There was another part of Coal, however, the non-official side of him, that thought with everything he already had heard about the dead man, perhaps he should give Curlie and Melissa a medal and send them on their way. It would save Lemhi County's taxpayers a healthy sum of money on a murder trial, and they would be rid of Everett, apparently a thorn in the side. This was the kind of thought pattern that Coal, as the county's head law enforcement official, could admit to almost no one.

Grant made Burks and Talty tell the entire story again, from when they arrived supposedly to see what appeared to be a man running from the area where Irene's body had been found, to their ill-advised foray into the trailer, and last of all their encounter with the three teenagers. After that, they had raced to the first house with a light on, pounded on the door until someone answered it, and then borrowed the phone to call the police.

Coal listened quietly to the whole story without interrupting. When it ended, he said, "I'm going to have one of my men ride with you back toward town—in your cab with you, that is." Of course he didn't tell them his main purpose in doing that was to keep them from getting into their glove box and ditching whatever might be in there that Curlie seemed bent on no one seeing, but Curlie and Melissa could probably guess. "I assume you can find the house again, the one where you used the phone."

"Sure I can," Curlie replied. "It was only a few houses toward town."

"All right. Well, we're going to need both of you to stick close to town for the next few days. Understand? Mr. Burks, after I jot down all your information, I'll send you both with Bob to see if you can point out the house so we can check out their side of this story." He turned to Jordan. "I'm going to have you accompany them down to the jail to fill out a report of what they saw while it's still fresh in their minds. I'll need you to ride in the cab with them so they don't have a chance to take out whatever they're so worried about in their glove box, but we'll get your car back down to you later. And then if you can I'd like to have you arrange to get the truck locked up someplace safe until we can get a warrant and dig through it."

Grant cleared his throat. "Coal, can I talk to you for a second over here?"

Coal followed him a ways off from the pickup. "What's up?"

"This is my case, right?"

Coal stared for a second, then realized what Grant meant. “Oh, yeah. Sorry about that. Old habits.”

“It’s all right. But I hate to tell those guys, we’ve got to get all the evidence we can off them tonight.”

“Evidence?”

“Yeah. Hairs. Blood. Whatever.”

“So . . .”

“So we have to take their clothes, too—not just the pickup.”

Coal grunted. “Well. It’s going to be fun explaining that to them. Then again, the way Melissa keeps eyeing you, she might be happy when you tell her you’re taking her clothes.”

Grant gave him a grin. “Funny, Coal. Yeah, that’s funny. But it’s actually kind of fun to watch someone’s face when you tell them you’re taking their clothes.”

“You have a sick sense of humor I never knew about, Grant,” Coal said. “I like that in a man.”

Grant laughed. “All right. Do you want to tell them, or do I get to?”

Coal motioned his deputy on. “Go ahead. I want to learn from the expert.”

They walked back over, and Grant laid out the plan for Burks and Talty. Coal hardly heard what he said, but he had to hold back a laugh when he saw how the color drained from Melissa Talty’s face at the mention of taking all her clothes.

Finally, once Grant managed to explain that Burks and Talty weren’t actually under arrest, but simply being detained in order to gather exigent evidence, and that someone would accompany them back to their house to get clothing, or loan them extra clothing from the jail, he was able to get them calmed back down. At least a semblance of calm.

“Bob,” said Grant, “I don’t suppose you could follow Jordan and these guys down to the house they called from, could you? So we can mark it and talk to them about Burks’s story. And then you and Jordan take them in and get their clothes, have them fill out statements . . . Oh—and the pickup will have to be impounded somewhere it can be locked up, where nobody else can access it."

"You don't ask much, do you?" Bob said, his face expressionless, but owing to his dark eyes and low eyebrows he looked more angry than accommodating, as he always did. It was a characteristic that could work either for, or against him. "You two staying here?"

Grant nodded, glancing over at Coal. "Yeah, we'll do some poking around. If there's anything left to see."

Coal had seen enough of how the crime scene was being handled on his arrival to know Grant probably meant that last as a thinly veiled reference to his displeasure at how the other officers had allowed the crime scene to be so badly trampled, but judging from Bob's reaction he didn't seem to catch it, which was probably for the best.

Jordan, looking none too happy about his assigned task, climbed into the cigarette and rancid grease stench of Curlie Burks's pickup, and Burks backed away, turned around, and headed off the hill, with Bob Wilson following after in his squad car.

Coal and Grant went back over to the body of Irene Boyer, and Chief George came over to observe, letting coroner Kerry Updyke sit in his car waiting for the release of the bodies. There were tracks all over the place around Irene's body. It looked like the scene of some sandlot baseball game. Ray Christian the detective would have been disgusted. Grant was a bit harder to read than Ray, but Coal could tell he was disgusted too.

"Did anybody get photographs of the yard before everybody trampled it all up?" Coal asked. "It was a big mess by the time I got here." He didn't realize until after he spoke how his comment might have sounded to Chief George, but it was too late to take it back.

"Gentry was here first," Grant said. "When we all started pulling in, it seemed like it all turned to chaos. I think I remember him having a camera. But I never saw him using it."

"He was using it at one point, but I was with him by then," Coal said. "The whole area had been run all over, though." By now, since Chief George had already heard his disparaging comment anyway, he was thinking maybe he should take the opportunity to make a point for future investigations.

The only light on Irene's body now was from Chief George's headlights. He looked at Grant. "Hey, can you grab me a flashlight? There's one in my truck if you don't have one."

When Grant brought his own light back, Coal shined it on the disturbed earth around the woman's body from several different angles. He saw once more the tennis shoe tracks. Cowboy boot tracks. Tracks made by Vibram soles. It was with a huge feeling of relief that he became certain there were none made by small-sized feet wearing moccasins, on this side of the body or on the other. There had been one strong suspect come to Coal's mind, a man he didn't want to believe would do something like this. But a man, he was sure, who could have, and who had the motive to because of recent events. The only thing was that never in all the time Coal had known Hunter Jack had he ever worn anything but moccasins—and everyone knew it. The other telltale sign was that none of the tracks Coal could see were overly small, and Hunter Jack was famous for the small size of his feet.

"Looking for something in particular?" Grant finally cut into Coal's thoughts after Chief George had gotten bored—or perhaps offended—and wandered over to Kerry Updyke's car, making him roll down the window to talk.

"Nope. Well. Yeah." He went on to tell Grant about Hunter Jack's overly small feet, and his moccasins. He might as well start getting everyone else used to the idea that Hunter Jack had not been in this yard—in case someone got the wild idea of pinning this on the Shoshone because of his recent fight with the man he called the Viking—the *dead* man.

When he had finished, Grant said, "I'm sure I can handle the rest of this, and I can let the coroner take the woman's body pretty soon. That's if you're thinking you need to go talk to Hunter Jack."

Coal chuckled. "That obvious, huh?"

"Pretty much."

Coal nodded thoughtfully. He didn't like the idea of having to wake Hunter Jack up in the wee hours of the morning. But just as Grant guessed, he felt like it was something that had to be done. In spite of what he knew in his heart to be true, there were going to be people who put the fight at the Lantern together with this ceremonial Shoshone spear, the kind of thing Jack was known for having all over his house, and decided to blame this killing on the big Shoshone. Coal had to do anything he could to nip that train of thought in the bud before it could gain any momentum.

Scanning the yard one more time, Coal let out a big sigh. It was indeed going to be a long night, and probably a long day tomorrow. There was no way he could justify releasing this crime scene now, and he couldn't release his deputies either. But he did need to go talk to Badger, no matter what else he did the rest of the night.

Coal stood away from the body, and Grant rose with him. Chief George had walked back over and had just lit up a Camel. He drew deeply on it, still holding the pack of cigarettes and a book of matches in his left hand. He squinted at Coal, then looked at Grant. "Smoke?"

Both shook their heads.

George drew on the cigarette again, held it in, then blew it out his nostrils. "Hey, listen. I apologize if we screwed up the scene, all right? Stupid on my part. Everyone's. I guess maybe everyone's already thinking who probably did this."

Coal's guts tightened. "Oh yeah?"

George shrugged. He peered at Coal. The light from his headlights was enough for all of them to see each other's expressions, even if it wasn't as good as daylight. "Well, yeah. That spear . . . And everybody knows about that fight at the Lantern between this guy and . . ."

"And Hunter Jack," Coal finished the chief's thought for him.

Again, George shrugged, this time with just one shoulder. "Yeah. Him."

"Hunter Jack always wears moccasins," Coal said, keeping his voice quiet, to make him sound calm.

George eyed him for a while. He drew deep on his cigarette again, seeming to try and draw strength in with the acrid smoke. "Sure. Sure. Hard to see moccasins tracks on ice though."

Coal thought about that comment. Finally, he cleared his throat. "Someone wearing cowboy boots ran this way, it looks like. Maybe a size eleven or twelve."

The chief only stared, trying to process Coal's comment.

"Badger's feet are probably an eight. Nine at best."

"Badger— Oh. Yeah. Hunter Jack. Well, sure, I know that. Anybody could have run out here, though. Those tracks could be from earlier today. Or yesterday."

Again, Coal felt his guts tighten up. "Well, anyway, I'm going to head down to Badger's and wake him up right now."

"You going alone?"

"Why not?"

"Well, what if . . ."

"What if what?"

"What if it *was* him? What if he did this?"

Coal shrugged. "I guess we'll see."

Grant followed Coal over to the GMC, and when he opened the door the deputy was in his way. He laid a hand on the door as Coal got in and opened the window. The slamming door sounded like a cannon in the crackling cold of the night.

"I'm glad you brought up the homicide thing again, Grant. Really glad. Listen, I'm sorry I didn't remember before."

"You had a lot on your mind then. I understand."

Coal nodded, thinking back on the sad death of his friend Slugger Janx. "Well, anyway, the way things are going in this valley, we're going to need your skills. In fact, I think you might have just given me some powerful ammunition to use with the County to try and keep your spot for you even if Todd Mitchell comes back to work someday—if you're still interested."

It was obvious that thought made Grant happy, for he couldn't hold back a smile.

Before Coal could turn the pickup around and leave, he heard Chief George hailing him, and he stopped and looked over, rolling down the window again. George stopped at the door, blowing warm breath into his hand.

"Hey, since you're going down to talk to Hunter Jack . . . Well, you know, it's been a long day for everyone. What do you think about me calling in some help?"

"Help?"

"Well, just until tomorrow. A couple of my reserves."

It didn't take Coal long to think it over. "That'd be fantastic. Maybe we can salvage some of this night yet."

George nodded, and Coal let him borrow his radio to call in to dispatch and have the dispatcher call out a couple of reserve officers, Horace Teal and William Verret. He told them to bring twelve-gauge shotguns loaded with buckshot to the scene.

Hearing that last, Coal decided to wait around until the officers arrived. He had some pretty plain instructions to give them if they thought they were coming up here for a manhunt.

Horace Teal was a mechanic at Quality Motors. Coal had met him once or twice but didn't know much about him other than to describe him as being compactly built with broad shoulders, sloping and meaty at the neck, and a head of thin, dark hair. He wore sharp-toed cowboy boots, flare-legged Levi's, and a huge silver ring on his right hand, inlaid with flat pieces of mother-of-pearl, red coral, and turquoise.

William Verret, on the other hand, he didn't know, only that Chief George had said he worked at Lemhi Lumber. When the black cowboy hat-wearing Verret got to the scene, not long after Teal, Coal's first impression was one of dislike. It was something about the man's eyes and his mouth. A huge horseshoe mustache, rather than hiding his mouth, seemed to frame it, and his lips, like his eyes, were hard and pinched. But it was his voice, which sounded every time he spoke as if his throat were full of wet gravel, and his cocky attitude, that grated on Coal the most.

"Hey, Horace. William," said the chief. "Listen, here's the deal." He explained what had happened and asked them to take turns watching the place. "Can you do that?"

"Sure," said Verret in his gruff voice. "In fact, maybe we can both stay up here at the same time. It'd be easier to stay awake with two of us."

"Okay, if you want to. I really don't even care if you sleep, if you want to know the truth. I just want a car here so nobody feels safe to come snooping around before we can get back in the daylight."

"Well, I ain't sleepin'," Verret averred. "Not unless Horace is here with me."

"Me either," said Teal. "I don't know what kinda whack-job is wandering around up here in the dark."

"Yeah, that's a good point," agreed the chief.

Coal quietly but strongly agreed and was glad the two volunteers had enough sense to suggest they both remain together. Secretly, he was hoping Chief George was just tired, and that all these little details he was missing weren't the normal way he did business. Telling a police officer it was okay to sleep at a murder scene up here in the middle of nowhere, with the suspect still running loose, was a potential recipe for disaster.

"Hey, guys," Coal cut in. "We're only watching the place, all right? Anybody shows up around here, it's not time to start World War Three. Just get their information and tell them to get lost. But watch your backs. Nothing's saying there wasn't more than just one killer up here."

Verret, his eyebrows almost hidden by the dipped brim of his black cowboy hat, stared Coal down. He appeared to be trying to decide what kind of a reply he could afford to make.

"Don't you worry, Sheriff. This ain't the first watch I been on."

"Good," replied Coal, as his initial dislike for Verret became chiseled in stone.

Once William Verret and Horace Teal were settled into Teal's pickup together, with Chief George's promise to bring a thermos of coffee and some Twinkies back up for them, Coal said, "Chief, I'm going to go make a visit before I head home. You need me for anything else?"

"No, Coal, I don't think so. You sure you don't want any backup?"

Coal stared at him. He wanted to think of something to say, but he was too tired.

Finally, the chief nodded. "Then I guess not. All right then. Just watch your back."

Coal looked at him squarely. "I'm pretty sure if Hunter Jack ever comes at me, he'll come from in front."

CHAPTER SEVENTEEN

Hunter Jack's house was dark, just as one would expect in the wee hours of the morning. Even though he was known to be a night owl, this was apparently too late even for him.

Coal crept through the neighborhood, noting that there were only a few lights on, and all those were dim. Any of them could as easily be seeing use as a nightlight as be the sign of someone still awake, or perhaps the owners had fallen asleep with them on.

He came back and parked a couple of residences down from Hunter Jack's, not wanting to mess up any tracks that might be in front. Other than the fifty-five Buick Special, Jack didn't own a vehicle, and the Buick was sitting in its place of honor under the awning, or at least what he assumed to be the Buick, although he couldn't see it because it was covered up with a tarp.

Descending from the truck with his flashlight, and the security strap undone on his Smith and Wesson, Coal turned on the light and shined it out ahead of his path, trying to keep from walking on any other tracks. He went up the wooden steps, which were surprisingly well-kept, and there he stopped.

In one flash of his light, he could see damage to the flimsy wooden door, right beside the knob. Leaning in closer, he inspected it with the beam of his flashlight cupped in his hand to keep the rest of the neighborhood from easily seeing it. He couldn't see any conclusive evidence of whether the damage to the door was new or old.

Taking a deep breath, he knocked on the soft wood with one knuckle, then waited. Silence greeted him, and then a few seconds later the barking of a dog. But it was a far-off sound, echoing along the frozen ground, against the frozen sky, and upon the frozen walls of houses. With the crisp cold of this night, it was probably some animal that had been left out unattended and was trying to remind its owner to let it back in. It didn't sound alarmed.

He rapped again, this time a little louder. Again, the barking dog was all he heard in the two minutes that followed.

Frustrated with the knowledge that he didn't dare walk on in looking for Jack, because anything he found without a warrant wouldn't be admissible in court, he turned and went around back, checking for sign under the windows. He knocked on each of the windows as he went, hoping if Jack was asleep he could rouse him.

Finally, he went back and sat in the truck, sinking back against the seat and reveling in the warmth of the heater fan.

This whole crime investigation thing wasn't Coal's forte, even with all the practice he had been getting since his return to Salmon, but certain things he knew. He knew the search and seizure laws forward and back, and he knew the rules of warrants. He also knew the longer a case sat before certain steps were taken, the colder it would get, and a cold case is always the hardest one to solve.

His first instinct right now was to wake up acting county prosecutor Bryan Wheat and tell him all that had happened, since before all was said and done he would be deeply involved anyway. Then he could find out if Wheat thought it prudent to wake up Judge Sinclair looking for a warrant.

He felt like he had enough, because as much as he hated to admit it, he knew Jack had several spears that looked very similar to the one they had taken into evidence at the scene of the murders. Most of Jack's Indian artifacts only fit that definition by their appearance, because Jack had made them himself. He had spears, gourd rattles, medicine sticks, knives, and bows and arrows. One of the bows was made out of the horn of a bighorn sheep, and it was Jack's proudest accomplishment. It was Jack's hunting piece, in fact, ever since the Gun Control Act had rendered it illegal for Jack to own a firearm.

But of course that wasn't all. Of greater importance was the fact that Jack had recently fought with one of the murder victims, had apparently received a couple of pretty good wallops on the head from him with the help of a billiard cue, and was in a bad legal situation thanks to the now-deceased Everett Sherman's actions. His potential desire for revenge, along with Coal's knowledge of his collection of Indian weaponry, would be more than enough at least to get the judge to issue a search warrant for this place, but still Coal hesitated. The fact was that in spite of everything he knew, he didn't believe Jack was guilty. In fact, knowing that intrepid Shoshone, he was somewhere down the river, right where he had told Coal he planned to go, and his home was standing empty right now. It probably had been for some time.

Coal looked at his watch. It was three-thirty. He drew a deep breath and looked back at the house. All right, so what was the worst that could happen if he went in without a warrant? No one had to know, did they? He would slip in, look for Jack, see if there was any sign he had been here recently, and ghost back out. If while he was in there he saw anything that begged further attention, then he could wake up the judge to get a warrant. It seemed like a foolproof plan—as long as no one saw him go in. Was it above-board? Of course not. But with the tools they had at hand for catching murderers in this county, sometimes a few rules had to be misshapen, bent, slipped over, under, or past. Or sometimes, with a man who truly desired justice at all costs, the rules had to be melted and poured down the drain. Whether it was honest or not, Coal knew one man very well who felt like that.

Scanning the area once more, he got out, shutting the door as lightly as possible. He went to Jack's front door and knocked, getting the same result as before. Steeling himself, and keeping the flashlight unlit for the moment, he reached into his hip pocket and pulled out his thin brown doeskin gloves, working them on.

One more glance about. The world was dead. When he tried the doorknob, it turned, and the door swung open. Thoughts and possibilities careened across his mind as he eased in and immediately turned on the flashlight, stabbing it around the dark room.

The room was empty except for furniture, and clothing strewn around and dirty dishes on the counter and in the sink. He walked to the sofa that had been here on his only other visit inside this house. That time, he had come here at Jack's invitation, to admire all his handmade Indian accoutrements and memorabilia. He had told himself he was only looking for Jack, but he had a powerful curiosity to satisfy.

Acid began to seep into his stomach when he saw the nails in the wall above the couch. A number of them. There were some items remaining there in the same spots they had taken up before: namely a couple of ceremonial rattles, a bison horn headdress, a wooden bow, and a couple of war clubs. But conspicuous by their absence were two lances, a quiver of arrows, and the sheep horn bow. All their places were marked now only by the rusted, bent nails that had held them on display.

Coal shouldn't be in here. He should have gone straight back to the bedrooms, knocked and yelled for Hunter Jack, then got out. Again he took a deep breath and moved down the hall, the light flashing before him. He knocked loudly on the first bedroom door and spoke Jack's name. No reply. Opening the door revealed a room with no furniture, only junk scattered around the floor and some Indian artwork on the walls. He went to the end of the hall, to the room he had figured would be Jack's bedroom. This time he knocked louder, and longer, then slipped away from the front of the door and into the bathroom, in case Jack came barreling out of his room looking for war.

After a couple of minutes, he returned to the door and spoke Jack's Indian name again. Then, gritting his teeth, he turned the knob and pushed the door open. The bed was in disarray, and empty. The mass of disturbed blankets didn't mean anything, of course. Jack could have last slept in here twenty minutes ago, or three days.

To satisfy his curiosity, Coal stepped closer, took off his left glove, and laid the back of his hand on top of the bottom sheet. It was cold.

A quick glance around the floor revealed no large-size boots or small handmade moccasins, although either could have been hidden anywhere in the house, or even discarded elsewhere by a murderer trying to hide evidence.

It was time to get out. Nothing Coal would find in here was going to help this case one way or another, now that he had ascertained that Hunter Jack wasn't home. The man had said he was going down the river, and that could be exactly what he did.

Coal went swiftly to the front door and started to open it, then froze, his flashlight unused at his side. He had heard a noise, and it could have been nothing, but it sounded like the crackling of gravel.

He had pulled the door shut by reflex, but now he pushed it open gently. Out in the middle of the street, just down from Hunter Jack's plywood shack, a pickup was stopped. He could hear it idling, and silvery steam streamed from the tailpipe. Its headlights were off.

The pickup began to creep forward, and then all of a sudden, just past Jack's house, it picked up speed. It hit twenty or twenty-five miles an hour fairly fast as its lights came on, and Coal about fell off the steps trying to get back to his truck to get it turned around.

He saw where the other pickup, a dark-colored late fifties Ford, went around a corner almost on two wheels as he threw open his own door and leaped in. He popped the clutch too fast and killed the engine, then fired it up again and spun the wheel hard, making him go up over a few feet of the lawn across the street in his haste.

Pulling on the headlight switch after twenty yards, he got to the street where the other pickup had turned, and made the corner even faster than the other vehicle had done it. The other one was no longer in sight.

As fast as he could without fear of careening right across the highway, Coal flew up to Highway 93 and looked both ways. There was nothing to be seen. He swore and slammed the heel of his hand on the wheel, throwing himself back against the seat. He started to pull out onto the highway, then swore again and sank back.

Taking a deep breath, he tried to put himself in the head of the other driver. First, could it be whoever it was had been drunk and was simply trying to get home undetected? Maybe they had seen Coal's truck idling and stopped to figure out what was going on. And after that, perhaps they had recognized it as his pickup and only meant to get home fast. Of course it could also be something more nefarious.

He gritted his teeth and turned to look back the way he had come. In his haste to get to the highway, he had passed at least two other streets. At the speed the other pickup had been going, he would have had to slam on his brakes to make it onto either of them, but after all, that's what brakes are for.

Putting the pickup in reverse, he went slowly backward to the first of the gravel streets, which cut off to the right, and looked along its length. It appeared to come to a dead-end perhaps ten houses down. He backed on to the next one, which also cut to the right. Pretty much the same sight greeted him.

He didn't have any other leads on the pickup. He sure hadn't been able to get a plate. So what did he have to lose?

Turning the wheel, he drove down the street, looking into each driveway because it was obvious at a glance the truck wasn't on the street.

He got clear to the end without seeing anything of interest, so he did a three-point turn and got going back the other way, returning to the second street.

Turning onto it, he proceeded the same as before. He was clear to the dead-end when he saw it: a dark fifties Ford pickup, parked in the starlight alongside a ramshackle log cabin with a concrete porch the full length of its front.

When Coal got out, he drew his pistol, carrying the flashlight in his left hand in case he needed it, but keeping it turned off. He probably should have called for back-up, but this was Salmon, Idaho. If a man called for back-up here every time he thought he might need it he would never get anything done.

As he got close to the pickup, a garbage can erupted from near the corner of the house.

It was the last place he had been looking, as he was concentrating on the cab of the truck, and the noise almost made him dive to the ground. A black and white cat raced away from the garbage for parts unknown, leaving Coal wanting to send a couple of rounds after it to help it on its way.

Breathing deep to get his heart back under control, he continued to the pickup, raising his light to flash it into the cab. It was empty. He went to the hood and laid a hand on it: warm.

There was no address visible on the front of the house, but he certainly wouldn't forget where it was. Stepping back, he aimed his light at the license plate and jotted down the number in his mental notepad: Idaho, 2L 752.

Whoever this was, there was no way Coal was going to talk to him—or her—tonight. He had been involved in law enforcement long enough to know that. But whoever owned this truck was going to have some serious questions to answer for him the next day. He would be back here, loaded for bear.

As he started to turn away, he had another thought, and he turned back. He felt his heartrate begin to pick up as he looked around, searching the shadows. He knew he shouldn't be having the thoughts he was having, but he couldn't help it. Too many times he had seen plans, and investigations, go awry when he or some other investigator went back to confront or interview someone and they had fled to parts unknown.

In the end, his conscience lost the battle to his desire to see justice done, and to find this truck right where he had left it, if possible. Stepping around to the side of the pickup that faced away from the quiet house it was parked by, he crouched down and screwed the cap off the valve stem of the rear driver's side tire. He used the fingernail of his pinky finger to let the air out of it, listening impatiently to the drawn-out, irritating hiss, and feeling the ice cold of it against his hand and against one knee. When that was finished, he went and did the same with the front tire, satisfied only when his hand was good and frozen stiff and both tires were nearly flat on the ground.

Putting the second valve stem cap back on, he stood slowly and studied the windows of the house, then pierced the shadows all around with his eyes. When he was finally satisfied no one was watching, he turned once more away.

Back in his pickup, Coal tried to decide if he should bother Nadine to get the registration information on the pickup. At last, he decided it could wait until morning, and he got a notepad out of his glove box and wrote down the license plate number like a white man. Even a trained FBI agent, this time of morning, couldn't be expected to remember everything.

CHAPTER EIGHTEEN

Coal couldn't sleep, and having Dobe and Shadow seem extraordinarily restless didn't help matters any. The second time he let the dogs out, his head had only hit the pillow, and Dobe was doing his irritating whirl-around on the bed before he could find out that his first sleeping position was his best sleeping position, when it hit Coal that he had never called Kathy MacAtee back.

Trouble sleeping then became the impossibility of sleeping, and Coal struggled off the bed to fumble his way downstairs and make coffee. The dogs didn't even have the common decency to come down and keep him company, and Coal's last farewell from Dobe was a quiet groaning as he slipped out the doorway and headed for the stairs.

Sitting in his mom's chair with coffee mug in hand, Coal looked at the clock on the wall, but he couldn't make out the hands, or the numbers. In fact, he wasn't sure he was even looking at a clock on the wall, or maybe just some flattened volleyball. His nighttime vision certainly wasn't what it used to be.

Sitting up is somehow different from lying down when it comes to sleeping, so Coal had to get up and go to the kitchen table when he almost fell asleep and spilled his coffee in his lap. That would have been preferable to spilling it on his mother's chair, however. He would never have heard the end of that, and it would have made the war over coffee in the house that much harder. His mother seemed to live under the delusion that one day she would convince him to stop consuming his life-saving nectar altogether.

Coal, now that he was sitting on a hard wooden stool, light glaring into his eyes, with both managing to keep him awake, tried to go over the murder case so far. Of course he had turned the case over to Grant Fairbourne, but that didn't change the fact that ultimate responsibility for it fell directly on his shoulders, as sheriff of Lemhi County. If Grant did an impeccable job, and the killer, or killers, were caught and arrested, Coal would look good. Conversely, if Grant botched everything horribly, no one but Coal was even going to notice. But in the public eye, Coal would be raked over the . . . coals. The play on his name managed to bring a half-hearted smile to one corner of his mouth.

Coal had an appetite for fried eggs and bacon, but what he couldn't drum up was the energy to get up and pull them out of the fridge. Instead, he sat sipping his third cup of ink-black coffee and stared up at the clock on the wall. He was waiting for some semblance of a decent hour that would justify his starting to make all the phone calls he feared would suck up at least two hours of his morning, and every last fluid ounce of his patience. He would rather crawl through a hive of giant bees than talk on the phone.

Down the hall, Coal finally heard the stirring of his mother. No matter the darkness of the morning, that woman seldom let five o'clock tick past without already being up and dressed, getting ready to head out and feed the horses.

Coal thought idly of how he should have some kind of guilt for not taking care of the horses for Connie, but that was a chore he wouldn't steal from her often. She actually enjoyed it, and if he did it very often, eventually she would chastise him for it. Instead, he rallied his energy stores enough to drag his butt off the stool and turn on a front burner of the stove, setting his favorite giant cast iron pan on it.

As he chased bacon, eggs, and whole, raw milk out of the fridge and onto the countertop, he glanced over at the clock again. He should have been running through all the calls he had to make to start buttoning down the progress of the murder investigation, at least in his head. Instead, he was thinking about Kathy MacAtee. As much as he kept trying to make himself feel aloof, he didn't. He had completely missed mentioning Luke's birthday to Kathy, and now he had been acting like a jilted lover toward her, when they weren't any kind of lovers whatsoever, but only really good friends—or at least so he had believed before finding the stranger, Gunnar Westerlind, at her house seeming so chummy with her. To make it worse, she had acted coolly toward him, and . . .

He stopped. What was he thinking? What was he *doing?* He and Kathy MacAtee, and her deceased husband, Larry, who had been Coal's best friend, had been in each other's lives almost as far back as he could remember. Kathy had always loved Larry MacAtee, it seemed. There had never been anything of romance between her and Coal, so why had he been feeling since he last saw her like she had given him the brush off? He didn't even know if there was any kind of relationship brewing between Kathy and Gunnar Westerlind, but even if there was, so what? She had every right to find someone new, someone who could be a companion to her, and even a lover. Who was Coal to take that away from her? Had he been feeling like she was disloyal to Larry? If so, it was something buried deep in his subconscious. The plain fact was, he had been acting like a fool, feeling jealous, he guessed, because Kathy seemed to have found someone else to be her friend.

After Connie came through the room, stopping to give her son a warm hug, then took her coat and hat and headed outside, Coal looked at the clock again. It was five-twenty. One benefit of knowing someone from childhood, and knowing them well, was you knew their habits intimately. Coal knew that Kathy, like his mother, was always up by five, and soon out feeding the stock.

Maybe he could still catch her . . .

Unfortunately, it wasn't Kathy's voice that finally came on the phone, but one of her daughters, sounding very sleepy. Coal winced. The girls would have to catch their bus all too soon, and he had stolen valuable sleep time from at least one of them.

"Milo?" He took a chance that he was speaking to Kathy's oldest daughter.

No, replied the voice. *This is Sara.*

"Oh, I'm sorry! You sound so big." He wasn't sure that "big" was a word thirteen-year-old girls liked to have describe them, but Sara took it well, letting out a laugh.

Is this Coal?

"It is, and I sure apologize for waking you up so early. I was hoping to catch your mom before she went out to feed."

She's not, said the voice. *She's— Oh, here she is!* He heard Sara say something to her mother in a muffled voice, probably with her hand over the receiver. Then Kathy's voice came over the line.

Coal?

"Hi, Kathy. I'm sorry for calling so early."

Oh, don't be silly! I've been worried about you. You know I never sleep in this late, don't you?

"I do, yes. I'd never have called this early otherwise. Hey, I apologize for not returning your call sooner. Things have gone pretty haywire around here."

I've been hearing, Kathy said. *I'm sorry you have to deal with that stuff again.* The tone of her voice subtly changed. Coal was in tune enough to wonder if her thoughts had gone back to the first time Coal had been forced to "deal with that stuff", when it was with her husband, Larry.

"Goes with the territory, I guess. So I won't keep you, Kathy, but was there something you needed, or did you just call to say hi?"

Oh, no! No, well . . . I guess I just felt like I should apologize for the other day.

"The other day? Apologize for what?" Coal felt sheepish. He was 100% sure he was the one who should be apologizing.

Oh, well . . . Oh, maybe nothing. It just felt like . . . Oh, let's just forget it, okay? I was probably overthinking things.

Coal wanted nothing more than to move on from this topic before any attention could be turned on how abruptly he had left Kathy's, and how coolly he had treated her. At the time, he had felt she was the one treating him in a less than warm manner, but now he was pretty certain it was the exact opposite.

Ignoring pretty much every single thing Kathy had haltingly stumbled her way through, he veered onto a sideroad he hoped she would appreciate, nonetheless. "How are the girls? And King?"

After a moment's hesitation, probably while she shifted mental gears, Kathy cheerfully replied that Milo, Sara, and little Jen were all well, and that they all missed seeing him. As for King, he had almost literally become king, at least of the three girls' hearts.

"What time does the bus pick up the girls?" Coal asked. When Kathy told him it was promptly at seven, he said, "Would you mind if I came over and said hello? Just real quick."

Mind! Her voice sounded almost startled. *Of course we wouldn't mind. You have to be crazy even to ask that, mister.* She punctuated that statement with a laugh, but the way her voice sounded, he didn't think she was joking. Maybe she really did miss him. Maybe his impression of how she treated him when Gunnar Westerlind was with her was all in his head, the way he suspected.

Restraining himself from calling anyone else to start delving into the murder investigation, Coal finished his coffee as Connie was coming in, then excused himself to change into some sweats and go down in the basement, where he did a fast-paced, heavy weight workout with little rest between sets, finishing up in only fifty minutes, even including stretch time.

Coal wasn't one to waste a lot of water in the shower, but this morning he did. He stood letting lukewarm water run down over his head and body, now and then scrubbing himself, almost absent-mindedly, with a bar of Irish Spring and letting the delicious aroma rise to his nostrils. It was going to be a good day.

He came out of his bedroom dressed in Levi's 501's, which fit him better than any other jeans made, his Vibram-soled Redwing boots, and a form-fitting maroon tee shirt. As he descended the stairs, he was shrugging into a dark blue stone-washed shirt to whose chest he had pinned his sheriff's badge.

Buttoning his shirt as he stood in the kitchen watching Connie work her magic on a pan of quiche, a dish whose recipe his father, Prince, had brought back from the war, Coal let himself bask in the warmth, both physical and emotional, of his mother's kitchen. As often happened, she seemed to sense his mood, and she turned and looked at him where he leaned up against the bar behind her.

Connie gazed up at him for a while as she continued to whip the mixture of eggs, sausage, green peppers, and whatever else was going to cover the base of her quiche. Finally, a little smile came to her lips. "What are you up to, Son? For such a little bit of sleep you've been getting lately, you sure look bright-eyed—and happy. Are you?"

"Um . . . I guess so." He didn't want to give himself away too much, partially because he wasn't quite sure to what he should attribute his feelings. Did he owe all of this to Kathy?

Connie smiled bigger and shook her head at him. "My. You guess so, do you? You know, sometimes I think you ended up with way too much of your father in you. So hard to let your guard down, isn't it?"

Coal grinned back at her. "Maybe."

"I guess it's pointless asking why you look so awake and happy," she said as she walked over and began to pour the egg mixture over two pans of prepared pastry.

"No reason," he said, keeping his planned visit to Kathy up his sleeve. He hated to have something go wrong and then have Connie assume later that it was because of Kathy. "It's probably just that euphoria you sometimes get when you're so tired your body starts running adrenaline through you to help you cope."

Connie looked at him and raised an eyebrow. "Now *that* I could believe. Son, I'm sure you have a lot you need to do today." He had already told her all about the murders, and enough about the investigation that lay ahead to satisfy her curiosity. "But I think you need to come home when all the kids are gone to school and try to get a nap in. I'm worried about you—even if you do seem wide-awake and happy right now."

"Thanks, Mom. I'll think about it." But he knew she knew better. Driving all this way back out here just for a nap wasn't a luxury Lemhi County's top lawman could afford.

To the tune of Charley Pride singing "The Day the World Stood Still", Coal drove down Kathy MacAtee's long, icy driveway around six-forty, while it was still dark. He pulled up to the front of the house, hearing the crunch and rattle of ice under his tires even through the closed windows of the dark green Thunderbird he had chosen to drive today.

Before he even had a chance to turn off the radio and try to push sudden, unfortunate thoughts of Maura PlentyWounds from his head, he was surprised to see the front door fling open, and eleven-year-old Jen MacAtee came running from the house. Her loose hair, the color of dark honey flew out behind her as she ran to greet him, in spite of the slick ice.

Scrambling to shut off the engine and get control of his sudden rush of emotion from the unwelcome intrusion of Maura into his thoughts, Coal threw open the heavy door and lunged up out of the car. To his surprise, without saying a word Jen ran right up to him and wrapped her arms tightly around his middle. Coal had to fight his emotions even harder as he put his arms around the girl and crushed her to him, thinking how miraculous the actions of a child can be when it comes to healing a broken heart.

The other girls, dark-haired beauty Milo, and her next-younger sister, Sara, came out on the porch all smiles but stopped short when they saw Jen had beat them to Coal's affections. Soon, Kathy appeared behind them. Smiling, Coal stared at her. The look on the woman's face he could only describe as beaming. Old Larry sure had been a lucky man. He had never allowed himself to think much about Kathy, other than the fact that she was his best friend's wife. But she really was a beautiful woman, there was no denying it. Every time he saw her he felt more shocked that he had never noticed it before.

When Jen finally had her fill of hugging, which took a good fifteen or twenty seconds, she took Coal's hand and proudly led him to the porch to greet all the people of lesser importance. Coal was touched to receive huge, tight hugs from both the older girls, and then one from their mother that almost crushed the breath of life from him. During the entire female assault, Coal was only vaguely conscious of a club whacking his leg repeatedly that could only be the tail of King.

Once finally inside the warmth of the house, it smelled much like the heaven Connie had been making back home, only here it was from pancakes, maple syrup, and bacon. As King fawned all over Coal, and he tried to accommodate him with as much petting as he could manage, one or the other of the girls kept an eye out the front window. Sadly, they didn't have the luxury of waiting for the bus to pull up, however. It was a good three-minute walk from their front door all the way out to the highway.

Coal had been looking forward to some peaceful time with Kathy, so it was only on a whim, the last time he looked at Jen's wistful expression, that he said, "Why don't I drive you girls to school today? The Bird's all warmed up out there, and it's a lot nicer ride than that big, drafty bus."

"Oh, no, Coal," Kathy countered. "No, you don't have to do that."

He looked over at her, trying to reconcile his feeling of pride that he had thought of such a magnanimous gift to Kathy's girls with the almost frantic look on Kathy's face—for lack of any better way to describe it.

In spite of his basic male inability to understand women, Coal managed to pull a miracle out of his hat this time. "You come with us, okay? After we drop the girls off, you and me'll go to Wally's or the Coffee Shop and grab a coffee and a cinnamon roll. Then I'll bring you back out."

"What about your work?" she asked, once the frantic look he had seen on her face metamorphosed into one of temporary confusion, then turned back to hope.

"Work? You do live in my county, don't you? Wherever I want to go in our county is my work."

Her deep chocolate eyes stared into his for a moment, and finally she let out a resigned laugh, a sound also of relief. "Okay then. Only if you're sure." Once again, with Coal's quick thinking, the woman was beaming.

After the bus had stopped out at the end of the lane for a few seconds, then pulled away and headed down the highway, there was plenty of time left for Kathy and the girls to have a nice visit. Not having to stop numerous times on the way in to school left a good forty minutes of leeway.

Coal managed to ward off any questions Kathy had about what she had heard on the early morning news concerning the murders. He didn't want to frighten the girls needlessly, and besides, any talk of fights, and bars, and murders only took away from the idyllic feeling of being here, feeling both the physical warmth from the combined efforts of the wood stove and furnace, and the emotional warmth of feeling so welcomed by these beautiful girls—all four of them.

Finally, they headed into town, and after all three girls proudly hugged the local sheriff, for their friends and fellow students to see, and took their books and departed, Coal and Kathy were alone.

They watched little Jen all the way to the front door of her school, where she turned one last time and gave them an exuberant wave, then disappeared behind the red metal door. The vanishing act left Coal feeling strangely empty, after being so overloaded with female attention.

He turned to find Kathy watching him, her dark eyes sparkling. "Quite a bunch, aren't they?"

With a laugh, he replied, "They sure are. Quite a bunch. You're doing a good job, Kathy. Larry would be proud of you."

Kathy looked quickly down, darting a hand out to clutch his. When she looked back up at him, her eyes were moist. "You think so? Sometimes I wonder. Sometimes . . ." Her voice faded away as she dropped her gaze again.

"I promise," he said, reaching out with his other hand to raise her chin up so she was forced to look at him through her tears. "Those are three great little girls. I'd put them up against any other girls in this valley—even my own."

She searched his eyes, badly wanting to find the truth in what he said. Finally, she laughed, and the laugh clashed with a new rush of tears. This time there were enough to spill over and run down her cheeks, and he reached out and wiped them away with a thumb.

"Do you want to wait a little bit for coffee?" He strived to make his voice soft. "We can go for a drive first if you'd rather."

"No! No, I promise, honey—I'm okay. Coffee would be good. Besides, I've been craving the taste of a cinnamon roll ever since you brought it up. Coal, I'm sorry about the tears. Sometimes they just . . . You know, sometimes they're just there. Before you know it."

"I know the feeling," he said. He could never tell her that her comment had got him thinking again about Maura. There simply were some tears that would remain forever close to the surface.

CHAPTER NINETEEN

Wally's Café was crowded when Coal held open the door to let Kathy precede him inside. Both crowded and warm. Wally Richardson and his wife Beulah greeted Coal with their usual exuberance and warmth, and the same warmth spilled over to Kathy, when Beulah pulled her close and gave her a tight hug.

As usual, many of the room's customers knew Coal, and most of them who did liked him as well, and greeted him amiably. The crowded room was no place for deeply personal conversations, so after all the greetings were done, Coal and Kathy mostly sat in silence, sipping coffee and pulling off bits of a warm, buttered cinnamon roll they were sharing.

Finally, they went back out to the Thunderbird, and by the time they hit the far edge of town the heater was already well on its way to getting the inside too warm.

Neither Coal nor Kathy spoke, and Coal wondered why. He also wondered what Kathy might be thinking about. Then a wry smile came to his own face as he was thinking about rancher Gunnar Westerlind and what might be between him and Kathy, for KSRA, with impeccable timing, started Jim Reeves singing, "He'll Have to Go."

Unable to let an opportunity like that go, as the last beautiful notes of Jim Reeves's perfectly timed song faded away, and Glen

Campbell immediately began crooning out "Wichita Lineman", Coal casually asked, without looking over, "So how are things with you and that Westerlind fellow?"

He felt Kathy turn to look at him. It was almost as if he could hear her heart beating as well—or maybe that was his. "Gunnar? Well … I don't know. What do you mean how are things?"

Coal shrugged, pretending to take great care studying a stocky bay horse out in a snowy field. "Well . . . I don't know," he echoed her words, then wondered if there was enough shoelace left exposed by which to pull his boot out of his throat.

"You're not worried about him, are you?"

Looking quickly over, Coal said, "Worried? Why would I be worried? I guess I was just curious. I don't know much about him, but . . ." Kathy didn't give him the common courtesy of allowing him to back away from the subject, so he figured he might as well bull on. Maybe he would learn all he needed to know about Westerlind when he talked to the state patrolman, Gentry, later, but for some reason he wanted to hear something about the man from Kathy.

"Coal, can I ask you something?"

He took his eyes off the road again to look at her. "Of course you can."

"It might be an uncomfortable question."

With that kind of an introduction, whether it was going to be or not, it instantly became uncomfortable, for Coal. "Umm . . . Okay. Go ahead." *Here it came,* he thought. *Damn all devious women and their uncomfortable questions.*

"I don't even know quite how to word it, but . . . Coal, what are we to each other? You and me, I mean."

"What are we?" Coal's put-on look of confusion hid the proliferation of curse words traffic-jamming on the highway of his brain. "I'm not sure what you mean."

Of course he was lying. Stalling for time, hoping maybe a deer would run out in front of them, or a UFO would land on the road and aliens would beam him up to remove his brain and study it to find out why he was stupid enough to bring up Gunnar Westerlind to Kathy MacAtee on such a formerly idyllic morning.

"Coal." The sound of his name came flatly to his ears, sort of like a teacher trying to jar a student's mind into actually listening to whatever she was prattling on about. "You know what I mean. Don't you?" Coal gritted his teeth and stole another look at her, seeing uncertainty in her face. Maybe even she didn't know what she really meant. Maybe he was about to get some kind of get-out-of-jail-free card or something.

Any good soldier knows there are a number of options in a battle: He can go on the offensive and attack; counter attack; or retreat to fight another day. Coal wanted to drop on the battlefield and feign death, but he chose a cloud of smoke to disconcert the foe—or maybe he was putting up a force field to deflect Kathy's round.

"I didn't mean to make things uncomfortable for you. You don't have to tell me anything about Westerlind if you'd rather not." *And I'm begging you to give me the same courtesy about us!* He screamed the words in his head, but of course he couldn't say them.

Kathy grew quiet and turned to look out her window for a while. Coal was conscious that his foot raised up slightly off the gas, the car slowed accordingly, and he wondered what stupidity made him do a thing like that. What he most wanted to do was put the pedal down and make the car's 429 Thunderjet barrel them home to the ranch at top speed.

"I guess you're the one who got uncomfortable," Kathy finally managed to say. "I apologize. It wasn't a fair question."

And it wasn't. To Coal, Kathy MacAtee, even as beautiful, warm, sweet, and attractive as she was, was still the wife of his best friend. And even if Larry was gone in body, he would always be there in spirit, always sitting firmly, like a block of hard cheese, right between Coal and Kathy—keeping them at a safe distance, as such great old friends should be.

In spite of Coal's reluctance to talk about it, he knew Kathy deserved an answer from him. However, when the news came on, he got a brutal unexpected reprieve when the commentator started reporting that Libyan Arab Airlines Flight 114, a Boing 727, had been shot down by Israeli fighters for straying over the Sinai Desert, into forbidden airspace. All but five of the one hundred thirteen people on board had been killed.

After Kathy's initial gasp, and then a long moment of reverent silence after the story ended and the weatherman gave his best guesses about what the weather was going to do for that day and in the near future, a singer by the name of Roberta Flack came over the airwaves, breaking KSRA's country traditions with the country's current most popular song, "Killing Me Softly With His Song".

"We've been friends as far back as I can remember, Kathy."

Coal's flat statement broke the long silence between them when they were only a mile or so out from her ranch. He saw a long-haired black and white dog on the opposite side of the highway from the MacAtee place, a dog he knew often to be running at large, chasing people's stock. A brief survey proved to Coal that a golden retriever mix, known to be a frequent companion of the black and white dog on his forays around the county, was with him today. At the moment, he didn't care. He cared only about Kathy.

He could feel the woman studying him. From the corner of his eye, he saw her hand budge toward him, but it stopped still several inches away. "So . . . friends? Is that what you're saying? To answer my question?"

He glanced over at her, knowing he owed her more than a casual glance, but also knowing many people had been scraped off the pavement for giving much more than casual glances to anything but the roads they were driving on.

"I'm a pretty broken fellow," he said. "Especially compared to Larry. The best thing I can be to anybody I care about is their friend."

He knew what he said was true, but it was also true that in his heart he knew he could never give Kathy his love, at least not the romantic kind, if that was what she was reaching for, because Larry would always be there watching them.

"Okay. I have to respect that. So what about Gunnar Westerlind?" she went on. "Why do you want to know about him? And what do you want to know?"

Everything Coal wanted to know about Westerlind he could never bring himself to ask Kathy, because he didn't understand his own desire to know certain things. All he could ask her was about who Westerlind was, and who his son was. He had a lot of feelings to sort out before he dared ask anything more personal about the rancher.

"Somebody saw a pickup that appeared to be fleeing from the scene of the murder last night," he said bluntly. "I guess it fits the description of Westerlind's truck."

Kathy took in a deep, contemplative breath. They had wasted valuable time in silence and were pulling up to the ranch drive now. Coal slowed almost to a stop and turned in, unable not to think of the time not so long ago when he had first seen Kathy's station wagon pulling into this same opening on her arrival back in the valley, after learning about her husband's murder.

Ice chunks crackled under the T-Bird's tires as they drove down the long driveway, then parked in front of the house, beside the station wagon.

"Would you like to come in, Coal? Or do you have any more time?" He wasn't certain, but it felt like any sound of enthusiasm was gone from her voice. Or maybe she was only preparing herself for rejection.

He turned off the engine, and the sound of Jeannie Seely singing her momentarily ironic song, "Don't Touch Me", died on the instant. *Don't touch me, if you don't love me, sweeth—"* Kathy looked down at the radio in the sudden silence, and he couldn't help but notice the little smile on her lips that seemed almost as ironic as the words of the song.

"I have time," Coal replied after a few more seconds. "As long as Westerlind isn't around."

She looked at him. Studied him. "Does he worry you, Coal?"

"Worry me how?"

"However, I guess. Mostly—do they think he might have had something to do with the murder? Because I don't believe that for one second."

In spite of the defensive way her voice sounded, Coal tried to believe Kathy wasn't starting to have feelings for Westerlind. "It was a teenage boy driving the truck, and he might have had a girl and another boy with him. So no. Westerlind isn't a suspect."

She nodded to that, looking cautious. "Do you want something to drink? Come inside for a while, okay? If you have time."

They opened their doors at the same time, and Coal didn't care. It wasn't like they were on a date or anything, and besides, these days women were opening their own doors more and more often, and Kathy was a pretty independent kind of woman anyway. In the current circumstances, she could sit in her car and freeze to death before any man came around to open her door for her.

They went in the house, which still smelled of pine smoke and that morning's bacon. Coal didn't want a drink, but he also didn't want to refuse. He had already hurt Kathy's feelings enough for one day—or at least he guessed he had, by the way she seemed to be having a hard time meeting his gaze. He wondered if she had only invited him in because it was awkward telling him he needed to go.

Kathy remembered that Coal couldn't stand the smell of beer and wouldn't even pose next to a glass of it, so she offered him peppermint schnapps, and that was good enough for him, a cup of it anyway. He sipped from his glass and watched Kathy build the fire back up, then jumped up on a whim and went out to get an armload of wood from where she kept it at the side of the house.

When he came back in, she was shutting the stove door, and she turned and watched him silently as he laid the new yellow logs down in the explosion of dust and hunks of bark from the last pile. "Thank you, Coal. Can I ask you one more favor? You said we're friends, right?"

"Of course we're friends."

"I just need a hug. A really long hug."

Coal couldn't help feeling warmed by the memory of that long hug twenty minutes later as they sat on the sofa, still sipping their drinks, watching the dance of the flames behind the fire screen, listening to the pop of pitch pockets exploding when the heat was too much.

For some time now, they had sat in silence, and Coal wondered if Kathy could hear his brain overheating. He didn't want to ask anything else about Gunnar Westerlind, but for some reason the man was all he could think about. He wondered if Westerlind would come driving up to the house while he was still here, if he was that frequent of a visitor for Kathy. He prayed he wouldn't. But why did he care? Kathy needed a man. What was wrong with her finding happiness? Maybe Westerlind was a good man. Maybe he was the one who could love her, and make her feel like a woman again.

Coal hated to think about it, and that was the feeling he despised most. He didn't know Gunnar Westerlind. He didn't even care to. Yet he didn't know why.

And when he realized the reason, a realization that came like a bolt out of the blue, he knew he had to leave, to go start his day of phone calls and report writing at his office.

He had to go because he couldn't handle the reason he didn't want anything to do with Gunnar Westerlind: Coal wasn't interested in Kathy MacAtee as anything but a friend, but for some reason he couldn't explain even to himself, it didn't matter.

Coal Savage was jealous.

CHAPTER TWENTY

Coal didn't make it far after leaving Kathy's. He was only half a mile or a little more out, on his way back to town, when he saw the big, long-haired black and white mongrel and his gold-colored mutt companion dart across the road some seventy feet along his path.

Cursing because he didn't have a rifle in his car, he still thought he might salvage something out of this morning and have some target practice with his .44 magnum to boot, so he gunned the engine and flew up to where the dogs had crossed, slamming on the brakes. It was time these two dogs stopped being *at large*, and in his experience with a couple of footloose animals like these, at least out here in the county, there was only one way to go forward. From everything he had been told, no one had ever been able to get close to these animals.

But Coal's Smith and Wesson could.

Throwing the Thunderbird in park and turning on the hazard lights because there was no place to pull off the shoulder, Coal leaped out and drew his pistol. It turned out that "leaping" wasn't the most advisable way to dismount onto the edge of this highway, which he learned when he slipped and nearly fell on the ice. Recovering, with a few choice curse words, he stepped off the treacherous ice and into the crusted snow.

The dogs, after crossing the heap of snow along the road edge, then making their way through a patch of thick willows that lined this side of a barbed wire fence, so far seemed oblivious of his presence. Either that or they were both completely apathetic, since they were nearly one hundred yards away from him now, across an open, snowy field bordered by more thick willows.

Coal took a couple of steps across the snow that plows had piled up on the roadside before realizing he wasn't going to make it very far. He was too heavy to keep his boots from breaking through the crust of snow, and the sound even at that distance from the dogs was much too loud. Besides, just ahead of him the ground sloped off down into the thickly interwoven willows, and by the time he could make it through them and back out into the open field, who knew how far away the dogs would be?

He raised the pistol in both hands, but before he could move his thumb to cock, his entire body jolted to a sound no human likes to be surprised by—the racking of a shotgun. How he didn't throw himself down in the snow and start shooting—or at least *fall* down in the snow—he would never know.

From across the empty highway behind him, a man's voice came deep and gruff and as no nonsense as the racking of the shotgun. "You shoot one o' them dogs, I'll gut-shoot you right here, you son of a bitch!"

Coal stilled for just a few seconds, instinctively. Then, knowing he could accomplish nothing by whirling around but to die, he moved his hands skyward with great caution, the revolver still in his right hand.

"Before you do anything stupid, friend, let me tell you—I'm the sheriff." Coal tried to make himself sound non-confrontational, but not mousy either.

"Sure! And I'm the damn Pope!" growled the voice behind him. "You just hold still right there till I get up close enough to blow a winn-der through you if you decide to move when I ain't told you to."

Shut down in such a blatant way, there wasn't much more Coal could say at the moment except to tell the man he had his badge in his wallet, where he had put it before going into Wally's with Kathy, in order to draw as little attention to himself as possible.

"Oh yeah? Well, first you throw that there pistol down in the snow, 'n' then you reach real slow fer that wallet—with your left hand."

For the briefest of seconds, Coal actually contemplated complying, but he chose against it. "I'll holster the gun and snap it in if you want," he said. "But I'm not throwing it in the snow."

"Why you damn—" The man stopped mid-sentence. There was a hint of grudging respect in his voice when he went on. "All right, I guess I c'n respect that. Then holster it—slow. One wrong move 'n' I'll ruin yer elbow forever."

Coal brought his arm down with exaggerated slowness. As he slid the Smith and Wesson back into his holster and snapped it, the dogs completely forgotten now, he thought with growing joy about how much fun he was going to have with the gentleman behind him once the tables were turned. He could hear the boots of the man behind him now, as he trod carefully across the highway.

"All right, good. Now stay facin' that way 'n' take out the wallet, left-handed, then hold it back'ards t'wards me."

There was no further reason to quibble. Coal reached back and worked his wallet out, then held it back, listening to the careful crunching of the man's boots on the ice as he moved close.

As the wallet slipped out of Coal's hand, he heard the man swear, then the sound of his wallet hitting the road. "Git forward a little—three steps!" the man said in a growl. "Go on, now!"

Coal did as he was told, moving farther up the snowbank. A second later he heard the man grunting. Even without looking, he could tell he was crouching or leaning down to pick up the wallet. He knew he could most likely whirl on him and get the drop, but he didn't see any reason to. This fool was going to know soon enough that he had made the wrong decision by holding the sheriff at gunpoint.

Another grunt by the man as he stood up, and then— "Aw, hell! Awright. So— Say, is that the widder MacAtee?"

Before Coal could reply, or the man could say anything else, the sound of a vehicle, passing way too close, caused the man to curse again, this time vehemently. There came a scrambling sound and a loud *thwump!* followed by a groan. At the same time that Coal turned his head to see the blur of a blue and white pickup sliding to a stop on the icy asphalt past his car, he spun around to see a pear-shaped, bearded man lying on his back in the near lane of traffic, a shotgun gripped tight in his right hand. The man seemed to be struggling to rise, but then his entire body relaxed, and his head fell back down against the asphalt.

The pickup door slammed down the road as Coal stepped cautiously to the fallen man, drawing his revolver out again, out of caution.

"Is that you, Sheriff?" came a voice from the direction of the pickup. "You need any help?"

Seeing that the downed man's eyes were shut, and to all appearances he had lost consciousness, Coal turned his head to see a man moving gingerly toward him. It was Gunnar Westerlind.

"Yeah, maybe. Come on over here, would you? I need to get this fellow off the road."

Westerlind, looking unfortunately every bit as dapper and handsome as Coal remembered, in his light gray hat, a navy-blue collar shirt and expensive sheepskin coat, skated up close. There was real concern etched all over his face.

"Man!" He stared down at the fallen stranger. "I guess I startled him a little, huh? That was some fall! What was he doing?"

"Holding me up," replied Coal, dryly. "At least that's how it felt. I think I was about to shoot a dog that must belong to him, by the way he was acting."

"I'm sure you were," Westerlind said. "This idiot's got the whole area in an uproar with those dogs of his he lets run loose all over the place. They already killed one of my calves that I know of, and I would have shot 'em myself if I could have got close."

"I'm sure a lot of people would have," replied Coal, glancing both ways along the highway for approaching traffic.

"Well, here—let's get him off the road," said Westerlind, merely reminding Coal what his original plan had been in first accepting the man's offer of assistance.

Together, they were able to get the man over on the icy road edge, behind the protection of Coal's car. Coal then went back and gathered up his wallet and its contents. The gold-plated star-shaped badge representative of Lemhi County's lawmen was right on top, and visible through a thick clear plastic window. His various cards and some cash were in the other pockets, most of them still securely in place. But one of the most important things he retrieved was a photograph, glued to a piece of cardstock, that had fallen from the man's fingers when he hit the road. A Remington pump shotgun also still lay there on the ice, and Coal put the photo in his shirt pocket, then picked up the shotgun, unloaded it, and slipped the shells in his coat.

Plucking the photograph back out of his shirt pocket, he blew residual snow off it, then returned it to its secure place in his wallet, but not before it was seen by Gunnar Westerlind. "What's that? It looked like Kathy MacAtee."

Coal had slapped the billfold shut too late. When he looked up and met Westerlind's eyes, the rancher gave him a sheepish look. "Sorry. None of my business, of course."

Glancing over toward where the stranger still lay on top of the snow, in insulated coveralls and a heavy coat, Coal looked back at Westerlind and gave a shrug with one shoulder. "Oh, not a big deal." He reopened the wallet and slipped the photograph out. It was a shot on a gradated white to gray background of a beautiful white and blue 1968 Camaro, with Kathy MacAtee, dressed in straight-legged dark blue polyester pants, and a wild print pattern shirt, standing in front of it with a huge grin on her face. Above her, under the business header of **QUALITY MOTORS**, it said, **Come down and get your own brand-new Chevrolet Camaro! What a catch!**

Westerlind studied the photo for a bit too long, then grinned. "Would you look at that? They're right, huh? What a catch!"

"Yeah. Nice car," said Coal.

"Kathy's, right?"

Coal nodded. "Yeah. Hey, listen, I'd better go call an ambulance if I can't get this old guy to wake up. Unless you feel like staying around, thanks for your help."

It was Gunnar Westerlind's cue to leave, as Coal carefully slid Kathy's photo back into its safe pocket of his billfold, with a faded, scratched photograph of Larry, and others of Connie and Coal's children.

"Right," said Westerlind. He had taken the hint. "You're welcome, Sheriff. I guess I'll see you around."

Coal nodded. *Not if I see you first,* he said in his head, while out loud he said, "Sure."

As Westerlind was jumping in his pickup and driving down the road, Coal got on the radio and spoke to Flo, the normal daytime dispatcher, who did double duty as a housewife when she wasn't on the radio or phone doing police business.

It was Jay Castillo and Ronnie Davis who showed up over half an hour later in the ambulance to collect Coal's patient, who had gone in and out of semi-consciousness three times since Coal made the call, and who had suffered a large goose egg on the back of his skull. In the meantime, Coal had dug the man's wallet out from a pair of smelly trousers well hidden under his grease- and manure-stained brown coveralls, and it was with a bit of shock that he was treated to a much more battered version of his Quality Motors ad featuring the smiling image of Kathy MacAtee.

While he was still getting over his shock at seeing the same photo in this man's wallet as he had in his own, Coal was ascertaining that the man's name was Wilford Bayless, a name he guessed he probably should have tried to get from Gunnar Westerlind, since he obviously knew the man, or at least knew *of* him. Bayless was only a year older than Coal, although he had the grizzled, scruffy-bearded looks and demeanor of a man in his late fifties. He lived right here on this highway, and was probably Kathy's next-door neighbor, to guess from his address. The license said the man weighed two-forty, and Coal wondered who was running the scale at the time the license was made. The man he was looking at, who had an amazing resemblance to the singer-actor Burl Ives, would go an easy three hundred.

"You got Smiley Bayless here," said Jay Castillo after a cordial greeting and handshake.

"Smiley, huh?" Coal had to chuckle. "He'd be better named 'Smelly'. Not a very friendly sort of cuss, is he?"

Jay almost smiled. "Sometimes he is. I always got along with him."

That surprised Coal a little. "Well, maybe because you weren't about to shoot his dog."

"Yeah, that might do it," Ronnie Davis cut in, looking as surly as ever. "But then again, a lot of other people in this area might give you a medal if you did."

"We'll see about those dogs when he wakes up," Coal averred. "Now that I have an idea whose they are."

"It's more than an idea," growled Davis. "He's got a whole pack of those mangy things, and everybody around here has played the devil trying to corner 'em."

Coal nodded. The information was duly noted, but he didn't feel obligated to carry on further conversation with a man he hadn't gotten along well with since coming back to the valley.

"Well, Jay," Coal turned to his friend. "You want any help tucking him in the ambulance, or are you two all right?"

"What do you think?" asked Davis again, making the question his own business.

"What do I think?" Coal drilled a hard gaze through Davis. He had done well to put up with him as much as he had, but his patience was coming to an end. "I think if you want help you should learn some manners—that's what I think. And if I help out, it will be because of Jay—or Bayless. Not because of a surly jackass like you."

Having spoken, there was no taking his words back. Coal and Ronnie Davis stared each other down, two big, hard men who were used to feeling the respect of their peers. Two hard men, neither of whom felt the respect of the other.

"Let's have a look at Smiley," Jay cut in, trying to calm the tense situation. He knelt to look the man over as Coal explained what had happened, and that Bayless had seemed to be regaining consciousness more than once but finally had succumbed. "Well, it sounds like we probably should get him back to Steele pretty quick," Jay said. "I don't like the looks of that bump on his head, and his blood pressure's too low. He's got that one enlarged pupil too. I'm guessing this is a pretty dangerous concussion."

"You sure you don't want help?" asked Coal.

Ronnie Davis grunted. "Surly jackasses like me should be enough to lift one little man."

Davis turned to his partner, whose trace of a smile said everything he needed to say. "You got his feet, Jay? Let's get 'im rollin'."

"I guess we're going, Coal," said Jay Castillo. "See you around."

Coal replied with a smile that took only one side of his mouth. "See you, buddy. I'll stop in and grab a coffee with you sometime soon."

"I don't drink coffee, but I'll do some hot chocolate, and you do the coffee."

Coal chuckled. "Oh, that's right! I forgot. The guy who owns the Salmon River *Coffee* Shop doesn't drink coffee. Right!"

With a sly grin, Jay replied, "Well, I'll bet there are a lot of guys who own strip clubs that aren't strippers."

That got a loud laugh out of Coal, which miffed him because he was supposed to be looking surly for Ronnie Davis. "All right, all right. Okay, so I'll come in and we can share a glass of milk straight from the teat."

"If that's your thing," Jay said. "My lips are sealed." And with the sly little grin still on his face, he went to take Wilford Bayless's feet so Ronnie Davis could prove how incapable of getting the man's upper half he was. Coal's spiteful side made him almost want to hang around just to watch Davis struggle with the burden he had brought upon himself, but there was no sense in rubbing the man's nose in it. Even a man with Davis's immense stubbornness should be allowed enough pride to choke on.

CHAPTER TWENTY-ONE

Coal cursed his own careless stupidity. He had gone no more than a mile and a half on his way back toward town, and had just started going over in his head the list of things he needed to do today, and to check on, when two matters struck him almost as one. First, he had yet to follow up on the pickup whose tires he had let the air out of in the Indian village. Second, he had gone well over the time when the judge would get to the courthouse, and he needed to see him and obtain a search warrant to go through Curlie Burks's pickup.

With those thoughts in mind, he availed himself of one of the few privileges he liked to claim as an emergency responder and slammed his foot down on the gas. Some three hundred and sixty horses roared to life under the hood, and it was good that he had already passed all the curves along the river and was well out on the straightaway toward town. Even a car as smooth as the Thunderbird didn't care for taking tight curves at ninety miles an hour.

When he finally saw a vehicle in his lane ahead, Coal had to slow the Thunderbird down. He knew he could pass whoever was up there, but being late to do a couple of chores, however important they might seem to him, didn't justify flying past someone who was doing the posted speed. He coasted on to the city limits at little more than fifty-five miles an hour, and it seemed to have taken half an hour before he finally pulled into the courthouse parking lot.

It didn't take a fitness expert to tell his blood pressure was higher than normal as he took the courthouse stairs up to the judge's office two at a time.

At her desk past the top of the stairs sat receptionist Wilma Frank, and she looked up and pushed her thick-framed glasses farther up on her nose. "Well, good morning, Coal."

"Good morning, Wilma. You look nice." It was his typical compliment to her, because she always looked nice—as in "kind"—and he could say it without feeling like he was telling her an untruth. "Is the judge in?" He knew he was. He had seen his Lincoln in the parking lot.

"He sure is. Do you want me to give him a ring, or just knock?"

"I'll knock. He's alone?"

"Yes, he is."

Thanking Wilma, Coal went and tapped on Judge Sinclair's door, got the come-ahead, and walked in, shutting the door after himself. Once past the initial greetings, Coal started out his business by explaining the events of the night before.

Judge Sinclair's face seemed to pinch up tighter and tighter as the story went on. Finally, he let a big gust of air escape his lips and shook his head. "This valley," he said. "It's always been lively, but mostly with fistfights. What's happening to this town, Coal? I thought we moved here to avoid the strife of the big city, but it seems to have followed us both."

Coal wasn't sure the judge had ever told him where he hailed from, and he wasn't sure it mattered. A big city, in Sinclair's words. That was plenty.

"It does," he agreed. "I'm afraid I brought it with me."

"It will pass, my friend. Nothing as bad as this place has been lately can last. You'll see. So what do you need me to do this morning, Coal?"

"Well, we impounded the pickup I told you about—under the exigent circumstances doctrine. It's locked up now, but we haven't done a deeper search, and we need to. I also think it's imperative to search Hunter Jack's house for evidence."

Judge Sinclair and Coal hashed out everything about the murder investigation, what Coal or other officers had observed, what witnesses had said, and Coal used the judge's own typewriter to type up a detailed affidavit for the warrant. The judge agreed to everything Coal wanted, then stepped out and turned the information over to Wilma to type up for him.

While they were waiting, Judge Sinclair went to a pot of coffee brewing on a hot plate that sat on a shamefully battered cupboard crouched in one corner. He picked up the pot and looked over at Coal. "Coffee?"

"I hoped you'd ask," said Coal. "Yes, please. It's been a long night, and I don't think this day's going to be any easier."

"You'll like this," said Sinclair, pouring a white ceramic mug almost to the brim. "It was roasted with hazelnut flavoring in it—my leftover supply from a Christmas gift my wife gave to me. We'll have to have you over to dinner sometime, Coal. You and . . . well, who would you invite? Anyone special? I'm sorry if it's none of my business, but I understand that you're a single man."

"Yes, that's true," said Coal. "But . . . who would I invite? My mother, maybe. She's the safest." He gave the judge a grin.

"Well, a fine choice. Fine choice," the judge said, starting to chuckle as he handed the mug to Coal before turning back to pour himself one. "She's the safest," he mimicked Coal's words, then chuckled louder, as if to himself.

Coal took a long sip of the jet-black liquid, relishing the taste of it on his tongue, letting it trickle gently down his throat, warming him. When the judge turned with his own mug and looked at him, Coal smiled and gave him a nod. "Your wife obviously loves you, Wiley. No doubt about that. Tastes great, especially on a morning like this."

"Yes, you are right," said Sinclair, then grinned. "My wife loves me. And she's also safe—like you're mother. You're quite a character, Coal. Quite a character."

After finishing his coffee, and once Wilma Frank brought in the two warrants, Coal took them and went downstairs, then outside and down the three yellow-painted steps into his dingy office. Grant Fairbourne jumped up from behind the desk as he was walking in, and Coal smiled at him.

"Relax, Grant. I don't have anything against you sitting down—even in my chair."

Looking embarrassed, Grant laughed. "Sorry. I guess I'm jumpy."

"I don't blame you. A lot of killing going on in this valley lately."

Grant nodded. "I made you coffee."

Coal didn't tell the deputy he had already partaken. The polite thing to do was thank him and go pour himself another cup, which he did. It was black as tar, and bitter, just as knock-you-awake coffee is supposed to be. Coal sighed. With enough caffeine in him, he might make it through this day after all.

Getting on the phone, he called Flo, the dispatcher, and got her to run the number of the license plate on the pickup he had disabled. It came back as a 1958 dark green Ford registered to a Joseph A. Teton, with an address in the Indian village. Coal couldn't recall the details, whether he was high on coffee or not, but he knew he had heard of Joe Teton before.

"Where's Curlie Burks's pickup impounded, Grant?" Coal asked as he hung up the phone.

"Down in the city lot," Grant replied. "They have a chain-link fence they put it in."

"Thanks. You're really on the ball," said Coal, nodding.

Grant chuckled and jerked a thumb at a note sitting on the desk. "That's what Jordan wrote. I just read it before you came in."

"Good detective work," said Coal with a grin. "Like I said—you're on the ball. Why don't you come with me down to the Indian village? I have to check a vehicle down there and maybe talk with a man, and then we can do a warrant service at Badger's place."

"Need anyone else?"

"Why?"

"No reason. Except I think Jordan's sleeping in the back, if you want him to go."

Coal blinked, trying to make Grant's words register. "He's—You say he's sleeping in the back? In the cellblock?"

"Yes, sir."

"Huh. Well, that's some dedication. Looks like I have the two best deputies in the county."

Grant stared at him for a few seconds, looking confused. Then he laughed, as Coal was nodding. "Yep—the *only* deputies in the county."

Coal walked to the door that led to the cellblock and looked through the window, seeing Jordan Peterson asleep on a cot inside one of the cells. He shook his head. "Man, he looks exhausted. Let's just you and me go," he told Grant. "Maybe we can grab Bob Wilson too."

"Uhh . . . You sure? I don't think he's too happy with you right now."

"Why?"

"I think he's still mad about you being nice to Hunter Jack."

"You're joking. Well, I guess we won't bring him to do a search of his house then, huh? That's okay. Two of us will be enough. I don't expect to find much at Badger's anyway." He knew that to be true, of course, since most of what they would be looking for Coal already knew, from his first visit.

The two of them drove their own vehicles down to the Indian village, on the off chance that something might happen that would require hauling someone to jail. They pulled up in front of the tar paper shack where Coal had flattened the two driver's side tires on the fifty-eight Ford. The address was different from the one on the registration, but there the vehicle still sat, looking forlorn and lop-sided. He wondered if its owner had swapped residences since registering the pickup, or if he had simply parked it in the first convenient driveway.

Checking his watch and seeing that it was ten-thirty already, and more than late enough that most people should be awake, he went to the front door of the shack and knocked. A medium-height, obese Indian girl somewhere between fifteen and thirty-five years old—Coal had found that people in the tribes aged strangely—opened the door a crack, just enough to allow both her glassy black eyes a view of him. She looked him up and down.

"Yeah?"

"Excuse me for the intrusion, but I wanted to have a word with the owner of the pickup out here."

Her eyes roved disinterestedly to the pickup, then back to him. "I don't know whose that is."

"Okay. Can you explain why it's parked by your house then?"

Without a reply, she turned her head and yelled back into the house. "Oman! Come to the door." She looked back at Coal. "Just a minute." With that, the door clicked quietly shut.

Raising his eyebrows, Coal looked over at Grant, who was already watching him. "Well. That was interesting," said Grant.

Coal chuckled. "Yeah, you could call it that."

Twenty seconds later, the door opened again, this time wider, to reveal a male of some fifty to seventy years of age—Coal was embarrassed that it couldn't be judged any closer than that, but he had learned the hard way. The man had the features of a Mongol, with a broad, flat nose, shaggy, poorly cut hair, and a would-be walrus mustache naturally bare of most hair in its middle. He wore a brown tee shirt that to judge by its slashed, faded appearance had been the party house of hundreds of silverfish, possibly for years.

"Are you Oman?" Coal asked, remembering what the girl had called him.

The man opened the door a little wider, the skin between his eyes pinching closer together. "Huh?"

Patiently, Coal said, "The girl called you Oman."

Now the man grunted. "Ol' man. She calls me old man," he explained. Coal had to hold back laughter, but he feared the start of it already showed on his face.

"You can laugh," the man said, his expression remaining flat. "Oman. That's pretty funny. And my name is Leroy. Leroy Bernard. You're that friend of Hunter Jack, huh?"

Coal nodded, feeling unsure if his answer would help him or not. What did the Shoshones think of their fellow tribesman, hell raiser that he could be? "Yes, I would call us friends."

"He's a good one," Leroy Bernard said. "Good man."

Relieved, Coal said, "Well, I came to ask you about the pickup parked out here."

"Don't know nothin' about it," Bernard said. "It was there when I got up."

"This village isn't very big, Mr. Bernard." It sounded like Coal was simply making a statement of the obvious, but what he intended by it was to give Leroy Bernard a chance to look helpful.

"Uh? No, not big."

"So I know you know who owns the truck."

Bernard, with his hand against the doorframe, pressed himself up straighter, shifting his shoulders around in his thin shirt, seeming oblivious to the cold flooding into his house. "Yeah?"

"I think so."

Bernard nodded. "So you want to know who owns it?"

"If possible."

"Skunk Teton," said Bernard simply. "Why didn't you ask that before?"

Coal couldn't help the smile that lifted one side of his mouth. "You know what? I'm just not real sure. Anyway, do you have any idea why Teton would have parked it here?"

"Maybe too drunk to drive home?" suggest Leroy Bernard, still straight-faced. "I can go ask him if you want."

It was only now starting to dawn on Coal who Teton was. "You called him 'Skunk'. Is that the guy who was driving the pickup that Hunter Jack jumped out of the back of on top of a skunk?"

"The same," Bernard said. "And that's the truck." He nodded toward the beat-up Ford. "Probably c'n still smell a skunk in there, on a good summer day."

"Do you want us to tow the truck?" Coal asked. "Get it out of your way?" He wasn't making the offer to be a nice guy, but he wanted it to look like he was. The real reason he wanted to tow it was so that in impounding it he would be able to search for evidence, which was always done on impounded vehicles, for purposes of liability. Anything illegal he found inadvertently in the pickup could be used as evidence in court.

"No. Not botherin' me. Is it botherin' you?"

Coal masked his disappointment. "Not bothering me either. I just thought you might want your parking place back." He knew Leroy Bernard was only covering for Teton. The Shoshones were for the most part pretty tight knit. As scarce as they were around here, Coal guessed they had to be.

"Nope. It's good."

"It has a couple flat tires," Coal pointed out.

Bernard shifted bored eyes toward the pickup, then looked back at Coal. "Huh."

"Well," Coal said, taking a deep breath. "I guess we've let enough heat out of your house."

Leroy Bernard looked blandly at Coal, then gave Grant a cursory glance before looking back. "Pretty good to know a friend of Badger's," he said. "Have a good day."

With that, Bernard pushed the door shut, and Coal heard the striker slip back into place. Giving Grant "the look", he turned away and walked back out to the waiting Thunderbird, which he had left running because he was in the mood to have someplace cozy to crawl back into. Grant followed him to the car.

"Well, before we go serve the warrant on Badger, and Curlie's pickup, let's see if we can have a word with Joe Teton."

Grant grinned. "Skunk?"

"Yeah. Skunk Teton."

CHAPTER TWENTY-TWO

Coal knocked on Joe Teton's door, or at least the door of the only house he thought could be Teton's—the only house around with no vehicle parked outside.

A man of medium build, with a long, drawn face lined with wrinkles and still bearing the deep brown of summer pulled open the door after three barrages of knocking that grew louder each time. He wore a cowboy hat that had probably started out before a few accidents and uncomfortable incidents looking like the silver belly hat worn by the Marlboro Man in cigarette ads. He wore a striped white shirt with every possible button done up, a black vest, large belt buckle, and Wrangler jeans belted over a waist too small for his torso.

The man didn't speak. Holding the door halfway open, he just looked back and forth between Coal and Grant, although like most Shoshones he didn't make direct eye contact with either.

Only then did Coal remember he hadn't returned his badge to open view. As he dug for his wallet, he said, "Sheriff Savage. And you're Joe Teton, I guess?" At that point, he had the wallet, and he flipped it open for the man to view his gold star—which all good school kids wore on their foreheads, and foolish, delinquent lawmen kept in their wallets, or, if they wished to be flashy, in plain sight on their chests. Either way, most people weren't fooled by their stars into thinking their teachers were rewarding them for winning some spelling bee or answering a math problem right.

"Okay, Sheriff. Yep, Joe Teton. C'n I help you with somethin'?" Like any Shoshone worth his salt, Joe was completely noncommittal, but Coal couldn't help his gut feeling that Teton was trying overly hard to seem casual.

"I'm hoping. I notice your truck is parked at somebody else's house, Joe."

"You did? Where?" The man seemed about as genuinely surprised as Coal guessed his expressionless face could accomplish.

Shifting gears to try and match the surprise Teton wanted to portray, Coal said, "You actually don't know?"

"I knew it was gone," replied Teton. That was easy enough to say with no big commitment.

"You knew— And that didn't bother you any?"

"Naw. I got a lotta friends, Sheriff. People borrow rigs around here all the time. You know? Ain't no big deal."

"What if you need to go to work?"

Teton shrugged. "Huh? Hell, I go borrow somebody else's rig. Most nobody takes their keys out. You know?"

Coal couldn't help chuckling. As long as Joe Teton could shoot replies like this at him, how would he get *any* questions answered? At least with real answers . . . *you know?*

"I don't suppose you have any idea in the world who would be driving your pickup at two or three in the morning, do you? And why they would come down Hunter Jack's street with their lights off—and then suddenly hit the gas like they were running from somebody. Then park in someone else's driveway."

Joe Teton kept staring his expressionless, almost sightless stare. Coal couldn't decide if the light he saw in the man's eyes was a sign of his mental wheels frantically churning, or if he was only amused by the line of questioning.

"Hey. Damn. That was a lotta questions. I ain't got enough coffee in my brain to remember all those—even if I had some answers."

Again, Coal laughed, but his own wheels had been churning pretty fast too, and he had a curve ball to throw at Joe Teton. He threw it low, and he threw it hard: "Somebody drove your pickup up by the cemetery last night, Joe. And chances are whoever it was murdered two people—a guy named Everett Sherman, and a little Bannock woman named Irene Boyer. So unless you want somebody to start wondering if it could have been you in that pickup, you might want to start racking your brain about who might have taken it."

Coal didn't know if there was a speck of truth to his off-the-cuff claim that Teton's pickup had been up by the cemetery. He only knew he had to say something to shake up Joe Teton. The formula could not have worked better. Coal still didn't get any answers, but he did get one thing: a sure sign—the *first* sure sign—in Joe Teton's face that Coal had struck far too close to home.

On a whim, Coal's eyes dropped to Teton's feet. He was wearing sharp-toed cowboy boots. To the trained eye, they were exactly the same shape and size as the ones that had left prints by the bodies at Everett Sherman's trailer, or at least too close to tell the difference.

"I don't know a thing," Joe Teton replied. "Guess I better go. Got bacon on the stove." With that, he stepped back and shut the door softly in the face of his interrogation.

Coal waited until he and Grant had walked out to the Thunderbird before he turned to him and slid his sunglasses on, trying in some way to mask his face from the world. Fortunately, no one could observe the beating of his heart.

He was holding in what he had to say, but Grant spoke first. "What was that, Coal? Were you making that up about his truck being up there, or did I miss something?"

Coal clenched his jaws. "It was an inspiration," he said, trying to keep all expression from his face and wishing he were as good at it as the Shoshones. "Grant, did you or somebody else get molds and photos of every tire track up there?"

"As much as poss—" He saw Coal's eyebrows start to raise and stopped. "Yes. We got molds and photos of every tire track up there."

"And of every shoe and boot track, of course."

"Of course."

"Did you look at Teton's boots?"

Grant nodded.

"Okay. I'm running on a hunch. We need to go right now and get photos and prints on the tires on Joe's Ford. And we need those boot molds and photos."

"Because now Joe Teton has come out of the blue, and he's our number one suspect," Grant finished Coal's thought.

Coal nodded. "Numero uno, Grant. Without a question. We're only missing one thing."

Grant's jaw hardened. "A motive."

It was hardly a decent stroll to Hunter Jack's place from Teton's, but Coal and Grant didn't go. Not yet. Instead, they returned to Joe Teton's pickup, took detailed photographs of all four of his tires, as far around as they could get. Coal was paying special attention to capturing any identifying marks like nicks in the tread.

The photos were about all they could legally get from Teton's rig, so they drove together to Hunter Jack's, hoping Teton's pickup would still be there if and when they were able to get a warrant to dust it for prints and go through it more thoroughly.

They had just pulled up at Hunter Jack's place when the radio crackled open, and Flo came over the air. *Salmon dispatch to Sheriff Savage. Salmon dispatch calling Sheriff Savage. Come in?*

Swearing, Coal jerked the mic off its hook. "Savage!" he said a little too brusquely.

—wreck down toward the end of the road, came back the truncated message.

With another curse, Coal grinded his teeth together. "Repeat that, will you, Flo? The first part broke off."

I said I just got a call from down the river at Northfork, Sheriff. They said there's a car in the river.

"Do you have a more precise location, or will somebody flag me down when I get close?"

They said they'll be waiting for you but to please hurry.

Coal almost laughed and almost cursed again, but he didn't think either would do him any good. *Please hurry?* What did they think he was going to do, ride his bicycle down there?

"I'm on it, Flo. Headed toward North Fork. I'll also have Deputy Fairbourne with me." He jumped out of the car, and when he started back toward Fairbourne's pickup, the deputy threw his door open and jumped up. Coal told him about the call, told him to follow him down the river, and they took off, leaving Hunter Jack and the in-depth search of Curlie Burks's truck behind. Coal just hoped Joe Teton's rig would be held in place by the two flat tires. Somehow, he just couldn't see that Teton wasn't their number one suspect right now, with all the evidence combined—not that *any* of their clues so far were all that stellar until all the lab work was done on the prints, blood, tire tracks and footprints.

It was twenty-one miles along the winding Salmon River road to North Fork, and with all the ice along the road, in the shadows of the mountain that loomed close over the asphalt, there was no driving particularly fast, but most of the time they were at least able to keep up the speed limit, with the one exception that they got caught behind an ancient pickup whose driver either couldn't find the gas pedal, or perhaps a cat was caught underneath it. Coal put his red light on the dash, flicked it on, and very cautiously on the treacherous ice, he passed the old truck, with Grant close on his tail.

With ten minutes still to go, the radio opened up again, and Flo very unprofessionally said, *Coal?* Maybe he should have been put out, but her informality made him laugh. "Yes, Flo?"

Coal, we've had a few more calls, and somebody said the car's in the Stillwater Pool. They said it's probably been there since last night, so if anybody's in it . . . well, there probably isn't any reason to go fast and get you hurt too.

"Okay, Flo," Coal said. "Thank you. We're driving safe. By the way, you have a wrecker on the way, right? And the ambulance?"

Yes, sir, Sheriff. Sure do. She seemed to have at least decided to correct herself on part of the informal communication. Coal made up for it.

"Good girl, Flo! I'll bring you a cinnamon roll from Wally's when we get back to town."

Cool! Love to see you, Flo replied. *Salmon dispatch out.*

Behind him, Grant flashed his lights. For a second, Coal wondered if his deputy wanted him to pull over, but he decided Grant was probably just acknowledging the funny transmission. Grant probably hadn't experienced a lot of such radio traffic in his last job over by Boise—but Salmon really was next to being the "Old West".

In another two minutes, Coal spotted a cluster of vehicles along the side of the road, all with flashers blinking like a cheap Christmas parade. He slowed way down until he was able to inch up within six feet of the closest car, a silver Pontiac LeMans that looked just as out of place out in this country as his Thunderbird.

As Grant rolled up behind, and both of them got out, a cluster of concerned citizens streamed toward them from the cars, most of them in appropriate cold weather backwoods attire. Coal recognized the first man in line, a tall, gangly fellow wearing a red buffalo plaid coat and Elmer Fudd hunter hat.

"Hi, George."

"Hey, Coal." They shook hands, and then George waved toward the river. "Hard to see from right here, but just around the bend back there you can see the rear end of a car stickin' up outta the hole."

"No tracks coming out on the ice?" asked Coal.

"Nothin' I c'd see. An' it looks weird, if'n you ask me. Like maybe it didn't even slide off."

Coal furrowed his brow. "What do you mean, didn't slide off? How'd it get in there?"

"Lookin' over them tracks, looks like they got lined up and then almost gunned it on inter the river," said George, then gave an expansive shrug.

Coal walked over and looked at the tire tracks, which he followed along for a ways. George appeared to be completely right. The wheels seemed to have been rolling the entire way along, not locked up as one would have expected.

The group of citizens had grouped up a ways back, and Coal saw that Grant had stopped them. Good lawman—he was keeping any evidence safe.

"You can come with me, George," said Coal. "Come along here, will you?" He started walking along the vehicle tracks in the snow. Eventually, the snow got too deep for him to tell whether the tires were still rolling or not, but at least at one point, right before the river, it almost appeared that the car had made a last effort not to stop here, but actually to propel itself forward at speed. Where its rear end stuck up out of the hole in the ice, it seemed to have sailed, at least for most of the way.

"What do you think, Coal? Think they'd go in the river on purpose?" asked George, gawking at him.

"Don't know, George. I just don't know," Coal replied. "I guess we'll know more when the tow truck gets here, if they can get this thing out."

Coal was hoping all the people who had stopped to see the fun would clear out, but only a couple of them decided to continue on into town. The eight remaining cars had burped out twelve passengers, and those twelve people stayed as closely within earshot of Coal as they could right up until the time that the tow truck and the ambulance rolled in, forty minutes later.

Andy Holmes, Coal's friend who owned one of the body shops in town, got out of the big white tow truck, saw Coal, and grinned. He came right out through the snow and gave Coal's hand a hearty shake. "Hey, buddy! Good to see you."

"You too. I had no idea you ran a tow truck service."

"Guy's gotta cover all his bases in a one-horse town like Salmon." Andy gave Coal his huge grin.

"Ha! Not me. My job keeps me running from dawn to dark—sometimes well after dark."

"That's true. You're a crap magnet if I ever saw one. So . . . what do we have goin' on here? Dispatch said a car in the river?"

"The only thing I know is you have that car rear end sticking out of that hole," Coal said and pointed. "Nobody knows who it is or how long it's been in there, but it looks to me like a suicide," he said, lowering his voice so the bystanders wouldn't hear.

"How do you figure that?" asked Andy.

"It's not a slide off. You can tell the wheels were still rolling when it hit the deep snow. And we can't see any tracks from anybody walking out of the wreck, so I guess they're still in the car."

"Wow. Fun way to go," Andy said. "Turned to an icicle."

"Yeah. So do you think you can get it out?"

"I can try," Andy replied. "It's going to be interesting."

"Good. Entertain me."

Andy paused. "You said you have no idea who it is? What did the registration come back as?"

Coal gave Andy a blank stare. After several seconds, it turned into a look of disgust. "Well, thanks for making me feel like an idiot."

"Didn't call it in, huh?" asked Andy, a twinkle in his eye.

"Guess I have too much on my mind. Maybe I need to retire."

"Then who'd I have to tease?"

Coal went and got his binoculars out, then came back to the riverbank and focused in on the car's plate. Jotting the plate number of 2L 1336 into his mental notepad, he walked back to his car and called it in to dispatch. After a few minutes, Flo came back over the air, identifying the owner of the car, a 1963 Plymouth Fury, as Burt Landry, an outwardly easy-going, fun-loving middle-aged man with an attractive wife and several kids. What in the world was a man like Landry doing driving down the river late at night? And why would he purposely launch his car into the river? Coal already sensed a sad story of marital upheaval in the making, and he was so tired of sad stories.

Coal thanked Flo for the information, but before he could get out of the car, she came back on, sounding appropriately like a backwoods dispatcher with no radio etiquette. *Oh! And Coal—*

Nadine made a note in the log early this morning after you were probably gone home. Want to know what it was?

Are you kidding me? Coal wanted to say, rudely. What he actually said, politely, was, "Yes, Flo. What did it say?"

It says she sent Deputy Peterson on a grand theft report this morning, and that's the car. Burt Landry called it in.

"Oh. Great. Thanks, Flo."

"Coal," he heard a voice beside him, coming out of the big shadow that darkened his door as he was getting back out of the car. "I'm starting to think you can't get enough of me."

Jay Castillo was looking down at him.

"Well, hi, Jay. We haven't even had that coffee yet—I mean cocoa, sorry. And here you are again."

Jay only grinned.

"I hope you didn't bring that surly jack—" Coal stopped. Ronnie Davis was just stepping around his partner, and their eyes met.

"Jackass. That what you were about to say?"

" . . . ass," finished Coal, the wind kicked out of his sails. "Yes. Howdy, Mr. Davis." It might have been the kindest thing he could think of to say to this man—and one of the most awkward.

Ronnie Davis had already picked up on the car sticking out of the river, and he turned away from Coal without another comment about their tense moment. "Man! That looks iffy. I guess we find the littlest guy around here to go out there and put a tow hook on that bumper," he said. "I guess that leaves you out," he said to Coal, almost smiling.

"You too," Coal replied.

At the same time, they both turned to look at Andy Holmes, who had walked up after Coal and stood waiting for instructions. He looked from Ronnie, to Coal, to Jay, then dropped his hands exasperatedly to his sides.

"Sheesh." For Andy Holmes, that was a nasty curse word.

CHAPTER TWENTY-THREE

Andy Holmes not only was the lightest of the men gathered at the river, but recovering vehicles was the business he had signed up for. So out onto the ice he went, after bemoaning the fact that he had no wet suit and after only somewhat jokingly beseeching Coal to try and warm his dying hypothermic body with his own should he happen to fall into the ice with the car before getting his cable hooked up to it.

Prior to Andy's getting on the ice, Coal had one of the area farmers who happened to mention that he had some sheets of plywood left over from a construction project bring them up in his pickup. Then, to Coal's surprise, Ronnie Davis stepped forward. "I'm not so big I can't get out there on plywood, Sheriff. Even if both of us are out there. You want some help placing these?"

Coal stared at the other man, who stood six-one, and weighed perhaps two hundred ten pounds. He wasn't in Coal's class, weight-wise, but still, the pair of them would put an easy four hundred sixty pounds out on the ice. Coal had seen February ice, even river ice, support a lot more weight than that, but it still both surprised him and impressed him that Davis would volunteer for such a nerve-wracking task when there were other, lighter men around.

"Well, thanks for the offer. Sure. Any help I can get is welcome." He didn't know how to address Davis, whether by his first name or by "Mr. Davis," so he avoided addressing him at all. But one thing was for certain: For whatever reason, Ronnie Davis was obviously making an effort either to apologize for being surly, or perhaps even to mend the rift that had been between them from their first meeting, way back in November. It wasn't something Coal could soon forget.

Andy and Coal could have done the same job together, and with less weight on the ice, but Coal was glad to let Davis help, mostly because the man wouldn't have offered his assistance if it wasn't important to him. He and the EMT got down to the ice carrying one sheet of plywood. They laid it down, then pushed it out onto the ice. Grant and Andy had come up behind them with a second sheet, and as Coal and Davis came back onto the bank, they laid that one down, and Coal and Davis slid it forward. George and Jay had the third sheet, and by the time it was laid out, they were a full twenty-four feet out on the river. Underneath the pale green ice, that appeared to be sloppily frosted with vanilla glaze in places, Coal could see the lazy movement of this slow section of the river they called the River of No Return.

He turned to Davis, not knowing quite what to say, but certain he had to say something. Davis's dark brown eyes, looking surly and hooded as always, met Coal's. "I really appreciate the help. Thank you."

Ronnie Davis came close to smiling. He held out his hand between them, perhaps more shocking than his offer of help. As Coal took the man's hand, Davis said, "You're welcome. Even us surly jackasses can be helpful from time to time."

Coal grinned, pumping the strong hand. "Yes. Yes, we can."

They walked back to shore with Davis leading the way, and Coal looking at the broad back of a man he might never think of the same.

Andy Holmes was waiting for them on shore. He grinned as they stepped off the board onto the crusted snow, now packed down tight by the tread of many boots. "Thank you guys. I actually don't feel like I'm about to commit suicide now."

"Here to please, buddy," said Coal.

"You owe me bigtime," said Ronnie Davis. "Don't make me regret keeping your sorry butt alive."

It was now with far less worry that Coal watched Andy drag his tow cable out onto the river, walking on the three solid sheets of plywood. They had tied a length of good nylon rope around Andy's waist, just in case, but Coal only let him get to the end before his worry nagged at him again. He decided to go out with him. Even with the safety rope, if Andy were to break through the ice, or simply slip and fall in the water, Coal wanted to be right there on hand to tow him out.

"You don't rest much, do you, Coal?" asked Andy when Coal reached him.

"Not much, I guess. A man like me has only so many friends."

Andy's laugh was almost a giggle. "For a filthy cop, I'd say you have more friends than anybody else in the valley."

"Just hook that cable on," said Coal in his best gruff voice. "Before I shove you in the ice myself."

Taking a length of chain he had looped around his neck, with a hook on one end and a stout eye at the other, Andy managed to reach far out. Coal hung onto him by wrapping his hand around the loop of rope, then leaned back toward shore. Andy wrapped the chain around the best place he could reach, which was the car's axle, to the inside of the right wheel. Then he took the cable Coal pushed toward him, and with a solid *click,* he connected the safety hook of the tow cable over the eye in the chain. A couple of ceremonial pats on the bumper, and he jerked his thumb backward as a sign for Coal to hoist him toward shore. When they were safe on the sheet of plywood together, Andy let out a long sigh. "Man. That was exhilarating. That should do it if anything will."

"Great," replied Coal. "Let's go find out."

Walking again in single file, but this time dragging the sheets of plywood with them as they came, they made it to shore without either of them so much as slipping. They stacked the plywood to one side, on top of a fourth one they hadn't used, leaving them waiting there in case they needed them again. As Andy climbed the bank up to his tow truck, Ronnie Davis looked once more at Coal. "I know you care about the people in this valley, Savage. I guess Lemhi County's lucky to have a guy like you wearing that badge."

"Thanks, Davis. I appreciate that—and your help."

"Call me Ronnie, all right?"

Coal smiled. No matter what else came of this day, a potential new friendship with a man he thought he would always be at odds with would make it worthwhile.

The screech of the tow truck's motor winding the cable back on its spool, and the always unnerving sound of the tight-wound wires in the cable straightening out under pressure, put everyone on edge as every part of the tow truck, whose tires were substantially chocked, strained and groaned trying to get the thirty-five hundred pounds or so of water-logged vehicle out of the death-grip of the River of No Return.

The straight line of the cable, in relation to the upraised tail end of the car, made it an almost forty-five degree angle, and seemed an impossible challenge. But just when the job seemed most hopeless, there came a deafening *crack,* like the explosion of a cannon. A huge chunk of ice some five inches thick, now broken away from the sheet connecting it to shore, loomed up out of the river like a great whale breaching. It slammed down onto the ice sheet, and the car's bumper managed to swing down an impressive amount, coming close to lining up with the tow line.

A cheer went up through the crowd, and Coal looked up toward Andy just as his expression turned to one of huge relief. Andy grinned and waved at Coal, trying to evince great confidence. Coal would never make his friend admit to the anguish that had been on his face only moments before. The tow truck operator seemed as shocked as anyone that his motor or cable had not become another casualty of the river.

Another five minutes, and the car had crept to the shore. After the first huge iceberg broke free, the car ended up crashing onto the top of the ice. It put a severe crack for five or ten yards along it, but fortunately the tires rolled up onto the ice before the bumper made any move to slide underneath it, in which case Coal had feared they might have to employ dynamite to set it free again. No matter for the car's driver. Whoever was inside, whether that was Burt Landry or somebody else, was long dead by now.

Coal's curiosity was as pitiful as anyone else's, the difference being that he, Grant, Ronnie Davis, and Jay Castillo had more rights to look inside the car than any of the onlookers who had simply stopped out of curiosity or, more darkly, for the bragging rights to say they were among the first to see whoever had taken a dunk in the river. Coal got to the car first, and he looked inside. Even though the windows were up, the car had filled with water, at least up to the point where it had been sticking out. The water was murky enough that he had no clear view of the seats, even with the upper portion of the compartment empty of water.

Standing safely back, he edged the door open, and water gushed out onto the ice.

Coal had feared what he was going to witness when the water cleared the car seat, but he didn't see it.

What he saw was emptiness. No Burt Landry, no member of Landry's family. There wasn't one soul inside this vehicle.

CHAPTER TWENTY-FOUR

They had the Plymouth up in the wide spot along the highway, most of the disappointed onlookers, deprived of the opportunity to ogle a water-logged corpse, had driven away, and Coal was just reading the VIN on the driver's side hinge pillar when the radio began to crackle, and an unreadable voice came over the air. He was a ways from his car, but he had left the window open for just that reason.

"Grant, can you go see what that is?" he said, turning with irritation away from his study of the VIN, with Andy Holmes hovering over him curiously. The deputy took off post haste. Just when Coal was staring at an incongruous fifteen-pound rock lying on the driver's side floorboard of the Fury, Grant came slipping and sliding down over the snowy trail that had been hard-packed by the treading of many feet.

"Coal." It was the succinct slapping down of his name, with no sound of a question mark behind it, that drew Coal's attention away from the puzzling rock.

"Huh?"

"Might be trouble in town."

Coal straightened up, waiting for more, without speaking.

"Call came in about a break-in and burglary. Going by my memory, it sounds like it might be Hunter Jack's place. The cops are headed that way now."

Coal's string of curse words echoing across the icy river might have made its way into a volume of macabre poetry, if only they could have been netted and brought into captivity. To his sadness, they simply vanished in ignominious solemnity in the willows on the far side of the river. All his poetic prowess might have been lost, except he thought he might be able to duplicate the exact wording later, in some quiet studio when he had time to reminisce.

"I'm guessing that news doesn't make you happy," said Grant.

Coal's eyes flashed up at his deputy. He caught the glint of humor in his eyes, and he couldn't help but laugh. "No, not exactly. Not when I know how the cops are feeling about Badger right now."

"You want me to stay here and deal with the car? You run back to town before anything goes south?"

"Huh." Coal took in a great breath, then let it sigh back out, at least for the moment clearing his mind. He thought back with great fondness on his recent attempt at dark poetry, now wasted on the river, and him too worn out to summon any energy to start over. He would have to let his curses build up again, until some perfect sequence of events called up his artistic vocabulary once more. "Yeah, Grant, I'll go. But I doubt it'll be quick enough to keep anything from going bad."

"No. Probably not. And having them call Jordan in won't help much either. He knows how you feel about Badger, but that Bob Wilson has a pretty strong personality—don't you think?"

"Yeah, I may have noticed that." Turning, Coal pointed down at the rock on the floor of the Plymouth Fury. "Give that rock some thought when you're doing your investigation, would you? I know my own convictions about why it's there, but I don't want to lead you on."

"It was in there when you opened the door?" Grant asked, to clarify.

Coal nodded. "Take it with you, huh? And wear gloves." He felt immediately foolish for making suggestions to a trained crime scene investigation, but he was too irritated with this day even to apologize.

Saying a quick goodbye to Jay Castillo and Ronnie Davis, who were just now loading up to head back to town, and to Andy Holmes, whose obligation to tow the car would force him to remain to the bitter end, Coal jumped in the Thunderbird, got it turned around, and roared back toward town, making sure the red light on his dash was glaring like a pitifully garish Christmas decoration.

He didn't dare call into dispatch, because everything he said would be over the air for every officer and anyone with a scanner or CB radio to hear. But he had heard three transmissions while rocketing home that displeased him enormously. The first time, it was Bob Wilson calling for backup. The second, it was Chief Dan George radioing back for Flo to call reserve officers William Verret and Horace Teal back in. On the third one, Bob Wilson was calling for the state bull, Gentry. All too often, calling for the state happened because local officers had been involved in a wreck or a shooting. Coal's only consolation was that no one had called for an ambulance.

Finally, just as Coal was hitting the Salmon River bridge, Chief George's voice came over the radio again. *Police chief to sheriff. George to Sheriff Savage. Savage, you out there?*

By the end of that frantic-sounding barrage, Coal had yanked the mic off the hook, nearly sliding through the intersection at Main Street in the process, and nearly in front of a fast-flying pickup coming off the Bar.

"What?" Coal almost yelled in the mic. It was hard to hide his irritation at having nearly been run over, and not even able to go after the speeder.

How far out are you, Sheriff? We need you at Hunter Jack's place as fast as you can get here.

“Two minutes!” Coal snapped back. “And tell Badger that—please!”

Roger, came the chief’s voice, sounding like he had caught on to Coal’s mood. *Chief George out.*

Coal whipped up in front of Hunter Jack’s ramshackle house amid a sea of vehicles. He could hear a siren’s wail somewhere far out on the highway, which must be Officer Gentry, trying to run innocent travelers into some roadside ditch.

The first person Coal saw was Chief George, in his nicest uniform minus the right sleeve, and a torn place on the chest where a badge might once have resided. The second person was Bob Wilson, one eye swollen shut, a fat lip, and blood all over his shirt front.

Coal remembered this time to say a few of the words he had been rehearsing, before anyone got within earshot.

He got out and braced himself to be tackled by Bob and the chief, who were barreling toward him. He had enough awareness about him to notice William Verret, his huge horseshoe mustache framing a mouth and chin covered in crimson, sitting on the tailgate of his pickup off to one side, his hat gone, thin strands of hair hanging down over his forehead, and face looking drawn and haggard.

Dark Badger had been hard at work.

“You get in there and get some cuffs on that buddy of yours,” Bob Wilson growled before the chief could speak, his one open eye glowering.

“What the hell happened?” asked Coal.

The chief reached out to put a calming hand on Bob’s arm, keeping him from speaking. “He called in a burglary, Coal. Bob came to investigate, and the fight was on.”

“Fight?” repeated Coal. “Fight over what? He didn’t want you doing the investigation?”

Bob's dark eye turned to the chief, and then looked back at Coal. "Well, I told him he was wanted for questioning for . . ." Bob's voice faded off. It seemed that Coal's knife-like glare sliced it off at the roots.

"You did *what?* Were you by yourself, Bob?"

"The chief was en route," said Bob.

"Great. Just great. You couldn't wait until I got here to talk to him about something like that?"

Bob swore, then winced, touching fingers gingerly to his swollen lips. "I guess I couldn't. Obviously."

"I guess you told him I was coming," Coal said.

"Why do you think we're all sitting around here and not doing a damn thing?" Bob said.

Coal glanced around. "Uh-huh. Just what the hell kind of fight *was* that, anyway? What—four of you against one? And he isn't in cuffs?"

"You try to cuff that man," blurted Chief George, for the first obvious time letting a semblance of petulance surface. Considering what Badger had made of all these officers, Coal could hardly blame him. "No wonder they call him Badger," George went on. "He's just like one—only man-size."

Letting out a gust of breath, Coal looked toward the house. "Well, I guess . . . Say—what was he using as weapons, anyway?"

"His damn hands," growled Bob Wilson. "I would happily have shot his sorry butt if he had picked up anything else."

Coal had to struggle to hold back the grin that tried to crack his face.

Walking toward the front door, which now hung from the frame by one hinge, Coal called out, "Hey, Badger. Coal Savage out here. Want to let me in?"

"Hey, Sheriff. Sure. Come on in and have a drink with me. I'm just sittin' around."

Coal had to force himself not to look at any of the other cops. He could only imagine the anger the casual sound of Badger's invitation had just caused to erupt on their faces.

Just as the state cop car, with Gentry at the wheel, squealed around the corner ready to go Badger hunting, Coal saw big Jordan Peterson strolling toward him from the end of the house, where up until now he had done a good job of laying low. From the expression on his face—his *uninjured* face, so Jordan must have gotten here after the fight ended—Jordan must have felt like Coal was about to walk alone into a den of silver-back gorillas, man-eating lions, head hunters looking for their next meal, or angry women who had just learned the early morning sale they had come for was not until the following week.

"You're not goin' in there alone, are you, Coal?"

Coal grinned. "I'm sure not going in there with any of *you* guys. You think I want to get in a fight?"

Jordan chuckled nervously. "But did you see those other guys?"

"Uh-huh. I'm glad I'm not them." He grinned. "Take it easy, buddy. I'll be okay as long as I don't tell him skunk hunting is no longer legal."

Almost as an afterthought, Coal took off his gun belt and handed it to Jordan. "Put that someplace safe, would you? Badger can't legally have guns on his property. Between you and me," he said, lowering his voice conspiratorially, "there are a few guys around here I could see using that just to get rid of him."

Calmly, he walked up on the stoop, looking in amazement at the loose-hanging door, now attached to the frame only by one twisted hinge. "You need some new hinges, Badger," he said through the open doorway.

"No kidding, huh?" a voice from the half dark inside the house replied. "Come on in, Sheriff. It's not much—but it's home."

"Not much *left* of a home," Coal emphasized as he stepped past the half-fallen door to see Badger sitting on the couch, both hands lying as casually in his lap as if they were a couple of sleeping cats—and about the same size, Coal noticed.

"Man! I'm tired," Badger said. "You hear what happened at all?"

"Only that somebody broke into your house. And then you called to report it and Officer Wilson came and told you you were wanted for murder. And then . . . Well, to be truthful, he didn't say much about any fight, but the way those guys look I'm guessing there must've been one."

Badger laughed, then sighed. "Yeah. Some fight. Those guys couldn't get the drop on a nursing rabbit, Sheriff. Not like you an' me. Boy, now *that* would be some fight, uh?"

"Some fight," Coal agreed. "A fight I'd be pretty sad to ever see happen."

"Me too. I'd hate to kill you, and I'm pretty sure you'd make me do it."

Coal studied Badger's face, trying to decide if he was serious. The shadows were fairly deep, so it was hard to make out the nuances of his expression.

"Well, Badger, I'd hate for you to try to kill me too."

The word "try" was the biggest part of his statement, and both of them knew it.

"Sit down, Sheriff." Badger waved him toward a chair that appeared to have been made out of a few dozen roadkill cats, some of them with mange. He didn't want to sit in it because he would probably have to burn his clothes later, but he didn't feel like offending Badger either. So he sat, sinking way down low as the stench of rotten gases escaping the depths of the chair made more and more room for his two hundred fifty pounds, until he almost thought his pockets would touch the floor.

"Sorry the springs ain't much," said Badger. "Time to put a board under it or somethin', I think."

Time to entomb it in the pet cemetery, thought Coal. "Yeah," he said. "A board ought to fix it." *Or a torch and a can of gasoline.*

"So somebody broke into your house. That's what your original call was?" Coal asked. It was something he had been wondering about ever since he had come in illegally himself.

"Yeah. They broke the front door latch, and they took some of my stuff off the wall." He jutted a forefinger straight up above his head, indicating the wall where Coal had already seen the missing ceremonial weapons during his midnight intrusion. "Took a knife too. One I made myself."

"I don't suppose you have photographs of anything, do you?"

"Course not. But I can sure describe every detail of every piece."

"I bet. Well, I guess you can come down to the jail with me and write up a list of everything that's missing, all right?"

"You just tryin' to get me to the jail, Sheriff? That's pretty sneaky."

Coal chuckled. "Let me tell you something I think would be pretty funny, Badger. Those guys out there—all four of them, or however many you had in here—they couldn't get handcuffs on you. They were taunting me when I said I was coming in here. They said something about how there's no way I could get cuffs on you, since all of them together couldn't. Funny, huh?"

Badger matched Coal's chuckle. "That is. Pretty funny. I guess it'd be extra funny if we both come walkin' out of here, all casual, with me in your cuffs—if you can even get them shiny little things on me."

Grinning, Coal said, "It would take two pairs, hooked together."

"I think we should do it," Badger said. "You know—just for fun."

"Yeah," said Coal. "Just for fun. Hang on."

It took several seconds to struggle up out of the roadkill cat skin chair. Coal walked to the front door and casually called out. "Hey! Jordan!"

"Yeah, boss," came back the big deputy's voice.

"Think you can round me up another pair of cuffs?"

"Sure."

Jordan approached the door, looking as if he thought a herd of wild witches would come flying out at him on their brooms any second. He held up his handcuffs, and Coal took them with a wink and turned back into the house.

"Well, my friend, why don't you walk around and make sure of everything you think was taken. Then we'll put these on you and go outside and have us a good laugh."

"All right, my friend," said Badger, standing up. "Done."

Coal was happy to know he could come back at his leisure now and serve his search warrant on Badger's house, once its occupant was securely in his cell until their next meeting with the judge. He didn't say one word about the warrant to Badger, however. Unlike his friend Bob Wilson, once in a while Coal knew when to keep his mouth shut.

CHAPTER TWENTY-FIVE

The Big Valley came on at four o'clock, and Joe Teton tuned into it every day. He loved watching the three Barkley brothers fight the battles of good and evil. He loved watching beautiful Audra Barkley find her way in the world, making bad decision left and right that her brothers always managed to bail her out of. And he loved how their mother, Victoria, managed to stitch the whole family cohesively together

But today, during an episode called "The Young Turks", which Joe fortunately had seen the year it first aired, and perhaps five times since, his mind was on anything but the television. Even a young, heavy-set Buck Taylor, guest starring as a bad guy on *The Big Valley* before ever finding his way to TV's most popular Western, *Gunsmoke,* couldn't pull Joe Teton's attention away from his problems at hand.

And Joe Teton's problems, he was guessing, were nothing short of the size of a fat dinosaur.

He looked at his little boys, Pete and Nathan, crouched in front of the television in their usual praying position, watching *The Big Valley,* thinking all was right with the world. He thought of the day red-bearded Everett Sherman had come racing through the village in his pickup, endangering every Injun in camp, and not caring one bit. It was easy to recall how satisfying it was to batter the side of Sherman's truck with that rock, but how painful and humiliating it was when Sherman retaliated. His privates had long since stopped hurting from the kick, but he still carried the ugly yellow and green remnants of the bruising around his eye.

Oh, what had he done! He was a fool! He was endangering his little boys, risking them getting taken away from him forever. And for what? Someone, sometime, would have killed Everett Sherman. It was a sure thing. *More* than a sure thing. But when? *When?* And what kind of damage would that cruel, careless fool have done in the world before then? Perhaps even to Pete and Nathan!

No! No, what Joe had done was not so bad. Even God would applaud him! Any good, responsible man would have done the same thing, given the chance, and especially having every reason to believe that no one would ever know.

Lying on his handmade couch, his bottle of Michelob in hand, Joe looked over at his little boys. Where would they be taken if he was caught? If they sent him off to prison? Who would watch over them? Who would love them the way their father did?

Why had he taken his pickup up there? Why had he not hidden his tracks better? Why could Joe Teton never mind his own business? But that little man had caused a lot of trouble for his best friend, Dark Badger, and Badger was probably going to go off to jail again, because of him. How could Sherman not be held accountable for that? Joe was only protecting his friend! What kind of man would not protect a friend in need?

Suddenly, he sat up. He knew suddenly what he had to do. He had to go, to leave. Go anywhere. Maybe Fort Hall. Maybe to Utah, or over to Wyoming. Somewhere where his *people—the* People—would hide him. There was nothing for him here. Not now. Not anymore. He had slipped up, and he had slipped up bad. He had seen before how the wheels of white justice rolled, and they would roll right over the top of him, as they had in the past. There was nothing here. He had to get to his pickup, grab the boys, and just leave everything they owned behind. He had to make a run for it—now, before it was too late.

* * *

Dale Moore and Dawn Kelly lived two blocks away from each other, close to downtown Salmon. Although Troy Westerlind was the glue that held the three of them together, because he was their self-appointed ringleader, and they accepted him as such, it was much easier for them to spend time together than it was to spend time with Troy, who lived so far out of town and often couldn't get his father to let him use either of his vehicles to come into town.

This day, after school, was one of those afternoons when Troy had been forced to take the bus home, because once again he was on the outs with his father, Gunnar, and he was being grounded from using the pickup or the big Chrysler 300 Gunnar also owned.

No one was home at Dawn's house. Her dad was out on the road somewhere between Salmon and Louisiana, if Dawn remembered right. And her mom? Who could tell? She could have been at work. More likely, she was with some man, somewhere. Dawn had long ago given up looking—or asking questions.

While Dawn lay on her bed, twisting her hair around her fingers and staring at the ceiling, Dale Moore sat in her chair, at her desk, his forehead down on his clenched fist, which rested on top of the desk.

"What're we gonna do?" Dale said, almost in a moan. "What the heck are we gonna do, Dawn?"

Apparently Dawn had listened to Dale's panicked voice for a little too long, because this time when she replied it was in a voice raised almost to a hurtful level. "Dale! Stop! There's no way they know anything! Come on! You have to get a hold of yourself."

He sat up straight and spun toward her on the chair. "Dawn! Listen! If they found out you're Troy's girlfriend . . . Come on! You've seen the cop shows. You know how they work. This is only the start. Tell me again what they said, Dawn—*exactly* what they said."

Almost spellbound, feeling like his guts were up in his throat, Dale sat there listening as Dawn once more tried patiently to explain what had happened that morning, how Officer Bob Wilson, from the Salmon Police Department, had come to the school and started asking questions around. She had seen him go into the principal's office. At the time, she only thought about it in passing. An officer might be at the school for any number of reasons. It wasn't any cause for alarm.

But then just before third hour, she heard her name on the intercom. She was being asked to report to the principal's office.

Dawn had gone to the office, where to no surprise whatsoever she was confronted by Officer Wilson. The policeman was friendly at first—perhaps overly so. He started asking about her friendships, about her schedule, and about certain things she might have observed at school, things she knew nothing about and wondered why anyone would think she did. He acted like he was only after routine information that had nothing to do with her being in trouble.

Then, just when she started to feel at ease, he started asking her about Troy Westerlind, and specifically about whether or not she had been with him the night before. She acted casual. And lied through her teeth. The way she reasoned, if she was caught in her lie, she could easily rescind everything later. After all, she was a teenage girl. A high school student. Who would question a girl of her age lying about being with some boy, when girls her age lied about that kind of stuff all the time, trying to keep themselves out of hot water with their parents? Her plan was foolproof. She had thought about it many times since, and there wasn't a loophole for Officer Wilson or anyone else to come through.

"You have to stop worrying, Dale! Serious!"

"You promise you never said nothin' about me?"

"I promise. He was only asking about Troy. Relax!"

Dale took a deep breath, wiping sweat off his forehead with his fingers. “Dawn,” he finally groaned. “We shouldn’t have done it! We should never have let Troy talk us into something like that—*ever!* We *knew* it was gonna come back and haunt us.”

“It’s not!” she said, almost angrily. “Not unless you cave in.”

Dawn Kelly was only pretending to be angry because she was scared. But she couldn’t let Dale know that. He was scared enough for all three of them. She at least had to *act* calm and self-assured, or Dale was going to fall apart. And if he crumbled, all of them went down together. Troy had always said Dale was the weak link. He had threatened many times not to let Dale do anything with them anymore. Now Dawn wished more than ever that he had listened to his own decision.

She had tried to call Troy when they first got to the house, but when his father answered she hung up. Then she realized there was no way Troy could have gotten home on the bus yet anyway. She had to wait. Wait and hope Troy was the one who got to the phone. Troy’s dad hated her, and there were times he wouldn’t even let her speak to his son. Sometimes he pretended he wasn’t there, or that he was out doing chores. Gunnar Westerlind hated Dawn, and she hated him back. But she couldn’t help herself—she was in love with his son.

Dawn stared at Dale, who had his head bowed again, and his forehead resting against both of his palms. Dale was going to fold. If Bob Wilson, or any other officer got to him, he was going to cave in and talk. She had to reach Troy. They had to do something about Dale Moore, and fast, or both she and Troy were going away to the juvenile detention center in Saint Anthony, and they were going to be there for a long, long time.

Down at the jail, Coal and Badger faced off, Badger still standing there with the two sets of cuffs holding his hands together behind his back.

"I guess the joke was on me all along, uh? I never thought you'd trick me, Savage."

Coal drew in a big breath. "Listen. Badger. I'm trying to explain the situation to you. I wasn't trying to trick you at all. I thought you knew the score. You were in big trouble before I got to your house. You know that, right? You fought the cops—again. If I hadn't shown up when I did, they were going to come in there with the big dogs—and a lot of clubs. It was going to go down really ugly if I didn't come in there, Badger. You have to believe me. But either way, you were going to be arrested and taken to jail."

Badger stared Coal down. For a long time, there was a dull fire in his eyes. Coal was relieved when he finally saw it begin to die away. A few minutes later, when he had time to process the situation, Badger let out a long, slow breath. He dropped his chin on his chest. The fight was gone out of him.

"I'm in trouble, huh?"

"You're in trouble," Coal agreed.

"They think I killed those people, huh?"

"They do."

"All of 'em?"

"I don't know about that. But I don't believe it, Badger. That must count for something. I know you were down at your traps on the river."

Of course Badger wouldn't meet Coal's gaze, but the Shoshones seldom would. Coal knew enough about them that he couldn't read them like he would any other suspects in a crime. "At least you're on my side, Savage. So what do I gotta do? How long am I gonna be in here this time?"

"That will be up to the judge, my friend. But I have to tell you, it's not going to be as easy as last time. I got you out before with a lot of promises. Now that you've been in another fight with the cops—and a stone cold sober one this time—I'm not sure what I'll tell the judge. I'm not sure how I'm going to spring you this time, Badger. I'm not going to lie to you."

"I know. You've never lied to me yet."

"Nope. Now I have to put you back there in a cell, big guy."

"So . . . you'll have to take off the handcuffs then."

"I'll be taking off the handcuffs."

Dark Badger stared Coal down. Coal had no doubt what the meaning was behind the light that had come into his eyes.

"We're alone down here, my friend."

"Uh."

"Anything can happen down here."

"Uh . . . huh."

"But what happens all depends on you. Understand? Every last moment of the next five minutes is a choice you will have to live with."

"I swore I would never go to the pen again," Badger reminded Coal.

Coal nodded. "I've thought about that promise. Many times."

"It's a short run, Savage, and then I'm up in the mountains. The mountains I know like a little kids' picture book—only better."

"I know you do, Badger. And do you want to know something?"

"Uh."

"I can't blame a man who never wants to live in a pen. But I do hold a grudge against a man that betrays a friend."

Badger stood with his eyes on Coal's cheeks for a long time. Finally, he raised them, and their gazes locked. "But who's really a friend, Savage? In this world, are there any real friends?"

Coal reached into the coin pocket of his Wranglers, his gaze never leaving Badger's solid face. He tugged out his handcuff key and looked Badger frankly in the eye.

"I guess we're about to find out. Aren't we?"

CHAPTER TWENTY-SIX

Just as Coal, with key in hand, started to step around the noncommittal-looking Hunter Jack, the outer door swung open. Both of them looked over to see Jordan Peterson walking in, his wide shoulders seeming to fill the doorway, his big hands swinging at his sides, his step the stride of a self-confident man.

Under what probably appeared to be sharp scrutiny from both sheriff and prisoner, Jordan stopped. He glanced from one to the other. "Something wrong?"

"No. Except you might be invading a private moment," Coal said. He felt surprisingly calm, considering the situation he had only moments before been waiting to see unfold.

"Private moment," repeated Hunter Jack.

Brow furrowed, Jordan stared at the two of them, then finally raised his eyebrows, bringing his hands cautiously out to the sides. "Well, hey, if it's that kind of thing, I wouldn't want to interrupt. I'll just step back outside."

Coal chuckled. "No, I think you can stay. Say, Jordan—you remember Hunter Jack. Don't you?" Of course he knew the answer.

"Oh, yeah. I think I've more than had the pleasure."

Reaching down, Coal took the middle of the linked cuffs between Jack's wrists. "Here we go, Badger. Bend a bit forward, would you?"

"Had to bring in reinforcements, huh, Sheriff?" Jack was looking down at the floor, as if his words would bounce up off the yellow-painted concrete, flash between his legs, and better reach Coal's ears.

Coal paused. "Do you need Jordan out? I can ask him to go if you're afraid he might get between what you and I have got to do."

After a couple-second pause, Jack chuckled and shook his head. "Naw. Savage, I ain't got too many friends. 'Specially not ones with badges. Besides, I kill you, or even just break your arms, then I gotta kill your deputy too, and then go spend the night up in the snow and ice. An' you know what? It's cold up there in that country. So . . . I can wait."

"Good," said Coal, inserting the key. "I sure wouldn't want to have to see you try to break my arms or kill me. I'm sure Jordan wouldn't like that either."

"Nope. Jordan wouldn't like that," said Jack. He pretended not to notice Coal's repeated use of the word "try". If Hunter Jack was anything, he was sure of his fighting prowess.

Hunter Jack trooped into the cellblock meekly, at least to all outward appearances. He stepped into the farthest cell when Coal opened the door. "It's like comin' home," said Jack, sweeping the little room with his black eyes. "But let's don't make a habit of this." Only a second later, the Indian's bear paw knifed out between them.

Coal looked down at the hand. He looked back up, and deep into the Shoshone's eyes, which uncharacteristically were meeting his more and more often. A wolf does that, or a dog—when they're growing bold, confident, and ready to kill.

Thoughts flashed through Coal's mind of all the things Badger could try if he once got hold of his hand. Braided all around those images were other plans of the things Coal would do to thwart every one of the Indian's big plans.

In the end, he took Badger's hand, and it swallowed his own, like the hand of a gorilla. They held firmly, looking into each other's eyes. There was no show of strength. No pumping. Just a mutual hanging on.

"Savage? You're the best white man I know, and I mean that. By the Great Spirit, I mean every word. It's a honor knowin' you."

Coal felt a strange emotion well up inside him. "I'm honored to be your friend, Badger. I've always felt that way."

The big left hand of Badger came up toward Coal's shoulder, and he couldn't help envisioning again all the things the man could do with the advantage of having both hands on him. But Coal was gambling his life on Hunter Jack.

The huge hand rested on Coal's shoulder and gave a squeeze. *"Tsaande daga,"* the big Shoshone said. "In Shoshone, it means 'good friend'."

Coal nodded, doing his best to imitate Badger's words, and the Indian gave him a patient smile. "I will sleep in here tonight, Savage. But I pray I won't sleep here long."

Out in the main office, Coal found Jordan hovering near the door. He looked at him for a moment, reading the concern in his deputy's eyes before he cleared his throat and tried hurriedly to hide it by whirling away toward the coffee pot.

"No faith in my fighting skills, huh?" asked Coal.

Sheepishly, Jordan turned and looked back. He chuckled. "Sorry. That guy's reputation is pretty big, though."

Coal gave his deputy an understanding smile. "Thanks, Jordan. The backup is much appreciated." He didn't feel any need to mention that his own reputation had been pretty big around here at one time as well.

Jordan continued on to the coffee pot, picking it up. He turned to look over his shoulder. "Cup?"

"Sure. Sure, buddy. It's stacking up to be a tiring day."

Jordan poured two cups and brought one to Coal, who sipped it like a dying man goes after water. Coal sat down behind his desk, in the worn-out chair that had become his favorite—the kind of white man chair you actually replaced with a new one before the old one disintegrated into rust fragments, and shreds of cloth that only resembled something once identified as a chair, a type Coal had seen a lot lately.

Coal waved toward the chair across from him, a stout wooden one with wheels. "Have a seat, Jordan. Take a load off."

Jordan took the seat, sipping his coffee. He turned his head to look back toward the coffee pot, where there was also a mushroom-shaped porcelain container full of sugar.

Coal caught the look. "Don't do it, buddy. Resist." Jordan looked back, surprised, and they laughed together. It felt good. And it was good to see that expression on Jordan's face, and hear the sound of happiness in his voice.

"Coal?"

"Yeah."

"You . . . heard anything from Maura?"

"Nope. Not one peep. I guess some people when they go really do just go, huh?"

Jordan nodded, his expression fading into one of sorrow. "Yeah. Yep." He sat there for a second, then drew in a deep breath and gusted it out again. "I just kind of thought she might at least call. Even if she didn't change her mind. You know? Just call and check on us, or something. I mean, she didn't leave any way for us to even find her. Did she?"

"Nothing." Coal shook his head. "Idaho Falls. That's it."

He sat there for a second, and for the first time he could remember in many weeks, he had an urge to have a cigarette between his fingers. Stupid habits from Nam. Some things hang on like that ugly, noisy, smelly stray cat you made the mistake of feeding one time, and then it never leaves your feet. Another thing that hung on like that was the memory of Maura. Damn Jordan Peterson for his foolish youth, for flipping the sheet off the ghost of Maura PlentyWounds, whom to Coal was better left unheard and unseen, lurking in every dark corner of his existence, but never coming out into the light.

Jordan sat nodding, taking in deep, long breaths. "Shoot. She just got under my skin, I guess. I really liked her. You ever feel like that about anyone?"

Coal wanted to look up at Jordan, but he had to keep staring at the scarred spruce top of his desk. Had he ever felt like that about anyone? Damn. Either Jordan was fishing, he was blind, or Coal was far better at hiding his emotions than he had ever dreamed.

"Nopc," hc licd quictly, likc a lazy old dog in the first warm sunshine of spring. "I don't get too attached." Before Jordan could think too much more deeply, or form a reply, Coal cut the whole conversation off into a whole other pen. "I got your note about Burks's pickup. Thanks for that."

"Sure."

"I have a warrant for it, so we can go dig through there in a bit, then maybe grab a bite to eat. Did you get all the other evidence sent off to Washington?"

By "Washington", Coal was referring to his old partner in the FBI, Tony Nwanzé. If it weren't for his friendship with Tony, and their ongoing relationship, doing any real investigations in Lemhi County that involved the likes of blood, hair, or fingerprints would have taken Coal ten times as long as it did—if it ever got done at all.

"I got it sent when I woke up this morning and found you gone. By the way—sorry for falling asleep back there."

Coal chuckled. "You boys have been working like dogs. Don't even think about apologizing. I just wish we could get old Todd Mitchell back again. It sure would be good having somebody else to share the load."

They got away from the job again for a few minutes talking about Todd Mitchell, and his family. Todd, hurt badly on an incident here in Salmon, was in a rehabilitation facility in Salt Lake City, but last Coal had heard he was actually up and moving around pretty well. Coal had high hopes of going down with his family soon to pick him up and bring him home.

"Hey, I didn't tell you about my talk with those people this morning," said Jordan.

"People?" Coal was so mentally exhausted it was hard shifting gears so abruptly.

"Yeah, the people at the house where Burks and Melissa Talty went to call in the murders?"

"Oh! Yeah. Sorry. What did they have to say? Did you write it all up?"

"I sure did. Sounds like they backed up the story pretty much all the way, for what it was worth."

"Oh yeah?" This didn't really surprise Coal too much, for he had already moved Joe Teton far up on his list of suspects in the murders.

"Yeah. They said they came pounding on the door, yelling about some killings up the hill. They wanted to use the phone, so those people, the Kmetzes, let them in. The husband was pretty nervous to talk to me, because he said he had his gun out ready to shoot them if they made a wrong move. He was afraid what I might say about that, I guess."

Coal laughed. "He shouldn't be nervous. I would have done at least that. So what else?"

"I asked them all the details. You know, like if Burks and the woman were acting strange or anything. They said they were pretty shaky, and looking around like they were afraid of something."

Coal shrugged that part off. "I can't blame any normal citizen who felt like that, if their story's true. That's about as scary as it gets."

"Right! One thing I thought was pretty weird, though? I asked if they noticed anything about their hands, and those people didn't have any idea what I was talking about. They never volunteered anything about the blood."

"You're kidding!"

"No. So then I specifically asked if they saw any blood on their hands, and they both said no. They just said they both looked really scared, and that their hands were as clean as anybody's."

Coal sank bank into his chair. Then what the . . .

"So, Jordan—did you ever hear anyone say if Curlie and Melissa were back at the scene when the cops started showing up?"

"I don't remember hearing either way."

"Why would somebody go back to a scene that grisly, once they were gone and knew the cops were coming?" Coal knew Jordan would have no answers. He was only thinking out loud.

Jordan sat there for a long time. The wheels of his brain seemed to make an actual noise that filled the room. "Only maybe if they thought about something. Something they forgot?"

"And maybe needed to change something about the crime scene." Coal flopped the words out on his desk between them. It seemed to actually make a noise, like the ringing slap of the flat of someone's hand.

Jordan swore. Coal stared at him until he found his voice again. "Exactly."

CHAPTER TWENTY-SEVEN

Coal got up and walked to the door leading back into the cellblock. He stood at the window, looking in at Hunter Jack, where he lay down on the bunk, sleeping or at least pretending to. Coal's mind was churning. He had so much to do! And it felt like so little time to accomplish all of it. He stared in at Jack, at his huge torso, his great big hands. The man in that cell was a volcano waiting to erupt, Coal knew. And he himself was the only person he trusted around him.

Turning around, he walked back to the desk and sat down, staring hatefully at the phone he knew was about to spend way too much time glued to his ear. He looked back up at Jordan.

"Jordan, I need to say something before I forget. Take this as a direct order, and if you aren't sure I've spoken to Grant about it, pass it on to him too. I don't want you dealing with Hunter Jack. All right?"

"Dealing with him?"

"Yes. No feeding him. No water, unless you can slip a glass between the bars, on the floor. He has to use the bucket in that cell, and it stinks, you leave it till I get back here. Understand? No contact. No opening that cell door, not under any circumstances, even if you have three or four people with you."

Jordan stared at his boss for a long time. "He's really that dangerous?"

"He's really that dangerous."

"All right. You're the boss. It's done, as far as I'm concerned. He seems to like you, for whatever reason, so that's good enough for me."

"Thanks. So hey—if Grant makes it back in soon, why don't you go with him down to the PD and do the search on Curlie's pickup? You probably know most of the drill, but if not, just follow Grant's orders. He has a really good handle on this kind of investigation, I think. I'll go down with the two of you if I'm free, but I have a feeling I'll be on the phone for a while."

"Sounds good. What should I do till Grant gets here?"

"Take a nap, if you can. I'm toying with the idea of having you hit some bars with me tonight. And if I run out of time for that, you just get a free nap out of the deal."

Jordan decided to go home for that nap, and he asked Coal to have Grant call him there when he got back into town. After he was gone, Coal flipped open his book of notes, including phone numbers and other items he had written down. Then he drew a deep breath, glaring at the black phone in front of him. Gritting his teeth, he picked it up.

The first call went to Steele Memorial, and it irritated him to feel how his heart picked up speed when it was Annie Price who answered. "Annie? This is Coal."

Oh! Hey, Coal! I was just thinking about you. Are you doing okay?

"I guess, other than one foot in the grave with exhaustion. I'd sure like to see you."

Aww. Okay, you just melted my heart, so thanks. You must want something really big. Is that actually why you called?

"Well, unfortunately I called to ask about a patient that came in this morning, probably around ten. Wilford Bayless, I think his name is. Heavy-set fellow?"

Oh yes, of course I know the man. He was in last summer, when he decided to mow over the top of his foot.

"Ouch! Well, how is he?"

Frankly? Unconscious.

Coal sat silent for a second, trying to digest that news. "Wait, Annie. You're saying he's asleep, or he's actually still unconscious from his accident?"

Yes.

Coal laughed. "Okay, smart aleck. I'm guessing the second one. That's really bad, isn't it? That's been hours ago."

He has a skull fracture—a pretty significant one. We had to drain some fluid out of his skull already, and Dr. Bent is watching him very closely. Maybe you could come in and we could watch him together?

Her voice sounded hopeful, but Annie was grasping at straws that might as well have been rushing down the Salmon River. "I wish. The whole rest of my day is looking about as bad as it started out. I'm not even going to get off the phone probably for at least another hour, and then I have to go serve two search warrants. I want to be a cowboy, Annie. This sheriff business is for the vultures."

I want you to be a cowboy too, she replied. *Coal?*

"Yeah?"

I really miss you.

After hanging up with Annie, Coal sat and finished his coffee, which had cooled to room temperature. He wished he could talk to Grant Fairbourne to see how far out he thought he might be, but there was so far only one radio in the department—two, if Coal counted the one he had bought with his own money for the Thunderbird. Two radios, and both of them were his.

Picking up the phone again, Coal rang Flo.

Hello, Salmon Dispatch.

"Hello, Salmon Dispatch. That's a funny name for a girl with a voice like yours."

Flo laughed. *Aww. Well thank you, Coal—I think. And hi!*

"Hi. You've been a busy girl lately."

Ha! Not busy like you, sir! How are you holding up?

"Barely. And starting to forget I even have a family at home."

I'm sure! So did you just call to flirt, or do you need some professional help?

Coal laughed. "Professional help? Now that is a loaded question!"

Flo was already giggling. *Okay, okay. That didn't come out how I meant it. Let me start again—besides a head shrink, what else can I get for you, hon?*

"A head shrink, and I need you to call Officer Gentry. What's his first name, by the way? I think I knew it, but I've forgotten."

Lyle. I can see how he rates with you county guys. Flo's voice had a teasing hint. She sounded a lot more rested than Coal felt.

"Yeah! Lyle. Sorry. So please call him and see where he is for me, will you? I have some questions for him if he can either call me down here at the jail or meet me somewhere. I know I could call him on my radio, but then I'd have to go out in my cold car, and plus I wouldn't get to flirt with you while your husband's at work."

Now that would be a crying shame, she came back. *Okay, Coal. Hang on a second.*

She set down the phone but didn't hang up. He could hear her reaching out to Gentry, and he heard the state bull come over the air and talk to her. He wanted to seem alert to it, but he almost fell asleep while trying to listen, jerked, and almost hit his head on the desk.

Coal?

"Yes, ma'am?" He hoped he sounded more awake than he felt.

He's not by a phone, but he's coming in from the slide-off down the river. He says he'll be in town in ten and can meet you at the jail.

After Flo hung up, Coal leaned back in his chair and shut his eyes. Twice, he almost fell off the chair when he fell asleep. The second time was startling enough that he got up and poured out all but the last three or four tablespoons of coffee into his mug, drank the top down, then emptied the rest of the pot and filled the mug back up to the rim. He glared at the sugar, wondering if he could even remember the taste of that white poison.

Resisting the sugar, he walked back to sit in his chair, leaned way forward, and sipped at his cup, trying to go over the case in his head while waiting for the sound of the door.

Lyle Gentry showed up at almost exactly the ten-minute mark and walked through the door adjusting his gun belt. He took one look at Coal and stopped. "Man, Savage, you look like something the cat left."

Coal laughed. "That's nice. And I believe you. How are things, Gentry? Lyle, right?" Now he would look amazingly smart and caring to the other officer.

Gentry did indeed look pleased. "Yes, Lyle. Everything's good. Good. I guess you probably want to hear how my interview with Gunnar Westerlind went, right?"

"This case seems like it's cooking right along, so yes. Might as well hear what they had to say. We've got some other interesting developments."

"So I couldn't raise anyone last night, Savage—or do you prefer Coal?"

"Either. I'm not picky."

"Okay. Well, I kind of like the sports team here, so I'll call you Savage."

Coal only grinned and nodded.

"So like I said, I couldn't raise anyone last night, and I knocked for a while. The truck was there, though, and a dark red Chrysler sedan. Both felt fairly cool to the touch, but as cold as it was last night, I'm not sure that means a whole lot. I don't think it would take an engine very long to cool down in those temperatures. This morning, close to noon, I finally caught up to him—the father, that is. Now, Bob Wilson went over and started asking some questions around the high school, trying to figure out who the other two kids might be, and he figured out who the son's girlfriend is—a Dawn Kelly. But she said she wasn't with him last night."

"Him who?" asked Coal. "You mean the son, right? What's his name?"

"Troy. Troy Westerlind. And it sounds like you are familiar with the father, Gunnar. Really nice gentleman, pleasant to talk to."

"Yes, he seems all right," agreed Coal. He had no reason to mention his gut feelings about Westerlind, partly because under the circumstances he wasn't real sure his gut feelings meant anything. Maybe Westerlind was everything nice and polite he pretended to be. Maybe the only reason Coal was suspicious of him was because he didn't like knowing he was trying to see his old friend, Kathy.

"So anyway, I talked to Mr. Westerlind, and he assured me that the truck didn't leave his property last night. He said his son was home finishing an assignment, they watched a movie together, and then around ten they went to bed."

Coal tried to digest the story. He didn't imagine Gunnar Westerlind had any reason to lie about where his truck had been or not been. But what about Curlie Burks? If a man was going to try to draw attention away, hoping to make himself look less plausible as a murder suspect, would he really point a finger at a real person if that person had not been at the scene? Unless it was a person he disliked and whom he wanted to see in trouble, what would be the benefit? Why not invent a possible murder suspect from thin air, someone no officer could possibly track down, because he or she did not exist? Someone who could not defend himself, nor, as a fictional character, would have any need to? It would be easy to do, and pretty foolproof, as long as Curlie didn't waver from his story. Coal himself could have invented a dozen vehicle descriptions in seconds, and the same for made-up people.

As much as Coal did not want to feel biased, because he was afraid of what his deep-down reasons might be, if he had to pick which story seemed most believable, as odd as it might sound to anyone who knew both Westerlind and Burks, Burks's story was the one. So Westerlind . . . what were the possible reasons for him to lie about where his truck was at the time of the murder, or where his son was?

The most obvious reasons popped into Coal's mind: Loyalty. Wanting to protect his son. Not wanting to have his family name in the news, being dragged through the mud of a criminal investigation.

Curlie Burks's reasons to lie about seeing Troy Westerlind and two friends, in a very specifically-described pickup, coming down from the area of the cemetery? Dig into his suspicious, cynical mind every bit as deep as he could, Coal still came up with nothing.

Either Westerlind or Burks had to be lying. And it wasn't to be Burks, not because he seemed like a model citizen, but simply because there was no obvious reason for him to pinpoint a real person, or a real vehicle, unless the story was true. Not that he wasn't lying about anything else, but Coal simply could not buy that he was lying about Troy Westerlind, in his father's light blue and white Dodge pickup, being at the scene of the murders—and with two other people.

Whether Coal needed a reason to dislike Gunnar Westerlind or not, he had one. Coal hated a man who lied in a criminal investigation, and his guts and common sense told him Westerlind was lying. Why, Coal couldn't guess. But he was sure going to find out.

CHAPTER TWENTY-EIGHT

"Are you thinking what I'm thinking?"

Coal was addressing Grant Fairbourne, who had come into the office from downriver, looking half frozen, especially about the cheeks, ears, and the dark pink tip of his nose.

"Well, I'm thinking that big rock was shoved down on the gas pedal while the emergency brake was on, and then when the brake got taken off, the car took off and launched into the river. Is that what you mean?"

Coal nodded, as he saw a little shiver run through Grant. "That's what I mean. No tracks coming out of that hole in the ice, right? And it's hard for me to guess how anybody could have gotten out of the car, out of the water, and back to shore anyway. Or at least if they did, I think we would have found them right there on the shore, frozen to death. Hypothermia from water that cold works fast."

Grant nodded, rubbing his hands together and blowing on them. "You're right on all counts. Somebody wanted that car in the river, but it's anybody's guess why. Right? Or do you know something?"

"Not a clue," Coal said, giving a quasi-shrug, with his hands. "I still need to get hold of Bob Wilson, to hash out the details of the theft with him—and maybe . . . who did they say owned the car?"

"Burt Landry?"

Coal slapped the desk. "Yes! Landry. Burt. Man, Grant, sometimes I think my mind is going."

"Lots of cold and no sleep might cause that," averred Grant.

"Well then, I guess I have perfect excuses. Sorry, I would have made you some coffee to warm you up, but I know you don't partake. I'll buy some hot chocolate next time I'm in town, so you'll at least have *something* here for days like this."

"Thanks, Coal." Grant rubbed his hands together again, then stuck them abruptly in his armpits. "My mom taught me this trick."

Coal laughed. "Old trick. It works a lot better if you stick them in a horse's armpits, though."

Grant grinned. "I bet the horse loves it too."

"Try it. Then put your icy hands on your wife's back. It won't take very long to see which of them loves you best."

They laughed together as Coal stood up. "Hey, I hate like heck to make you get moving again when you just got back, but we really need to serve the search warrant on Curlie Burks's pickup, and we probably should hit Badger's place today too. You think you're up for it?"

"I don't think I have a lot of choice, right? It has to be done. Soon."

"Right. Jordan went home to get a nap in, and he said to call him when you got in. Man, I hate to do it, but he could sure use the experience."

"This time I agree. He can sleep after he's dead, right?"

By the time Jordan got back to the office, looking about as lively as a zombie, Grant had warmed up considerably. He had heated water in the coffee pot and drank two cups of it while Coal watched him and cracked jokes about it, but between holding the hot cup in his hands, and the warmth of the liquid going down his throat, and into his belly, it seemed to work wonders—and Grant managed to keep his religion intact, to boot.

They went to Hunter Jack's place first, where they ran through two rolls of film, and fingerprinted the doorknob, the door, and all around the doorframe. They also printed all the light switches, but none of the prints were complete enough to use. They found no cowboy boots there. Only one decent pair of moccasins and two worn-out pairs that Badger was keeping either to use for spare parts, replace the soles of, or was just too lazy or nostalgic to throw away. The entire search didn't take forty minutes.

Next, it was down to city hall, where they got the key to the chain link enclosure out back from the chief, and they started the laborious search of Burks's pickup.

As Coal had half suspected, they found contraband almost immediately, in the glove box. Not only was there a 9 mm Heckler and Koch VP70 pistol in there, one of the ugliest handguns known to man, in Coal's opinion, but there was a paper sack containing at least a pound of marijuana. Coal hefted it up and down in the palm of his hand, looking over the seat at Grant.

Grant gave out a long whistle. "Dang! That'll get Burks a felony for sure!"

Jordan was looking over Grant's head, as Grant leaned across the pickup seat, about to look underneath it with his flashlight in hand.

"Pot?" asked Jordan.

"Yep. Here," said Coal, tossing him the bag. "Give that a good sniff. You won't soon forget it. And later maybe we'll burn some at the office for you. That's another memory that will come in handy, if you stick to a career in law enforcement."

"Whoa!" Grant's voice cut in. "What's this?" As Jordan backed away from behind him, so Grant could straighten back up out of the cab, he hefted a piece of paper that was crusted with a dark brownish, maroon substance.

Leaving the glove box open, Coal came around. The afternoon was growing long, and light was no longer great, so Grant was shining his flashlight along the folded paper as Coal stopped beside him.

"It's a title," Grant said. "Nineteen . . . The title to this truck," he said, looking at Coal.

"Let me see," Coal said, and he took the paper from Grant. It had been folded neatly in half, about the right size to fit in a shirt pocket. It seemed certain that the maroon substance on it was blood, which appeared to be heavily concentrated along the crease in the middle, then nearly faded out by the outer edges.

"How many people keep their title in the vehicle?" asked Grant.

Coal grunted. "How many people soak their title in blood?"

Troy Westerlind got off the bus that afternoon on Highway 28, at the mouth of the long driveway that led to his house. Troy, who had reached his full height of six-foot-two as a sophomore, was now a senior, and although he still had a way to go to fill out his frame, to judge by his broad shoulders, large hands, and narrow waist, he was going to end up being every bit the figure of a man his father was, only taller. He was dressed in a heavy black leather coat, lined with flannel, and Levi's 501's, comfortably faded, but in flawless condition. The boots on his feet were of top cowhide.

With two books cradled in his hand, Troy started toward the house, seeing that his dad's red Chrysler 300 was not in the driveway. That was a relief, but it didn't much matter. His father wouldn't be gone forever, and there was no doubt that when he got home he would find something to be angry or upset about, some reason to berate or abuse his son over. It had become at least a weekly habit—sometimes three or four times a week. Troy would have loved to jump in his dad's pickup and get out of there, but they had shuttled it together to the shop, and even if his dad was willing to let him drive it again, who knew when it would be done?

Troy went inside the house, which was still warm compared to outside, but where the ashes of the fire in the stove had mostly turned white. His father either hadn't bothered to build it up, or he had been gone at least a few hours.

Digging a ham out of the fridge, he cut off two big slices, throwing them in a cast iron frying pan on the electric stove and listening to them start to hiss. He had just put two pieces of Wonder Bread in the toaster when the phone rang, making him jerk.

With a long sigh, he stared at the phone as it rang three more times after the first. Finally, he took another deep breath and took it off the cradle. "Hello?"

Hey! Troy!

"Hi, Dawn."

Is your dad there?

"Not yet."

Can you come over?

"Sure. If I wanna get killed. When I left this morning he was still havin' a cow about me bein' out so late last night. I told you that."

Yeah, sorry. I forgot. She lowered her voice way down. *Hey, Troy?*

"Yeah, what?"

I'm worried about Dale.

Troy's jaw hardened. His toast popped up, and absently he took it out, burning his fingers and dropping it on the countertop. "Why about 'im? And why're you whisperin'?"

Because! He's here!

"Damnit, Dawn! I told you I don't like you hangin' out with him when I'm not around. How's that gonna look to everybody?"

I don't know, but . . . Her voice faded off.

Growing suddenly angry, Troy asked, "Is he right there now?"

Oh, yeah, Troy. Yeah, me an' Dale are just hangin' out. Too bad you can't come in. How's your dad doin', anyway?

Troy swore again. "Hey. Put him on the line, Dawn. Tell him I gotta talk to him."

Okay, sure. Here he is. Dawn's voice sounded as casual as could be.

Hey, dude, Dale's voice came over the line. *What's crackin'?*

"What's crackin'? I'll tell you what's *going* to be crackin'—*dude.* Listen, man—you stayin' cool?"

The entire tone of Dale Moore's voice changed. *What do you mean? What's up? 'Course I'm cool.*

"Okay. Positive? I mean, you haven't talked, right? To anybody?"

No, dude! Come on! Who would I talk to?

"That's right!" Troy growled. "Get yourself thrown in juvie, right with me an' Dawn. Put 'er back— Oh, crap," said Troy. He had just heard the slamming of a car door at the front of the house.

What, man? You want Dawn back? came Dale's voice.

"No, jerk off! My old man's back!"

The front door flew suddenly open, before Troy could even say goodbye. Gunnar Westerlind stood there in the doorway, his silver belly hat brim low over his eyes. "All right, you little idiot. It's time to fess up. Where were you really last night?"

"Huh?" On a whim, Troy lay the phone down on the counter, turning so he was in front of it. "I told you—just cruisin' in town."

"At two in the damn morning?"

"Well, I—"

Troy didn't even get to finish his sentence. One second, his father was across the room, and it seemed like the next, with the front door still open wide, he was closing on his son, his hands reaching for the front of his shirt.

Dawn Kelly saw the terror in Dale's eyes as he whirled toward her. "What? What, Dale?"

"I think Troy's dad's beatin' the hell out of him."

Dawn jumped forward and snatched the phone out of Dale's hand. Just as she lifted it to her ear, she heard a string of curses, and a loud *thud.* "Hey!" she yelled into the mouthpiece. "Hey! You leave him alone! STOP!" But as loud as she could yell, the ruckus on the other end of the line continued.

Panicking, she pushed down on the disconnect button in the cradle of the phone, but when she let go, she could still hear the commotion. She pushed the button down again, holding it longer this time. When she let go now, there was only silence. No dial tone.

"Come on!" she yelled at Dale.

"What? Where we goin'?"

"To the neighbor's! I have to call the sheriff, before Troy's dad kills him!"

They took off together out the front door, running next door. When Dawn pounded on the door, an older man in a red flannel shirt pulled it open. "Dawn?"

"Mr. Moger, I need to use your phone! To call the police."

"What? What's wrong with *your* phone?" the man stammered, looking confused.

"The line's dead. *Please!"*

Relenting, Moger led Dawn to the kitchen, jerking the phone off the hook and hitting the zero for her. When the operator came on, Dawn frantically told her it was an emergency, and she needed the county sheriff. Soon, the phone began ringing again, and in two rings a woman's voice came on: *Police dispatch.*

"Yes! I need to report a fight! My friend's dad is beating him!"

Slow down, miss. Take a deep breath, came the voice from the other end of the line again. *You'll—*

"I can't calm down!" Dawn practically screamed into the phone. "It's bad!"

I'm sorry, miss, but listen to me: I won't be able to help you unless you can slow down and give me an address. Okay? Try to take a breath, and tell me everything.

Coal was finally on his way home when the call came over the air. *Salmon dispatch, calling any county unit. Anyone on the air, please respond?*

Cursing, Coal pulled the mic off its hook. "Sheriff Savage here."

Oh! I'm sorry, Sheriff, but I just took a call from a very panicked young lady, reporting a battery in progress. It's out past your place, I think.

"Okay, Nadine. Give me the address, all right? You can fill me in on the details when I'm en route."

Nadine gave the address, which meant nothing to Coal. But the details did. He swore when he heard the name of the suspect, and he was hoping he had a good full pot of curse words boiled up for whatever lay ahead.

CHAPTER TWENTY-NINE

Coal took the fight call alone. He doubted there were any other officers close enough for backup, and as any lawman in Lemhi County well knew, if you were going to wait around to have help, you wouldn't go on three-fourths of the valley's emergency calls.

Taking the corner into the Westerlind driveway a little too fast, he fishtailed on the ice, correcting his mistake just shy of sliding the Thunderbird's rear-end into a length of barbed wire fence. He eased up next to the blue and white Dodge and leaped out, grabbing his flashlight as he went. He didn't carry any kind of club, so the flashlight was as close as he would get if he needed anything besides his feet, fists, and the .44.

He listened for only a few seconds at the front door and heard no sound within. Pounding on the door, he stood to the side and waited. Soon, he heard footsteps inside, heard the rattle of a lock, then the clicking of the door handle. A rectangle of warm yellow light burst out onto the ice and snow as the door edged open to reveal Gunn Westerlind standing there, looking cautiously out.

All of a sudden, the man's eyes widened. "Sheriff! Man, you scared me. What brings you out here in the middle of the night? No, wait—don't tell me: Something about my neighbor. Bayless?"

Coal studied the rancher's face for a moment. He seemed completely at ease. "No, actually not, Mr. Westerlind. In fact, I called down to the hospital today, and Bayless is still unconscious." It suddenly hit Coal that he had been planning on stopping in to Steele Memorial, if only to see Annie. That was another item on his cluttered list for the day that he had missed.

"Still unconscious!" repeated Westerlind, looking startled. "That's terrible! But look at my manners! Would you like to come in and warm up?"

Glancing past and to either side of the rancher, Coal said, "Sure, I guess for a minute."

Westerlind stood out of the way, and Coal passed him, stepping into the entryway, which had a very Western flair about it, with reddish clay tiles on the floor that might have been brought in clear from New Mexico.

"So, Sheriff, exactly what do I owe your visit to then? I'm sure you didn't come out all this way just to tell me Bayless is unconscious."

"No, I definitely didn't. In fact, this is probably going to sound really strange, but somebody called in a fight in progress here. Or at least a *battery* in progress, if not an actual fight."

Westerlind stared for a moment, then laughed, as he swung a bewildered look about the room. "Umm . . . Well, I don't even know what to say to that! Are you sure they had the right address?"

"The caller mentioned you by name, according to dispatch."

"Well, I'll be . . . So just some smart aleck playing games then, huh?"

"I guess it must be," said Coal, with a shrug. "Say, I don't suppose you have any family about, do you?"

"No, no. I mean I do have a son—Troy—but he's out with friends tonight. It's just me alone, batching it."

Coal glanced around once more. The room seemed well ordered. There was no sign that a fight had ever taken place here. "Well, I'm guessing somebody your son knows was probably playing a trick on him, Westerlind."

"Gunn, remember?" said Westerlind with a patient little smile.

"Yes, right. Gunn. Anyway, I'm sorry to have bothered you. I'll let you get back to your evening."

"Thank you. It'll be a quiet one, that's for sure. Have a nice night, Sheriff."

"You bet. See you around."

Coal opened the door and stepped back out into the frigid air, walking to the car and climbing in. For half a minute, he sat there collecting himself, feeling the brutal heat collect from the very effective Ford heater. He wondered what was worse—being involved in an actual fight, having to arrest the participants, or trying to come down from an adrenalin high once it turned out the call was bogus.

Then again, could it be the call was *not* bogus? He sure wished he could at least have seen Westerlind's son. That would have settled everything. But of course there was nothing for it. If Troy Westerlind was out, he was out. Coal had no reason to suspect foul play. No evidence of a crime. It was time to go home to his family.

Then, on a whim, Coal had a thought. He looked toward the front door of the house again, sat for only a few seconds longer, then threw open the door once more and got out. Going back to the door, he knocked. It soon was answered again by Gunn Westerlind.

The man looked the obvious question at him, then said, "What did you forget, Sheriff?"

"I'm just curious if you have any idea when your son might be back."

"Why's that?"

"Oh, just on the off chance I could talk to him for a minute, so I could write in my report that I did. The county gets picky about this stuff."

"Oh, sure. That makes sense. Well, I wish I had some idea, but I don't. Sorry about that."

Coal shrugged. "Well, no problem. It was just a thought." With that, he thrust his hand out between them, and as he did, he dropped his eyes to Westerlind's hands, giving them a quick, practiced scan.

Westerlind smiled and took Coal's hand, they shook, and then the rancher's hand fell away. Coal already knew what he wanted to know from Gunn Westerlind. Tomorrow, at Salmon High School, he would learn the rest from his son, Troy.

Back at the house, Coal didn't know whose greeting was happiest—that of the twins, Wyatt and Morgan, the dogs, or little Sissy Miley. Maybe it didn't have to be a contest. Maybe in their own way, from the licks of the dogs, to the hugs of Wyatt and Morgan, to the meek little hand of Sissy reaching up to rest on his belt, the five of them gave Coal every last little bit of love they were able to manifest in one greeting.

Even as worn out as Coal was, and as ready as he was to lie down and sleep the sleep of the dead, he enjoyed every moment of listening to Wyatt and Morgan jabber on about their day. Wyatt, as always, was a little more reserved—dare Coal use the word "mature"?—in his presentation. Morgan was somewhat like a child's audible dictionary had exploded into the room, and every word was flying about, randomly trying to find a home, striving to fall into some sort of cohesive order. Meanwhile, the dogs were happy to hover around him with their tongues lolling out, taking his rubs and pats when he could get a free hand, and Sissy stood there with her cryptic little smile, happy to once again be in his presence.

While Connie was finishing supper, the whole rest of the family, even quiet, contemplative Virgil, went out to feed the horses together, Coal because he had to get back out in the cold to try to force himself to stay awake at least until after the evening meal, and all the children because, quite simply, they wanted time with their father, and their guardian. It would have been hard for Coal to tell them all how much their presence meant to him.

Flaking off hay and throwing it out to the horses was a much bigger job than it used to be since Maura PlentyWounds had run off and left her four animals here. Coal had often thought of selling them, as Maura had suggested he do, but somehow he hadn't been able to. He guessed he was still hanging on that little shred of memory of the woman he had loved—and still did, he was afraid.

When the horses were happily munching on their hay, Coal picked Sissy up, letting his forearm act as a seat for her as they watched the horses together. They were both looking at Cody, the big gray that had belonged to Coal's father, Prince, when Sissy piped up, in that sweet, timid voice. "Pop Coal, is Code old?"

He looked at her, still often surprised when he heard her speak, as shy as she had been from the start. "Cody? Old? I don't know, why do you think that?"

"'Cause he's a-gettin' all gray—like Mama Connie. An' she says she's old an' gray."

A rush of tears came into Coal's eyes before he knew it. "Well, Sis, now that you mention it, he *is* actually pretty old. In fact . . ." Coal's voice trailed off. He didn't want to finish his thought, and he didn't even want to think about how old Cody was. The truth was, Cody was getting close to the normal useful lifespan of a horse that was still rideable. The old warhorse was one of the last living links to Prince Savage, and Coal wasn't ready for him to go. But he wondered just how long the old boy had left. There was nothing anyone on earth could do to stop his eventual passing.

"Pop Coal?" He looked down into the girl's wide, innocent eyes. "You gon' do like my pop? You gon' go off too?"

"Go off? You mean go away?"

"No. You gon' go off an' down under the ground?"

Coal's throat tightened up, making him swallow hard. "I'll tell you what I'm going to do. I'm going to fight hard to stay right here with you, Sissy. I'm going to fight hard, so I can always hold you whenever you need to be held. And that's a promise."

After a long, solemn stare up at him, Sissy gave Coal that smile few seldom saw, and then she leaned over and lay her head against him. Coal looked over to see Katie Leigh and Cynthia Batterton both beaming at him.

Family. Coal drew a deep breath of icy air, blew it back out, and smiled at the girls. How could any man be luckier than Coal Savage?

Late at night, Dale Moore lay awake, staring up at the ceiling. What had become of Troy? He and Dawn had both heard what was happening in his house. There was no question what the sounds meant. And now there was the awful waiting, wondering.

Had old man Westerlind found out what they did? Or, more accurately, what Troy did? Because technically, it was Troy who had wielded the spear, not Dawn, whose laugh had turned to horror the moment the blood first began to flow, and certainly not Dale, who hadn't even wanted to go up to that place from the beginning. All Troy had kept telling him was that "it would be fun", and that "he had good reason". It seemed at first as if he had convinced Dawn too, which was a big shock to Dale, who would never have believed she could be so bloodthirsty—not the girl he had secretly loved for so long. But in the end, Dawn didn't like it either. Dale could see it in her eyes, even if she wouldn't admit it, not to him, and certainly not to Troy.

But now, both he and Dawn were in it up to their necks, almost as much as Troy. They had gone along with it, and that would be enough for the courts. Troy had sworn that was true, and Troy knew about things like that. Troy had already spent time in what everyone called "Saint Anthony", more precisely the juvenile detention center in that little town. Why did he seem to have such a drive to go back?

And then Dale remembered, as he always eventually did. Troy was anxious to go back to Saint Anthony because any place was better than going to be home with Satan, who was his father.

The ringing phone jolted Dale almost enough to fall off the bed. He fumbled around in the dark, trying to find his way to the light switch, and when he did, he hit it, and the two bare bulbs hanging askew from the ceiling threw a blinding light into his eyes, and over the entire room.

Dale had pulled the phone from the hallway into his room and set it on his dresser by the door, since there was no one else in the house anyway because his dad was still down at whatever bar he had chosen to haunt tonight—whatever bar hadn't already decided to kick him out. It wasn't until the fifth ring that he answered it, wondering if anyone would still be on the line once he got it to his ear. It must be one in the morning!

"Hello?"

Dale? I'm sorry for calling so late. It's Dawn.

"Dawn! What the heck are you doin'? Are you okay?"

Yeah, yeah. Dale, I'm fine! I'm sorry! I didn't mean to scare you. Is your dad home?

"What, you mean the damn worthless old wino? No. He's still down hittin' the bars."

Oh, sorry. Hey—if I can get out of the house, can I come back over?

"Wh— What for? You said there's nothin' wrong—right?"

Dale, come on! Stop! No, there's nothing wrong. Except . . . Hey, I just want to talk, that's all.

Far be it from Dale Moore, for as long as he lived, to turn down any chance to hang out with Dawn Kelly, who was leagues beyond his station in life! If she just wanted to talk—to *him,* not Troy—well, that was wonderful!

"Yeah, come on over. Just don't get caught, okay?"

I won't. I'm going through the window. Mom's got some guy in her room anyway, so I doubt she'd even care if she heard me leave. See you in a few minutes.

The line went dead with no goodbye. Dale picked up his jeans and got them back on, buttoning them and pulling his cleanest dirty shirt out of the drawer. He grinned at himself, thinking how clever he was to find a good way to put to use those poetically great words from his favorite Kris Kristofferson song, "Sunday Morning Coming Down". He slipped the shirt on, then left the room and went down the hall to wait by the front room door.

It was less than two minutes before Dawn Kelly was tapping hesitantly at the door, probably thinking Dale's drunk father might have made it home since they hung up. Dale jerked open the door, looking up the street toward Main. There was no wavering, dark shadow headed toward them, so he looked back at Dawn just as she fell against him and threw her arms around him.

Dawn was squeezing so tight Dale wondered if he would be able to keep breathing. He also didn't care.

Stepping backward, Dale pulled Dawn with him, slamming the door behind her. He made good use of his opportunity and put his arms around Troy Westerlind's girl, the girl he wished was his. His guess had been right—something was wrong. Dawn wasn't a hugger. Something had happened. As much as he loved this physical connection with her, it scared him to death.

"Okay, I'm good," Dawn said as if reading his mind. She let go of him and backed off a few steps.

"What's goin' on, Dawn? You promised nothin' was wrong."

"Well I called the cops back, and the dispatcher woman said the sheriff went to Troy's house. Nothing was happening. She said Troy's dad said he was by himself—that Troy was out with friends."

Dale felt the blood rush from his face. "He's lyin'!"

"Well, I know that! We both know that! But . . . Dale?"

"Yeah?"

"I'm scared. Bad scared. I didn't know who else to talk to but you."

" 'Cause there ain't nobody else to talk to," Dale said. "Dawn, what are we gonna do? What if Troy's hurt bad—even dead? You think his dad knows he was talkin' to us? Think he knows we heard what was goin' on?"

"No!" Dawn's reply was too adamant. She stared at him for more than five seconds, looking almost angry with him for even suggesting such a stupid thing. Then the brave mask fell off her face, revealing the terror underneath. "No. No, I do think he knows. He has to!"

"He could come after us too then," said Dale. "What're we gonna do?"

"Hold it together," said Dawn, becoming the bold one again, the one who never let much bother her, because she was the toughest girl in the high school—maybe the toughest girl in this entire pathetic town.

"Hold *what* together?" Dale shot out. "If the old man comes lookin' for us with a shotgun, there won't be anything left to hold together!"

"You have to stop panicking," said Dawn. "We'll figure this out."

"How?" The panic had risen high into Dale's throat. He wanted to play a tough guy, to do the same thing Dawn was doing. But he couldn't. He knew they should go to the cops, but he didn't even dare suggest it.

Dawn stared Dale down for several seconds. She was trying to make her eyes look rock hard, trying to show him how callused she was, and how nothing could get to her. But wasn't it too late? Hadn't she already admitted she was scared? She cursed herself. What a fool! You don't let on about things like that, girl! You especially don't ever admit to a guy like Dale when you're scared.

Then he thinks he has good reason to be scared too. Inside, she swore. She had made a big mistake. A mistake just in coming here!

When Troy jumped back into her mind, she whirled away from Dale. She couldn't let him read her face. She couldn't let him see any more of her fear. Without looking at him, she said, "Hey, let's go back in your room, in case your dad comes home."

With that, she turned and went past him, walking down the hall without letting him get a good look at her face. She went in his room and felt him following behind, basically a lost puppy who needed direction for every single move he made. Dale was a coward. But he sure had a soft spot for her. A soft spot she had always used to her advantage.

Dawn continued to avoid Dale's eyes. She went over and started rummaging as nonchalantly as she could portray through his pile of 8-track tapes. At last, she pulled out Kris Kristofferson's *Borderlord* album, smiling ruefully to herself. This was one of Dale's favorite albums, so he played it often when she was over here listening to music with him. She was pretty sure Dale never saw how she had to fight tears when one particular song came on, a song she couldn't believe Kristofferson didn't write just for her.

Taking the tape, she slid it into the slot in the player, hoping she wouldn't have to wad up paper to put on one side as Dale had to do sometimes, to keep the music from sounding warped. She pushed the power button, then the play button, then fought back the surprised tears that tried to flood her eyes when as fate would have it her song, less than half a minute in, began first to play:

> " . . . She's waiting for someone, and knowin'
> there's no one who cares if she comes or she goes.
> Just a soul in the shadows the world never sees.
> She's somebody nobody knows.
> Someone no one's ever known,
> Cryin' where no one can hear.

Somebody's dyin' alone,
In a city where nobody cares . . ."

Dawn gritted her teeth as the song continued, talking about some homeless man dying in a gutter. She gritted them so hard it felt like they would crack, putting a hard, callused frown on her face. Where in this world was there anyone who really wanted Dawn Kelly, who really cared whether she lived or died?

She thought often about Troy Westerlind, the one toughest, most beautiful boy she had ever seen. But she wished she had never met him. She wished she had seen the evil, bloodthirsty hate in him, the desire to kill anything and everything that moved. She wished she could have known, from the very start, that Troy was the devil.

CHAPTER THIRTY

Coal, a good, high intensity weight-lifting session under his belt, a pound of beef steak and three cups of coffee in his belly, was sitting in his Thunderbird at Salmon High School the next morning even before the principal arrived. He sat watching, sipping out of habit from a big light green thermos of hot coffee, as he watched the faculty arrive. One by one, they slowly pulled past him in the dark, parking in their accustomed places, disembarking and going into the dark school, where lights began to flicker on behind the windows that had been glaring out at him, so dark and foreboding.

In time, buses began to come up and stop, and students, like minnows escaping from a net, piled out and hurried through the frigid air to get into the relative warmth of the waiting school, which swallowed those minnows like a giant brown trout, lurking in some deep pool in a river.

A few students also rolled past in vehicles, those who lived far out in the boondocks, or even somewhere in town, whose parents had the means, and the desire, to let them drive their own vehicles to school. It wasn't such a common practice that Coal would not have noticed the white and light blue Dodge pickup, if it came. But it never did.

As silvery light began filtering over the school, and the last several vehicles trickled in and parked, Coal finally pulled across the street and parked at the school, right in the lane of traffic behind three vehicles he was essentially blocking in if they needed for whatever reason to leave.

He pinned his badge to the pocket of the blanket-lined blue jean jacket he had chosen to wear even though it was too cold for it. Going into the school, he watched the trickle of the last students making their way into the guts of the rooms so many of them despised, the same way he had at their age.

At the school office sat a woman wearing an olive-green dress outfit, whose raggedly seamed face belied the deep reddish black of her hair. She looked up at Coal through too-large glasses with a gold chain that attached to the stems, drooped down, and disappeared behind her neck.

"Good morning, Sheriff. How can I help you?"

"I'm not sure we've met, have we?" asked Coal.

"Most certainly not," she replied. "I would never have forgotten a face like yours. I'm Sally Edwards." She smiled and held out a hand that he shook and found surprisingly firm.

"Please call me Coal. The reason I came in was to see if I could have a word with one of your students—Troy Westerlind?"

Sally Edwards's brow furrowed. "Hmm . . . Well, I can't claim to be all-seeing, Coal, but I usually keep a pretty close eye on the comings and goings here, and Troy really stands out in a crowd—which you already know if you know him. I'm telling you that because I don't think I saw him come in yet this morning. But would you like me to have one of our aides run down to his class and see if he's in? We'd be happy to look."

"Could you? I'd sure appreciate it."

Sally Edwards summoned a cute little brunette in flare-legged jeans from the back of the room. With a big, shy smile for Coal, she slipped past him and hurried down the hall toward Mr. Barnhard's biology class. Three minutes later, she returned alone.

"I'm sorry, but Mr. Barnhard told me he hasn't seen Troy yet."

"Thank you, miss." Coal turned to catch the gleam in Sally Edwards's eyes. "I guess you do keep a pretty good eye out, don't you, Mrs. Edwards?"

"Oh, now—you need to call me Sally. You don't want the students to start thinking I'm old, do you?"

Coal grinned. "Heaven forbid! You're not much older than they are."

"Right! Talk like that would get you an A, Coal—if I were a teacher. And if you were my student."

"I'll keep that in mind—if you ever take up teaching. Well, thank you anyway—Sally. I don't suppose you could make a call to the police dispatcher if you see Troy make it in later, could you? I'd sure like to know."

"I would be delighted to."

Coal stepped back outside, adjusting his gun belt around his waist and peering up and down the block. He couldn't deny that he had been hoping to see Troy Westerlind this morning. The fact that he hadn't made it in was a bad sign he had been hoping not to see.

Pulling off his hat, Coal vigorously scrubbed his forehead with his hand, then slid the hat back on, drawing a deep breath of icy air that almost burned his throat. He tried mentally to go over his to-do list for the day, wishing fervently that it was a vacation day, or that Everett Sherman and Irene Boyer had been living inside the city limits when they chose to be murdered.

Sometime today, he needed to talk to Curlie Burks and Melissa Talty. He had to go make sure Hunter Jack was fed breakfast, since he had made his deputies swear not to open his cell door without him there. He needed to check on the fat farmer, Wilford Bayless, and see if he had regained consciousness yet, and it would be nice to have a long overdue visit with Annie Price, if she happened to be on duty when he went. If he found any spare time, he would make a call out to Kathy's, too, although he probably wouldn't be able to spare the time to go see her—as much as he wanted to. And he really needed at some point to start making the rounds of all Salmon's drinking establishments, asking about Everett Sherman and trying to see if he could turn up anyone else who might have a motive strong enough to want to see him dead. He didn't even think of Irene Boyer, whom he was almost positive was only collateral damage in the crime. She would probably still be alive today if she had not been friends with Sherman, or if she had stayed sequestered in the bathroom when the killing took place.

More important than everything else, however, Coal needed to follow up on the call from yesterday afternoon. What had become of Troy Westerlind, and where was he today? He prayed that the answer was going to be a simple one. *Something* had to go right in this county—sometimes.

The first move Coal made was to veer sharply away from his list of chores. He drove over to the city building, going inside to try and find Bob Wilson.

Bob, with his face looking like a bruised and swollen shambles, sat at a desk filling out paperwork. He heard Coal come in, but he didn't look up until he heard the door shut. When he saw Coal, he frowned.

"You look like used meat," said Coal.

Somehow, that got a grin out of Bob, a grin Coal hadn't been expecting to see for some time to come. "No doubt. You should see the other guy."

Coal laughed. He didn't want to rub salt in Bob's wounds by mentioning that "the other guy" looked like he had just stepped out of a health spa.

"What's up, Coal?"

"Well, I actually just came in to check on you and the chief. And whoever else got roughed up yesterday."

"Well, thanks," replied Bob dryly. "I guess we'll all live. How about you?"

"Never felt better on an hour of sleep," Coal said, wiping at his mustache. "Thanks for asking. So hey—there's no hard feelings about Hunter Jack, right?"

"Oh, hell no," Bob said. "No, I know you're just doing your job. It's probably a good thing you're around. That big jerk doesn't seem to have any respect for any other badge in this valley."

"No accounting for taste?" said Coal.

"None."

Grinning, Coal turned around, but he almost immediately turned back. "Oh! They told me you went to the school and found out who Troy Westerlind's girlfriend might be. True?"

"Yes. I talked to her yesterday."

"Great. I'd like to go over your notes with you. And did you hear about the battery call I went on out on Twenty-Eight around five-thirty or so yesterday evening?"

"I did hear something. What was that all about? I thought Nadine mentioned Westerlind."

"She did, and yes—he was the one the call was about." He went on to tell Bob about the call, including the red marks he had seen on Westerlind's hands when he went back in, then revealed the suspicious, significant circumstance of Troy Westerlind's not showing up for classes this morning. "Of course it's not your purview, so you won't have to deal with it, but sometime today either I'll have to go back out there, or send somebody else. I really need to see Troy Westerlind, face to face."

"I'll keep an eye out at the school," Bob volunteered. "Hopefully he's just playing hooky."

Coal nodded, raising his eyebrows. "Yes. Hopefully."

After leaving the police station, feeling overwhelmed, Coal finally did the smart thing and sat to jot down a list of priorities on a notepad. He got a solid list written, but try as he might he wasn't able to put it in any order of priority. So he would simply start putting a line through each of them as he finished.

First on the list, he stopped at Steele Memorial Hospital. The dark-haired, brown-eyed receptionist, Mandy, was at her desk, and she gave Coal a huge smile. "Aww . . . It's so nice to see you, Coal!"

"It sure is, Mandy."

They exchanged pleasantries for a few minutes before Mandy said, "Well, anyway, it's so nice to see you, but I don't imagine you came in just to talk to me!"

"Of course I did!"

She giggled, flipping her ponytail back behind her with one hand. "Nice answer. Well, I'm sorry to say Annie isn't in yet. We have two other nurses, though, if you'd like to get to know them."

"You're just giving me a hard time now," Coal said, feeling disappointed that Annie wasn't in, but not in any mood to allow Mandy to see it. "What I really need to do is check on a patient. Wilford Bayless?"

"Oh, my yes! Mr. Bayless. I heard he woke up early this morning!"

Coal stared at her until she started to look like she was feeling self-conscious. "Is everything all right?" she asked.

"Uh, yeah. Sorry! I'm a little out of sorts. Don't mind me. So you said he's awake! Can he have visitors?"

"Yes, I think so." She gave him directions to the room where they were keeping Wilford Bayless, and Coal headed that way, anxious to see how the man was doing after his hard fall.

Bayless, the man who could have passed for Burl Ives in his role as a semi-bad guy, in *The Big Country,* was alone in his room when Coal peeked in. Seeing no one else close by, Coal went in. Bayless's eyes were shut until Coal spoke his name.

The man turned his head gingerly. His vision obviously wasn't very clear, but after a few seconds his gaze focused in on Coal. "Sheriff," he said weakly.

"Mr. Bayless."

"Why are you here?" Unlike Mandy, Wilford Bayless didn't believe in pleasantries.

"To see how you arc."

"Looks like I'm fine, don't it?"

"Not so much," said Coal, matching the man's surly attitude because he saw no reason to act friendly.

"I'll be out of here soon," Bayless said. "So they tell me."

"Maybe I'll wait."

"For what?"

"To talk to you about pulling a shotgun on the local sheriff."

"Shotgun! Hell, I didn't pull no shotgun on nobody."

"Oh, come on," said Coal.

The man stared at him. After a while, Coal started to understand that the look in his eyes was that of a baffled man.

"You sayin' I pulled a shotgun? On *you?"*

"Listen, Bayless. What's your game?"

Bayless kept staring blankly.

"I'll be right back," Coal said, stepping out of the room. He wandered around until he found a nurse, and she took him to where

Dr. Levi Bent was cleaning up some instruments from stitching up a patient.

"Well, good morning, Sheriff. Can I help you?"

"Maybe. What's the story on Wilford Bayless?"

"The story? They told me you were there when he fell."

"I was. But that's just it—he's acting like he wasn't."

"Oh. Yes, that. No surprise at all. We're waiting to see, but it's not a sure thing he's going to gain his memory back of whatever happened right before he fell."

Coal stared at Dr. Bent, then finally let out a long sigh. "Well, great."

"What's wrong?"

"I came to write him a citation for pulling a shotgun on me, but how do you cite a man who can't even remember what he did?"

Dr. Bent grunted. "Right. Well, you might come back tomorrow. He's gained back more of his memory than we thought he might, in a fairly short time."

"Okay. I'll be back. Do me a favor, Doc."

"What's that?"

"Call me before you let him check out—that's *if* you can hold him."

CHAPTER THIRTY-ONE

Coal went back to Salmon High, armed now with the name of a girl whom students Bob Wilson had interviewed seemed pretty confident in saying was Troy Westerlind's girlfriend. He stopped at the main office, and the secretary, Sally Edwards, looked up from writing in a notepad when she heard him stop and saw his shadow loom across her desk. A bright smile burst over her face, crinkling the corners of her eyes.

"Well, hello, Coal! My, two visits in one day. I would start thinking you may be sweet on me if I didn't imagine you already have a bevy of girls to call on."

Coal laughed. "Oh, yeah. They're just falling all over me. Hey, Sally—I'm guessing Troy Westerlind hasn't shown up yet, right?"

"Right. Sorry."

"Okay, then the next number on my list is a little girl named Dawn Kelly? What about her?"

"So . . . Yes, I know Dawn. Sort of a surly little gal, Coal, and not your type at all."

Coal grinned. "Out of my age group, too. Is she here today?"

"I can't say as I actually saw her, but we can sure find out really quick. Hold on."

Once again, after looking at records to see what class Dawn Kelly was registered for, Sally Edwards called the little brunette over. "Miriam, could you do me one more big favor and run down to Mrs. Stalnaker's class? I need to see if Dawn Kelly came in today, and if she did, we need to see her." She looked up quickly at Coal for confirmation. "Right? You need to talk to her?"

"Yes, ma'am, if possible."

The sound of Miriam's dainty feet went pattering off down the hall, and Coal looked back at Sally Edwards. "Mrs. Stalnaker . . . Cynthia Batterton has her as well, doesn't she?"

"She's the senior English teacher, so yes, I'm certain she does."

It was another two minutes before Coal heard footsteps coming back from the direction Miriam had gone in, and she returned, now with a second girl. The friendly, helpful look normally about Miriam's face now looked strained and guarded, and Coal noticed that she seemed to make a point of avoiding getting too close to the other girl.

The girl with her was a little heavy set, although not in a way that would make her unattractive. She simply would not have been known to anyone as being dainty. She had sleek, shiny, honey-colored hair, straight as a wire fence, and pulled behind her head in a loose ponytail. Her eyes, a beautiful gray blue in color, with dark gray rings surrounding the irises, had a hard, mistrusting look, the kind of look that doesn't come and go, but resides permanently.

"This is Dawn," Sally seemed to feel obligated to introduce the girl when she stopped in front of Coal, looking up at him defiantly. "Dawn, this is Sheriff Savage."

"Okay," Dawn replied. Her eyes, if anything, grew harder, more hooded. Inwardly, she was preparing to shut down, or to shuttle away any and all of Coal's questions with seething anger and blatant disrespect for authority.

"Is there some place Dawn and I could talk that's more private?" Coal asked Sally.

"Oh, sure, you bet. Both of you follow me around the counter, okay? I'll put you in the principal's office for a little while. He's in a conference for an hour or so anyway."

Coal let Dawn, looking stiff and edgy, go in front of him, then he followed her and Sally to a nicely arranged office at the far back of the office area. Stepping inside, Coal caught the faint, pleasant odor of men's cologne, a scent he didn't recognize. But of course he wouldn't, since he wore none and couldn't name a single cologne, men's *or* women's. He only knew this one smelled nice, and because it lingered so, it was obviously a reputable brand.

"Why don't you have a seat?" suggested Coal.

"Do I have to?" Dawn stared him down.

"I'd appreciate it, let's put it that way."

With a disgruntled sigh, the girl turned to the chair closest to her, took a step sideways to grab the back of it, straightened it around, and sat. Coal went behind the principal's desk and wheeled a nice, wooden chair with a seat padded in red- and white-striped fabric around in front of the girl. "Your principal looks pretty into the school colors," Coal said conversationally.

Dawn glanced at the chair, looking far too busy to care about such mundane topics. "Sure, I guess."

Coal sat down. He had thought about offering Dawn to trade chairs, since this one was much softer, but he was pretty sure she would have scoffed at the offer, and the gesture would gain him nothing.

"Dawn? I've been told by a good friend of mine, Bob Wilson, that you and Troy Westerlind are pretty close. Is that true?"

"Maybe. Why?"

"Well, I'll tell you. I took a fight call out to their house yesterday afternoon, around maybe five or so. More like a battery call. Do you know what that is?"

"Battery?" Her wheels turned fast behind her eyes. "I guess like hitting and stuff."

"Exactly. So the way the call came in was that maybe it wasn't really a fight, but more like one person beating on another one."

She watched him as long as she could, then looked away after she couldn't stare him down anymore.

"Have you heard anything from Troy since last night?"

"Uh-uh."

"Does that seem normal for you and Troy?"

"Sure. There's a lot of days we don't talk unless we're in school."

"Does he miss a lot of school? Just not show up?"

She shrugged, looking affectedly bored. "I guess so. Maybe. I'm not really sure."

Coal smiled. "We could go pull up his records, I guess. Do you want to wait?"

She quickly shook her head. "No. No. So no, I guess maybe he doesn't miss school all that much."

"Do you think it's concerning that we got a battery call at his house and then the next day he doesn't come in?"

"I guess so. Sure."

"Do you know his father?"

He was watching the girl closely when he asked, and the hooded look about her eyes seemed to deepen, while her eyes themselves seemed faintly to darken.

"A little, I guess. I mean I've seen him."

"But you haven't spoken to him?"

She hesitated far too long, during which time she tried to meet his gaze, but failed, looking disgusted to be bothered with such a question. When he kept waiting on her, the pressure for Dawn was simply too much.

"I guess I've kind of spoken to him. Or it was more like he spoke to me."

"What was that about?"

"Nothing important. Just stuff."

"It would be nice to know more," Coal pressed. "Did he seem like a nice father?"

Dawn scoffed, then hurried her glance away from him and closed her expression off.

"No? Not a nice father?"

"Hey." The girl's voice had gotten huskier. "I don't know how I can really help you with this. Can I go back to class?"

Coal gave nothing. "Dawn? I'm pretty worried about Troy. I saw something at the house that makes me think his dad might have beaten him, but unless somebody helps me I'm not sure how to help Troy."

"Why would you want to help him anyway?" Dawn asked, meeting his eyes head-on.

"Why? Because he's in my county, and because he might be in trouble. That's what I do. I've got my own kids, Dawn. I hate to see them in trouble, and I hate it when anyone else's kids are in trouble."

Coal saw Dawn's jaw muscles grow tighter, just before she dropped her gaze to her hands, which were folded in her lap.

"Dawn?"

"Stop calling me that!" the girl burst out. "Okay?"

"All right. Sorry about that. I didn't mean to offend you." Coal was almost thankful for his experiences with Katie Leigh right now. She had helped form the patience he was using now, when he would have liked to snap back at Dawn. But there was one sure way to get this girl to clam up forever, and snapping at her was it.

After a while, Dawn drew a deep breath, and sighed it out. Then another. She looked up at him. "It's all right. Sorry I got mad."

A warm feeling went through Coal, as he felt the slightest bit of the ice between him and Dawn Kelly start to melt away. "You don't have to be sorry. I hate it when salesmen keep saying my name over and over again. It just sounds fake, right?"

She looked up at him. "Yeah, kind of."

"Well, I'm about the least fake guy around here. When I say your name, it's just what I do with my kids. But I won't do it anymore if it bothers you."

"No, it's all right. I guess I don't mind too much."

"All right. And I'd like it if you call me Coal, too. Deal?"

"Sure, I guess."

"Good. Well, what do you think about Troy? Do you know if his father has ever hit him before?"

She hesitated for five or ten seconds this time.

"Dawn? Oh—sorry!"

This time the girl smiled. "No, it's fine. *Coal.*" She gave him a smile, the first real smile, and it warmed his heart.

"So . . . what do you think then? Do you know if Troy's father has ever beat him?"

She nodded, not meeting his eyes this time.

"Yes? He has?"

She nodded again, more vigorously. He could see this time that she was fighting against emotions.

"Bad?" he asked.

Another nod. "Yeah. Pretty bad."

"Do you know if it was reported?"

She instantly shook her head.

"You don't know? Or it wasn't?"

"It wasn't."

"Okay. Did he come to school right after that?"

"It was a couple days that time."

"All right. Well, do you think it could be serious enough that I should go back out there? Do you think Troy would answer the door for me if his father wasn't around?"

She shrugged. "I guess. I mean . . . he might."

"Hey. Dawn? Can you look at me?" Coal wheeled his chair slightly closer, close enough that if she put her hand toward him he could have raised his own and touched her fingertips.

Her gaze flickered across his lower legs and knees, judging the distance by which he had grown closer. Any fear seeped out of her eyes as she raised them to his. He could no longer detect any anger. Now there was only mistrust.

"You seem frightened about something."

"I'm not scared of anything." Her voice had grown husky again.

"I am," he said. "Do you want to know what?"

She shrugged.

"I'm scared that any kids could be in trouble in my county, and if I don't know enough about it to help them, it could get worse." When Dawn had no reply, he went on: "I've seen a lot of bad stuff. Way more than I could ever tell you. I don't want you to go through things like that, Dawn. I wish you'd trust me."

For several seconds, Dawn's chin began to quiver, but her jaw hardened again, and she got herself back under control. "I've seen a lot of bad stuff too, Sheriff." She tried to look up at him but dropped her eyes once more. It didn't get past him that she had slipped back into calling him "Sheriff".

They both waited out a long silence. At last, the girl's eyes came slowly back up to his. "Hey—there's a new girl here. Her name's Katie Savage?"

"Yeah?"

"Well . . . Is that your daughter?"

"It is. And Virgil is my son."

Her eyes said she was searching her memory banks, but she finally shook her head. "I don't know him. But I know Katie. She seems like a really sweet girl."

"Thanks," he said with a smile. "That means a lot to me, Dawn."

"Sure."

"Do you want to tell me anything else?" he asked.

"No. Not really. I guess I should probably get back to my class, right? I'm not really so great at English as it is."

Coal laughed. "Yeah, that's a tough one, especially when you get to be a senior, huh?"

Dawn Kelly gave him another smile. "Yeah. Especially."

Coal stood up, so Dawn stood too. They walked to the door of the office, stopping together before Coal touched the doorknob.

"Hey. Dawn?"

"Yeah?" She looked up at him.

"I want you to know I'm here for you, any time you need. Okay? You just call, and I'll be there as fast as I can. Just like I would for anyone else in my county."

"Yeah?" she repeated. "Okay. Okay, I guess I can dig that." Without any warning, the girl hesitantly brought her hand up, holding it out to Coal. Surprised, he took it and gently shook.

He let the hand fall, met the girl's smile, and opened the door for her. "I guess we'd both better get back to work."

"Okay. Thanks . . . Coal."

They walked to the counter, where Sally Edwards, seeming surprised at the change in Dawn's demeanor, held out a slip of paper to her. "You just take this back and show it to Mrs. Stalnaker, sweetheart. See you later."

"See ya later," replied Dawn, and with one more soft-eyed look at Coal, she walked off down the hall as fast as she could without breaking into a run.

Sally turned and looked up at Coal. "Coal, I have to tell you I have never in the three years I've known her seen that girl act like that around an adult. Whatever did you do?"

"I just treated her like a human being, Sally. A human being who needed a friend."

CHAPTER THIRTY-TWO

Coal went up to the jail to bring Hunter Jack a big roast beef sandwich and a bowl of soup from Wally's. The Shoshone acted more recalcitrant toward him than Coal had ever seen before, making him doubly glad that he had ordered the others not to open his cell.

"I have to ask what's going on with you this morning, Badger. This is Savage here, remember? We're supposed to be on the same side—at least as much as possible."

Jack lay there on his bunk working his jaw muscles, his left paw dragging on the concrete floor like the oar of a canoe. His tray of food sat untouched on the floor several inches from his hand. The Shoshone finally looked over at Coal, his eyes dark and hooded as Coal had seen them before, but never for him.

"You're done talking, I guess. Sure wish I knew what I did."

Jack let out a long sigh. "Ah, it ain't you, Savage. Hold up." The big man struggled up to a sitting position on the sagging cot. "It ain't you, man."

Coal felt relieved. "What happened, Badger? This isn't like you."

"Yeah. Sorry. I had a bad medicine dream, all I can say. Dreamed I was gonna get hanged, an' ever'body was laughin'. You was the one leadin' me up on the gallows, an' you had this grin on your face you was tryin' to hide. But I could see it, Savage—plain as day."

"That's a heck of a dream," said Coal. "That would sure set a fella off. Don't you worry. We're going to do whatever we can here to get you off. All right? I'll be up talking to the judge later on your behalf."

"Yeah. Sure. After this last thing, though . . . Ah, hell, Savage. You know I got nothin' left to put up anyway. Nothin' but maybe my house. An' I think my car's worth more than that house."

"We'll see," Coal replied. "Don't lose hope."

Coal took a chance and let Jack out so he could go down the hall and use the restroom, then put him back in the cell, all without even a hint that the big Shoshone might be thinking about doing anything stupid.

"I told the other guys not to let you out, Badger," he told him as he stood outside the locked cell door. "Just so you know. They can give you water through the bars, if you want, and that's it. It's for your own protection, and theirs."

"Uh. Okay, good to know. Don't blame you. I'd prob'ly kill those two dumb big oafs."

"Talking like that won't help your cause any," Coal said frankly. "If the judge or prosecutor ever hears anything like that out of you, it's going to be ugly."

"Sorry. I'll shut up."

"I'll be back with supper sometime before I head home. Any requests?"

"Food," said Jack. "Some kind of food I can chew an' swallow."

Coal chuckled. "Food it is."

Coal spoke with Judge Sinclair not long after leaving the cellblock. They had a nice cup of coffee, and both of them agreed on the taste of it. Judge Sinclair had a fat Cuban cigar, and agreed not to make Coal have one too. They agreed that it was cold enough to freeze the balls off a brass monkey, a saying which had originated during the Civil War, Coal informed the judge, and which had nothing to do with primates or their reproductive organs. They agreed on that story.

But the agreements ceased there. When it came to what the two of them thought about Hunter Jack, and his current status as prisoner of Lemhi County, they did not see eye to eye. Coal wanted Jack free, and the judge wanted him to rot in his cell until the trial.

Judge Sinclair, one, Coal Savage—zero. Hunter Jack remained a big bird of prey in a cage, and Coal didn't even have the heart to go back and let him know.

Among the more important things Coal accomplished that day was to arrange and facilitate a meeting down at Jay Castillo's Salmon River Coffee Shop of all the local law enforcement, including Lyle Gentry, who was more than happy to get out of the outlying environs of his jurisdiction and into the semi-civilization of Salmon for a while. William Verret and Horace Teal, the police department's highest-ranking volunteers, were even invited, although that was a decision Coal lived to regret.

The meeting started out amiably, mostly because the beginnings of it were dining and sipping coffee—or in Coal's case, slurping coffee. They pushed three tables together clear in the back, then talked Jay Castillo into making that area off limits to other diners. Coal sawed through and gulped down over a pound of smoky brisket and six fried eggs, drank two glasses of milk, and then, knowing his muscles had been replenished for the day, he opened the meeting.

There wasn't a whole lot of information brought up that was new to Coal, unfortunately, except that Bob Wilson had gone to Dawn Kelly's residence, after talking to Coal, and managed to get from Dawn's makeup-sullied mother, Amber, the name of a kid who lived a block or so away that her daughter seemed to spend a lot of time with, with or without Troy Westerlind around. He had also managed to locate the address, and it was that of one of

Salmon's frequent boozers, Zack Moore. His son, Dawn's friend, was named Dale.

Bob also told Coal that Tim Lacey, although he hadn't made it to this meeting, was out and about, and although he couldn't actually take up full-time law enforcement duties until fully healed up, he had started asking questions around about the murder victim's relationship to Curlie Burks and Melissa Talty.

It seemed, according to rumor and much to Coal's surprise, that there was bad blood between Burks and Everett Sherman.

"Bad blood?" Coal echoed once his initial reaction was passed. "What kind of bad blood?"

"Something about Curlie losing a game of pool against Sherman."

Coal stared for several seconds, digesting this. "You're kidding."

Bob almost smiled, which for Bob was usually his "smile". "All right, it's a bit deeper than that. Somebody told Tim he heard Curlie actually lost a vehicle to Sherman in that game, and then he welched."

"Oh. Okay. That's pretty big. Is that all Tim got?"

"Yes."

"Okay, well, I guess I should be hitting the bars tonight, instead of going home," Coal said.

"I don't know why the hell y'all are even going through this stuff," said William Verret suddenly, his hard mouth framed by his graying horseshoe mustache. As Coal had first noticed about Verret, his gravelly voice, sounding like it needed to be cleared, was to Coal's ears akin to the screeching of a bobcat. Verret, black cowboy hat firmly settled on his head, sat just down from Coal and to his left.

"You don't know why what?" Bob Wilson asked, cutting off the angry reply Coal was forming.

Verret turned to glare at Bob. "Come on! We all know who killed Sherman. Why the hell is everybody wastin' time an' good money on this bull when the guy who did the killing is already sittin' up there in the county calaboose?"

"I agree," inserted bull-necked Horace Teal, seated right across from Verret because the two of them seemed to be connected at the brain stem. "Don't we got better things to do than chase fake leads around the valley? We c'n sure try hard as hell to pin stuff on a dozen or more people it wouldn't be hard to prove hated Everett Sherman, but only one of them people has proven himself willing to kill people."

Coal was seething inside, so he was loath to speak what was on his mind without thinking it through extra hard. He was surprised to hear Jordan Peterson speak up—mild-mannered Jordan, who as the youngest one here, and a "newbie" to boot, generally didn't seem to feel welcome to throw his opinions out there with long-time peacekeepers.

"You fellas know why Hunter Jack went up to the pen—right?" Jordan looked all around the table, trying to meet every eye he could. "Is anybody not clear about that, because it seems like a pretty big deal."

Everyone stared at Jordan, from Coal on down the line. It was slit-eyed William Verret who finally growled a reply. "No, rookie. Why don't you just inform all the rest of us Salmon hicks so we're as educated as you?"

Grant and Jordan both looked at Coal at the same time, but it was Bob Wilson, seated across from Coal, who gave his boot a hard kick at the very moment Coal was about to come up out of his chair.

Coal glared at Bob, the only person in this meeting he had known for more than four months, and a man he loved like a brother. Bob gave him back a little nod, holding up a placating hand, then turned to give a withering look to both Verret and Teal.

"You two can just simmer down a bit and listen to what Peterson has to say," Bob said, his voice far more level than Coal's had been about to be. "You're in over your heads here on this case, so you'd better listen close."

"Oh, that's rich," growled William Verret. "You were the worst of everybody here when that Injun stabbed Tim Lacey."

Bob continued to stare, all his attention now directed to Verret. "That was a stabbing. It has nothing to do with this murder case."

"Boys, Bob's right about this," Chief George finally cut in, seeing his job clear, to keep the peace at least between his underlings, if it couldn't be kept anywhere else in the valley. "Deputy, why don't you go ahead and enlighten these two?"

Jordan nodded and turned back to divide his attention equally between Horace Teal and William Verret. "When Hunter Jack went up to the pen, it was because he punched a guy—with his bare hands. The guy raped his little sister."

Verret glared Jordan down. It was plain he hated being called on the carpet right when he was talking so tough. "Yeah, I heard some kind of bull like that once. Nobody never proved it was true, though."

"Make a call if you don't believe it, Bill," said Bob Wilson. "Go do some research before you make a bigger fool of yourself. Jordan happens to be right, and it isn't just a rumor. But go check on it yourself if you don't want to believe us."

Verret scoffed. "Well, hell, I gotta get back to work. I ain't got time for this bull anyhow." With that, the angered would-be policeman jabbed himself up from the table, turned, and stalked to the counter. The rest of them waited until he had paid his bill before anyone spoke.

"You have any questions, Horace?" asked Chief George, apparently warmed up now to keeping his troops in line.

"I guess not, no." But he turned to Bob anyway. "So that story's true, huh? One punch an' that Injun kills a guy that raped his sister?"

"Yes. It's true."

"Okay." He shrugged with his hands and laid them on the table as he took a deep breath and gusted it out. "I wish somebody woulda said that sooner. Bill had me pretty much convinced that was a made-up story."

"Anybody else have questions?" asked Coal, ignoring Teal. "Or anything to add?"

No one did. They got up and paid their bills, then filed out, and Coal had just stopped at the Thunderbird with Jordan and Grant when Tammy, the beautiful blond waitress from the Coffee Shop, came rushing out after them. "Coal, wait!"

He turned to her as she rushed up. "Yeah, Tammy. What is it?"

"Your dispatcher just called for you. Shc said they just called from the tire place to say a guy was in there getting tires filled. Some guy you had asked them about?"

"Oh! Shoot! Thanks, Tammy. I appreciate the message."

As Tammy turned to go back in, Coal looked at Grant and Jordan. "I might need to have you two tag along. That's Joe Teton getting the air put back in his tires. Follow me down there, will you?"

Coal raced the Thunderbird down to the tire store, with Jordan and Grant close behind him. They all pulled into the lot and didn't bother parking in any way special before jumping out to go inside. Joe Teton was at the counter with his wallet when Coal walked up directly behind him. Jordan came up on Teton's left shoulder, and Grant closed upon the right.

"Getting some tires fixed, huh, Mr. Teton?"

Joe Teton whirled around at the sound of Coal's voice. Looking from Coal, to Jordan, to Grant, the Shoshone quickly and accurately assessed the situation.

"Circle the wagons around the redskin, uh?"

Coal smiled. "Something like that. So Joe—you wouldn't be planning on taking any trips, would you?"

Joe could only stare. "No. I mean, no sir. Just need to get my tires fixed an' get startin' to work again."

"Those your boys over there by the window?" asked Grant.

Two boys with the same color of skin as Joe sat on the vinyl-covered bench in front of the sunny south window of the shop. No one else was in the place, and the boys looked like little Tetons. There was no denying them. So Joe Teton said nothing.

"Those boys look old enough to be in school," Coal judged. "Stay home sick, did they, Mr. Teton?"

"No. Just . . ."

"It's illegal keeping your kids out of school if they don't have a good excuse," pressed Coal. "Why aren't your boys in school?"

Teton's face was noncommittal. He kept his eyes on Coal's chin, because heaven forbid he might look challenging by looking him right in the eyes.

When it became obvious that Joe Teton had no answer for Coal, Coal said, "Hey, Mr. Teton, how fast do you suppose that old pickup of yours can go, anyhow?"

"I never tried to see," said Teton.

"I have one about the same shape," said Coal, casually. "I'll bet if I get it running fifty-five miles an hour it's a really good day. And shoot—the gasoline it puts down, I can hardly drive past one service station when I'm traveling."

Teton patiently stood admiring Coal's chin and chest. He had nothing to say. The store clerk, wearing a gray uniform shirt that said "Darrin" above one pocket, stood silently waiting behind him to settle the bill for checking the Shoshone's tires and filling them again with air.

"That Thunderbird of mine, now. Man, that thing can fly. Ninety on a straightaway is nothing for that 429 Thunderjet under the hood. Shoot, I'll bet it wouldn't be a problem going one-twenty."

Joe Teton's eyes seemed to keep getting duller and duller, as he listened to Coal tell him way more information than he really needed.

"Takin' my boys back home, as soon as I pay for the air in my tires."

"What's that, Mr. Teton?" Coal pressed.

"I said—I am not leavin' town. But also—I didn't do nothin' you wouldn't have done for a good friend, Savage. Guess I just take whatever you can dish out. But what about my boys? Where do they go if I ain't home no more?"

"Exactly what are you trying to tell me, Mr. Teton?" asked Coal, his heart starting to race. Was this the end of the line for the investigation into the murders of Everett Sherman and Irene Boycr? Could it truly be this simple?

"I'm guessin' I need some kind o' lawyer, huh?" Joe Teton said. "That's right, uh?"

Coal drew a deep, calming breath. "Yes, Joe," he used the man's given name for the first time. "I'm going to guess that might be the best idea you've had in the last two or three days."

CHAPTER THIRTY-THREE

Coal, Grant, and Jordan gathered together in the Thunderbird after Joe Teton and his boys headed for home, because the Bird had the best heater.

They sat there together, watching Teton's pickup roll down the street, then finally turn on 93, headed, hopefully, back to the Indian village. Coal would be following up on that within minutes, just to be sure.

After what seemed an extended silence, Jordan spoke from the back seat, leaning forward to rest his arms across the back of Grant's seat. "All right, guys, I don't want to sound like a total retard, but . . . Did he just confess? Are we actually wrapping this case up?"

Coal turned his head to look at his former night jailer. He stared at him for several seconds, knowing what he believed in his heart, but not daring to say it. He finally looked over at Grant, making no reply to Jordan.

Grant seemed to have been waiting for Coal's and Jordan's attention. "There's something weird here. I don't want to burst anybody's bubble, but there's more here than meets the eye. Unless we can bring Teton in and get an actual, signed confession, I don't think we dare charge him and write Curlie Burks off completely."

Coal let out a long, discontented sigh. "Yeah, you're right. I hate to say it, but you are. And I also don't feel great about closing this case out and starting to prepare it for court until we've caught up to all three of the kids that were supposedly in that pickup Curlie saw. What if the whole case rests on them? What if they saw something that could wrap it all up in a nice, tidy package? What if they turned out to be our key witnesses?"

"Right," agreed Grant.

"So we're sure those kids were up there?" Jordan asked.

Coal gave him his theory about that, about how he didn't think Curlie would have mentioned a specific truck and a specific description of its driver if the truck and the driver weren't really there, when he would be much smarter simply to make up a fake truck, and a fake description of a driver.

Jordan nodded at the end of Coal's explanation. "Yeah, you're right. That makes total sense. They had to have been up there."

"You two have any plans for this evening?" asked Coal.

They both said no, although Coal knew Grant would be antsy to get home to his wife and kids. He made his plan for the evening out of respect for that.

"All right. Jordan, why don't you take five or six hours off and come back this evening? Grant, if you can give me just one hour, maybe around seven o'clock to eight, then Jordan and I can handle the rest. What I'd like to do is start hitting all the bars, and especially the ones with pool tables in them. I want to find out if there's anyone who can feed us some detail about that big bet Curlie and Sherman supposedly made over the pool game. I honestly don't believe Curlie killed anybody, but with that blood on his hands, and now that vehicle title covered in blood, I just really want some answers. If nothing else, Curlie might not be the murderer, but I think he has several other charges coming. We just need to figure out for sure what they are."

After finalizing plans to meet up again at the jail around six-thirty, the two deputies got out to go to their own vehicles, and Coal headed down Main and turned on 93. He turned in at the Indian village and drove down to Joe Teton's address. Sure enough, the pickup was there. Coal was a little surprised that Teton had caved in so easily to everything he had said about trying to get away. He hoped he wasn't missing something, but if he was he couldn't think what it might be.

He had started to drive on down the road when a thought struck him, making him pull a little ways down the street, to one of the nicer shacks in the neighborhood—but still little more than a shack, all the same.

Glancing up and down the street to give all the other residences the once over, he went ahead and threw the transmission in park, shut off the engine, and got out.

Going up to knock on the door of this residence, he waited slightly off to one side, hopefully out of the line of fire if someone decided to put a load of buckshot through their door. At one time he might have felt like he was only being paranoid. In this valley, now? He felt like he was merely being safe.

A heavy-set woman whose cheeks pressed up so high they made her lower eyelids disappear came to the door. She looked him up and down. "Yes?"

"I'm Sheriff Savage, ma'am. Would you mind if I had a word with you?"

"I don't think so. About what?"

"To clarify," Coal said, "you . . . don't think you would mind?"

She stared at him, not trying to hide her confusion. Finally, she said, "I don't mind. But what is it about?"

"I want to ask you a few questions about Joe Teton. Do you know who that is?"

"Of course." She pointed at Teton's house. "He lives right there."

"Good. How long have you known him?"

"I don't know. Many years."

"Is he a nice guy?"

"Sure. He is always nice to our family."

"He has kids, right? What about a wife?"

"His wife died of the liver thing," she replied. "But he does have two kids. Two little boys, Pete and Nathan."

"Good kids?"

"Yes, I like them."

"What does Joe do for a living?"

"He worked on a ranch for a long time. But I think he got hurt or somethin'. He hasn't been workin' much these days."

"So he's lived right there as long as you've known him?"

"Yes."

"Do you know if he has any other family?"

"Not like blood family, if that's what you mean."

"Yes, blood family."

"No. Just them two boys."

"So what did you mean when you said 'not like blood family'? Does he have someone else who's like family, somebody that could look out for his boys if something happened to him?"

"Yeah, I think. Or maybe. I mean, I think me an' my husband would take them two boys if Joe was gone."

"But you were thinking of someone else?"

"Yes." She looked up and down the street. "Hey, you can come in for a little while if you want. Pretty cold out, uh?"

"Thank you," said Coal, and he went in with her. A man who appeared to be appreciably older than the woman sat on a broken-down sofa watching a rerun of *Bewitched.* He looked over and raised a hand in greeting to Coal.

"How. Say, you old Prince Savage's boy? What's your name?"

"Coal. Yes, Prince was my father."

"My knees are bad, Savage, or I'd get up. Sorry. I'm glad you come home to the valley. Always liked old Prince."

"Hey . . . are you Buck? Buck Darnell?"

The man's face broke into a grin that made his eyes disappear, and his face turn into a deeply creased road map. "Yes, sir. Yes, sir, that's me. Old Prince an' me, we was both in that war," said

Buck Darnell. This made Buck the father of the woman Coal had been talking to, because Coal knew who Buck's wife had been and she had died several years earlier.

"I remember, I remember." Coal walked over and held out his hand, and Darnell reached up and shook with him. "It's good to see you again, Buck. It's been a lot of years."

"Yep, sure has. Back when you saw me before, I could still set on a bronco. Not no more."

"Well, you have a well-broke one under you now," said Coal, indicating the couch with a grin.

"Sure, sure. Broke down, anyhow."

After the exchange of niceties with his father's old friend, the heavy-set woman who turned out to be Darnell's daughter, Renée, warmed up a few notches. As was usually the case, once one tribe member accepted a white man, others usually followed.

"Outside, you were about to tell me about somebody else you had thought of, Renée. Somebody else like family to Joe Teton."

"Yes. Maybe you already understand about the People, as us Shoshones call ourselves. Maybe you understand about how we're all like a big family. We try to take care of our own people. But Joe Teton has one man who's like a brother to him, and I think if he had to, he would take Joe Teton's boys."

"Hunter Jack," said Coal before Renée could say it.

She nodded, almost smiling, but with the size of her cheeks a smile might have rendered her sightless, so she didn't. "Yes, Hunter Jack—Dark Badger, we old members call him."

After Coal finished talking to Buck and Renée, he went out and decided to go up and down the street a little more, talking to other people. He got much the same story from the few others, not only on this street, but throughout the village, who answered the door: Everyone seemed to like and respect Joe Teton, all of them swore he loved his boys dearly, and almost to a person they said they would care for Pete and Nathan Teton, but that Joe would most likely choose the man who was like a blood brother to him to take them in: Hunter Jack.

In the Shoshone village, Coal never managed to connect with another person who was good friends with his father, Prince. That friendship made him return once more to the Buck Darnell residence before driving out of the village. He simply felt like he could get more open answers from a man who had a previous connection to him.

Renée let Coal in again, and with her permission he went straight over to Buck and crouched down. “One more question, Mr. Darnell. If it’s all right.”

“It is all right—if you will call me Buck instead of Mr. Darnell. That is what your father called me.”

“I’m happy to, Buck. Listen. I don’t want to make you feel like you are hurting a friend, but I need a truthful answer from you about Joe Teton.”

“I only tell true answers,” said the old man, his eye corners crinkling up, even though this time he hardly seemed to be smiling.

“Do you think Joe Teton feels strongly enough about Hunter Jack, as his brother, to kill somebody for him?”

Buck Darnell had drawn all his attention away from the television now. He studied Coal for a long moment. “Yes. If he thought Jack was in bad danger.”

“Has Teton ever acted before like he would kill somebody?”

“Joe *has,* Coal Savage.”

“Has what?”

“Joe Teton has killed people,” said old Buck Darnell, with a completely straight face. “Lots of people.”

CHAPTER THIRTY-FOUR

Coal wasn't sure what to think, even once he got over old Buck Darnell's more than startling statement and heard the rest of the story—that Joe Teton had been in the Army and had fought valiantly in the Korean War, with a collection of medals, including two Purple Stars, to show for it. Coal couldn't help his estimation of Teton going up.

On the other hand, he also couldn't ignore a simple fact of nature: Having killed before, and killed often, made it easier for most people to kill again.

All in all, in Coal's mind, his case against Joe Teton was greatly strengthened by the time he drove away from the Buck Darnell home, and one of the surest nails in Teton's coffin was the way Darnell answered Coal's question about whether or not Teton had ever had any interaction with Everett Sherman.

"He damn sure did," Darnell said, and then he proceeded to tell Coal about the recent day when Sherman had come racing recklessly through the village with Irene Boyer in his pickup, driven up on Teton's lawn and got stuck. "Joe hit that old boy's truck with a rock 'bout as hard as he could, an' that little red-haired guy smacked him in the eye real good. That's why Joe's still got what's left of that shiner now."

"What did Teton have to say about that?"

"You're one o' the good fellows, right, Sheriff? 'Cause I like Joe Teton."

"I'm on his side if he's innocent, Buck," he said.

"Good. The thing is, Joe yelled at that guy that he was gonna kill 'im, if he ever come back here again. Ever'body on this street heard that—not just me."

After leaving the Sho-Ban village, Coal decided to take a little bit of a break, which he called part of his job because of still needing to talk to Wilford Bayless, and he stopped at Steele Memorial. Annie Price was in now, looking unreasonably beautiful for a woman whose job was dealing day in and day out with blood and guts. She was having a good day, too, and their conversation, such as it was, remained light and playful. But she was also pretty busy, so they didn't have too much time together before Coal decided to make the most of his visit and go down to see Bayless.

"He's still about the same," Dr. Bent told Coal when he ran into him in the hallway and the doctor informed him that Bayless was sedated and sleeping. "He's showing good signs, overall, but he still doesn't seem to have picked up much memory of anything that happened before he fell."

Coal drew a deep breath. "Doc, any chance that he might have seen a way to get out a citation and possible jail time by pretending not to remember things?"

Bent shrugged. "I can't say no. No one could know that. But I doubt it. I think that big boy is cantankerous enough that if he had pulled a shotgun on somebody he'd be proud and loud about admitting it."

Nodding, Coal said, "I guess that's about what I figured too."

After the hospital, Coal returned to the high school. Sally Edwards laughed out loud when she saw him walking up to her station at the counter. "Well, Coal Savage, I'm going to have to be more careful about my makeup and hair from now on if this keeps up. I'm starting to believe you're only coming here to flirt with me."

"Oh, man, you caught me. Well, since the jig's up about that, Sally—since I'm already here, I don't suppose you might be able to scare up a student by the name of Dale Moore, would you?"

"Now that one I can help you with," she said proudly.

"Great. Why the big smile, if I might ask?"

"Oh, that Dale. Such a nice, polite kid," Sally said. "He always says hi to me when he comes by. Sometimes in the spring or fall he'll even bring me a flower."

"That's kind of strange for a high school kid," remarked Coal.

"It is. Yes. But he seems very sincere. I always got a feeling he doesn't get too much attention at home. When I used to work at the grade school is when I first got to know him, and you never saw a kid who hung out in here more, always coming up to talk. Later on, he started making a point of sidling around behind my desk and stealing a quick hug from me, when none of the other kids were around."

"Aw. Sounds like a kid that just needs some love. So he's still like that?"

"Oh, well, he doesn't do too much hugging anymore. I mean, he will, but he's a lot more timid about it. You know—trying to keep up the tough guy image. It's a hard job, they say. I'm sure you know all about that." She gave him a big grin and a wink.

Laughing, Coal said, "You nailed me to the wall, right there. So, Dale . . ."

"Oh, yes! Sorry," said Sally, letting out a laugh. "I'm like 'Old Lonely', the Maytag Repairman, I guess!"

Sally sent a different aide down the hall after Dale Moore, and a kid returned with her that Coal would have put at a glance in the group of kids who never did anything spectacular in school, never gleaned a lot of attention, from girls *or* other boys, and always flew "just under the radar", as the saying went. He wore tan polyester pants that were a little too short—what kids referred to as "floods", or "high waters", and a short-sleeved shirt of Salmon Savage orange, with a large, bold black number 50 centered in the middle of it.

Sally put Coal and Dale in a different room this time, because the principal was back in his office. The room was darker, dingier, with no window in the door through which to look out on the world. When Coal shut the door and turned to Dale Moore, the fine-haired blond boy was staring at the closed door and starting to fidget, as if he had just been shut behind bars.

"So you're Dale," Coal started out. "Well, Dale, I'm Coal. I got stuck in the sheriff's job here. Silly thing to do, huh?"

Dale tried hard to meet Coal's gaze, and he tried hard to smile. "I guess so."

Coal chuckled. "Maybe you know my daughter, Dale. Katie Savage?"

Dale's eyes brightened with recognition. "Oh, yeah. Sure. She's a real nice girl."

"She didn't pay you to tell me that, did she?" Coal asked, then grinned and winked at Dale.

Dale's laugh was the sound of a kid starting to warm up. "Naw. Everybody knows she's nice. You adopted Cynthia Batterton too, right?"

"Oh, you know Cynthia too? Well, I didn't actually adopt her, but yeah, she does live with us. Her dad was a good friend of mine."

Dale only nodded that time. Coal sensed that the boy wanted to say something about K. T. Batterton, maybe offer condolences. But as with most kids his age, the words didn't come.

"So, Dale, do you have any idea why I wanted to talk to you?"

The question might have been too soon, but maybe with questions like this there never would be a good time. It was a question he hadn't asked Dawn Kelly at all, because his guts had told him to make friends with her first, before dropping the bomb of asking what she could tell him about the night Everett Sherman and Irene Boyer died.

Dale's eyes darted toward the door, but he quickly tried to bring back a semblance of nonchalance. It never took.

"I'm not sure," the boy replied, again trying to meet his eyes, again only managing to do so for a few seconds.

"Well, it's about a drive you took the other night, with Troy Westerlind and Dawn Kelly."

Coal's bold statement, pulled on a whim out of thin air, got a result from Dale Moore about like he had told him his favorite dog had been run over. The color drained from Dale's face, his mouth gaped open, and he took an involuntary step toward the door Coal now stood directly in front of, as if he had done it on complete accident.

"I'm pretty concerned about your reasons for going up that road at that time of night, son."

Coal was skating on thin ice right now, and he knew it. The one thing he wanted least to do was make Dale clam up on him out of fear. He also didn't have any desire to tell him something he knew wasn't true, because once a trust was broken, especially in a brand-new relationship, it could never quite be forgotten, and Coal refused to be known in this town as a liar. So he couldn't flat out inform Dale that someone had recognized him, but he was going to push it as far that way as he could without telling a lie.

"I was just . . . I, uh . . . Well, it was Troy's dad's truck, you know? And we were all together, Troy an' me an' Dawn, an' . . ." The boy was working himself up to full-blown panic mode, barely able to form sensible phrases. Basically, he was only trying to fill the empty space between himself and an authority figure who to a kid no more than five-foot-seven probably seemed about the size of Goliath.

"Hey, Dale. Would you like to sit down for a minute? You don't look too good."

"I'm, uh . . . No, I'm fine. I just—"

Coal couldn't lie even to himself. About now he was really starting to feel bad about this kid. But something was seriously wrong here. This was not the kind of reaction that came out of a kid who had only been out for a joyride.

"All right, Dale. Maybe we should start over, huh? Let's sit down for a little bit. Do you want to go get a drink of water? We could even go grab a pop or something if you want."

"No, sir, I'm . . . Well, I don't feel too good. I've been startin' to get sick today." Coal wouldn't lie to Dale, but he could hardly blame a scared teenager for lying to him, which Dale was, without a doubt. It was the kind of excuse a kid pulled up who was scared out of his wits. Dale might be feeling sick, but it was the kind of sickness that came out of mental torment.

"We could go check you out of school," Coal suggested. "I don't want you to have to stay here if you're sick. I'd be glad to give you a lift home."

Dale stared at Coal's midsection. He could no longer even pretend to want to look at his face. His sheer panic now had locked his jaw up tight. Coal took a step forward, putting his hand softly on the boy's shoulder. He didn't even flinch.

"Come on, son. Come over here and sit down. Everything's going to be all right. I promise. I'm going to help you, if I can. But you're going to have to talk to me."

Like a walking vegetable, Dale let Coal guide him to a gray metal folding chair, which Coal opened. He eased him down onto it, then did the same with a second one, sitting down close to Dale's side, rather than directly in front of him blocking the door.

"Take some deep breaths, Dale. You're all right. Breathe deep. And let's just sit here for a while, huh? We don't have to even talk."

Now Coal's own mind was racing, although nowhere near as fast as the boy's had to be. What in the world had these kids done that night, exactly? And how in the world had Dawn Kelly acted so tough and cool, and in the end even almost relaxed and friendly, when her friend looked like he was going to pass out? Of course Coal hadn't asked Dawn the same questions, but even so, she had to have been involved in the same activity that was apparently scaring years off Dale Moore's life right now.

It was a good two minutes, in the gloomy light of that room, that Coal and Dale didn't make a sound, at least not a sound beyond breathing, and that was only Dale, who was fighting not to hyperventilate.

Coal waited as long as he felt prudent for Dale to crack and break the silence, and the boy didn't. At last, Coal knew someone had to say something, because Dale's head or heart were going to explode if the silence continued much longer.

Carefully choosing his words, he said, "Hey, son. Sometimes we see things we can't ever get out of our heads. Sometimes there are things so scary to us they change our lives forever. Believe me, I've been there. I've seen blood like you can't imagine. Dead animals. Dead people. Bad things. You can't hold that stuff inside, Dale. You have to find somebody you can trust, and get it out."

It finally hit Coal why he was saying all this. He suddenly knew what was eating out Dale Moore's soul. These kids had either witnessed the killings, or they had at least seen the dead bodies. But what was keeping them silent about it? Did they feel like they were in danger? Were they trying to protect someone? Anything Coal could come up with was going to be guesswork, unless he could make Dale Moore crack. And right now, making Dale crack was taking the wind out of Coal's sails. That must be the worst part about having children of his own.

Feeling suddenly at a loss, Coal stood up. Dale's eyes jerked up to his face, and for a moment Coal thought the boy was going to bolt out of his chair. He thought about calling Dawn in here and letting her see how Dale was acting. He thought about sending a unit out to the Westerlinds' to see if they could find Troy and bring him in too. Maybe if Troy and Dawn saw Dale in this condition they would break down and tell whatever they must have seen that night. On the other hand, maybe together they would find strength.

"I'm going to have them call Dawn back down here, Dale. Would that be all right with you?"

Open panic seemed to swirl around Dale's features. He only stared, and Coal didn't know if he was trying to collect himself or if he had mentally checked out. The second choice seemed to be the right one.

"Dale?"

"No, don't bring her. Please! I don't want to see her!"

"Why, son? I thought the two of you were friends."

"We are! But . . . I just don't . . ."

"What? You don't what? You don't want her to see you like this?"

Dale shook his head back and forth. Coal noticed a film of tears collected inside the boy's lower eyelids that he hadn't seen before.

"Will you be all right here for a bit while I step out? I'll be right outside."

The boy nodded, sitting close to the front edge of his chair.

Coal turned and went out to the office, where Sally seemed to have been waiting anxiously for him. "How much trouble would it be to get Dawn Kelly back?"

"Maybe quite a bit," the woman replied. "She went by here not long after you brought Dale in. She was moving pretty fast and looking upset about something. I called to her to see if she was okay, and she just ran out the front door."

Coal swore in his head. It didn't have the same wonderful therapeutic value it would have going across his tongue, but he couldn't hold it that long, and he couldn't let his new girlfriend hear his gutter mouth.

Thanking Sally, he turned back into the room and shut the door again. Dale's hands were clenched in his lap now, and he was staring at them like they were a rattlesnake coiled to strike. To all appearances, Dale didn't even know Coal had come back.

"Well, Sally tells me Dawn Kelly ran out of here looking pretty upset a while ago, Dale," he said. "Do you have any idea why she would be so upset?"

"Uh-uh." Dale kept staring at his imaginary rattlesnake.

"Do you want me to run you home, Dale?" asked Coal. He hated to think about Dale getting a chance to put his head together with Dawn and Troy, to get things sorted out and arrange their story, but it didn't look like he was going to get anything out of Dale Moore without changing tactics, and he wasn't sure he had the heart for that at the moment.

Dale's voice was shaking when he replied, looking up at Coal and meeting his eyes for the first time in many minutes. "Do you think I'm gonna go to jail?"

CHAPTER THIRTY-FIVE

Dale Moore broke down before Coal could manage to answer his question about jail. The boy was so shaken up he was inconsolable, and his emotional state eventually made Coal start to question much of his take on the murder investigation so far. To listen to and watch Dale Moore, blubbering like a two-year-old, his eyes red, his cheeks and the front of his shirt soaked in tears, and snot running down his lip until he swept it away with his forearm before Coal could get tissues for him, it would not have been hard to convince Coal that Dale was the one who stabbed the murder victims rather than Joe Teton.

Coal stayed with Dale in the dingy room until the end-of-day school bell rang. He couldn't simply leave Dale to go out and face his schoolmates in his present condition. Maybe if he didn't have children of his own, maybe if he hadn't gone through the recent things he had with Katie Leigh, with Cynthia, and with Sissy . . . Maybe the former Coal, the tough, calloused Marine, could have walked out. But the Coal who had been re-forged in the fires of emotional trauma could not walk out on this boy.

Handing Dale another handful of tissues as the boy began slowly to calm down, Coal said, "I'm stepping out, son, but only for a minute. I'll be back, all right? And you'll be all right. We're going to sort this out. Whatever has you so upset, I'm going to help you through it."

Coal went out long enough to report to Sally Edwards, and this time also to briefly meet and speak with the principal, Wade

Carlson. "I don't know how long I'll need the room I have Dale in, but it might still be a while," he told the administrator.

"You just take all the time you need, Sheriff," Carlson replied. "We're not going anywhere."

Returning to the room, Coal clicked the door shut. Dale was leaned far forward in his chair, his head on his folded arms. This time he had a round metal garbage can close by. By the sour smell in the room, Coal didn't have to surmise long to know why, so he didn't go look in it. He could handle a lot of things, but vomit was high on his list of substances to steer far around.

"Come on, son. Let's go get you a drink of water, all right? You up for it?"

Dale hesitated for a moment, then finally stood up. He didn't even bother with a nod in reply.

Coal peeked out the door to see a trickle of students still in the halls. He turned back to Dale. "Why don't you rest up, and I'll go get you a drink. Sound okay?"

This time Dale nodded, then fell back onto his chair and stared at the ever-interesting stained linoleum floor.

Coal brought back water. He reached the door and had to take a deep breath before opening it, not because of the smell he knew would assault him again, but because he had to steel himself against what might be inside. He had walked in on a successful suicide more than once, the first one being a fellow Marine, in Korea. The way Dale was acting, he knew every time he left the room there was a danger of what he could return to. He made up his mind not to leave the boy again.

Dale Moore was still sitting quiet in the room, apparently drained of all tears. Coal handed him a paper cup of water, and the boy sipped it all down before Coal spoke.

"You ready to talk, son?"

Dale shook his head in reply, not looking up from the bottom of the empty cup.

"You have something pretty heavy on your heart, don't you? I've known that feeling, believe me."

Dale nodded, still interested in the ant farm that must have formed in his cup, or whatever was so intriguing down there.

"Who do you have at home, Dale?" Coal asked. "Your dad?"

"Not sure. He prob'ly ain't there."

"You interested in going home with me? My mom puts on a heck of a supper."

Dale gave an adamant shake of his head. "No, sir."

"All right. Dale? We'll have to talk again. You know that, right?"

The boy nodded, inspecting his shoes now, apparently losing interest in the water cup.

Coal almost told the boy he needed to tell him what he had done, but he feared that would close Dale off for good. Instead, he said, "Son, I want you to know I'm here for you. We can talk next time with your dad, or whoever you feel safest with. But we do have to talk again. Just know I'm going to do everything I can to help you. You ready to go home?"

Dale nodded and stood up. As an afterthought, he dropped the cup in his garbage can. At least Coal thought of it as Dale's because if anyone puked in a garbage can he owned, he would give it to them permanently.

Dale moved toward Coal in what he could only think of as a shuffle. With the door still shut, Coal waited until the boy reached him. He put a soft hand on his shoulder again. "You good to go out now? Because we'll wait till you are."

Dale nodded. Then suddenly he threw his arms open and grabbed onto Coal's midsection, squeezing him like he would never let go. Coal was fast to return the embrace, patting Dale softly on the back, fighting his own amazement.

Dale finally released his hold and stepped back, unable to meet Coal's gaze. "I can ride in your car, right?"

"You bet. It's a Thunderbird." He almost mentioned that it had suicide doors, but that was terminology he thought best left silent right now, because this boy seemed as fragile as anyone he had ever seen.

Dale Moore stood in the front room of the little home he shared with his father, watching Coal walk back to the dark green Thunderbird. He had no idea why, but he loved that sheriff. He had never met him until today, but he loved him. He wished his dad could be Sheriff Coal Savage.

The sheriff got in his car and glanced back at the front door one more time. Dale imagined him being hopeful to see him still there. When the sheriff missed Dale peering through the sheer curtains at the front window, he stared at the house for half a minute more, then threw the car in gear and drove slowly off.

The last thing Dale watched, the thing he couldn't take his eyes off, was the back passenger door of the Thunderbird. They called those backward back doors suicide doors, Dale knew. The dad of one of the other students had one just like it, only it was white.

Suicide doors. Suicide . . . The word rang like a big, angry bell in Dale's head. Suicide . . . There were so many ways a kid could take his life. Dale had spent an awful lot of time contemplating them all, but until this moment, seeing that "suicide door", none of those thoughts truly seemed like an option. But now, suddenly, seeing those doors seemed like the strongest of signs from God.

What was that word? Divine! A divine sign. The answer to all Dale's woes was to take his life. He had blood on his hands. It seemed like it was burning holes in his skin, like he could never wash it all off because it had burned him and left permanent stains.

But death . . . Death would take away all that pain, all that burning.

Death would make Dale Moore free at last . . .

Dawn Kelly had to run the gauntlet when she came through the front door. Her father's semi-truck still wasn't parked out front, which sometimes made her sad, but she didn't want to face him now anyway. Instead, her mother Amber's beat-up Pontiac sat in the driveway, like an ugly, taunting toad.

She pushed open the front door, and her mother turned from the kitchen table to stare at her, her makeup looking even heavier than normal, only partly because she had the kitchen light off.

"Why are you in the dark?" Dawn asked, only realizing how belligerent her voice came out after it was hanging like the smell of factory smog in the air.

"I'll sit in the dark if I feel like it," Amber Kelly snapped. Then her voice softened, but only a little. "The light was hurting my eyes."

Dawn started to walk past, then made the mistake of looking at her mother closer. It wasn't only the light hurting her mother's eyes. Both her mother's eyes were black, and the makeup she had tried to use to hide it was only partly why it looked like she had applied eyeshadow with a spade.

"I got homework," said Dawn, starting toward the hall.

"Dawn! Don't you walk away. Get back here."

Dawn paused. "Why?"

"I want this damn house cleaned up, you little whore. I go off and work hard to bring food home, and heat this house. Least you can do is have it clean."

Whore? Who was this woman, of all people, calling a whore! Dawn stared at her mother until her own eyes hurt, from the bruises not only around her mother's eyes, but on her neck and the little she could see of her upper chest as well. By then, the harsh word she had called her had faded completely out of her consciousness.

"Okay, Mama. I'll clean it. As soon as I get my homework done, I'll clean everything up. Don't you worry. It'll be okay."

Her mother stared darts at her. Her mother knew it wouldn't be "okay". Dawn knew it wouldn't be okay. Dawn's father would be home soon, and his mother's bruises would not be gone. He would demand answers, and he deserved them. But he wouldn't get them, and he wouldn't even know where to go to look for justice for his wife.

"What are you up to?" asked Amber, her voice on the verge of hysterical anger. "Why are you talkin' to me like that?"

"I just want to make you happy, Mama," said Dawn. "Just once."

She turned and walked down the hall, jerking the phone off the table, unplugging it, and taking it with her into her room. She could hear her mother screaming at her from the other room. She heard her coming down the hall yelling. Reaching over, she turned the door lock and locked her mother out of her ruined little life. But she couldn't lock out the din from her.

For a while, Amber Kelly pounded on the bedroom door, screaming obscenities. Dawn went and turned on her record player almost as loud as it would go and listened to Pink Floyd's first album, *The Piper at the Gates of Dawn,* every bit as loud as she could turn it up. The sound drowned out her ferocious, drunk mother, until finally the noise of her mother faded away.

Dawn loved this Pink Floyd album, released in 1967, not only because it had her name in it, but because it screamed out all the radical things she wanted to say for herself. After a few minutes, her mind almost numbed by the music, she went and opened the bedroom door and eased it open. Her mother had collapsed in the hall, and she lay in the fetal position against the far wall, her hands over her head to block out Pink Floyd.

Dawn shut the door quietly and locked it again, then picked up the phone. With shaking hands, she dialed Dale's number. On the other end, she heard it begin to ring. It rang, and rang, and rang.

Then it rang some more. Twenty rings. Thirty. *Where was Dale?* He couldn't still be with the sheriff! School was long since over.

Ever since she saw Dale and the sheriff walk past together in the hallway, the acid had been building up in her stomach. Dale was going to crack! He would tell the sheriff everything! He was going to crack, and then Troy, she, and Dale were all going to juvie in Saint Anthony—or worse!

Dale, pick up your phone! In her head, she was screaming the words. *Pick up the phone!*

The alarm bells began going off in her head. Dale had already confessed! He was headed down to the jail, handcuffed in the back seat of the sheriff's car!

Next, the sheriff would be coming back for her. And then it would be Troy's turn—if Troy was still alive after his father got through with him for ruining the family name, or whatever his reason was for beating him this time. It didn't seem like that evil Gunnar Westerlind needed much excuse at all.

"Dale!" She growled his name out loud this time. "Dale, you little jerk, pick up the phone!"

CHAPTER THIRTY-SIX

Coal drove away from Dale Moore's house but only made it as far as Steele Memorial before pulling up and stopping in front of the emergency entrance. He reasoned that if he stopped here it would keep him from overstaying his welcome, because he would feel guilty about blocking the way to anyone who had a real emergency. After sitting there for five minutes, however, he started to realize that his only real reason for stopping was because he missed Annie Price. He had already been here twice to check on Wilford Bayless, and that was a fish he could just as easily fry tomorrow.

With a sigh, he pulled away from the hospital just as the deejay at KSRA radio was spinning "Tie a Yellow Ribbon 'Round the Ole Oak Tree" for what felt like the twentieth time that day. He had Dale Moore and Dawn Kelly on his mind, since they were his most recent interactions, and thinking of them made him start thinking about Troy Westerlind, the only one he hadn't spoken to from the late-night foray of Gunnar Westerlind's pickup. It was three-forty-five now, so he had a while before his meeting with Grant and Jordan to go start peppering the local bars with questions about Curlie Burks and Melissa Talty. Maybe since Lyle Gentry seemed to be taken in a little by Gunn Westerlind's polite manners, it was time for Coal to go back out and see if he could find Troy. After all, they couldn't hide that kid forever. And besides the desire to interview him about the night of the murders, Coal wanted to check the boy's welfare.

It was a bit of a drive out to Westerlind's place, but Coal decided to make the drive. This was a puzzle piece he needed if he was going to put the Sherman-Boyer case completely to rest.

Coal made the corner into the Westerlind drive much more sedately than his last reckless forty-five degree near-disaster. He was pleased to see only the red Chrysler 300 in front of the house, and the pickup nowhere in sight. That made it likely that either Gunn or Troy were out somewhere, and no matter which one it was, it would serve a purpose for Coal. If it was Gunn, he might be able to roust Troy out and talk to him, and if it was Troy . . . well, it meant he wasn't dead.

He knocked on the front door, not completely sure why his heart began to pound faster. It wasn't ten seconds before the door swung open, and Gunn Westerlind was standing there with his typical look of pleasant surprise on his face.

"Why, hello, Sheriff. You keep this schedule of visits up, and I can see we're going to end up being best of friends. What do I owe this visit to?"

Coal, hiding his disappointment not to find Troy home, said, "Well, I was hoping to catch Troy home. I'm not sure why, but they're pretty worried about him down at the school. I guess he's all right though, huh? You wouldn't happen to know where I could catch him, would you?"

The faint shadow crossing Westerlind's face was barely discernible, and gone in one or two seconds. "Well, actually I would."

"Oh, great. Where's that? I'll pay him a real quick visit and put this whole thing to rest."

Westerlind's smile looked a little uncomfortable. "Actually, I'm not sure you'll be visiting him *or* putting anything to rest, because that's where he is—resting."

After a couple of seconds to process what Westerlind said, Coal shook his head. "I don't understand."

“He’s in his room, Sheriff. He’s caught some kind of flu bug, I think. I hear it’s been going around.”

“Oh. Well, darn.”

Coal’s mind churned in a couple directions before he could get back on track. One of those directions was back to Salmon High School, where Sally Edwards had told Coal just that morning, during their gay repartee, how happy she was that the usual flu season hadn’t seemed to be materializing yet, and she didn’t know of anyone missing school who was out because they were sick.

The other direction, of course, was the absence of the blue and white Dodge.

“I guess I assumed because the pickup isn’t here that he must have it.”

“Oh, no, no,” said Westerlind with a chuckle. “It just needed some tuning up, so it’s in town for a day or two.”

“Oh, all right. I don’t suppose you’d mind if I just peeked in on Troy real quick, would you? Just ask him a question or two—make sure he’s okay?”

“Umm . . .” Gunn Westerlind stared at Coal, his eyes almost spinning. Coal had been around long enough to know when somebody was stalling for time, fishing for something to say. “Well, sir, I guess we can only ask, right? Why don’t you come on in.” Westerlind turned away from Coal so fast it was almost as if he spun on his heel. Unlike Coal’s last visit, he let him shut the door for himself, but after only four steps away from Coal, he turned back, smiling a smile Coal wasn’t sure he saw any reason for. “Why don’t you wait there, and I’ll see how he feels, all right?”

Westerlind walked off again without awaiting a reply, stopping at the corner of the entry wall. He yelled out, more than loud enough to make sure Coal and anyone else in the house could hear. “Hey—Troy? We have company. Sheriff Savage is here, and he was hoping to have a word with you. Are you feeling up to any company—or are you still in bed?”

There was a long moment of silence.

"Troy, son?"

Coal didn't know what he expected. He was half certain they would get no answer and that Westerlind would claim his son was fast asleep and tell him to come back some other day. So when he heard the voice, it almost gave him a start.

"Hey, Dad." The voice did indeed sound weak, and perhaps barely awake. "I'm pretty sick. Could you see if he'll come back tomorrow or something?"

"Sure, Son. But . . ." Westerlind turned and looked at Coal, shaking his head with exasperation. "Hang on a minute, Sheriff. Let me see if I can be more persuasive. I don't want you to have to make that long trip out again."

"Sure, go ahead," said Coal, although inside he was thinking how funny it was that Westerlind thought he was only here to check on Troy's welfare. Did they really think the other night, and Curlie Burks's testimony that he had seen Troy, and the pickup, up by the cemetery was simply going to go away?

Westerlind walked down the hall, and Coal heard a door crack open. "Son? I think you should at least let the sheriff lean in here and talk to you. He just wants to make sure you're all right. I guess they're getting worried about you at school." Coal heard the boy mumble something in reply, but whatever it was was completely lost to him.

"Come on in here, Sheriff," came Gunn Westerlind's voice. "I wouldn't go in the room, but you can talk to him from the doorway if you'd like. You really don't want to get what he has."

Coal went in and turned down the hall. When he got to where Westerlind was, he stepped around him and looked into the dim-lit bedroom, where a mound under the covers of the bed showed Coal he could find Troy.

"Son, I just came out to check on you. The school's worried about you, and so are your friends."

An overly weak voice spoke back. "Thanks, Sheriff. Will you tell everybody I'm okay? I just got this bug really bad. I been pukin' all day and night—and other stuff."

Coal sure didn't need those details. He had seen plenty of sickness in his day, especially with four kids. Then again, this bedroom didn't smell anything like the bedroom of a person with influenza, or at least not any of the bedrooms in Coal's experience.

"You don't feel strong enough even to sit up and let me see you?" Coal asked, knowing he was pushing his luck.

"Well, I—"

Beside Coal, Westerlind's voice cut his son's words off. "All right, Sheriff. I think we've bothered the boy enough. Let's let him rest, all right? I'd appreciate it. Son, you'll be okay in a day or two, don't you think? And the Sheriff can see you then?"

"I think so, Dad. Yeah. I'm pretty sure."

"All right. You just rest. Son, do you need anything? Some more tea, or broth or anything?"

"Uhh . . . No, thanks, Dad. Thanks for askin', though."

"All right, Son. I'll check on you soon."

He quietly slipped the door shut and turned to Coal. "I'm really sorry about that. I'm sure he'll be better soon. You know kids. They recover fast, huh?"

"Sure, sure," said Coal. "I know kids."

They walked together back to the entryway, which split off to the kitchen. Here, they stopped, and Westerlind jerked a thumb toward the kitchen. "Say, can I get you a beer or anything?"

"No, thanks."

"Oh, shoot! Sorry! I'm sure you're on duty and all," said Westerlind, with a sheepish look.

"It wouldn't be a big deal. I just don't drink." That wasn't exactly the truth, of course. He drank now and then, but at least he didn't drink beer. And if he had, it wouldn't be with Gunnar Westerlind.

When Coal got back into the warm Thunderbird after thanking Westerlind and telling him goodbye, he heard the last of a radio transmission that sounded like the voice of Jay Castillo, saying the ambulance was on the way to the hospital.

Nadine's voice came on immediately after. *Ten-four, Salmon IRU. Hospital trauma staff will be standing by at the door.*

Thank you, Salmon, said Jay's voice. *Ambulance out.*

Curious, Coal stopped out at the highway. He had been thinking about making a left and going to see Kathy and the girls for a bit, but the ambulance went out so seldom that it was big news in Salmon, and Coal hated to be left out of the news. Besides, he had a bad feeling whenever he heard a trauma unit was standing by at the hospital.

Reaching out, Coal snapped the mic off its hook and brought it to his mouth. He paused it there, unsure he wanted to make this call, but knowing he must.

"Sheriff's car to Salmon Dispatch. Salmon Dispatch, come in?"

Sheriff, this is Salmon. Nadine's voice sounded badly shaken.

"Nadine? I'm just now getting back in my car. Could you fill me in on that last call the ambulance had?"

There was a long pause before Nadine's voice came over the air. *Sheriff, stand by.* It was a good ten seconds before she crackled over the airwaves again, obviously trying very hard to control her emotion. *I'm sorry, Sheriff. I tried several times to reach you. There was a young girl . . . she was asking for you specifically—by your first name.* Nadine paused so long this time Coal wanted to scream at her, but she had the line still open, so he couldn't even say anything to rush her. Had something happened to Dawn Kelly?

Again, Nadine's voice, sounding overly husky—and no one would ever have said Nadine sounded husky—*Coal, you should get back to Steele as fast as you're able. The ambulance was on an attempted suicide, and . . . Is there any way you can call? I don't feel comfortable putting this over the air.*

Coal had already spun out onto the highway in front of a fast-approaching car, and he had gunned it up to eighty without even thinking about it, leaving the car far behind.

"I'll be to the hospital in less than ten minutes, Nadine. If there's any way you can reach that girl, please tell her to hang on!"

Roger, Coal. I'll try to reach her. But this call . . . If you could find any place to stop, it would be good.

"I'm coming fast, Salmon. I'll be there right away."

Nadine, after another pregnant pause, came back sounding almost hurt, or at least deeply disappointed. *Roger that, Sheriff. Salmon out.*

The Thunderbird's tires on the pavement and the roar of the engine were loud, but the lonely silence left inside the car was almost heartbreaking, so Coal reached down and punched the radio back on. It seemed fitting for the deejay to announce and then start playing Donna Fargo, on a song called "Little Girl Gone".

When he slid up to the emergency room, the ambulance was still sitting outside with its back door open. Coal threw the car in park and jumped out. He hadn't even made it to the front door when to his shock he saw a person appear behind the glass, and that person was a girl, rushing his way.

The door flew open hard, and Dawn Kelly came rushing out. "Sheriff Savage!" she said with a sob, and she threw herself against him, her arms taking him in a crushing embrace. "I tried to call for you! They tried to find you." That was all she got out, because she broke down sobbing, holding onto him like he was her last hold on life.

It was still in the thirties, although a low around zero was predicted that night, but as Coal stood there holding Dawn Kelly, he could feel the cold seeping deep into his bones. He knew what it meant that Dawn was standing here crying into his coat, and he wished he had taken the time to stop and call dispatch from the Baker Store, or somewhere else along the way. He wished he had given himself more time to prepare himself mentally.

He let Dawn cry as long as he could stand before taking her shoulders and pressing her away from him, making her release her powerful hold on him. "Dawn, what happened? Is it Dale?"

She nodded, trying to look at him and probably barely able to see him through her tears, and her swollen eyes. "He used his belt. On the doorknob!"

CHAPTER THIRTY-SEVEN

Catching movement past Dawn's head, Coal looked up to see EMT Ronnie Davis coming toward the front door from inside the hospital. Davis came out looking angry, furiously stuffing his lower lip with tobacco. It seemed like he only became aware of who Coal was as he pushed out through the double doors into the cold evening air.

"Hello, Savage."

Coal nodded, pushing back his numbness. "Ronnie."

"You doin' okay? They said you know this kid, huh?"

Coal could not keep himself from being taken aback at Ronnie Davis acting decent toward him. "Well, sort of. Yeah, I'm all right." It wasn't exactly true, but tough guys can't reveal their hearts to just anyone.

Davis nodded, studying Coal's face for a moment. Coal studied the EMT back, and knew that was one tough guy who didn't buy his story. Holding up his snus can, Davis said, "Chew?"

"No. Thanks anyway, though."

With another nod, Davis paced away, staring out into the street lights on Main. He came back around, studying Dawn as she stood there with Coal, then looking back up at him. "Well, don't hold crap in, Sheriff. It ain't good."

The advice shocked Coal. In a day and age when men still made an art out of "holding things inside", it certainly wasn't something he expected to hear from a man whose crust was as hard as Davis's. He swore that to him it didn't matter, but it sure did to this little girl, whose hard surface had sluffed away like the last creek ice of spring.

"Hey." Davis's hard-sounding deep voice drew Coal's attention away from the top of Dawn's head. Coal guessed the EMT had been working himself up to being able to offer something more substantial. "For what it's worth, I don't know if you've ever been around this kind of injury, but I've seen it before. I think the kid'll recover okay. Thanks to your friend here."

Coal stared at Davis, trying to process his words. As the truth began to register, he said, "Thanks, Ronnie. That means a lot."

He suddenly sensed Dawn Kelly staring at Davis as well, and then her face whipped up to Coal. Ronnie Davis's words hadn't only come as a surprise to Coal!

Jay Castillo came striding out as Davis walked over as if on an afterthought and quietly closed the back door of the station wagon ambulance. "I think you could go see him if you want," Jay said, looking at Dawn. Then he raised his eyes to Coal. "Both of you."

Coal forgot to thank his friend as he hurried after Dawn, who had whirled and bolted for the door. Without running, he couldn't catch up to the girl before she was through the doors and off down the hall. Trying to act at least a little tougher than a seventeen-year-old girl, Coal made tracks down the hall to where a small cluster of women in short white dresses, white shoes, and nurses' caps stood outside the door of a room.

As he reached them, he realized the farthest one away from him was Annie Price, and she turned, recognized him, and grabbed his hand. "Coal! Are you doing okay?"

He nodded. "Yeah. Are you?"

She matched his nod. "I'm good. He'll be okay, too. Did they tell you?"

"A little," Coal said, looking in at Dawn Kelly, who stood beside Dale Moore's bed and had once again lost her battle with "tough".

"He was using a belt. His dad's, they think," Annie said. By the look of her face, she was trying to talk her way through her own trauma in the aftermath of the incident. "He did it on the doorknob, but that young lady found him really fast. It couldn't have been more than a minute."

A wave of emotion rushed all through Coal. Poor Dawn! She had seen nothing in her life of the death and destruction he had. This incident would stay with her for the rest of her life.

A commotion erupted down the hall the way Coal had come. He and the nurses whipped around to see a man rushing down the hall, with Bob Wilson trying to keep up with him. By sight only, Coal recognized the man as he got close. He was a bone-thin man dressed in plaid flannel, with drooping red eyelids and a face full of hard lines.

"Where's he at? Where's my boy?" the man said, his eyes spinning across everyone gathered there.

"Dale?" Coal managed to find his voice first. "In there, mister."

The man took the white-clothed nurses like a bowling ball through pins, barreling into the room and stalking to his son. As he got close, a string of name-calling spewed out of his mouth, but by the time he had grabbed Dale's hand, basically forcing Dawn to quick-step backward, he was sobbing.

"You stupid kid! Stupid kid!"

"Dawn?" Coal called quietly, motioning to her with his fingers. "Come here with me."

Eyes still shocked, as if in a trance, Dawn peeled away and made her way out to Coal, throwing her arms around him again. Maybe for lack of anything to do, while Coal held onto her, Annie stood there softly rubbing and patting Dawn's back, intermittently.

Dawn seemed unable to stop weeping openly, so Coal asked Annie to get some Kleenex, and then he turned and led the girl down the hall, finding the first open examination room and guiding the girl into it. He stepped out only far enough to catch Annie's attention when she came back bringing a handful of tissues. "You two stay in here as long as you need," Annie said, giving the girl's shoulder a rub of comfort. "He's going to be okay, honey. I promise." With a last glance up at Coal, Annie stepped out, shutting the door softly behind.

The closing door gave Dawn Kelly unspoken permission to break down harder, and Coal simply allowed her to cry out her pain and sorrow, letting her hold onto him because she didn't seem capable of letting go.

It was a good twenty minutes before the last of the girl's sniffles faded away, but she still stood holding onto him, as if she would float away into space and vanish if she relinquished her hold. Another five minutes, and she gave out with a last sobbing sigh. "I gotta try to call Troy," she said, her voice quiet.

"I'll try him for you," suggested Coal. "I think his dad is more likely to give him the phone if it's me."

Dawn didn't even argue. She already knew what Coal knew—that Gunn Westerlind had no use for her, or any of Troy's other friends.

As Coal took the girl with him back out in the hall to the receptionist's desk, she refused to be out of physical contact with him. If he didn't hold her hand, she was clutching his elbow. The receptionist gave up her station to them, and Coal dialed the phone number Dawn gave him. Westerlind picked up after three rings.

Hello?

"Mr. Westerlind. Coal Savage. I'm down here at the hospital with one of Troy's friends, Dale."

A long pause. *Okay? So . . . you say you're at the hospital? What happened?*

"Attempted suicide." Westerlind swore in reply to that. "I'm here with Dawn Kelly. She'd like to talk to your son."

Well, I don't know if that's such a great—

Coal knew he sounded rude cutting the man off, but he didn't have time not to be rude—nor, with Westerlind, the inclination. "Will you just let the girl talk to him? His friend just tried to kill himself. Have a heart."

After another pause, Westerlind said, *Hang on a minute.*

It was fully two minutes later, after Coal was certain Troy Westerlind had had a good coaching, before he heard a different voice come on, a version of Gunn's voice from twenty years earlier.

"Troy? This is Sheriff Savage. I have someone here who needs to talk to you." With that, he handed Dawn the phone, reached up and gave the side of her head a pat. "I'll be just down the hall if you need me," he said in almost a whisper.

Her nod and mouthed *Thank you* were filled with gratitude.

Dawn! Troy's voice came over the phone line scratchy, and as frightened as Dawn had ever heard it. *What's goin' on? Did Dale really try to kill himself?*

At the sound of those blunt words, Dawn had to bite her lip to keep back her emotions. She was surprised she had the ability to cry anymore. "He did, Troy. He's in here at the hospital with his dad right now. And I'm with the sheriff."

Dawn? The boy's voice was instantly filled with angst. *Dawn, we all swore to secrecy, remember? You gotta keep it shut. Don't you go welchin' on me!* When she didn't reply, he asked, *What about Dale? How is he? Is he sayin' anything?*

Dawn listened to the voice of the kid she had called her boyfriend for well over a year. It was as if she were listening to someone she didn't even know. In mere sentences, a hard truth was coming out that she had known for some time, but wouldn't admit to herself until this. "You don't even care how he is, Troy. Do you? Be honest. You only care if he's going to tell on you. Same with me, too. You don't care. You just want to get what you want and then throw us both in the trash."

Now stop, Dawn! Stop! You know I care. How is he? Is he awake?

Dawn drew a deep breath, taking a step backward and leaning back so she could look down the hall. She saw Sheriff Savage leaning against the wall, out of earshot, because he was polite, and he actually cared about her feelings. It was a kick to the stomach. Not because Sheriff Savage's concern for her well-being shocked her, but because all of a sudden she realized that an almost complete stranger cared about her more than the boy who claimed her as his girlfriend.

She pulled back out of sight of anyone in the hall. "You know what, Troy? Forget I even called. Go back to whatever you were doing."

No! Dawn! Don't hang up on me! I want to see you. Come out here, okay?

"Oh, stop, Troy. Why don't you just freakin' stop? You know I don't have any way to get out there. Unless you want Sheriff Savage to bring me."

Dawn! Come on! You're my girl!

"I'm not your girl, Troy. Not anymore. I'm done. I am so done with you."

No! Dawn, stop! You don't mean that. Just stop! I need to see you!

"Don't worry, Troy. I'm not cracking. I'm not telling anybody about what we did. Okay? So just go back to being who you are and stop freaking out. I know you. You're going to be just fine."

No, Dawn, wait. Just—

Reaching out, she pushed down softly on the disconnect button, holding it in place for a good fifteen seconds, as if that would ensure that the evil of Troy Westerlind was shut out of her life forever.

"Dawn? Dawn!" Troy Westerlind, standing in the kitchen, slammed the phone down on the base, cursing Dawn Kelly, calling her every foul name he could think of. Before he could get the last of them out into the formerly quiet air of the house, his father appeared from down the hallway.

"All right, Troy. All right."

Troy's one good eye he could still see out of snapped over to his father, where he stood in the entrance to the hall. To his shock, he recognized the object in front of his face. His father was holding up the Shoshone lance he had been keeping hidden in his closet.

"Just what is this? Where in the name of—" Gunn Westerlind stopped, mid-rage, staring at Troy. "Where did you get this, you little bastard? And I won't ask you again!" He raised his fist to his son, savagely shaking the lance in his left hand.

"It's not mine!" Troy stammered, stepping nervously backward. "It's not!"

"Well, clearly, Troy. Clearly. And I'm asking who the hell you got it from!"

"From Dale, man. I got it from Dale!"

CHAPTER THIRTY-EIGHT

When Dawn came back down the hall to where Coal was waiting, he smiled at her. “Everything all right?” Her face already told him the answer.

“Yeah, it’s fine.”

He studied her for a bit, but it was obvious she wasn’t going to volunteer anything more, so he let it drop. “Want to go down and see if we can get in the room with Dale again?”

The girl’s eyes turned worried. “I don’t know. I don’t know if I want to see him like that.”

“Yeah. I get it. Do you want to go grab a pop or something then? I can get us into the nurses’ lounge, or we can go to the café.”

“I don’t have any money for anything,” she said.

He laughed. “I’m not going to make you pay when I’m the one who offered. My treat.”

She gave him a shy smile. “Sure then. I guess so.”

They chose the nurses’ lounge because neither of them felt like being in a public place. Annie Price let them in and got them two Pepsis out of the fridge. She stopped at Dawn’s side and put her hand on her shoulder. “You okay, honey?”

Dawn nodded. “Yeah. Thanks.”

“Sure.”

“Okay, well if you need anything else, you just let me know.” Annie looked over and winked at Coal, then left. When she was gone, he got up and returned his Pepsi to the fridge, then poured himself a cup of black coffee and put the pot back on the burner.

He sat back down across from Dawn and grinned, raising his coffee mug to her in the manner of a toast. "Darn nurses don't know what's good for them."

She smiled back at him. She even tried to laugh, but it didn't come out as being full of much humor. Dawn kept concentrating hard on the yellow vinyl top of the table they were sitting at. Her hands were down in her lap. Coal held his silence, trying to be patient, sipping the coffee that had obviously sat on the burner too long and thinking he should have kept the Pepsi instead. He looked at Dawn, studying her. He wished he knew her better. He needed to wait until just the right time to start with questions again, and he needed to plan his questions carefully. Dawn was a girl who could be his friend for life, or with one wrongly worded, or wrongly timed question he could lose her forever.

Finally, he took a deep breath, preparing himself for whatever was to come. "Hey, Dawn? Do you want to talk about anything?"

She looked up at him, her gaze faltering. "No. Why?"

"I don't know. It just feels like you've been having a hard time lately, maybe."

She nodded thoughtfully but failed this time to meet his eyes. He could see behind her veiled eyes that her mind was racing with thoughts. She was trying to decide—open up, or lock her heart tight. Finally, she shrugged. She still didn't bring her hands up into sight.

When after five more minutes of quiet it became plain that she had decided not to speak, he cleared his throat. "Dawn, I want to ask you about something. I don't want you to get scared, but you do need to know this."

That was it. He saw a curtain close over her eyes, even though this time she met his gaze head on. "Yeah?"

"Well, there are a couple of folks, a man and a woman, who claim they saw you up by the cemetery with Troy Westerlind and Dale, on the night those two people were murdered." The statement wasn't exactly true, but it was close enough for Coal. He had studied for a long time on exactly how to tell her that, and the words he had chosen were as close as he could come to a way to tell her the score while at the same time not sounding like he was trying to accuse her of anything.

The girl held his gaze until it seemed like her eyes glazed over. "Oh. How do they know me?" she asked after a long hesitation. Her voice sounded tight now. Her eyes betrayed her fear.

Coal swore, but only in his mind. He hated situations like this, where it felt like he was trying to lure in a wounded animal, and any wrong move could send it scurrying away, to die alone in some hole where he could no longer reach it to help it.

"They only knew Troy for sure," he admitted. "But they described you and Dale." He knew it had to be dark up there, and he doubted Curlie Burks and Melissa Talty would stand any chance of identifying Dawn or Dale in a real-life situation. But he certainly didn't dare admit that to Dawn right now, not when there was still some chance of her talking to him about that night. Besides, if Curlie had recognized Troy, then maybe he really did have enough light to see Dawn by. Maybe he really could pick her out of a lineup.

"Okay," she said softly. She could no longer meet his eyes.

"Don't be frightened, Dawn," Coal heard himself say over the pounding of his heart.

She looked up, trying to meet his eyes. Her gaze was still veiled, untrusting. She was ready mentally to bolt, to go into hiding. To shut down.

"I'm not frightened," she said, with a weak shrug of one shoulder. Coal gazed at her, feeling the fear in her that she denied so strongly. Dawn was an attractive young lady, but she was a poor liar.

"I hope you feel like you can trust me," Coal threw out. "I trust you."

She chuckled, raising her eyebrows as she studied the hands she now brought up and folded on the table between them. She blinked exaggeratedly. At last, in a weak voice, she said, "Thank you."

"There will be a prosecutor asking you a lot of questions pretty soon," Coal revealed. "They also might have you take a lie detector test. So anything you tell me before will help you. And Dawn?"

She tried to meet his eyes again but didn't reply.

"I'll do everything I can to protect you, okay? Just be truthful with me. That's all I ask. Whatever truth you feel safe giving me."

He found the girl's eyes in his now, studying him, trying to find the truth in him that he could see she so desperately needed to see. Finally, she nodded, and tears dimmed her eyes. She stood up awkwardly, and he stood too. Staring at the floor, she said, "Can I hug you?"

He smiled, even though she couldn't see it. "Of course you can."

After Dawn had stood in Coal's comforting embrace for as long as she needed, she said, "Can we go try to see Dale now?"

"You bet. Come on." He threw away her Pepsi can, dumped out the remainder of his muddy, burned coffee and rinsed the cup, and then went down the hall to the room Dale was in.

To Coal's surprise, Dale's father, Zack Moore, had already left. Dale lay unconscious, sedated. There was hardly more than a red welt on his throat now to show where the belt had been tightening that in minutes more would have ended his life. Weeping now in silence, Dawn went to the side of the bed and put soft fingers on Dale's forearm, just inches from where the IV tubes fed into his left hand.

"Do you want some time alone?" asked Coal.

"No! Please don't leave me," she pleaded.

"Okay. I'll be glad to stay here with you," he said, and instinctively he moved closer, putting his arm around her waist to support her in this time of grief. "He seems like a real nice young man," Coal said after a while. Dawn could only nod in reply.

The door suddenly swung open, and Coal looked over, out of habit more than anything. Striding in were Troy and Gunnar Westerlind, and as a shocked look passed over both their faces at sight of Coal, they fanned out to stand side by side. One of Troy's eyes was swollen shut, his left cheek had a large red bruise on it, and there was a scab on that same side of his nose.

"Hello, Sheriff," said Gunnar, clearing his throat. "How is the boy?" Coal was very aware of Troy's one-eyed stare in Dawn's direction.

"He'll be all right, they say. Thanks to Dawn."

Gunnar's faltering glance shifted for a moment to the girl, and the look in it was not a kind one.

Gunnar slid his eyes sideways to the face of Dale Moore. Carefully, he said, "So has Dale been able to talk at all? Or has he been out the whole time?"

"He's been out. They have him on meds, but I think his throat's probably too bruised to talk yet anyway."

"Oh," replied Gunnar. "That's too bad."

After studying the other man's face for a few seconds, Coal shrugged. "Yeah, too bad, I guess. Not sure what he'd even say at this point anyway."

Gunnar met his shrug. "Of course. Who could know, right?"

Coal looked down at Dawn, who was mostly hidden from Troy because he was in the way. He had thought she might run around him to hug her boyfriend, but she made no move that way. That was when he knew for sure that the phone conversation Dawn and Troy had had was not the kind of conversation she had been hoping for. He had suspected as much.

"So, Troy, you must be feeling better, huh?" Coal asked, trying to sound nonchalant although he was anything but.

"Yeah, I'm fine. I think it might have been just from . . ." The boy's voice faded out, and his eyes flickered over to his father, as if he had lost track of exactly whatever he had been commanded to say.

"Troy got in a fight over in Leadore," Gunnar said. "I guess I should have told you that—save you the shock of seeing him like this. Also, I got to thinking later that maybe what I was thinking was him having the flu could have been from the beating."

"No doubt," said Coal. "I thought it was kind of odd that you thought the flu was going around the school, when they told me at the school that it wasn't."

Coal turned his attention fully on Troy. "What kind of fight was that, son? It looks like it was bad enough that I should go talk to them."

"Oh, nah," Troy sputtered instantly, his eyes darting away. "It was just as much my fault."

"Still, anybody who's willing to be that brutal needs to get a talking to." He meant his words to sound every bit the warning to everyone in the room that they were.

"Well, I'm not even sure who they were anyway. And I think I might have seen they had Idaho Falls plates." That last part was an obvious afterthought. Troy Westerlind had just made certain there was no way Coal could follow up on his story.

"That's too bad," said Coal, not looking at the boy's father. "Sorry bastards sure did a number on you, all right. I'd love to get my hands on them if I could."

The four of them stood there in awkward silence until Coal asked, "How did you even drive home in that condition, Troy?"

The boy shrugged. "Well, it wasn't easy. Yeah. I could hardly see the damn road."

"I'll bet not," Coal said.

After another couple minutes of silence in the room, the door opened a cautious several inches, and then pushed the rest of the way in. Annie Price peered in, scanning the room. “We’re going to need to do some stuff real quick, everybody. If you’d like to hang around in the waiting area I can come and get you when we’re done.”

“No,” Westerlind said quickly. “Looks like the boy’s out for a while anyway. Guess we’d better get going.”

Coal agreed, and he snatched Dawn’s hand and pulled her with him as he followed Gunn and Troy Westerlind into the hall. He was moving fast, trying to stay alongside Westerlind enough that the man knew he was there. Casually, he said, “Say, Gunn, who do you use for your mechanic work in town, anyway?” It was a question he had been meaning to ask Westerlind, and this was the perfect opportunity to ask it.

“Umm . . . Well, I like Jerry’s. Does good work.” Westerlind didn’t meet Coal’s eyes.

“Oh, okay. Never had any experience with him. What’s he doing to your pickup, anyway?” Coal couldn’t say even to himself why he was asking this stuff now. Originally, he had intended to see if the pickup was really at the shop, or if Troy Westerlind was out driving around in it. Now that he knew Troy was here, it seemed like a moot point, and yet something told him to ask anyway. Maybe it was only because something had seemed so off in Westerlind’s manner when he told Coal the truck was being worked on.

“He, uh . . . Well, just a tune-up, sounds like. It was running a little rough.”

“Oh, that’s not too bad,” said Coal, conversationally. “I got to where I do all my own tune-up work, but if you’re always busy, it sure is good to have a mechanic you trust.”

“Sure is,” said Westerlind.

“Say, I’ve been meaning to have you tell Kathy MacAtee hello for me next time you see her,” said Coal. “I’ve been so busy I don’t make it out to check on them much anymore.”

"Oh, sure. You bet. I'll tell her," Westerlind replied. "Well, we'll see you later, Sheriff."

With that, the Westerlinds were off down the hall and out the door that emptied onto the street.

Coal turned and looked down at Dawn, who was squeezing the blood out of his hand. She looked up at him. "Do you think boys in Leadore did that to Troy?" she asked.

"No."

"It was his dad, right?"

Coal nodded.

"But how can you be sure?"

"Because I saw marks on Westerlind's hands that night. And because Troy didn't even have a pickup to be out in Leadore the night I took that call in the first place."

CHAPTER THIRTY-NINE

Coal didn't want to leave Dawn Kelly that day, but eventually he knew he had to. As much as he would have liked to stay by her side, to keep her safe, she was one of millions of people on the face of the earth who needed help of some kind. He couldn't help them all, and it was one of his most bitter pills to swallow.

Stopping at Dawn's house, he walked her to the front door. A woman in heavy black makeup and too much rouge opened the door as the girl was about to grab the handle.

Everyone was surprised by the sudden appearance of everyone else. The woman stared from Dawn to Coal, and they both stared back at her.

Coal found his tongue first, but only enough to say, "Ma'am," and to tip the brim of his hat.

"Who are you?" she asked, peering closer, then seeing the corner of his badge peering out from beneath his coat. "Oh, hell!" She turned her eyes to glare darts at Dawn, then looked back up at Coal. "Now what's she done?"

"Nothing, ma'am. She didn't do a thing—except save a friend's life."

"She's . . . not in trouble?"

"No. Far from it. Your daughter is a friend of mine," he said. And he meant it.

"Well, I'm going out," the woman said, turning her attention back to Dawn. "You need to stay home tonight and clean up."

"I said I would."

"Okay." The woman didn't look ready to go out, but she had already made the statement, so she went, right on past them and out to her car.

They watched her pull away without once glancing back, even to wave.

"My mom," said Dawn quietly. "You can tell she loves me so much, huh?"

How did he even reply to that? He wasn't going to lie about what he had observed. "You're a good girl, Dawn," he said. "That's the important thing, and I hope you won't forget it."

"Thank you," she said, and she gave him one last, long hug.

Before she shut the door, Coal said, "If you ever need anything, you call me, okay? If you're ever in trouble. Call me first. And if you want to talk about the other night . . . Well, think about it, okay? Whatever happened that night, we'll get through it together."

"Okay. I'll remember."

The door closed softly, and Coal walked away, wishing the world were a different place for a young woman like Dawn Kelly.

Back in the Thunderbird, Coal heard Nadine's voice come over the air. *Salmon dispatch to Sheriff Savage. Third attempt.*

He swore, ripping the mic off the hook. "Sheriff here."

Coal, the hospital called and needs you to report there right away if possible. Someone there to talk to you.

"Roger that," he said, speeding away from in front of Dawn's house even before bothering to hang up the mic.

At the hospital, he parked in the same place the ambulance had now vacated and hurried inside. The first two people he saw at the desk were Annie Price and Wilford Bayless. Bayless looked at him out of those angry blue eyes, with his eyebrow hair hanging down over them.

"Sheriff. How do I get a ride home?"

Coal looked at Annie, who shrugged. "That's what I was called back here for?"

Annie nodded, making an embarrassed face. "Sorry!"

"I come in on the ambulance," Bayless cut back in. "Not my choice that idiot Westerlind made me fall an' crack my head."

"You're right." Coal looked over at the clock behind the receptionist's desk. He still had plenty of time to get Bayless home and then get back for his rendezvous with Jordan and Grant. "I'll take you home. We need to talk anyway."

"I don't see about what," said Bayless, his tone surly.

"You will."

When they were seated in the car, Coal called dispatch to advise Nadine what he was going to be doing. Then he turned to Wilford Bayless.

"We need to talk about you pulling shotguns on people, Mr. Bayless—particularly on the sheriff."

"Oh, judas priest!" growled Bayless. "How's I s'posed to know you was the sheriff?"

"You shouldn't be pulling a shotgun on anyone," said Coal.

"Well, I damn shore will to protect my dogs!"

"You damn sure better start keeping your dogs under control," Coal said, his voice darkening.

"That's all you want to talk about?" said Bayless angrily. "Start drivin' me home." Coal complied, pulling away to head for Bayless's ranch mostly because he just wanted this cantankerous buffoon out of his car.

"I'm probably going to write you a citation for brandishing a firearm," Coal said when they were well on their way out of the town limits. "I'm guessing from the way you talk that you've got all your memory back just fine."

"I damn shore do. But you wanna write tickets, go write one to that Gunn Westerlind. He drives like a bat out of hell! You saw for yerself!"

"You thought he got too close to you, and you slipped and fell. I'm not sure that was his fault, Mr. Bayless."

"Oh, my hell! Let's talk about last Monday night then! When he tried to pass me in his pickup when there was another car comin' head on, and he went right between the two of us so close he hit the side of my damn cattle truck!"

Coal was just getting the Thunderbird up to speed. He turned and looked at Bayless. "You say he actually hit you?"

"Darn sure did!"

"Can you prove that?"

"I can!"

"Why didn't he wreck? Why didn't you *both* wreck?"

"He only hit his side mirror," replied Bayless.

"You're sure of that?"

"Hell yes. I went back an' picked it up off the road!"

Coal's heart was beginning to pound harder. He drove in silence for a while, only vaguely aware that his foot was creeping lower and lower on the gas pedal.

"Speakin' of breakin' the law," Wilford Bayless finally said. "You always do seventy-two in a fifty-five?"

"Oops!" Coal eased back on the gas. "Sorry. My mind was wandering."

"They call that inattentive driving, if I remember correct," said Bayless.

Coal laughed. "You got that one down pretty good. So listen, Mr. Bayless—are you telling me that on Monday night, Gunnar Westerlind passed you? And knocked off his mirror doing it?"

"I never said it was him, but it was shore his truck."

"What time would that have been, about?"

"Hell, I don't remember. After the bars closed and I was headin' home. So maybe two? Three?"

"Two or three in the morning. You'd swear to that? Sign a statement?"

"Don't see why not. 'Cept . . . You wanna trade?"

Coal laughed. "Your citation for recklessly brandishing a shotgun against an officer of the law in exchange for signing a statement about what you witnessed that night. And giving me the rearview mirror?"

"That's a deal. I shore got no use for it—less'n it's to look in an' see how perty I look."

Again, Coal laughed. "Looks like you just bargained your way out of a ticket—this time."

Coal dropped Wilford Bayless off at a ramshackle residence that looked like something straight out of *Gunsmoke,* except the longhorns had been traded out for Herefords, and sagebrush abounded in place of rolling tumbleweeds. Coal took the badly bent rearview mirror fixture Bayless gave him, whose mirror was shattered beyond use, and said goodbye, then headed back toward town.

He had only made it partway before, in the failing light, he saw a vehicle approaching from town that appeared red in color, and looked from the distance like a high-end automobile. Slowing down, he recognized Gunnar Westerlind's red Chrysler 300 as it flew past him at well over the speed limit, and he recognized the cowboy hat on its driver, who was alone when he should have had his son Troy in the passenger seat. Glancing in the rearview mirror, he saw the car take a bow as the brake lights came on too harshly. He had no way of knowing how fast Westerlind had been traveling, but he had more important things to think about anyway.

Keeping his own foot off the brakes, to make it look to Westerlind like he hadn't noticed him, Coal kept cruising on until the Chrysler passed out of sight in the twilight. The first driveway Coal found afterward, he pulled into it and turned the Thunderbird around, then stopped on the side of the road. He had been having a hunch that while Westerlind and his son were in town they might get the pickup from the shop and bring it home. Now it was time to see if his hunch was correct.

Sure enough, Coal soon spotted a pickup speeding his way from the direction of town. Tom T. Hall was crooning "That's How I Got to Memphis" when the rig flew past, and it was indeed Westerlind's Dodge.

Stomping on the gas, Coal spun out of the driveway and back onto the highway, heading south. As he drove, he clicked his red globe on and set it on the dash, then called dispatch to let them know he was in pursuit of the pickup.

The Dodge pickup had more get-up-and-go than Coal expected, and its driver, whom Coal assumed to be Troy Westerlind, decided to use every inch of pedal. Stupidly, the kid must have seen Coal pull out, and whether he recognized the Thunderbird or not, apparently he didn't want it catching up to him.

But the Dodge was no match for Coal's 429 Thunderjet in the ability to eat up miles, and it certainly wasn't built to stick to the road the same. Coal was flying up on the pickup when the deer, four of them to be exact, bounded across the highway right in front of it, and a fifth stepped out and stopped.

The pickup's brake lights came on as the vehicle went into a smoking skid, then began to slew sideways, eventually hitting a patch of ice. The whole vehicle did a donut, slamming backward into the pile of snow the plows had built up on the side of the road.

As Coal jerked the mic loose to call for another unit, the pickup was trying to pull free of the snow pile, but it was inserted much too deeply. After making his call, Coal drew his revolver, just in case, and stepped out of the car, clicking his brights on to shine into the face of the pickup's driver.

With the door as imaginary cover, Coal leveled the Smith and Wesson at the driver's side of the pickup's windshield, where the dark shape of a big person's head was weaving back and forth as if trying to make some monumental decision.

"Get out of the truck!" Coal commanded in his loudest voice. "Make it fast!"

After only one or two seconds' worth of hesitation, the pickup door flew open, and a man spilled out the side with his hands high in the air, slipped on the icy cap of the snow and fell to his knees. "Don't shoot! Don't shoot!"

"Troy?" called Coal. "Troy Westerlind?"

"Yes, sir! Yes, sir, it's me!" Coal was surprised to hear the boy sounding so deferential. It wasn't a sound he would have expected out of this kid, but then again, the bore of a .44 magnum can make respectful people out of the most belligerent pieces of work.

"Stay on your knees, Troy. Got it?"

"Yes, sir. Yes, sir, I'm staying!"

Coal reached back into the car and flipped his hazard lights on, then straightened back up to see Troy still kneeling on the ice. "You buried it good, huh?" said Coal as he walked close, amused at how high Troy Westerlind was able to reach his hands. "Why were you running, anyway?"

"I wasn't runnin'," Troy said, his hands edging down ever-so-slightly.

"You sure weren't strolling. I'm surprised a pickup can drive that fast."

Troy just stared at him. "Well, go ahead and stand up, Troy. Got any weapons on you?"

"No, sir. Not unless you count a pocketknife."

"A man can get killed by a pencil," replied Coal. "Or a paper-clip. Yes, your pocketknife is a weapon. Take it out and throw it in on the seat, then come over here."

Troy did as he was told, but as he obeyed, Coal could see a change slowly coming over his face. It might be in part because Troy had figured out Coal wasn't going to shoot him, but Coal's guts told him it was more because Troy was deescalating from being scared to feeling a surly, troubled teenager's greatest need—to look tough. Seconds more would reveal the truth.

"Where are you coming from, Troy?"

Wiping away a temporarily puzzled look as his hands came down even farther, Troy said, "From town"—as if that were news to Coal.

"Where in town?"

"Can I put my hands down?" The boy had done it—made it all the way from scared rabbit to cornered, angry coyote.

"No, why don't you keep them up for a while? Where in town are you coming from, did you say?"

"What's the difference?"

Coal stepped closer. "It could be a lot of difference."

"What are you gonna do? You know my dad's gonna be back here pretty soon." Troy's look was brazen now, and his eyes full of defiance.

"Do you know how long it would take me to rearrange your face with this gun barrel, Troy?"

Troy glared back. In his eyes, Coal could see him trying to decide if he could possibly be serious.

"You think you're in some Clint Eastwood movie? You got any idea how long it would take for my dad to rip that badge off your shirt?"

"A lot longer than it would take me to have you in cuffs on that snowbank, kid—and with your other eye swollen shut to match the one your old man gave you."

That comment stopped Troy cold. "You wouldn't dare hit me. And my dad didn't give me this eye. We told you—I got in a fight in Leadore."

"Did your friends try to help you?"

"I was by myself," sneered Troy. Bingo! Coal had already cut off any chance Troy might have later of trying to say he had been with friends in Leadore. The truth was, only one person had beaten Troy Westerlind, and as much as Coal instantly didn't like this kid, he knew the effect an abusive parent could have on a child, and he liked Gunnar Westerlind even less.

Coal had no idea if any other law enforcement unit would be coming along, but maybe it didn't matter. They had already been passed by three other vehicles, and now a fourth one, a green late sixties Chevrolet, slowed up and stopped just past where Troy had the Dodge stuck. The Chevy backed up, and someone in the passenger seat rolled down the window and leaned out. "Hey, Sheriff. Need any help?"

Coal didn't recognize the speaker, but he recognized the friendly Lemhi County attitude. "I'll take you up on that, if you have a few minutes. I'm going to need to pull this truck out of the snow. Do you have a tow chain?"

"Hold tight," said the man, and they backed up even farther, until they were back some ten feet from the front of the Dodge, and nearly to the front of Coal's car. Two men, ranchers, from their looks, descended, and one jerked a chain out from under the seat. They quickly had their rig hooked up to the Dodge's front bumper, and then the driver got back in. As the other man stood there watching, the Chevy's gears started to whine, and it backed slowly up and sucked the Dodge right out of the snowbank.

The driver got out and unhooked the chain, and the two men introduced themselves. "Need anything else?" the driver asked.

"Nope. Your timing was perfect, boys. Look me up at the courthouse sometime, and I'll buy you a cup of coffee."

After the Chevrolet drove off, Coal turned again to Troy, whose hands were barely up now. "You think you're gonna beat me now, Sheriff?" asked the boy with a sneer.

"I don't have any reason to, Troy," Coal replied. "But I'm definitely going to need to ask you some questions."

"Like what?" The tone of the boy's voice ground down hard on Coal's nerves, but he kept his cool.

"We'll go back to town. Then I'll ask."

"What about my dad's truck?"

"How about I follow you?"

"My dad's gonna . . ." Troy stopped himself. "Well, he'll be comin' back soon—to see where I am."

"He will," Coal said. "No doubt about it."

"You think he's not gonna—" Again, Troy cut his words short. He looked as if he were trying to rearrange his thoughts and say something important—and of course tough. At last, he clamped his mouth shut. The kid knew he was in trouble. Coal could see that in everything about his face.

"Troy?"

"What?"

"You know I can chase you down in that T-Bird no matter where you run—right?"

Troy only shrugged, holding onto his manly indignation.

"So I'm going to drive up a ways and turn around. Then you're going to drive the speed limit back to town and up behind the courthouse. I expect you know where that is."

"I'm not tellin' you nothin'," Troy spat. "I want a lawyer."

"If you want a lawyer, I'll sure get you one," said Coal. "The crappy thing about that, though, is you'll have to spend the night in jail."

"What? Hey, you got nothin' to hold me for!"

"That's not true, Troy. I have reckless driving, which is a misdemeanor, and an arrestable offense. In less than a minute, I might have resisting an officer, which is another one. And then I have aiding and abetting."

"What's that?" asked Troy.

"Meaning I think you helped murder somebody. Or at least you didn't come forward with knowledge you have of the facts. Either way, you decide to fight me, you're going to jail."

"I'm only seventeen," said Troy with a sneer. "Let's see you get away with this bull!"

Coal smiled thinly. "That's for a judge to worry about. Poor dumb county sheriffs just don't give a damn."

CHAPTER FORTY

All the way back to the jail, Coal was going over the facts of the case in his head, and going over what he so far had on Troy Westerlind. When it came to the killing, and Troy, he had next to nothing. He didn't even believe Troy had killed anyone, but for some reason he certainly wasn't admitting that he had been up and down that dark cemetery road the night of the murders. Why? What did he have to gain by lying, and what could he have to lose by telling the truth?

Another thing Coal spent a lot of time going over in his head was exactly how he was going to approach questioning Troy back at the jail. The biggest part of him thought that questioning him at all, prior to the boy having a chance to get a lawyer, was going to backfire on him. But Coal had never actually told Troy Westerlind he was under arrest. If he made sure the boy knew he was only being interviewed as a witness, rather than interrogated as a suspect, he would be legally covered—wouldn't he? And if he discovered anything on accident, well, that would be admissible in the case, would it not? As long as he made sure Troy knew he was free to go any time. But that was the hardest part: As soon as he told Troy he was free to go, he was going to go. Coal didn't know the boy well, but he knew that much about him.

By the time they were climbing the drive to the back lot of the courthouse, Coal had made a decision. He was going to hold Troy for reckless driving. He wanted at least to see how his father acted when he had to drive in and pick him up. But in the interim, he would read the boy his rights, then see if he wanted to sign a statement. If Troy could provide some good reason why he had been up by the cemetery that night, even if it was something stupid he shouldn't have been doing, Coal didn't care. He was willing to cut the kid a break, even though he wasn't sure he deserved one. But first, he had to milk him for any fact he might know that would help in solving this case and getting it out of his hair.

Coal parked the Thunderbird next to Westerlind's Dodge, and they got out at the same time. "I guess I'm probably not telling you anything new, but the jail's down those stairs," Coal said.

With sullen eyes, Troy turned toward the stairs, then looked back at Coal. "I know I get to make a call."

"Sure you know it. I'm sure you've watched at least *that* much television, when you weren't out and around wreaking havoc on the world."

"Go screw yourself," said Troy, curling his lip. He turned and strode to the stairs, going down them and pushing the jail door open. Jordan Peterson was already there waiting.

"Hi," Jordan told the boy. Troy merely stared at him, his jaw hard. He had made up his mind not to talk.

"This is Troy Westerlind," said Coal as he followed the teenager in and shut the door behind himself. "The driver of the white and blue Dodge Curlie told us about."

Troy's eyes hooded a little more. "Where's my phone call?"

Coal grinned. "Oh, your phone call? Don't get all worked up about that. There's no law that says you have a right to a phone call in Idaho."

"What?"

"Yeah. Welcome to Hollywood. But don't worry—when I'm ready, I'll let you call your dad. He needs to come get you anyway, so I can talk to him about his truck."

"What about it?"

"Well, first off, where did you just pick it up?"

Troy tried his utmost to stare Coal down while at the same time frantically searching his memory banks. "How should I remember? Some place here in town!"

"On what street, Troy?"

"I don't remember. On Main, I think."

"You think? How long've you lived here, anyway?"

"A couple years is all."

"A couple of years? Troy, this town has less than three thousand residents. It's not a big place, and you aren't some little snot-nosed kid. You're seventeen, right? And you expect me to believe you don't know for sure if that shop was on Main?"

"I'm not answering any more questions." Troy's eyes were belligerent, but at this point Coal was starting to understand that most of it was put on. He had a hunch it was mostly because the kid was afraid of saying something wrong and getting his father in trouble.

"It's okay. Before you make your call, I'll just ring up Sylvia's and talk to them about the truck. Does that sound familiar? I think that's where your dad said he took it to have a tune-up."

Troy's eyes flashed around the room. "Whatever! Yeah, I guess that sounds right—Sylvia's."

"Wrong choice. He told me Jerry's."

"Oh, wait! Yeah. Jerry's!" Troy sputtered. "Yeah, it was Jerry's. I was thinkin' about somethin' else."

"Sure," said Coal. "All right, just hang tight. Jordan, entertain him for a bit, would you?"

"You bet," Jordan said.

"I have to use the bathroom," Troy growled.

Coal lifted his chin toward the cellblock door. "Let him use the john back there, Jord. Just keep him back from Badger, huh? Wouldn't want the kid getting his head cut off or anything."

"Sure thing," said Jordan. "Come on—Troy, is it?"

Troy only glared at Jordan until Jordan shrugged and walked with him to the door.

Coal had just reached over to pick up the phone book and look up Jerry's when he heard a commotion back in the cell block. It grew into a roar by the time he stepped the door and threw it open, seeing Hunter Jack with his big hands wrapped around the cell bars and staring out at Troy.

"Hey, Sheriff!" Jack growled. "Who is that damn kid? He was in my house! It was him stole my stuff, I bet you a hundred bucks!"

"Huh? Badger! What are you talking about?" Coal asked.

"That kid! He came over a while back with a bunch of damn Boy Scout of Americas. They were doin' some kinda merit badge thing, and somebody told 'em I had a bunch of Indian artifacts, an' weapons an' stuff. I seen this kid eyeballin' everything I owned. I *knew* he'd be comin' back! Kid! When I get out of here, you're dead! You hear me?"

Coal jerked his thumb at the cellblock door, looking at Jordan. "Jordan, get him out of here, all right? Let him use our toilet."

Once Jordan and Troy were gone, Troy looking visibly shaken although he tried to keep up his angry, tough front, Coal turned back to Hunter Jack and stalked close to him.

"Badger, what was that all about? You really think that kid was in your house?"

"Aw, hell, Sheriff! Look at the size of that kid? You think I'd forget a kid that big comin' in my house with a bunch o' little twelve-year-old Scouts? It was him. I guarantee. He was drivin' a blue an' white pickup."

"Okay. You're right about that. But why do you think he came back and stole things from you?"

"I told you," Jack proclaimed. "He was eyeballin' everything real close. But it wasn't like them other kids. This one was casing the place. I been around law breakers all my life, Sheriff. I know the look."

A chill ran down Coal's spine, a chill he wasn't sure he could explain. He turned and looked back at the closed door that led out to the office. The first thought that hit him, and it hit him hard, was: Did Troy Westerlind own a pair of cowboy boots?

"As soon as I make a couple of phone calls, I'll get you something to eat, Badger. Any preference?"

"Food," growled the Shoshone. "Meat. But what're you gonna do about that kid? I got a broke-in house, an' stuff missin'. I guarantee you it was him that took it!"

"Okay, I'll see what I can do, Badger. I promise." And that was a promise Coal was going to keep, because all of a sudden he was getting far more curious about Troy Westerlind's reasons for being up at the cemetery the night of the killings than he had guessed he would be. And he was thinking about Dawn Kelly's reluctance to talk . . . and Dale Moore's attempted suicide . . .

Coal went back out and looked up the number to Jerry's Automotive, then made the call. Jerry Riggs himself answered.

"Hey, Jerry, this is Coal Savage. How are you doing?"

Good! Good, Sheriff. What can I do for you?

"Well, I wanted to ask you about a vehicle that might have been picked up from you today. And by the way—do you do body work too?"

Sure, sure. Some little things, anyway. What was the vehicle?

"A 1970 Dodge. It was blue and white, and belongs to a rancher named Gunnar Westerlind. Sometimes he goes by Gunn."

Oh, yeah, yeah. I know him. Nice guy. Beautiful truck, too.

"Okay, so the next question is did you do a tune-up on that truck, and did you put a new passenger side mirror on it for him?"

Well, hang on a second, Sheriff. You said he would've got the truck today, right?

"Yes. Probably about an hour ago."

Sheriff, I ain't seen Westerlind in here in a good month or more. Maybe two or three.

After hanging up with Jerry Riggs, Coal stared at the phone for twenty or thirty seconds. This was a new twist. No Jerry's? Why would Westerlind have lied about that? On a whim, he turned to the *Yellow Pages* to look up auto body shops in town. There were only two of them, Andy's, and one other. He glanced at Andy's phone number to make sure he remembered it right, then called it up. Andy was picking it up as Troy Westerlind came out of the bathroom.

"Hey, Andy, this is Coal. Can you hang on for a second?"

Coal turned to Troy. "Your dad had a tune-up done on the truck—right?"

Still looking surly, but suddenly in a cautious way, Troy nonchalantly said, "Uh, yeah. I think that's right?"

"Okay. Hey, Andy," he said into the phone. "By any chance, did you have a Dodge pickup in there today owned by a Gunnar Westerlind?"

Sure did.

"Oh!" Coal was surprised. "Did you do a tune-up on it?"

Andy laughed. *A tune-up? Coal, are you losing it? You're getting me mixed up with Ken Parks.*

"So you don't do tune-ups? I kind of thought that was the case."

Well, I can *do tune-ups, I guess. And if anybody asked, I probably would. But no, that Westerlind fellow was in here for me to put a new mirror on the truck. The old one got knocked off by a tractor, he told me.*

"Oh. A tractor, huh? I see. Was it an insurance job?"

Nope. Paid cash for it. And he told me it was pretty embarrassing how it happened, and he didn't want me to tell his wife any of the details about it, so he said he'd give me an extra twenty just to keep quiet about it if she or anybody else called to get any details.

"Really? Very interesting. Thanks, buddy."

Coal hung up and looked over at Troy, trying to sound as casual as he could. "So, Troy, where is your mom, anyway?"

Troy sneered at him. "Why?"

"I'd just like to know."

"Yeah. So would I. She left when I was seven, and nobody knows where she went."

"So I guess she wouldn't care too much if somebody gave her the details about how you whacked the rearview mirror off the passenger side of your dad's pickup then, right?"

Troy, staring hard at Coal's face and pretending to be big and bad, probably didn't mean to curse out loud. But he did.

CHAPTER FORTY-ONE

"You still want to call your father, Troy?" asked Coal.

The boy tried hard to stare him down, but the fire was gone from his eyes. He glanced over at Jordan, then back at Coal.

"Hey, Jordan," said Coal, "would you do me a favor and go upstairs for a little bit? Maybe say hi to Cindy Hardlinger for me?" Cindy was the secretary up in the court clerk's office.

"Um, sure thing, Coal. I just hope she doesn't think I'm hittin' on her."

"Oh, come on, Jordan. You're both single, right? You can't be that superficial. She's a really nice girl."

Jordan's expression was the closest Coal had ever seen to being defiant. "Uh, yeah."

"Besides," Coal added. "She really knows her way around a pot of coffee."

"Great. That's how I plan to pick a wife. Call me when you're done, huh? I need plenty of time to get our date set up."

With Coal's laugh echoing after him, Jordan left, and Coal was alone in the room with Troy Westerlind.

"Troy, do you want to talk? I'm here to listen. Or you can call your dad."

"He ain't my *dad,"* said Troy, sounding belligerent again.

"What is he?" asked Coal.

"My old man, if I call him anything."

"I'll have to talk to . . . *your old man.* You know that, right?"

"Why?"

"Because he's been lying. To the state police, and to me. He told us you were with him all night the night of the murders."

"I *was!"* said Troy, sounding desperately angry.

"Troy. Stop now, man. It's not worth it," Coal said. "It's all going to come out anyway. Understand?"

"No."

"Well, let me cut it into bite-size pieces for you. Dawn's going to talk to me. And Dale's going to talk to me. And they were both in the pickup with you that night. I have an eyewitness who recognized you, and another who saw you clearly and would probably know you if she saw you again. And I have the pretty strong testimony of a man you tried to pass at two or three o'clock in the morning that night, when you broke off your mirror going home on Twenty-Eight. I have testimonial evidence of that, and your old broken side mirror outside in my car. There's an awful lot stacked up against you, Troy. The only thing I don't have is the whys.

"And now," Coal went on, "I have a guy telling me he thinks you're the one who broke into his house and stole some Indian weapons from him. Do you have any idea how bad this is starting to look for you? If all the fingerprints come back from the FBI, and yours are on the murder weapon . . . Troy, you could be going to prison for life."

Troy Westerlind was starting to look green. He looked around the room, and for a second his gaze settled on Coal's metal garbage can, which sat beside the desk. Coal remembered too recently when Troy's friend, Dale, had used a similar garbage can.

"You feeling okay, son?"

Troy shook his head. "No. Can I sit down?"

"Of course." Coal pushed the chair toward Troy Westerlind that his deputies and others used when in conference with him. On an afterthought, seeing the green around Troy's gills again, he slid the metal can close to the chair and watched Troy slump into the chair.

"Troy, you need to understand something," Coal said, trying to think ahead and cover all his bases. "You aren't under arrest for anything. You know that, right?"

Troy stared blankly at him. Finally, he replied with a nod.

"That means if you had a way home you could get up and walk out any time, except after what just happened with your driving, I can't let you leave just now with the pickup."

"Why am I here then?"

"You're here to wait for your fa— Your 'old man' to come get you. And for me to get some answers from him."

"He ain't gonna talk to you," said Troy. The words could have sounded belligerent, but all the bellicose tone was gone from Troy's voice, and his manner was defeated.

"He'll have to if he wants any easy way to get that truck back."

"Why? It's his truck, right?"

"It is. But it was used to flee a traffic stop today, Troy. A lawfully attempted traffic stop. That means I get to keep it if I want to—until the whole case makes it through court." Coal was speaking harsh things to Troy Westerlind, but none of them spoken in a harsh voice. As he always did, he tried to match his tone to the person he was conversing with, and Troy's current attitude was submissive. He knew he was potentially in serious trouble, both from the law, and probably from his father.

"What's gonna happen to Dale and Dawn?" Troy asked. "I mean, if they talk."

"It depends on what they'd be talking about. You know that."

Troy nodded. His fingers were laced together now, and his hands in his lap. He stared at them as if they were a confusing puzzle he was bent on figuring out.

"Am I old enough to go to prison?" Troy asked in a quiet voice.

Coal didn't want to give the answer to the Troy he was talking to right now. He would have loved to say it earlier, but it was hard to say to a young man so visibly shaken. "You are. Plenty. It all depends on what the crime is. Do you need to tell me anything?"

"I . . . I can't."

"Why?"

"I just can't." Troy's chin began to tremble, and he lowered his head even farther, as if he was going to sleep.

"Eventually, we have to call your father, Troy," Coal said in a soft voice. "Either you do, or I do. Your choice. Unless there's anything you want to tell me before that."

Even though Troy was trying hard to hide his face, Coal could see him blinking rapidly. Finally, the boy said, "I think I got a eyelash or somethin' in my eye." Coal understood that. He had had plenty of eyelashes get in his own eyes—mostly since the trouble first began with Laura, the wife he had lost.

"You want to go try to get it out with some warm water? That usually helps me."

"Yeah, sure. I guess I'll try that." Troy jumped and hurried to the restroom. When he came back out, his eyes were red, but he said, "Yeah. I think I got it."

He came and sat back down in the chair Coal had offered him. "What can I do to help you, son?" asked Coal. "I have to call your father soon unless you want to. It's only going to get worse the longer he has to wonder where you are. After all, you *were* supposed to be right behind him."

Looking down at his hands again, Troy nodded. Finally, he forced himself to look up. "Is there any way you could put me in jail?"

Coal stared at the boy. "How's that again?"

"Could you put me in jail?"

"Why?"

"Because . . ." Troy's voice trailed off.

Realization finally came to Coal, who was a little bit dense perhaps because he had never had to suffer the kind of fear Troy Westerlind was suffering. "It's that bad with him, huh?"

Troy nodded, unable to meet his eyes. He finally managed to say, "I gotta get out of there. I can't go back."

"I understand. But you have to talk to me."

"About what?" Troy asked, raising his head. "About that night?"

"Well, yes, about that too. But right now I'm talking about something else completely. I'm talking about how your face looks, Troy. And how I'm guessing a lot of your body might look too. That has to stop. You can't keep allowing it to happen to you and not say anything."

Troy looked down. He had obviously decided there was no point pretending about the attack in Leadore anymore. Even a bunch of identity-less boys from Idaho Falls couldn't cover for his situation now.

"Do you want to talk about that night up at the cemetery, Troy? Maybe that would help you. I know it would help me."

"How?"

"Because it would answer some questions. Son . . . You remember you're not under arrest, right? You remember you can get up and leave any time, as long as you're on foot?"

The boy nodded.

"Okay. I'm going to write a statement to that effect and have you sign it. And then I'm going to ask you some questions."

Again, Troy only nodded in reply.

Coal got out a notepad, and upon it he wrote, in his best penmanship, *I, Troy Westerlind, understand that I am not in any way being detained. I am not under arrest. I have been made completely aware that I am free to leave at any time, and that any question I answer is answered of my own free will. Signed,*

In the space following the last word, Coal drew a line, then took the pad around the desk and handed it and the pen to Troy Westerlind. The boy couldn't keep his hand from shaking as he signed his name.

Coal went and sat down again, pulling the big, awkward-looking tape recorder out of his desk drawer, setting it on top of the desk, and plugging it in. He hit the *play* and *record* buttons simultaneously. "Now look at me, Troy." Troy looked up. "Troy Westerlind, were you or were you not, on the night of Monday, February 19th of this year, driving up by the Salmon cemetery with your friends Dawn Kelly and Dale Moore?"

Without warning, the outside door flew open, coming just shy of slamming into the wall. Startled, Coal lunged up, his hand going to the butt of his gun.

There in the doorway stood Gunnar Westerlind, his hat low over his eyes.

"Sheriff, I'm a pretty reasonable man," said Westerlind, his face looking dark from more than just the shadow of his hat. "But I'm not above getting angry. Would you mind telling me just what in the hell is going on here, and why you're holding my boy? And just why the hell was I not notified that he was down here?"

No sooner had those words left Westerlind's mouth when his dark gaze pivoted, settling on the scabbed, battered face of his son.

CHAPTER FORTY-TWO

"Afternoon, Mr. Westerlind," said Coal. He had long since ceased any attempt at being familiar enough with the man to call him by his first name, as he had once requested he do. "We were going to call you, but we were just trying to settle a few things first."

Coal had planned to reach over on his desk and shut off the tape recorder, but he changed his mind and left it running. At that moment, Troy Westerlind almost lunged out of his chair.

"Sorry, Dad. I was going to call you as soon as I could."

The father looked at the son, his eyes still in the shadow of his hat, but darker still than they should have been. "What've you been discussing, might I ask?"

"Nothin', Dad. Just talkin' about . . . stuff." The boy's eyes started to go to Coal, then quickly fell away.

"Like I said, I was about to let him call you," said Coal. And then he saw the look of terror in the boy's eyes, and he lost his sense of caution.

Moving around the desk, Coal motioned the boy over closer to him. "We had an incident with the pickup today, which is why the boy is here. He kind of went into a spin on the highway and ended up in a snowbank."

"Okay?" said Westerlind, his eyes full of burning suspicion.

"And while we were talking, it turned out your son didn't recall all the same details you did about your pickup, and why it was in the shop."

"Huh?"

"I called Jerry's, Mr. Westerlind. And I called Andy's, which my friend Andy Holmes owns."

Gunn Westerlind's face went still and cold, his eyes hardening even more than before. He said nothing, because there was nothing he could say.

"Listen. I sure as hell don't care where you take your pickup, mister. But what I do care about is you lying through your teeth to me, and when you start lying about one thing, I begin to think I have reason to suspect lies from you about *everything*." Westerlind apparently still had trouble finding anything to say in return.

"You've been lying about where you took your truck, and why. You've been lying about where your boy was at what time. You lied to the state patrolman running a lawful murder investigation, and you lied to me the other day about your son being in Leadore when we both know he was home, in the house with you, but for obvious reasons you couldn't let him come to the door."

Westerlind's eyes flashed over to his son. "What have you been telling him?"

"Shut up, Westerlind. You shut your mouth and listen to me. I can see what your son looks like right now, and I saw the marks on your hands the night of that call. I'm going to start paying you a visit. Every—damn—day. And every day you had better let me see your boy. If one new mark shows up anywhere on this boy—and I mean *anywhere*—you had better have a damn signed affidavit from the person who put it there. Do we understand each other?"

Westerlind glared. "Well, I guess we do. Pretty well. Anything else?"

"Yes. Your boy and I have an awful lot still to talk about. I wouldn't even know where to begin. But you had better make damn good and sure he is somewhere that I can locate him any time I please. Am I making myself clear?"

Westerlind nodded. Coal couldn't remember ever seeing more hatred in any man's eyes.

"We're conducting a murder investigation. Double homicide. But you know that already. Now know this, and your boy already does: He has just gone high on the list of suspects, for murder and burglary. Let that sink in good and deep."

"All right," said Westerlind, finally having found his tongue. "Now you hear this, you high and mighty son of a bitch. You might think you are God's gift to law enforcement. You might think you have the right to run roughshod over other people and do just as you please. But every bit as powerful as you think you are in this valley, you can't even come close to having the friends I have, Savage. And you, my friend, are about to come up hard and fast against a brick wall. I would suggest you start looking for another job—and maybe in another state."

"I have two things to say to you," Coal said. "One—I am *not* your friend. And two—I'll take you apart with my bare hands if you lay another finger on this young man, and to hell with who you think you know, in this state or any other state. We good?"

After the Westerlinds walked out, Coal turned and looked down at the tape recorder on top of his desk. The twin reels were still spinning around and around, even in the deathly silence left in the room.

Reaching over, he hit the stop button, and then *rewind.* That was one tape recording that was going to be of absolutely no value to him now.

When Jordan Peterson came back downstairs after Coal called him, he stopped and looked around the room, then gave Coal an odd glance. "Something happen?"

Coal looked over at him. "What do you mean?"

"Umm . . . I'm not even sure what I mean! Something just feels weird in here."

Coal looked at his deputy for a long time, then suddenly started laughing, and he could feel the tension from the last half hour seeping out of his every pore. He finally went over and plopped down on his chair behind the desk. He looked up at Jordan, who was staring at him as if he had gone insane.

"What?"

Jordan shook his head. "You. Who's going to be the new sheriff after they commit you to Blackfoot South?" The actual institution's name was State Hospital South, a mental institution where many of the southern half of Idaho's legally insane ended up being residents, and which was generally used as a joke by Idahoans who thought one of their friends—or enemies—had cracked.

Coal let out a long sigh, wiping his eyes. "Don't mind me. While you were gone, Troy's dad showed up unannounced."

"And?" Jordan stared at his boss for a few seconds. "Oh, crap. It went over that good, huh? And I missed the whole thing."

Coal chuckled. "Well, if you get bored, it's all on that tape. Just make sure you delete it afterward, or at least hide it someplace really special."

The door opened, and Grant Fairbourne came in. "Am I early?"

Coal looked over at the clock. "A bit. Not bad. No reason we can't start now."

"I can think of a reason," Jordan cut in.

"What's that?"

"So we can also listen to that recording. I swear I'm not going to sleep a wink until I do."

Grant and Jordan had a good laugh the whole way through Coal's recording of his surprise meeting with Gunnar Westerlind, while Coal sat there cringing for much of it.

"Well," said Jordan when it was over. "I guess you and Westerlind won't be going out to any dinner parties together any time soon, huh?"

"Nope, I guess not. Now can we get to work?"

They got together at the desk and wrote up a list of all the bars in town, and then Coal divvied them up into thirds and tore each list off the page, handing one to Grant and one to Jordan. They both looked down their lists, and when Jordan had read his, he looked over and scanned Grant's. He looked at Coal blandly.

"You got the Lantern?"

"Maybe. I didn't really notice," Coal lied.

"Probably didn't have anything to do with the bartender down there," said Jordan, winking at Grant.

"Probably did," said Coal. "I'm trying to protect her from the two of you." With a grin, he led the way out, turning to make sure Jordan, who was bringing up the rear, locked the door.

Out at the Thunderbird, Coal paused to tell the others he was going to go get some food for Hunter Jack and then later might run into them down in town.

After feeding an obviously very tense Hunter Jack, who was still brooding over the sudden appearance of Troy Westerlind, alive and in person, Coal headed back down the hill. Thanks to the early hour, he found a parking spot directly in front of the Lantern and went on inside.

Elisa Doan was behind the bar, wearing a tight red plaid shirt of thin cotton, silver hoop earrings, and with her walnut brown hair sculpted tightly about her face and just covering her eyebrows. She gave Coal a big smile.

"Well, if it isn't Coal Savage himself!"

"It is. And if it isn't Elisa Doan."

Elisa Doan scanned Coal's attire, resting too long on the edge of his coat. "I guess that little spot of gold I'm seeing is your badge. Meaning you're on duty?"

"I'm afraid I am."

"Damn."

He laughed. "Sorry. Hey. I have a long list of annoying questions for you."

"My favorite kind."

"They're all about a guy named Curlie Burks and his girlfriend Melissa."

"Uh-oh. My favorite kind—of losers."

They both laughed. "So I take it you don't care for them."

"Oh, not really. I mean—sorry! I don't mean I don't care for them. They're all right, I guess. I'm sort of a loser myself, right? Or else I wouldn't be working in a bar."

"No comment to that."

She frowned, cocking her head. "So that means you agree."

"Stop! We can discuss all that some other time. I just need some answers, and I have a feeling if anyone would know them it would be the person who works most often at Curlie's favorite hangout."

"Okay, fair enough. I'd rather not hear about how you think I'm a loser anyway."

"Have you ever seen the movie *The Born Losers?"* asked Coal.

"Oh, yeah, I think so. You mean the first Billy Jack movie?"

"Uh-huh."

"What about it? Well, being a loser isn't always bad, right?"

She laughed again. "Okay, you got me again. Now that you've buttered me back up to where I can be in love with you again—what are your questions?" She gave him a wink. He hoped that meant she was playing around with him.

"So how well do you know Curlie Burks?"

"I've never slept with him, if that's what you mean."

Coal cringed. This was going to be a long interview. "Actually, I never even thought about that. I hope that's not how you judge how well you know everybody." He said it with a playful smile, but he was actually quite serious. He could see one thing: No matter how nice Elisa Doan seemed, they were not going to get very well acquainted, at least not on a personal basis.

Elisa's expression turned more business-like. "Well, I've been seeing him in here pretty much since I started—so two years ago? He's pretty regular. Comes in at least twice a week. And I mean at *least.* Some weeks maybe five times. And hits on me at least every other time."

"Okay. I assume when he's not with Melissa."

"Oh, he doesn't care. I'm not sure she does either. She always has other guys buzzin' around her too. It's bar life, you know?"

That was great. It was another reason Coal had for being glad he *didn't* know all that much about bar life.

"I guess. So you've had talks with Curlie, I guess, if he's familiar enough to be hitting on you."

"Listen, you don't have to be all that familiar with somebody to hit on them, buster." She grinned, then went serious again. "Sorry. I forgot, this is all business." She squared her shoulders and saluted him playfully. "But seriously, yeah, we've had some nice talks—or at least interesting ones—when he isn't too drunk yet."

"Have you ever seen him be violent? Or overly argumentative?"

"No. I don't recall anything like that."

"How about Melissa?"

"Oh, no! No, she's a sweetheart. Kind of an airhead, but a nice girl."

"All right. Next question. Does the name Everett Sherman mean anything to you?"

She gave him a playful frown. "Well, duh! Of course it does. It was all over the news."

"Oh. Right." Now Coal felt the fool. There probably wasn't a soul in town by now who ever turned the TV or a radio on who didn't have the names of Everett Sherman and Irene Boyer memorized. "So a better question would be—did you know them?"

"I actually did."

"So you were just messing with me."

"Yeah, sorry. Yes, I knew them both a long time before the news came out."

"You don't seem very sorry."

She cocked her head sideways at him, pretending to try and decide if he was crazy. "Are you for real? Of course I'm not sorry. That guy was a jerk. And Irene? What a total boozer. Loser boozer, to put it kindly. Every time they came in here I knew it was going to be a long night."

"So let me cut to the chase. Did you ever see anything happen between Curlie and Everett that might have led them to have hard feelings for each other?"

"Well, sure."

"Enough for Curlie to want to kill Everett?"

Elisa scoffed. "Listen, I'm not a murderer myself, but I doubt there was one person who ever spent much time around Everett Sherman who didn't wish they could kill him at some time or other—or at least didn't wish somebody else would kill him."

CHAPTER FORTY-THREE

"Well, Elisa," said Coal. "I don't know that I'm getting any closer to pinning a murder on Curlie or Melissa, but it's been entertaining to try."

"Then I guess that's a success," said Elisa Doan. "But we're not done, are we?"

"Not if you think there's more."

"No, but I just want to hold you."

Coal laughed. "I could take that two ways."

"I know." She winked at him, then suddenly looked over toward the front door. Promptly, she swore.

Spinning around, Coal saw Annie Price standing in the doorway glaring at him and Elisa. She scoffed, left behind the stench of a rotten, disgusted look, and backed out, shutting the door.

"Oh, crap," said Elisa, looking back over at Coal. "Umm . . . Sorry about that."

Straightening back up to the woman, Coal let out a long sigh. "Yeah. Well, not your fault—and it's not like Annie and I are married."

"Okay. Well, I'm sorry anyway. You know what they say about a woman's scorn."

"Uh-huh, and I guess I'll find out in person all too soon. Can we go back to the question about Curlie and Sherman? Did anything ever happen to make you think Curlie could end up hating him?"

"Actually, yes."

"More than anyone else?"

"Well, I'm not sure about that, but it was pretty ugly. See that guy over there?" She pointed to a man in a white tee shirt with a great big Tweety Bird printed on the front. "He can tell you more of the story than I can, but here's what I know. One night Curlie was playin' pool with Ev Sherman, an' it was gettin' pretty heated. Of course they were both drunk as skunks by then. Curlie was in to Ev quite a bit of money. And I mean *quite a bit*. It was gettin' heated. Finally, Curlie started to turn the tables on this one game, an' he was on fire. It seemed from what I could see, and from the cheers comin' from there that pretty much every weird shot he tried, he made."

"So he won?"

"No. He won just that one game, but he still owed Ev real big. Maybe too big to pay him back. He tried to laugh it all off and say he wasn't really playin' for money and he didn't think Ev was either. But Ev was, and he got pretty ugly about it. They had a scuffle, and some of the other guys—Lane was one—pulled them apart. Curlie got all huffy and said he'd bet his pickup on the next game."

"And he lost."

"He lost," she echoed.

"So then why was Curlie still drivin' his pickup that night at the scene?"

"That part I'm not sure about. Anything I told you I'd just be guessing—but educated guessing."

"What do you mean?"

"Well, it's pretty well known around the Fish that Curlie's fairly well connected when it comes to the drug scene—you catch my drift?"

"Wait—the Fish?"

Elisa stared at Coal with amused eyes, waiting. He never got the joke. "Come on, dude. The Fish? You know—*Salmon?* I guess you don't hang around my kind of crowd too much."

Coal laughed. "Oh, jeez. Guess I should have seen that one."

Elisa matched his laugh, looking over toward the front door as it opened. It must not have been Annie returning with a flamethrower, because the bartender smiled.

Turning casually, Coal watched a thick-set man in a green John Deere cap and blue buffalo plaid shirt strolling toward them. "Hey, Sunshine! How's my main squeeze?"

Giggling, Elisa said, "Oh, I'm great, Verd. Wired on caffeine and ready for the night. How about you? Can I get you anything?"

"Aw, you cut me to the core, baby! You know what I want."

"Okay, but I'm workin'. I'll just get you a drink instead."

Verd let out a guffaw, glancing over to appraise Coal. "Real funny, woman. Watch how you're talkin', Elisa! You don't want the fuzz to start gettin' the wrong idea about me."

"What, that you're a Casanova?"

Verd's laugh was the next thing to a giggle. "Right! But I keep hearin' the sheriff is the Casanova." The man grinned at Coal, but there was a glint of a challenge in his dark blue eyes.

"I'm grabbin' you one of those disgusting Buds, Verd, unless you've changed poisons," said Elisa as she turned away. "An' I'm guessing you'd like me to hook you up with a pack of Winstons."

"You know me too well, baby."

As Elisa went for the beer, Verd turned to Coal. "Just havin' fun with you, Sheriff. Verd Butler. How you doin'?"

The man held out his hand, and Coal took it, hiding his reluctance in doing so from his face.

"Coal," he introduced himself.

Verd Butler grinned. "Aw, hell, Sheriff—er, I mean *Coal.* Ain't nobody in the valley don't know by now who you are. You come in right off an' start stealin' up all the foxy chicks."

That comment made Coal chuckle. "Yeah. I guess that would be me," he said, not trying to hide the sarcasm in his tone.

Elisa stepped back over, sliding an open can of Budweiser across the bar, with a pack of Winstons balanced on top of it. Without hearing a price, Verd handed her some folded cash. "Keep the change, doll."

She gave him a wink, setting the money behind the bar. Then she turned and indicated Coal with a wave of her hand. "Hey, Verd. I don't suppose you have a minute."

"Sure, baby, what's up?"

"Well, weren't you in here the night Curlie lost his pickup in that pool game with Ev Sherman?"

"Ha! Boy, was I!"

"Okay, so Coal has some questions about it, and maybe you could help him more than me."

"Oh, sure. Sure." Butler looked at Coal, rubbing a hand across his dark whiskers. "Anything to get some credits with the local fuzz, brother! Oh—and . . ." He scanned the smoke-filled back of the room. "I see two other guys that were here that night, too. You already talk to them?"

"Nope. I'm just starting on Elisa."

The man let out a boisterous laugh. "Well, dang! Ain't we all?"

Coal chuckled, out of politeness. He was guessing Verd Butler was more or less harmless, but he certainly was a mouthy one.

At the back of the room, a jukebox suddenly cranked up, and The Rolling Stones began to pollute the atmosphere with "Brown Sugar," whose title was sweet, but whose sound was not, at least not to the ears of a dyed-in-the-wool country boy. Trying to ignore the noise, Coal started questioning Verd Butler about the night of the big pool game. As he had expected, Butler kept feeling the need to insert off-color humor and flat-out stupid observations into his commentary, besides the fact that he didn't tell Coal much more than Elisa already had.

"That ruckus, though," said Butler with a big laugh. "Now that was a fight, huh, sugar?" he exclaimed, looking over at Elisa.

"Oh, whatever," she replied. "You know I'm not much for fightin'."

"Sure, sure. I know—flower power, right?" Verd laughed and turned back to Coal. "But man, did that little faggot lay into Curlie. He wasn't much for size, but whew! Could he pack a wallop! Split Curlie's eyelid right open, for sure. He'd a won that brawl, too, if me an' some o' them others didn't drag 'im off an' get 'im to chill out."

"What happened then?"

"Well, of course Curlie was pretty heated up, right? I mean, he didn't ever even make no physical move t'ward that chump, an' he laid into him. So Curlie starts to yellin'—of course while we all was holdin' Sherman back—that we should let 'im loose—that he's gonna kill 'im. Honest truth? We would've too, if we thought he could do it. I don't think there was nobody around that really liked that piece o' work. I was happy as a clam when I heard the news, but I sure hoped the killer wasn't Curlie."

"Why would you care?"

"Why? Because I like Curlie. He's my bud. Hell, Sheriff, *everybody* likes Curlie. And he wouldn't hurt no one—I swear it."

"Okay. So that night—did Curlie end up giving his truck to Sherman? After he lost?"

"No, an' that was weird, because that little faggot was like a badger, man, an' he sure wouldn't have forgot about somethin' that big, even if he *was* drunk when it happened. But Curlie kept on drivin' the truck, an' it even seemed like he got to be chummy with Sherman. I'd see 'em around together quite a bit. So whatever. I don't judge nobody, but I don't know how a good guy like Curlie could be pals with a jerk-off like that idiot."

When Coal had had enough of Verd Butler, he excused himself to let Verd do all his hitting on Elisa Doan, but Verd stopped him before he got far.

"Hey, Coal—one thing you should be careful about with old Lane there—the Tweety Bird guy? I heard Melissa Talty might be involved in all this crap, but I wouldn't say anything to Lane about her. The two of them are kinda havin' a . . . a *thing*. You know?"

"Melissa and Tweety Bird?" asked Coal for clarification.

"That's a big rumor around here," Elisa confirmed with a shrug. "So tread careful."

Coal thanked them and waded through a sea of tables to get to where Tweety Bird, the guy Elisa had called Lane, and some guy who resembled a wrinkled old snake with arms were matching up at the pool table. Coal watched for a while until Lane, who had the appearance of an ex-jock, maybe twenty-five years old, with big, powerful-looking arms that like his belly had taken on a lot of fleece since his high school football glory days, glanced over at him. The look in Lane's eyes was one of irritation at someone studying his game too closely, but when he saw the gold badge, he straightened up. For the moment, he seemed to have forgotten his shot.

"Can I help you—Sheriff?"

Coal shrugged. "Yes, but go ahead and play out your game. I don't want to ruin your concentration."

"Ah, heck," said Lane. "No prob. My partner can handle my end." He turned and held his pool cue out to another man. "Here, Smitty. Mop him up for me, huh?"

While Smitty and the erect snake went on to play the game already set up, Lane lit up a Camel, shook out the match, and carried it over to throw away in a metal garbage can. He reported back to Coal.

"All right, Sheriff. What can I do for you then, exactly?"

Lane—*Tweety Bird*—amused Coal. He wondered if he was all that tough, as tough as he looked, or at least looked like he had been prior to a few hundred bags of chips and boxes of Oreos. Maybe he was, if he was brave enough to go around dressed in his little sister's shirts. He told Lane he was working on the murder case, specifically trying to learn more about Curlie. Taking the last advice from Elisa and Verd Butler, he left Melissa Talty out.

Lane drew deep on his cigarette, leaned back his head and blew a funnel of smoke toward the ceiling. On the jukebox, the Bugs started jamming on "Hey, Jude", making Coal wish he could finish up this interview before he knew the repetitious and grating end of the song would make him want to put a hole in the Lantern's music machine.

"I ain't gonna be no narc, man," said Lane. "Understand? Before I say one other thing, I'll flat-out tell you, that ass needed killin'. He needed it every day. I don't blame Curlie if he did it."

"Do you think he did it?"

"Hell, no. Curlie wouldn't even go deer hunting. If he saw a rattlesnake, he'd walk around it. He didn't kill anybody. He don't have the gonads."

Coal mused upon Lane's words. The man obviously had no respect for Curlie Burks, which made complete sense if he had no qualms about carrying on a relationship with Curlie's girl that was open enough for seemingly everyone to know about it. But still, Lane was making sure that nothing he said would hang Curlie, either.

"How much have you heard about the murder case?" Coal asked.

"I don't know. Man, you hear stuff around—you know? Little stuff. I did hear that Curlie and his girlfriend are the ones who reported it. That they went up there and found the guy and that fat little Injun girl dead. And I heard they saw the killer run from the scene too."

"Maybe," said Coal with a nod. "People claim a lot of things, some of it to cover up other things they don't want people knowing."

Lane's eyes hardened a little. "Yeah, I guess. You got anything else? Other questions?"

"You in a hurry to get back to the game?"

They both knew the pool game was already over, but Lane looked over anyway, then shrugged again, this time with the other shoulder. "Well, whatever. The game's done."

"I just have one more question, but it could be a big one."

"Shoot."

"Do you remember where you heard all these things about the case?"

"Maybe."

"But . . ?"

"Well, come on. I don't wanna get anybody in trouble."

Coal already guessed who it was. So he threw it out there. "Did you talk to Curlie? Or was it Melissa?"

Lane stared Coal down, his eyes hooded and flinty. "Maybe I'm not remembering," he said finally, but Coal caught the suspicious glance he cast toward Elisa Doan and Verd Butler, who were still deep in conversation at the bar, where four more newcomers had gathered.

Coal thanked Lane stiffly, then walked back to Elisa and Verd Butler. "He didn't have much more to tell me, except he's certain Curlie couldn't kill anybody. That seems to be the consensus everywhere."

"Listen," said Verd, "I like Curlie a lot. Great guy. But let's face it. He's kind of a puss. I mean he talked real big about killin' Ev Sherman. Anybody who was in the bar that night could tell you that, so I don't feel guilty admittin' it. But if it came right down to it? I think some little old dude could walk up and slap Curlie's face, and he'd just take it. He's what you could call a lover, not a fighter—as they say."

"All right. Thank you both." Coal looked over at Elisa Doan. "Have a peaceful night."

"I will. And hey—why don't you come around more often?"

"For . . ?"

Elisa frowned. "Well, for . . . You know, a drink. When you're off duty."

Coal glanced over at Verd Butler, who was grinning at him. With a smile, Coal touched his hat brim to them both. "I'll try to do that, Elisa," he said, all while he had no intention of it. Elisa Doan seemed like a nice girl, she was beautiful beneath the sheet of makeup, and built like the proverbial brick house. But Elisa Doan was not a woman Coal could see any future with. She had her lifestyle, and he had his—and never the twain would meet.

He had no more than stepped out the front door when his eyes fell upon a blue Buick parked across the street, in the glow of neon lights. He swore. It was Annie Price, and she was watching him, at least until he spotted her. Then she whipped her head the other way.

Before he could act, the door behind him opened again, and Verd Butler was standing there. "Hey—Coal? I just wanted to say one more thing."

"Okay?"

"Just that you might want to have a talk with Melissa Talty, if you haven't already."

"Why do you say that?"

"I'm not saying why. Just talk to her. Could be you'll get more than you bargained for—but do me a favor and don't mention to anybody that we talked."

With that cryptic statement, Verd nodded, then headed back inside.

Coal turned again, and again caught Annie Price watching him, but this time she didn't turn away. With a deep breath of icy cold air, he looked both ways along Main, then started across.

CHAPTER FORTY-FOUR

As Coal neared Annie Price's Buick, he had a gut feeling she was going to speed off, when she looked forward and put her hands on the wheel. But she didn't. He reached the car, and she looked up at him through her closed window. When he went to grab the door handle, she hit the electric window switch, and the window came down halfway.

"Hi, Coal."

"Hi, Annie. Listen—you know I'm on duty, right?"

"Sure. So?" The woman's demeanor was stiff, and cold—even colder and stiffer than it should have been in the February air.

"So I was in there asking questions about the murders up by the cemetery. That's it." He wasn't sure why he felt the need to explain. It sort of rankled him that he even had to. He was only doing his job, and here Annie was acting like she was his wife and he was out trying to make a date with Elisa Doan.

"That's fine. It's none of my business." Which Coal agreed with but would never voice out loud—or at least had not come to that point yet. "I just saw your pickup there on my way up to see if you were still at the courthouse. I was going to tell you that kid woke up."

"That— You mean *Dale?"*

"Yes, sorry. Dale Moore."

"Is he able to talk?"

She shook her head, and he could see and feel her softening. "No, his throat is pretty bruised, and still swollen. The doctor had to sedate him, and he also has a nasal cannula in, so he can breathe better. Hey—Coal?"

"Yeah?"

"I'm sorry about how I looked a bit ago. I was just excited to talk to you, but then . . ."

"Then you saw me with Elisa Doan." She nodded, looking ashamed. "Well, let me tell you, Annie. There is absolutely nothing between that woman and me, and there never could be. I have a certain type, and she's not even in the ballpark."

"But she sure is very pretty," Annie admitted.

Coal was forty-two years old, closing fast on forty-three, and he had made plenty of stupid mistakes in his life. Even so, one man could only display so much stupidity, and Annie's comment was an ugly snare he would not fall into in a million years. "To some guys, maybe."

She smiled. "Oh, sure. I didn't mean you thought she was pretty." Reaching out, she lay her hand over his, which had come up to rest on top of her door when she rolled the window the rest of the way down. She gave it a pat. "I'm not doing too great, am I?"

Coal gazed down at her. "Doing too great? What do you mean?"

"I mean I feel like I screw up every time I see you anymore. Like my jealousy is hanging out of every pore, and I'm just irritating to you."

For several seconds, all Coal could do was stare. Finally, he said, "All right, Annie. Is there room for one more in this car?"

"Well, of course," she sputtered, "but . . ."

"No buts about it. I'm coming around." Having said so, he walked around the front of the car, threw open the passenger door, climbed in and sat down. Boldly, he reached over and put his hand on Annie's thigh. "Now you listen good, young lady. You haven't done anything wrong. All right? If you come across a little jealous, that's flattering, to an older gentleman like me."

She giggled and echoed, "Older!"

"Yes. Older." He gave her a big smile. "Annie, I might be really gun-shy, to say nothing of being up to my eyebrows in the sheriff's job, but it makes me happy every time I see you."

Annie's eyes were glistening. "Really?"

"Really. I'm not going to lie. I think about you all the time. I've tried to come visit you, and other times when I want to something comes up, and I can't. But you're on my mind a lot. Please don't forget that."

She nodded quickly, putting her hand over his and squeezing it hard. "I'm sorry for acting like a woman, Coal. It really isn't me to be this way."

He leaned back a little. "Well dang! I'm here to tell you if you start acting like a man, I'm gone!"

After saying goodbye to Annie, this time with only a kiss on the cheek, Coal started along the street, until he finally located Grant Fairbourne, in the Smokehouse.

"Get anything?" asked Grant.

Coal told his deputy quickly everything he had learned.

"Well, that's more than I have—except two women twice my age who want to go out with me. And a guy too, I think, but he didn't come right out and say it."

Coal laughed. "Well, you can keep that one to yourself, brother. Where's Jordan?"

"I think he went in the Coffee Shop. None of the bars were turning anything up for him."

"Well, I'm thinking I've got a good start, from the Lantern. I had a hunch that would be the right place. I'm going to go pick up

Melissa Talty, I think. At least see if she'll go down to the jail with me so I can record our conversation."

"What do you need me and Jordan to do?"

"Nothing. You just go home and hug that little wife and those babies of yours. I think I've got the rest of this. Well, go home *after* you go tell Jordan the same."

Coal went back to his car after Grant left, and he pulled the manila folder full of reports from the various officers over into his lap. Flipping on the light, he went through the list of suspects, pulling up Melissa Talty's information.

He remembered her saying she lived up on the Bar, above the courthouse. He found her address on Fairmont and drove up there, finding only a dim light shining through a heavy curtain in the front window. The only car around was a cream-colored early sixties Ford Falcon, a once-nice family sedan, but beat up and rusting around the rocker panels and at the rear of the front wheel well.

Coal went up and knocked on the door. After half a minute, he saw the curtains part, only a few inches, and he saw the movement of a hand, and possibly part of an eye. The light was dim enough it was hard to make out anything for sure.

The curtain fell back in place, and Coal soon heard clicking at the door, presuming that a deadbolt was being unlocked. The door opened a little ways, and a woman peered out. "Sheriff Savage? Is that you?"

"It is. Miss Talty?"

"Yes!" She jerked the door open now. "Sorry! I must look totally paranoid. Come in, please."

Coal stepped through the doorway, and Melissa shut the door behind him. "Is everything okay?" she asked.

"Oh, sure. You bet. I just wanted to ask you a few questions."

"Okay. No problem. Do you want something to drink?"

"It would actually be better if you come down to the courthouse with me, if it's all right. And I have sodas and coffee down there. We can even stop and grab you a donut or something if you want."

"Oh. The courthouse?" Her gaze faltered. "I'm not under arrest or anything, am I?"

Coal smiled. "No. I promise—nothing like that. I actually just want to mark you and Curlie off the suspect list, but I hope you understand why I'm not able to do that until I get a few more things answered."

"All right. Well, can I change clothes real quick?"

She was dressed in sweat pants and a loose sweatshirt, with her hair pulled back and bound lightly behind her neck. "What you're wearing is fine, but if you'd feel more comfortable, that's okay. Nobody will see us, though."

"Not even those deputies of yours?"

Coal grinned. "Okay, you're right. I guess maybe them. Grab you some clothes. I'll wait."

After Melissa changed, coming out wearing flare-legged jeans with flowers embroidered on the fronts of both thighs, and a lime-green, sleeveless shirt, Coal looked back fondly on the relaxed, non-rebellious sweats she had been wearing before. Running the river definitely suited Melissa Talty's look.

He was going to suggest she grab a coat, but she beat him to it, picking up a heavy leather jacket lined with sheepskin, and heavy with long fringe. Out the door they went, and down to the courthouse, which seemed deathly quiet at this hour.

When they went in, Coal seated Melissa in front of his desk and got out his tape recording machine, setting it on the desk between them. He looked over at the clock, then started the recording, stating the date and time. After that, he shut the machine back off.

"Any questions before we start to record?"

Melissa Talty looked at the machine on his desk. "Just . . . do I have to be recorded?"

"Yes, we do. Is that a problem?"

"I . . . Well, I just hate my voice."

Coal smiled. "I won't play it back and make you listen."

She smiled back uncomfortably. "I'd rather no one else hear it either."

"Miss," said Coal, painting patience over his face, "the recording is really a tool for me so I don't forget anything for the report. I don't know shorthand, and I could probably type with my tongue about as fast as with my fingers."

Melissa Talty finally nodded, looking ultra-nervous. "Okay. We can go then, if you hurry."

Coal had no idea what that actually meant, unless she thought she would chicken out if too much time passed. He had her state her personal information, and then he delved right into questioning. Unfortunately, he soon began to learn that she wasn't much more helpful than she had been the night of the murders. She still couldn't give any reason why she thought Curlie had tried to pull the spear out that was buried in Everett Sherman's chest. She couldn't give him a reason for their being there, other than "they had come to visit their friends". From everything Coal had learned, he found that proposed friendship very strange indeed, especially as it had been ascertained that Sherman was drunk that night, and he had yet to talk to anyone who wanted to be around him when he was drunk.

"Did Curlie give you any reason why he drove back to the murder scene the second time?" asked Coal.

"Umm . . . no," Melissa spoke, but her eyes faltered, and when she forced herself to look back up and meet his gaze, there was no strength in hers. She was trying to *appear* strong, but failing.

"Let's rephrase that, for the recording, okay? You *did* return a second time to the scene, right? After going down the hill to report the crime."

She nodded. "Yes. Yes, we went back."

"And that's when Curlie went in the trailer. And you said he tried to pull out the spear?"

Looking flustered, this time she said, "Well, I'm not really sure he tried to pull it out, since I've been thinking about it."

"Oh. Really? You seemed sure before."

"Well, it was a pretty scary night. I think I'm forgetting a lot. You know—maybe blocking it out."

"Did you know for sure that Sherman was dead when you saw him?" Coal asked.

"Yes."

"How?"

"His eyes were open, and . . . the pupils were really big."

"So there probably wouldn't be a reason to pull out the spear, right? Unless you were trying to hide it so no one could find the murder weapon?"

"I . . . Well, I guess, but Curlie wasn't doing that. He— Wait. Sheriff, can we stop the recording? I think I should stop now."

Coal left the tape running. "Why? Are you all right?"

"I just . . . I feel like maybe I'm saying too much."

"Are you frightened, Miss Talty? Is there something you think you might have left out?"

"No, I don't think so, but . . ."

Coal took a deep breath, and a big chance. Reaching out, he clicked off the tape machine. "No more recording, Melissa. Do you mind if I call you that?"

The woman's eyes had filled suddenly with tears, and she wiped them furiously away, tried to meet his gaze, but ended up staring at the top of the desk instead.

"Melissa, I'm going to ask you a point-blank question. It's off the tape, okay? I told you all about the fight at the Lantern. A night Curlie didn't have you with him. It was a bad fight. Curlie got hurt, and in his mind he might have thought Everett Sherman stole his truck from him. You know, he was pretty intoxicated, from what I hear. Melissa, did Curlie put that spear in Everett Sherman? Did he stab Irene Boyer?"

"No!" she exclaimed. "No, Curlie didn't kill them! I swear! He could never hurt anybody! She was dying when we found her! You have to believe me! We saw a man running—a big man in a cowboy hat. Everything I've told you is true. Please! Oh, please believe me!"

Melissa buried her face in her hands and openly started to weep.

Getting up quietly, making just enough noise not to startle the woman, Coal went around and laid a hand gently on her shoulder, patting it. "It's all right, Melissa. It's all right. I do believe you."

His words only made her bow her head onto the desk, on top of her forearms, and cry louder.

Feeling awkward, Coal remained next to the woman until her sobs subsided. He gave her shoulder a rub and a pat. "Melissa? Look up at me, okay?"

She raised her red, tear-stained face. "Melissa, I haven't told anyone this, but we found a whole lot of marijuana in Curlie's glovebox. We found a concealed pistol too. And we found the title to the pickup under the seat. It was covered in blood."

Melissa started nodding furiously, but she seemed to have no voice.

"Melissa, why did Curlie still have the pickup, when everyone knew Everett Sherman won it from him fair and square? And why was the title all bloody? You have to come clean. If you want to make sure Curlie doesn't get charged with those two murders, you have to tell me what really happened that night."

Melissa lunged up out of her chair, covering the lower part of her face with her hand. She stared with eyes that looked startled, but vacant, at the machine on top of the desk. "Okay. I'll tell you. I'll tell you! But please don't put Curlie in jail."

"I have to turn the machine back on, okay?"

Melissa nodded, looking defeated. Slumping back onto her chair, she took a deep, sobbing breath. Coal started up the recording again, making a vocal note that it was being continued and that nothing recorded was being recorded over.

"This is everything, Sheriff." Melissa's voice had steadied now. She took two deep breaths. "This is everything I know, and everything that happened that night. I swear it on my mother's grave."

CHAPTER FORTY-FIVE

It was after eight-thirty when Coal showed up on Curlie Burks's doorstep on Water Street, after letting Melissa Talty off at her house. He would not soon forget the sad-eyed, broken last look she had given him before pushing open her door and going inside.

Coal gave four solid knocks on the front door. He had small hope of finding the man in tonight, since there was no vehicle in the driveway even though after their warrant service the pickup had been turned back over to him.

When the expected lack of reply came true, Coal got back in his car and started cruising Main Street. The pickup was parked on South St. Charles Street, around the corner from the Lantern Bar. It made sense, since this seemed to be Curlie's preferred hangout.

Stepping once again into the bar, the first person Coal saw was Elisa Doan, walking away from the bar toward a table.

Standing at the door, he scanned the room carefully. His eyes found Curlie Burks seated at a table, already watching him. He had a resigned look on his face.

As Elisa Doan delivered a couple of drinks to the table she had gone to, and turned around, surprised to see him there, Curlie Burks was also standing up from his own table, his fingertips white on the tabletop.

"Well, Coal! You really *are* stalking me!" Elisa said as she got close. Then she must have read the look on his face, and she turned and followed the line of his sight to where Curlie stood. "Oh. You didn't come back to see me after all. Well, darn. Anything to drink, Coal? Or are you a man on a mission?"

"I guess I'm a man on a mission, Elisa. But thanks."

By now, Curlie Burks was walking slowly toward Coal, and a number of people stood farther back in the smoky room, watching Curlie and Coal from where Hank Williams was wailing about being so lonesome he could cry from inside the jukebox.

Curlie stopped in front of Coal. "I'm guessing you found Melissa."

"I'm guessing so," confirmed Coal. "Do you want to come with me, Curlie?"

The man nodded, looking numb. "Can I get my coat?"

"Of course."

Curlie walked slowly back to his chair and slipped a blue jean coat off the back of it, shrugging it on. Turning, he waved to the people watching, and some of them gave him tentative waves back.

"I guess I'm goin' in your car," Curlie said.

"Yeah."

"What happens with my truck?"

"What happens? I guess we'll decide that before the night's over."

Appearing completely beaten, Curlie went out the door in front of Coal. Coal could feel Elisa watching him, but he didn't bother even to wave goodbye. Out at the Thunderbird, Coal turned to Curlie. "If you're promising to be good, I won't have to cuff you, Curlie. And just so you know, you aren't under arrest."

Curlie stared at him. "I'm not?"

"No, not for now. But we have a lot to sort out."

Curlie got meekly into the front seat, and Coal drove back up to the courthouse. Down in the basement, Curlie took the same seat Melissa Talty had been in, and Coal explained the tape recorder to Curlie the same way he had to Melissa.

Once all the opening details were out of the way, Coal sat back a little in his chair. "I'm not going to do any pressing here, Curlie. Okay? I'm just going to sit quiet while you tell me everything that happened that night. If I stop you, it will only be for a clarifying point. Understood?"

"Yes, sir."

"Begin when you're ready then."

Curlie began talking. He admitted to Coal how he had technically lost the pickup to Everett Sherman in a state of drunkenness, and in that same state he had tried to welch on the bet. Everett Sherman had struck him in the eye, and on a close inspection Coal could see the scar.

Curlie had initially given the truck up after sobering up and being told by too many people that he had lost fair and square to Sherman. He had Melissa take him to work for a couple of days, but then Sherman came to his house one night with a proposition. He knew that Curlie had connections who provided him with drugs, mostly marijuana, but sometimes acid, heroin, and even LSD. Sherman told him that if he could provide a certain amount of those drugs to him, he would eventually consider the debt even, and Curlie could have the title to his truck back—to all of which

Curlie readily agreed. In the meantime, he was allowed to drive the pickup, but only as a loan, and he had signed a paper to that effect.

On the night of Monday the 19th, President's Day, Curlie was to deliver at least a pound of high quality marijuana to Everett Sherman, and then their deal would be complete. Sherman would sign the title to the pickup back over to Curlie, and he could be on his way.

As a witness that night, Curlie brought his girlfriend, Melissa Talty along. He also brought his pistol, in case things went south.

As they were pulling up to the trailer that night, Curlie's eyes fell upon a big man dressed in a light-colored cowboy hat, a heavy denim coat, and blue jeans, running uphill away from the trailer. Then, in the middle of his headlights' beam, he saw someone on the ground, their arms flailing around.

Jumping out of the truck, with Melissa coming behind him, Curlie ran to the person on the ground. He reached her just as her body went into the final twitching of nerves prior to death. In shock, Curlie started yelling out to Everett Sherman, who wouldn't reply from the trailer. Curlie ran back, turned the pickup so its headlights shone on the trailer, then got out his pistol and went up to the trailer.

At that point, Curlie claimed he only glanced inside, seeing Everett Sherman with the spear through his body. He ran back out to the pickup, dragging Melissa with him. That was when headlights came over them, and they turned to see a pickup bearing down on them from the upper part of Cemetery Lane. Startled, Curlie brought his pistol up, and the pickup jerked to a stop in front of him. Curlie ran over to the pickup, which he recognized as belonging to a rancher named Gunnar Westerlind, and he recognized Westerlind's son as a star football player from Salmon High. He had a young lady with him, and a much smaller kid against the passenger door.

When Curlie told the Westerlind kid there had been a murder, the boy just stared at him, then stomped on the gas, swerved around him, and headed down the lane as fast as he could go without running off the road.

Curlie drove with Melissa down the hill to the first house he saw with the lights on inside, and that was where he called the police from. That was when he started thinking about the title to his pickup. He raced back up the road and went into the trailer, where he searched everywhere frantically, but to no avail. Finally, as a last resort because the plan had been for Sherman to give him back the title that night, he went to Sherman and dug into his shirt pocket.

There, of course, he found the title. He meant to drive off the hill then, but before he could he saw two pairs of headlights flying up the road from below. And that was when he was accosted by Officer Bob Wilson.

With the dull hiss of the tape recorder in the background, Coal stared at Curlie Burks as he finished speaking. He pulled in a lung-filling breath. It was quite a story. And this time a believable one, told in a voice that came from a face Coal had no reason to disbelieve.

"That's all of it, right, Curlie? The whole story."

The man nodded. He was defeated, and he knew it.

Coal looked at the recorder, then stated the date again, and the current time, and reached over to shut it off.

"Now what?" asked Curlie after a long moment of silence. "You won't do anything to Melissa, right? She didn't have nothing to do with any of this. I promise. I just brought her as a witness—you know, in case things went south."

"Melissa might need to be a witness," Coal said. "That's all. Curlie, can you tell me anything more about the guy you saw running? Anything at all?"

"No, sir. My headlights aren't all that good. I could only see so much, but I told you all of it."

"Okay. Okay, I believe you."

"What about me?" Curlie asked. Coal could tell he didn't want to, but suspense was killing him.

"Needless to say, I'm holding the dope, Curlie. And I'm not happy about the concealed pistol, but hey—I'm from the backwoods too, you know? I understand needing to keep yourself safe. The title to your truck, as far as I'm concerned that's yours. It's a bloody mess, but you already know that."

"Yes, sir. It is. And I'll have to go to court for the dope?"

"We'll be talking about that dope again, Curlie. Believe me, we will. I'm holding it in evidence. It's in the report. But I'm not charging you."

Curlie stared at Coal until the suspense was too much. "I don't understand. Why?"

"Why? Because if there's as much dope in this county as you say, you have a new calling in life, Curlie. A lot bigger calling. And with a felony marijuana charge hanging over your head, you're going to want to give that calling your all—believe me."

After taking Curlie back to his pickup, Coal sat at the curb trying to decide whether to head home and make a couple of phone calls from there, or to go back to the courthouse, where it was peaceful and quiet.

His favorite choice was home. Home where the people and the dogs loved him without reservation. But he chose instead to go to the jail, because he needed to make sure Hunter Jack was still doing all right.

He pulled into the dark parking lot, where now the only lights were the dim ones left glowing from upstairs offices, and the thin light spreading through the trees from the scattering of residences across the creek behind the lot.

Coal was tired. So tired. Weary, even. Wiped out or fried, as kids today liked to say. He went down and unlocked the outside door to the jail, wishing Badger wasn't here. By all rights, the big Shoshone shouldn't be. He just couldn't seem to stop hurting cops, and for some reason the local authorities frowned on such behavior.

Shutting the door behind him, Coal looked over at the coffee pot, and swore. He had left the burner on. That was going to be some tasty coffee in the morning. After dumping out the last of the burned coffee, and rinsing the pot, he went and peered into the cell block. Opening the door, he said into the dimness, "Hey. Badger, you awake?"

"Ugh," came the reply—Dark Badger's attempt at sounding like a true stereotypical "Injun", Coal guessed. "I'm awake. If I wasn't before, I would be now, with all this noise."

Coal grinned, although Jack couldn't see him in this light. "Hey. Do you eat Twinkies? Don't ask me why, but I have some in my desk."

"I eat live rats when I get this hungry," said Jack. "Bring it on."

Laughing, Coal went and got a package of Hostess Twinkies out of a desk drawer and took them into the back, stopping at the end of the hall. "Here you go. They could be forty years old, but I'm sure they'll still taste the same."

"Uh," said Jack, simply.

"Want some light?" asked Coal.

"No. Hell, no. Don't want you to see me eatin' on junk food."

"Okay. Well, I'm going to make a phone call or two. I'll be out here. You need some water?"

"Naw. Don't wanna have to get up an' pee."

Coal chuckled and went out. Not bothering to turn on any glaring lights, and letting the two little lamps back by the rifle rack weakly light the room, he sat and threw his feet up on his desk and called Nadine at her house. He knew this number by heart.

Hi, Coal! Her voice sounded excited to hear him on the line. *Hey, honey, you doing okay? It sounds like it's been another rough day for you.*

"Par for the course," he replied. "I don't know which way is up or down. Thank you for asking. That means a lot to me. Say, Nadine, did you happen to take any calls for me today that I don't know about yet?"

I did, in fact. I was just going to tell you. Some man from Washington, D. C. called and said he was an old partner of yours from "the Bureau". Tony Nwon-something? Is that the FBI?

"Yes, ma'am," replied Coal, happy to hear the news. "Tony Nwanzé. What did he say?"

He said he'll be sending some facsimile reports to you, and to look for them in the clerk's office in the morning. And he wants you to call him and said—and these are his exact words, because I wrote them down—if you don't call him tomorrow then you ain't no white man. The words made Nadine giggle. *By the sound of his voice, I'm guessing he is a Negro?*

Coal laughed. "He is, Nadine. One of the blackest Negroes I've ever seen, whose ancestors came straight out of Nigeria. And one of the best friends a man could ask for. Have a good night, Nadine."

Sweet dreams, Coal Savage.

CHAPTER FORTY-SIX

Troy Westerlind was home, where Coal had allowed him to drive the pickup, only as long as he stuck right with his old man. He lay on his bed, his light still on, staring at the ceiling. His door was shut firmly, but what did that matter? His old man had disabled the lock on his doorknob over a year ago, and he had proven many a time that he would walk right in whenever he felt like it. Usually what ensued was harsh and ugly, and always Troy was the loser.

Thoughts of Dale kept running through Troy's mind. Dale, and Dawn. What had he done? He had lost his friends. The only two friends he had in the entire world, and they were gone now. Forever. No girl said goodbye to someone like Dawn had said it to him if she didn't intend to stay gone.

He longed to call Steele Memorial, if he could just make the call without his old man hearing it, only because he couldn't stand having the old buzzard listen in on his conversations. His old man was always judging him. He always had. It had been that way before his mother left, but in the years since it had gotten so much worse.

Where was his mother? Had she remarried the man she ran off with? Did she have other children? Did she ever even think about the son she had abandoned? Did she ever wish she could see him again? To anybody who would listen, and even to himself, Troy swore he didn't care. He swore he hated his mother. The deep-down truth was that on some really deep, dark nights, when he was all alone, and safe some place where no one could reach him, tears came to Troy Westerlind. Actual tears. He had even cried himself to sleep before, but he would kill anyone who ever caught him.

Dale . . . Dale! How was his friend? Would he recover? Would he still be the same nice, innocent kid? Stupid damn kid! Why would he try to kill himself? He had a father who cared about him, at least when he was sober. He lived right in town, no responsibilities, just a few houses away from Dawn Kelly, Troy's favorite girl in the whole world. Dale had everything. And he was stuck with a murdering piece of trash for a friend, a piece of trash whose foolish acts had driven him right to the point of wanting to take his own life.

Tears came to Troy's eyes, and he swore and scrubbed them away. Dawn . . . Where was she tonight? Was his girl spending the night in that house alone? Or had her slovenly truck driver father finally made it back home from the road? He wished he could go to her. He wished he could beg her to come back. But there was no way anybody was ever going to see Troy Westerlind crawl. He would go the way Dale Moore had before he would crawl.

He thought of the lance he still had. His old man had ordered him to get rid of it, or at least to scrub it clean and somehow put it back where it had come from. He thought of the blood on his hands, and of that horrible moaning bawl as that lance sank home. He thought of Dawn's hands when he grabbed them, putting them on the wooden shaft. He thought of the suddenly almost crazed look on her face as they looked at each other, with Dale screaming at them that he wanted to go. The blood . . . It was everywhere. The thrashing legs, uncontrollable. He recalled the dying look in the eyes, of how the wetness pooled there, then finally spilled out the corner of one eye, down the twitching cheek.

Most of all, right now, he remembered the numb look that had come over Dawn Kelly's face, how she had struggled back to her feet, how she had slapped his bloody hands away when he tried to touch her.

Troy had stopped in front of Dawn's house that night, and before he could even say goodbye, she and Dale flew out the other side of the truck and ran for her front door. By the time he got out, all he heard was the slamming of her door, and he was left in the deep silence, complete except for the booming rattle of the pickup's engine.

Jumping back into the pickup, he squealed the tires getting out of there, bombing east down Highway Twenty-Eight. And then there was that damn cattle truck, right in his way, taking up more than its half of the road. He wasn't going to wait for whoever that was. Troy Westerlind waited for *no one!*

So he slammed his foot down on the gas and started around, and there were the headlights. From out of nowhere—headlights! There was no turning back, no way to get past the cattle truck. All he could do was try to shoot the gap, and hang on . . .

Troy felt breathless. He stared at this ceiling he might have looked at for more minutes total than any other thing in his entire life, and he hated it. He hated this entire house, and everything, and everyone in it.

Most of all, Troy Westerlind hated himself.

Something came to Coal as he sat there in the half dark, something on which he had never followed up. He thought about putting it off until tomorrow, but it was important enough that he decided to make the late call. Reluctantly, he got up and turned the bright lights back on, then came back to his desk and thumbed through all the reports. He found nothing in there written by the volunteer police officers, William Verret and Horace Teal, but he did locate phone numbers for the two of them.

Deciding which of the men to call was like choosing between kicking a wet cow pie or squishing it with his boot, but he decided to try Teal, the Quality Motors mechanic, if only because he was more familiar with him. Teal seemed all right anyway, he guessed—as long as he didn't have William Verret around to keep him riled up.

The phone rang four or five times before picking up, and a rough voice on the other end of the line said, *Yeah-lo!*

"Horace Teal?"

Yeppers. Who's this?

"Savage. You got a minute?"

Oh, yeah. Sure. What am I gonna do but slug another couple brewskies anyway, right? What's up, Sheriff?

"Well, I'm looking through all the reports from the murder investigation. I didn't see anything from you and Officer Verret, so I'm guessing you didn't have anything to report, but just to cover my bases, did you see anything that night after everyone left? Any more activity?"

Shoot, man! We did, we did. I started to write it up, but then when nobody ever asked, I just kinda lost track of it and set it all aside. Work's been pretty hectic, so my 'pologies.

Trying to keep his impatience out of his voice, and wondering if Teal might be already too intoxicated to help much, Coal took a chance anyway. "If you can finish writing up whatever you saw, I'll come pick it up from you tomorrow, Horace, but fill me in real quick, would you?"

Sure thing. So we was up there for a bit, you know. Well, till it started gettin' daylight, actually. Then we both had to go get ready for work. Man! That was a long night.

"Okay?" Now Coal was starting to lose his battle with the desire not to let his impatience show.

Oh, yeah, yeah. So there was a couple cars that drove up there. We talked to 'em. Got their information and stuff. Nothin' big. Just the same old nosey lookie-loos, you know? But then sometime around two-thirty or so we saw headlights comin' down from the cemetery. They stopped up quite a ways and just sat there, then after about five minutes they come on down, real slow. I could almost tell right when the driver spotted our car sittin' there in the shadows because he pretty much slammed on his brakes. Then he did one o' them 'let's keep drivin' on by real casual so we don't draw attention to ourselves' kinda things.

"And you stopped the truck, right?" said Coal breathlessly.

Sure did. It was just too weird that he was up that road so long. What was he doin', anyway? And why would he be comin' outta there that time of morning?

"So who was he? What did he tell you?"

I'll have to wait to get to work to tell you his name—unless Bill remembers. But he was a Sho-Ban, right? Maybe mid-fifties? You know, with them folks you can hardly tell. Nice enough guy, though—or seemed like it.

"What was his story? Why was he up there?"

Oh, yeah. Said his wife's buried up at the cemetery and he'd been missin' her, so he was just up there sittin' in his truck, listenin' to music, and smokin'. Me an' Bill figured he prob'ly had him a peace pipe, added Teal, laughing. Coal wasn't in the mood to match the laughter, so Teal cleared his throat, an embarrassed sound. *Anyway, we got his plate and such. Didn't call it in, but it's in the report. That's about it, I guess. I didn't know if we were really allowed to do any searchin' of his truck, so we didn't.*

"No, you did all right, Horace. This guy wasn't wearing a cowboy hat, was he? By chance?"

Nope. No, sir, bare-headed. Of course the usual black hair, pretty long and some gray. Not much. Wore a coat.

"What kind of coat?"

Heavier. One of them with the sheep fur collars?

Coal smiled at the idea of sheep having fur, but he didn't embarrass the policeman by saying anything. After thanking Horace Teal and telling him he'd come over to his work to pick up the report, Coal hung up. He thought about calling William Verret too, he guessed a phone call a night with a semi-intoxicated individual was plenty. Not that he knew Verret would be drinking, and perhaps he was judging a book by its cover. Either way, the main thing was he simply didn't much care for William Verret, so he put off the call and headed home.

On the way, driving slow to give himself the best chance not to hit any more moose or deer, Coal went over in detail in his head what he was dealing with so far. He was pretty positive he could mark Curlie Burks and Melissa Talty off his suspect list. But no one else.

Joe Teton was still number one, and high on the list, especially after his conversation with Horace Teal. He wouldn't know for certain it was Teton that Teal and Verret had stopped that night coming down the road from above, but if he were a betting man he would put money on it. The suspect who ran from the scene wore a cowboy hat, a heavy coat with a sheepskin collar, and cowboy boots. Joe Teton? All of the above.

One thing was sure: When Coal got the fingerprint analysis back in the morning and talked to Tony Nwanzé, he would know a lot more. He was going to see if he could secure a warrant from the judge to lift Teton's prints off his door handle or from Joe himself, and if any of the prints on the murder weapon were Teton's, Coal was going to be making an arrest.

At the moment, he was ninety percent positive that the murderer of Everett Sherman and Irene Boyer was going to turn out to be the friendly neighborhood Shoshone, Joseph A. Teton.

In the morning after his intense workout, Coal decided to spend some time with the kids. It was always hard when they were getting ready for school, but at least he made the attempt, and he got to share time with every one of them, at least in passing. He even got a hug from each of them, including Cynthia Batterton, but the one that meant the most, because it was so rare, was from Virgil, his quiet teenager.

"Everything going okay at school, Virg?" asked Coal, taking a sip of his coffee.

"I guess, sure." The boy's eyes were evasive.

Coal, sitting on one of the kitchen stools, cranked his torso around. "Hey, buddy."

Virgil turned around, looking reluctant to do so. "Yeah, Dad?"

"You sure everything's all right? You look like something's bothering you."

"No, really," insisted Virgil. "Everything's good."

Coal studied his boy. He remembered how he himself would close up at that age. In fact, he sometimes still did. "Okay, Virg. Well, you know you can talk to me about anything, right?"

"Sure, Dad. I know." And then Virgil turned and dodged away, leaving Coal feeling uneasy. He hadn't been spending as much time around his kids as he would have liked to, that was for sure. But still he thought he knew them well enough to know when something was up. There was something bothering his oldest boy. He knew it, but of course there was nothing he could do about it if Virgil wouldn't talk.

Leaving only Sissy Miley home with his mom, after one of the little girl's great big embraces that always warmed his heart, Coal drove all the other kids to their schools. When he dropped Virgil off, he watched him closely. He didn't want to read anything into the boy's behavior, but he seemed to be scanning the schoolyard in an awfully careful manner for a normal teenager. When he finally headed for the school, after Katie and Cynthia had gone on far ahead of him, he did it with his head down, moving faster than even the nippy February air warranted.

Trying to put his son out of his mind until he could get back with him hopefully in the evening, Coal stopped at the Coffee Shop to get Hunter Jack something to eat, then drove on up to the jail and went in. He cranked up the radiator heater a little higher, then went back to give Jack his breakfast.

Jack was sitting on the edge of his cot looking like the proverbial cat in a cage. He leaped up when Coal opened the door.

"Man, Badger, you act like you haven't eaten in a week," said Coal.

"I ain't so hungry, Savage. I'm just . . . Man, when am I gonna get outta here? I'm gonna go crazy if I have to stay in here one more day."

"Sorry, Badger. I can't do anything about that right now. If I could, I would. Why don't you try to eat this food? You need anything else?"

"No. Just out. Hey—you talk to that damn kid that was in here about my lance and stuff?"

"Not really."

"Why not? I know he took it. I know he was in there, Savage. I could tell by the way he was actin' with them Scouts that he was gonna be comin' back. An' I could feel him in the house later—you know, after it got broken in?"

"Next time I see him, I'll ask about it. But I wouldn't get my hopes too high. If I were you, I'd quit letting the Boy Scouts come over. I know it's sad to punish all of them, but it hardly seems worth taking the chance. One apple can spoil the barrel, as they say."

"Uh," replied Jack.

"Hey, Badger?" Coal had turned away, but he spun back now.

"Yeah?"

"What do you think about Joe Teton? I mean you two are pretty good friends, right?"

"Sure. Like brothers."

"That's what I figured."

"Well? What?"

"I have to tell you he's worked himself up really high on my list of suspects in the murders. How do you feel about that?"

Hunter Jack stared at him, his face blank. "Uh. I don't think so."

"Why?"

"He ain't no killer."

"You know he was in Korea, right? You know he killed a lot of soldiers."

"I guess, maybe. Yeah. But . . ."

"But what?"

"Savage. He's got them two boys, uh? Little boys. An' his wife's gone. I think you should leave Teton alone, Savage."

"A killer's a killer, Badger. You know that."

"But that guy deserved killin'!" Jack burst out, losing his cool for the first time Coal had observed in person. "Can't you just let it be? Can't some things just be left alone?"

"They can't, Badger. I'm sorry. If I'm going to be the sheriff here, I don't have any choice but to keep looking into this. You should know that."

When Coal left Hunter Jack and went upstairs to the clerk's office, he was feeling bad. In a perfect world, he would almost have sided with Jack. He couldn't deny it. Some people, people like Everett Sherman, seemed to have no purpose on the earth but making other people's lives miserable. But what individual had the right to pass that kind of judgment? And then there was also Irene Boyer to consider. Maybe neither she nor Sherman were the salt of the earth, but they were still human beings, with the same rights to justice as anyone else. He would hate to see Joe Teton's young sons have to go to an orphanage, but he guessed they wouldn't. He guessed the Sho-Bans would take care of those boys in their own way, the way of their people.

Pushing the plight of Joe Teton out of his mind for the moment, however self-made it might be, he stopped in front of the desk of

Cindy Hardlinger, the jovial, poorly dressed court secretary with the heavy brown eyebrows, and smiled down at her. Cindy had been watching him walk all the way to her, a warm but shy smile growing on her face.

"Well, good morning, Coal Savage. My. You sure look handsome in that hat."

He grinned at her, "Well, thank you, Cindy. I guess I should have brought you a donut, to pay off a compliment like that."

Cindy giggled. "I guess you're up here to pick up a couple of telecopies that were dropped off here yesterday by the newspaper editor. They're from Washington, D. C."

"I am. Indeed. Thank you, Cindy!"

"My pleasure," she said, straight-arming a manila envelope out to him, which he took.

"Let's go grab a cinnamon roll at Wally's sometime, huh?"

Obviously taken by surprise, Cindy stared at him for a moment. "Really?"

"Well, sure! All the work you do around here? It's only fair for me to pay some of it back."

Cindy's bright smile turned her almost plain face into an almost attractive one. "Okay! You're on."

He left feeling good for making Cindy happy—and hoping she wouldn't get the wrong idea. Of women in his life, he already had too many, and complications were ready to overflow in his life like an overfilled sack of potatoes.

Coal returned to the jail to sit at his desk, with his notepad and his phone. Thinking about Tony Nwanzé, with a grin, he reached over and picked up the handset of the phone, hugging it in place between his head and shoulder, and dialed a number that would be etched in his memory until the day he died.

A secretary answered, and the voice was familiar. "Mary Wright?" said Coal.

Yes? Who is this?

"Mary, Coal Savage here, out in Idaho!"

Oh, Coal, Coal! How wonderful it is to hear from you! The two of them exchanged pleasantries for nearly five minutes on the county's dime before Coal got around to asking if Tony Nwanzé was in.

Well, of course. He's been standing here staring at me impatiently for most of this conversation. Here he is, Coal. It was so nice talking to you.

Hey, my brother! What's shakin'?

Coal laughed. "My whole world, it seems like. You?"

Same old bureaucratic b. s. on a different day, man. Same ol' same-o. So did you get all the stuff I sent you back?

"I did, but I haven't looked at it yet."

Well, let me say, it'll be some fun! My lab guys were a little put out at me—you might even say pissed off! Tony's gleeful laugh erupted, over the miles. *But hey—good to keep them chumps on their toes, right? Anyway, it took some good sleuthin', but they got all your prints lined up for you. You got any kinda good tech there?*

"Good question," Coal replied. "I might have to go to one of our bigger cities for that."

Well, just look these over, brother. They made 'em 'bout as clear as possible, so if you're able to get some good ones to compare to, you're in like Flynn!

"Thanks, Tone. I owe you—again."

Well, one o' these days I'll be out there to collect, you c'n bet your lily-white hiney! Later days, brother!

Tony Nwanzé always left Coal smiling, no matter how off his day might be. While the warm glow of friendship was yet flowing through him, he pulled all the paperwork out of the manila folder, making a mental note to call the editor at the Recorder-Herald later to thank him for his assistance. He studied the prints, but to him they were only prints. He would have to get a judge's order now to bring in all his suspects for fingerprinting, then see if he could get any kind of a match. Then even if he thought he had a match, he would have to have his known fingerprints matched up to the ones from the spear. All of this led to the hardest part in any criminal investigation: the waiting.

Going to the coffee pot to pour himself a cup, Coal sipped at it and paced the floor for a few minutes. Hunter Jack was strong on his mind. He wanted to figure out a way to get Jack back out of jail, but considering what had happened the last time he went to bat for him, he was a little nervous about going to Judge Sinclair about it.

As if the very act of thinking about Hunter Jack had called up the event, the door suddenly swung open, and Coal was surprised when he looked over to see volunteer policeman William Verret looking at him, his left thumb hooked in his pocket.

"Sheriff."

"Good morning, Verret. Something I can do for you?"

"I hear you need some reports," said Verret, moving his right hand around from the shelter of the door to reveal some papers. "Teal called me this morning, and I figured I'd save you the trouble of trackin' me down."

Swaggering to the desk, Verret dropped the papers unceremoniously, then dipped the front of his already low-hung black hat brim to Coal. "That good?"

"Sure. Thanks. Anything else?"

"Yep. You lettin' visitors in?"

"Visitors . . . for who?"

"How many people you got back there, anyway? Hunter Jack is the one I want to visit."

Coal studied the man, his suspicions rising. "What do you want with Badger?"

"A visit. I don't have to say what about. Do I? And no, I don't have any weapons on me."

With a shrug, Coal jerked a thumb. "Well, you know where the cellblock is. Make it quick—and quiet."

Coal wasn't sure, but he thought Verret smiled at him from under his overbearing mustache. It was a smile like a hyena smiles.

Coal followed Verret to the iron door, and when the man went in, Coal let him shut the door behind him, but he stayed at the window, wishing sound carried better.

William Verret walked right up to Hunter Jack's jail cell, piercing him with his eyes. Like a slow, lazy bear, Jack came up off his cot, meeting Verret's slitted, glassy eyes.

Verret wrapped his fingers around the bars of Jack's cell. "Redskin? You're dead."

Hunter Jack simply stared back at Verret. He emitted no sound, not even his typical, "Uh".

"Listen, you red bastard—I didn't care one thing about Everett Sherman. Nobody did. But I know Injuns. You kill one man, you're gonna kill more. You get out from under this murder, you get back on the streets, a free man, you better be watchin' your back. Every step you make. Every building you go in. Every one you come out of. You be watchin', red man. Because someday, there's gonna be somebody waitin' for you. Don't you ever forget that."

Hunter Jack took a deep breath and walked slowly toward the bars of the cell. The closer he got, the more he made William Verret look like a child. When he got close enough, Verret let go of the bars and backed away.

"Cowboy?" said Hunter Jack. "When Coal Savage gets me free, I'll be lookin' for you first—so you find a hole, an' you climb down in it. And don't ever dare come out."

CHAPTER FORTY-SEVEN

Grant Fairbourne showed up just as William Verret was leaving, and Verret only gave him a nod as he went out.

"What's wrong with him?" Grant asked Coal. "You'd think I just kicked his dog."

"I think Badger might have just kicked his dog," Coal replied, and he told the deputy about the reserve officer's visit to Hunter Jack.

"Man. That's bizarre. Too bad you couldn't hear what they said."

Grant went over and got a Pepsi out of the little fridge and popped the top. Hiding his smile, Coal watched him sip it. He didn't bother saying anything to Grant about his belief that coffee would harm his eternal soul, while sipping on the unknown substances and overload of sugar in a Pepsi Cola was just fine.

Grant had just put on his badge and buckled his gun belt around his waist when he turned idly to Coal. "Hey, Coal? You know, I've been thinking about something. It's been gnawing on me, actually."

"Well? Shoot."

"It's that Troy Westerlind kid. Does anything about him and those other two make you wonder? I don't know, do you think maybe you're . . ." Grant stopped, obviously realizing he was about to say something ill-advised.

"Go on. I'm . . ?"

"Well, I don't mean any offense, but do you think you might've gotten too close to those kids? A little?"

"Too close? What're you talking about? Am I close to them?"

Embarrassed, Grant shrugged a shoulder. "I don't know. Maybe. Maybe too close to see all the possibilities? Sorry. I'm probably way out of line."

Coal grunted quietly, looking down at his empty coffee cup. Feeling unjustifiably irritated, he got up and walked to the coffee pot, pouring his mug three-fourths full and taking a swallow. It was too hot, so he drank some more, wincing.

Turning, he caught Grant's eyes on him, and the deputy looked quickly away, realized he had been caught, and looked back. "Sorry, Coal. I'm just brainstorming."

"No, Grant. Maybe you're right. So what exactly do you think I might be missing?"

"Well, here's the thing I'm thinking. Why were those kids up there late at night like that? School the next morning and all. What's up there? Anything?"

"Not much. The cemetery, and then two or three ranches, back farther. The road dead ends back there a bit farther."

"So I guess here's what's been gnawing at me. We were looking at Curlie as a suspect—him and Melissa Talty. Now we're thinking Joe Teton, right? We've always just thought those kids were up to no good and happened to be in the right place to see something. But have we ever thought about them as suspects?"

The question hung in the coffee-tainted air for a long time, while Coal and Grant studied each other. Coal finally let out a long sigh. "I'm not going to lie. That thought has crossed my mind a few times. But . . . I don't know, Grant. I guess I don't have any excuses. Not really. Maybe you're right. Maybe I got too close to some aspects of this case."

The thought hit Coal that he had given Troy Westerlind a can of Pepsi when he was interviewing him, and Troy had thrown the empty can in the trash. Coal stepped quickly to the can and looked down. True to their nature, no one in the jail had emptied the trash, and the Pepsi can gleaned up at him. Bending down, he stuck his finger in the hole at the top and pulled it up and out.

"Mr. Crime Scene, why don't you do me a favor and get some fingerprints off this? I just got all the prints from the lance back from D. C. Let's satisfy some curiosity, shall we?"

While Grant was lifting prints off the Pepsi can, Coal went back into the cellblock to see that Hunter Jack's bag of food still had not been open. He looked at Jack.

"You and Officer Verret have a nice friendly chat?"

"Uh."

"That means . . . yes? No? You don't remember?"

"I wanna kill that white man," said Jack. "It means that."

"Badger? You have to stop talking about the people you want to kill. Do you understand? At some point they could be asking me to testify against you in a murder trial. And I will have to tell them every single thing I know. Every single thing I've heard."

"You don't *have* to."

"If they ask me point-blank I do. So stop talking about killing. It's not helping your case."

"Uh. Good. I'll stop."

"What did Verret say when he came in here, if you don't mind my asking?"

"He said, 'Good day, Mr. Jack. Nice to see you'."

"Oh. Nice guy."

Jack looked up at Coal, seeming to focus on his chin. "I can't stay in here much longer, Savage. It's killin' my spirit—you know? You gotta do somethin'. I thought we were friends."

"We are, Badger. But anymore I'm not sure anybody will listen to me. There are a lot of guys around here who've decided you're a murderer. And with you going around stabbing and beating up cops, I'm having a real hard time convincing them otherwise."

"Uh. Then I guess I gotta get my own way out."

Coal stared at Hunter Jack for a long time after that.

"Badger? If you find a way out of here, they're going to kill you. And some of them might enjoy doing it."

"Well. At least I would die with the wind in my hair."

When Coal went back out to the office area, Grant already had several prints, lifted with clear tape and laid out on a piece of white construction paper. "Take a look, Coal. What do you think?"

Coal looked over the prints. "Pretty clear, most of them. Looks like you've done this once or twice."

"Maybe."

Coal took the paper over to his desk and snapped the desk lamp on, wishing as he always did that he had some kind of shade to put over that blinding bare bulb. "Pull a chair around here, Grant," he ordered.

When the two of them were side by side, and Coal with a magnifying glass in his hand that he had gotten out of a drawer, they laid out the prints Tony Nwanzé had telecopied back to them, the prints pulled by Grant from the Shoshone lance.

"I guess the prints on that lance were a pretty jumbled mess," Coal said, surveying all of them. Two sheets were obviously all prints of smaller individuals, and a note on top of both pages said, "All kids?"

"Boy Scout fingerprints," Coal muttered to himself, and he slid those pages aside.

The others, he sorted out by size, and when he had several that matched the size just taken from the Pepsi can, he began comparing them. The job was far more tedious than he would have guessed, and when he finally started to feel a tension headache coming on, he set down the magnifying glass and pushed everything toward Grant. "Here. Take a turn, would you?"

He got up and started for the coffee pot, and Grant's polite voice stopped him, making him turn. "How much of that stuff do you already have on board?"

"What, the coffee?" Coal knew he looked irritable.

Grant stared back for a while, then shrugged. Any answer probably seemed as pointless as the question. Coal went and started to pour a cup full, then swore and poured it back.

He came back and sat next to Grant again, leaning back in his chair.

The phone rang, and Coal jerked and swore again. Grant remained aloof, studying prints with a close scrutiny. Coal picked up the phone. "Savage."

Yeah. You sound like it. It was the level voice and dry humor of Bob Wilson.

"Mornin', Bob."

Morning—but not so good.

Coal sighed, not in the mood for cryptic comments this early in the morning. "What does that mean, Bob?"

I need you to come over to the high school office, Coal. Make it quick, if you can. And please—no questions.

Coal let loose with the quietest, most polite string of curses he could manage. "I guess I'm taking another trip to the high school. Hell, as often as it seems like I'm in that damn place, I might as well get registered and see if I can catch up on my credits." After a few seconds to gather his wits, he clapped Grant on the back and stood up. "I don't say it much, Grant, but I sure admire a man who can handle the sound of a phone ringing. And a man who doesn't swear."

Grant looked up and smiled. "Thanks, Coal. I used to swear too, believe it or not. If you apply your mind to it, you could stop, if you wanted to."

"The hell I could."

Grinning at his own cleverness, Coal walked to the door, buckled on his gun and picked up his coat, putting it on and adjusting the edge of it around the gun butt.

"The problem is I don't want to quit. I like the taste of the words too much."

When he sat down on the frigid vinyl of the Thunderbird's seat, he swore again, and then he sat there feeling a little guilty. Maybe he *should* attempt to quit cursing, at least to say he had given it a good try. But the easier option was to fire Grant, so he no longer had anyone around to make him feel bad about his language.

Firing up the Bird, he let it idle for a couple of minutes to get the oil pressure up, then drove out of the lot and down off the Bar.

Coal walked through the front door of his old alma mater and breathed deeply. He wasn't sure if he liked the smell. Did it make him feel nostalgic, or did it bring back bad memories? He guessed it was a little of both.

Walking to the office, he tried to smile at Sally Edwards, but this time Sally wasn't smiling back. "Sorry, Coal. This isn't a visit that's going to make you happy."

He kept his swear words inside. "Where am I headed, Sally?"

She stood up. "Back here, to the principal's office. Mr. Carlson is already in there, and so is your friend Bob. With the boys."

The way she said that, Coal wondered if she thought he knew why he had been called, but he didn't say anything. Maybe the shock of what he was about to find out would stir his creative juices to new heights with the curse words. All the old ones were tasting a little stale anyway.

The blind was drawn over the window in the Principal Carlson's door. Great. Might as well make the fun surprise last. Coal knocked and heard a mumbled invitation, so he pushed the door open.

Straight into the room and at the back, seated behind his desk, was Principal Wade Carlson, and he stood up deferentially. "Sheriff. Come in and have a seat."

Coal looked to his left. There were four boys he didn't know, all of them with some mixture of scuffs, red marks, or dried or sticky blood on their faces, seated there in a row of hard plastic chairs. Clenching his jaw, he turned to the right, which was sheltered a little behind the door. On that side sat Bob Wilson, his friend, and Virgil Savage, his son. Virgil had dried blood crusted on the side of one nostril, and a bad bruise over his right eye that eventually would be a whale of a shiner.

Coal showed no reaction. He simply stepped the rest of the way in, shut the door behind him, and took a seat that made a sandwich out of Virgil, with Coal and Bob being the bread.

Mr. Carlson took a deep breath. "Sheriff, I really apologize for bringing you down here. The first thing I want you to know is your son is in no trouble."

Coal felt his eyes flicker, and his heart jumped. He felt the urge to reach over and squeeze Virgil's knee, but he held back, afraid it would embarrass him.

"All right. That's good."

The principal went on to tell the story of how apparently the four boys across from Coal had taken it upon themselves to become shy Virgil's daily tormentors. Their abuse had mostly taken the form of verbal slurs, tripping, or an occasional punch in the arm or the back of a hand to his groin. All normal high school kid stuff, even if it wasn't acceptable.

Today had been different, and the principal got two of the boys to confess at least partially to a more brutal attack, because this morning apparently Virgil had decided to push back.

Coal looked the boys over, then glanced at Virgil again. Finally, he turned his attention past Bob, to Mr. Carlson. "I'm missing something, Mr. Carlson. I'm not going to deny that I have done my best to teach my son how to defend himself, but . . . this?" He indicated the four boys with a wave of his hand.

The principal cleared his throat. "Well, that's the part we've managed to leave out so far. Sheriff, I'm sure your son was making a good show for himself, but this?" Like Coal, he indicated the boys with a wave of his hand. "Most of this happened after Troy Westerlind stepped in."

Coal's eyes widened. "Troy— You're telling me . . . Troy Westerlind stepped in? On Virgil's side?"

"The honest truth," said Carlson, with an expansive shrug. "I know. I know, Sheriff. I've had that boy in this office at least a dozen times, but never for anything like this. Never for any time when he came to someone's rescue."

His heart pounding hard, Coal said, "Where's Troy now?"

Again, the principal cleared his throat, looking over at the boys. "That's the reason we had to call Officer Wilson in for this rather than handling it ourselves. Aggravated battery, Bob tells us—a felony."

Coal lunged up out of his chair. *"What? Aggravated assault? Troy?"* Turning his head, he scanned the four boys for any injuries he might have yet to spot, then whirled to swing his eyes up and down Virgil, evaluating him. He looked back at Carlson, shocked and dumbfounded.

Principal Carlson pushed up off his chair, his eyes filled with concern. Patting the air down in front of him, as if to placate Coal, he said, "No, Sheriff! I misspoke. Troy is at the hospital. Dirk, down there on the end, well, he took it upon himself to take a rifle butt to the back of Troy's head."

CHAPTER FORTY-EIGHT

Coal didn't ask to take his boy with him when he left the school. He just took him. And he left knowing the case was in good hands, and that his friend Bob Wilson would do the right thing, where Dirk was concerned. That boy had a strong felony charge coming, and Coal felt confident knowing Bob would see it through.

Racing to the hospital probably too fast, even though it was a very short distance away, Coal and Virgil had no time to talk. It wasn't until Coal slid up in front of the emergency room entrance that he thought to look over at his boy. Of course Virgil was not looking at him, but out his own window.

"Virg?"

Slowly, his son brought his face around. Coal saw him blinking rapidly as he did, and at the last second he brought a hand up and rubbed his eyes. "Yeah, Dad?"

Coal stared, realizing suddenly that he didn't know what to say—at least not without a few hours in which to say it. He said the one and only thing he knew how, the one thing that losing Laura, and almost losing Katie Leigh as well, had taught him he must say, because nobody knew what day was going to be his last.

"I love you, Son."

No sooner had he spoken than he knew it might be the wrong time, for tears flooded his son's eyes, and Coal could see he lost his voice. Virgil nodded vigorously, reached down and squeezed the hand Coal had laid on his thigh.

"You stay out here as long as you need, Virg. Or I'll take you in with me and we'll get Annie to take you to a private room where you can be alone for a while."

Nodding adamantly at that idea, Virgil threw open his door. He didn't want to be alone with his emotions in this big car with all the large, very clear windows, and Coal didn't blame him one bit.

They went through the front door, and relief washed over Coal when the first person down the hall to turn and see them was Annie. She came almost running, immediately assessing the situation when she looked at Virgil. Coal passed his request for his son on to her, and Annie, putting her arm tightly around Virgil's shoulders, smiled at Coal and led the boy hurriedly away.

Coal stepped to the receptionist's desk, where dark-haired Mandy had stood up to greet him. "Hi, Sheriff. This day sure has started out insane! Do you want to see Troy Westerlind?"

Following Mandy's direction, Coal rushed down to the emergency room. Behind the closed door, he could hear a commotion of voices, and he opened the door and peeked around the corner. Troy Westerlind, with a grimace on his face, lay on a bed with the head raised halfway up, and dark-haired Dr. Jace Koslowski, along with the help of a nurse dressed in white, was trying to wrap the boy's skull in a wide white strip of gauze, while a second white-clad nurse Coal didn't recognize held thick dressing in place.

Coal backed away and shut the door softly. Stepping two doors down, where they had been keeping Dale Moore, he found an open door, and an empty room.

Walking as fast as he could back down the hall, he found Mandy trying to put together a pot of coffee. She spun when he spoke her name, and he had to apologize for frightening her. "Can you tell me if Dale Moore is still here?"

"Of course. They're keeping him for observation." She glanced around, as if to make sure no one else was within earshot. "You know—for suicide watch."

After Mandy gave Coal the location where he could find Dale Moore, he turned and went down the hall, took a left, and passed through a set of double doors. The first door on his right was open wide, and inside, on an upraised bed like Troy Westerlind's, lay Dale. The surprise to Coal was to see Dawn Kelly sitting with him, side by side on the bed.

Both kids recognized Coal at the same time, and Dawn leaped up. "Sheriff Savage!" She practically ran to him, throwing her arms around him tightly.

"Hi, girl." He hugged her as tight as she was holding him and looked over the top of her head at the patient. "Hey, Dale. You're looking pretty spry."

The boy smiled a tentative smile, and in it Coal sensed residual fear. Where Dawn had surprised Coal by melting into an entirely different girl from the one he had first met, Dale still didn't know quite what to think, or feel. Coal guessed the boy was going to take years healing from his past, if he ever could.

After a few seconds, Dale pointed at his throat. He tried to say something, but it came out as a squeaky whisper. "Don't try to talk, buddy," said Coal, moving close to the bedside with his arm around Dawn, and her arm around him, holding on so tight he wasn't sure she would ever let go.

When Coal was close, he put his free hand on Dale's arm and gave it a squeeze. "You sure gave us a scare. How are you feeling?"

Dale gave him a sad smile and a nod. "Good," he squeaked out.

"I see you have a loyal nurse here," Coal commented. "Playing hooky, of course—but I guess if there's any good reason this would be it."

Dale nodded and blushed. Dawn blushed too, and dropped her eyes.

"Hey, girl, why don't you and I grab a chair, huh?"

Dawn looked up at him and nodded, then let go of his waist and turned to the only chair in the room that wasn't taken. "Might have to go get another one," she said.

"Why don't you just sit on the edge of the bed?" Coal suggested. "I can't stay too long anyway."

When the girl was seated, Coal glanced back and forth between them. He felt suddenly uncomfortable about the news he had to share. Did these two know about Troy?

He was trying to work up how to tell them when Dawn, intuitive as so many of her gender seemed to be, said, "Is something wrong?"

Before Coal could reply, he saw the door open from the corner of his eye, and Virgil stepped in, followed closely by Annie, who had her hands on the boy's shoulders. When Dawn saw the boy's face, she gasped.

"Coal?" said Annie, and he met her eyes. "Mandy just took a call from one of your deputies. Maybe we should step out in the hall."

Feeling his pulse speed up, Coal nodded and went out with her, leaving Virgil standing inside.

"I guess your deputy found a match, he said to tell you. A match between a Pepsi can and a wooden handle? He said you would know what he meant."

Coal felt sick. A match. A match . . . Troy . . . Of course there were more questions to ask, but suddenly he felt all too sure he knew the answers.

"Okay, Annie. Thank you."

The concern all over her face may as well have been written in bold letters. "Coal? Is everything okay?"

"No. It's not." He wanted suddenly to pull Annie to him and squeeze the breath out of her. He didn't want to go back in to Dale and Dawn, and he certainly didn't look forward to his next visit with Troy Westerlind.

"I'm due for a break soon." Annie's voice, like her eyes, was soft. "Come get me, okay? If you need to talk."

Feeling numb, he thanked her and watched her walk away. His thoughts were jumping all over the place. He had been so certain about Joe Teton, for so many reasons. Teton had killed before. He had fought with and been injured by the murder victim, very recently, supposedly to protect two sons he doted on. He had also been publicly shamed by the victim in the same fight, in front of his entire neighborhood, and Joe Teton came across to Coal as a very proud man. He had claimed he would like to kill Everett Sherman. He fit every bit of the description of the man who had fled the scene of the murders. And then he had come driving down from the cemetery, at an hour when no person possibly could have had any good reason to be up there. Every last piece of circumstantial evidence had pointed to Joe Teton as the killer, and the only thing that had remained was to get a warrant from the judge, fingerprint him, then compare the known prints to the prints on the lance handle.

But now, out of the blue, came Troy Westerlind, along with Dale and Dawn, turned from potential witnesses to high on the list of potential suspects, all at the drop of the proverbial hat.

Stepping back into the room, Coal's eyes fell on Dale. He gazed at him with a sodden heartbeat, then turned his gaze to Dawn. Coal had seen lost people before. He had gone to school with some, and even been friends with some. He had seen them in Korea, and in Nam. Not psychopathic killers like the murderer, Hague Freeman, but people, usually young people, who had taken so much abuse in their lives that they themselves had finally turned to the abuser, sometimes as a perceived means of self-preservation.

Were Dawn and Dale those people? Were they killers? Were they even the kind who could watch someone like Troy Westerlind take the lives of two other human beings, and then keep the secret to themselves?

"Sheriff?" said Dawn finally, standing up and taking a step toward him. "What is it?"

"I have to go check something," Coal replied, stone-faced. "But I'll be back. Dawn? You'll still be here in an hour . . . won't you?"

"Yes. I'm not leaving Dale."

Coal nodded. "Okay. Before I go, I need to tell both of you something. This is my son, Virgil." He introduced the other two to Virgil. "Virgil looks like this because some boys at the school attacked him this morning." He quickly pushed away Dawn's concern for his boy. "Thank you, Dawn, but let me finish. Troy came to Virgil's rescue. I'm not sure why. But when he did, one of the other boys from your school hit him in the head with a rifle butt."

Dawn gasped and took another step toward Coal. "Is he all right?"

Coal shrugged. "They're treating him now, and bandaging him up. I haven't had a chance to talk to anyone. But . . ." He suddenly found it hard to go on, but he forced himself. "There is a time coming soon that I think you both have known about for a while. I've given you kids as much time to think about it as I can, but we're about out of time. I have to go look at something from the crime scene, but I'll be back within an hour. Both of you should prepare yourselves to talk to me. Do you understand? I'm going to need to know everything that happened the night those two people were killed, and why you and Troy were up by the cemetery at two o'clock in the morning. I'm sorry." He directed that comment between the two of them. "I'm really sorry. But it's time to talk. It will go over a lot better for both of you if you tell me everything you know."

Taking Virgil, Coal went out of the room. There was no goodbye between him, Dale, and Dawn.

In the hall, Annie Price was waiting, and she must have read the feelings he couldn't hide from his face. "Coal? Is everything all right?"

He shrugged. "It's going to take some time, Annie. But it will be. I have to leave, all right? But I'll be back, hopefully before an hour. I'm going to need you to keep both those kids here until I get back. Can you do that?"

She shook her head. "I can try. But if someone comes in needing a nurse . . ."

"I understand. Just try then, okay? I really need them both to be here when I get back."

Coal and Virgil rushed up to the courthouse, where Coal found Grant awaiting him. Coal's first order of business was to call out to the house and arrange for Connie to bring little Sissy into town and pick up Virgil at the jail. He had a gut feeling it was going to be a long day from here on, with ugliness in it that Virgil didn't need to see, although he hoped there would be a time before long when he might get his boy together with Troy Westerlind for some kind of proper thank you for Troy's coming to Virgil's rescue. Instinctively, he knew that time would have to be soon, for somehow he knew Troy was going to be going away—for a long, long time.

While Virgil sat down near the wall and picked up a copy of *TIME Magazine,* Grant took Coal to the desk and flipped the lamp on, highlighting a fingerprint he had taken from the Pepsi can earlier, sitting next to one of those that had come back from Tony Nwanzé. Patiently, with the point of a pen, Grant went over all the telltale signs in the ridges of the two fingerprints, then looked up at Coal. "We'll have to have this corroborated by an expert, of course—just for the trial. But I can promise you right now, this is a match. Troy Westerlind had his hands on that lance—the lance that killed Everett Sherman."

CHAPTER FORTY-NINE

Dawn Kelly said she had to go see Troy, if she could. She said she hoped he understood why, and then she left, and Dale Moore was left alone.

He lay in the hospital bed, which he had laid down almost flat because the door was halfway open, and he didn't want to see anyone passing by. If he thought about his reasons for that for very long, it hurt his head. He should have been the opposite. He should have been *wary,* and vigilantly watching for anyone to approach. So often in the past days he had dreamed of some evil, huge presence coming for him. So many times he had awakened to expect them there, standing over him, with a lance in their hands—the lance that would end his miserable life.

Sweat was beaded up on Dale's forehead, his cheeks, and chin. He could feel it running down his sides, beneath the sheets. He stared at the ceiling, part of him now wishing Dawn hadn't come to his house so fast. He had been so close . . . And she had brought him back—to *this.*

She had brought him back here, to feelings of crushing guilt, to memories of horror, of blood. Memories of that look of life fading out of those eyes.

He had to come clean. He couldn't worry about Dawn and Troy anymore. No matter what his confession did to them, his guilt over the sin of being there, of standing by and watching, without trying to stop it, was too much. And the only way to rid himself of that guilt was either by the means he had already tried . . . or by confessing—telling Sheriff Savage where he had been, and what he had seen, what he had allowed to happen, without a single word of protest.

With Troy, he wasn't sure what to think. After hearing what Troy had done for Virgil Savage, how he had come to the rescue of a shy, lonely boy when he easily could have joined in, or at least turned and walked away, he just didn't know. Ever since the killing, he had been so sure Troy was hopeless. But how could a hopeless, heartless boy turn around and fight for another human being in need? That was a puzzle Dale had not been able to conquer, and maybe never would. He didn't want to be the one to put the final nail in Troy's coffin, his coffin made of all the wood and nails of the sins and crimes Troy had committed. But that wasn't his to worry about anymore, not if it was going to eat his own soul away.

One thing about Troy: Ever since Dale had stumbled on the little story, the one he was sure was written by Edgar Allen Poe, about a man who started out killing some innocent little canary, in a very detailed, bloodthirsty way, and then later went on to killing people, he couldn't help thinking that was a story about a person like Troy Westerlind. He was destined to end somewhere in a penitentiary, or in some dark alley with a cop's bullet in his heart.

It was Dawn Kelly Dale truly hated to be part of bringing down. No matter how tough she tried to act, Dale knew Dawn Kelly. She had a heart hidden inside her that was bigger than a house. But maybe if he told the story now it would help her change. Maybe whatever punishment she got would be the best thing that happened to her while she was still young.

Anyway, it didn't matter. Dale had to talk. He had to confess. He had failed in taking his own life. He was too frightened to run away and try to find his mother, and didn't know if she would want him anyway. He had to stay here in Salmon, and that meant there was only one way forward.

Since Jordan Peterson hadn't come to work yet, after his late shift, and he had the only other radio because he was driving Coal's old truck, Coal swapped Grant his pickup for the Thunderbird, so Grant could monitor the airwaves.

He told his deputy to try calling Gunnar Westerlind, to get him to the hospital as soon as possible even though the very thought of seeing the rancher again made Coal's blood pressure rise. Then he told Grant to give Flo a call and have her keep trying the rancher, while he headed east for his house. Flo would call Grant and turn him back toward town if she made contact.

Then Coal headed back down to the hospital, leaving Virgil to wait for his grandmother.

The first person Coal saw in the hall as he came into the hospital was Dawn Kelly. She was walking the other way, leaving the emergency ward. He didn't want to yell out and startle the entire hospital staff and patients, so instead he picked up his pace to try to catch up with the girl, avoiding making eye contact with anyone he passed so no one would attempt to stop him.

Dawn made the corner long before he got there, and she was standing inside the doorway to Dale Moore's room by the time he caught up with her.

Dawn stood rigid, apparently staring at Dale instead of going in the room. That startled Coal, making two thoughts race through his head at once—either that Dale was gone, or dead, or perhaps Troy had died and she wasn't sure how to tell Dale.

The girl started slowly, stiffly, around the bed, and Coal saw Dale's pale face. The boy's eyes flashed from looking at Dawn to looking out at Coal. Dale's expression was almost one of relief, but for a second it looked like he was going to cry.

Stepping to the door, Coal's boots sounded loud in the hollow hall, and Dawn whirled around, a look of terror on her face. Even when she realized who he was, Dawn's face only deescalated from looking terrified by a fraction. This time the girl didn't run to him.

Carefully, Coal shut the door behind him. He took a deep breath. "Guys, you have to tell me what happened. I know the gist of it, but I have to know the details. And they'd be so much better if you told them to me voluntarily."

With her chin quivering, Dawn said, "Sheriff? I'm scared."

"I know, Dawn. I'm sorry," Coal replied. He couldn't tell her there was nothing to be scared of. If what he believed was true, they had much to fear, from here forward. "I'll be here for you kids any way I can. But you have to talk to me. There are some other suspects you have to set free, because it's the right thing to do."

This statement caused confused looks to come to both their faces, and they glanced at each other before looking back at him.

"Sheriff . . ." Dawn started, then stopped. "Sheriff Savage, please . . . Please don't think . . ." Her chin began to shake again, and then tears started running down her face. Her tough girl mask was melting too fast to stop.

"You kids get yourselves together, all right? I'm going to make a phone call and get Officer Wilson down here. I don't want to make it more uncomfortable for you, but I should have a neutral witness here for when you sign your statements."

They both nodded, still looking frightened, but now resigned. Coal went out and called Bob, who was still in the middle of dealing with the parents of the four boys involved in that morning's fight. But Bob knew where to find those boys, so when he realized the importance of this phone call, he released the boys into their parents' custody and headed down to be with Coal and the kids.

Coal had almost made it back to the room when he heard a commotion behind him. He turned to see Dr. Koslowski and Annie Price struggling to restrain Troy Westerlind, who was pushing at them and speaking angrily, words Coal didn't make out.

Suddenly, Troy whirled toward Coal, with an IV line dangling free from one elbow. "Sheriff!"

Coal hurried back toward the cluster of people. "What's going on?"

"Thank heavens, Sheriff," said Jace Koslowski. "We've got to get this guy back to his bed. He should not be up at least for several hours. That was a nasty hit he took."

"No!" growled Troy. "No! Sheriff, listen! Can you make them let me go? I have to get out of here."

"Why, Troy? Where do you plan to go?"

"With you! I want to go with you. Is Dale still here?" The boy had a frantic look on his face. Coal figured Troy was guessing the hammer was about to drop on him, if he couldn't get to Dale and convince him to keep his mouth shut.

"He's here," Coal said, evenly. "Dawn's here too." He wasn't sure how to process the look that came over Troy's face. For a second, it almost looked like relief.

"Troy, we're trying to find your father right now. We're going to need him to come down here."

Troy scoffed. "He's not at the house?"

Coal shrugged. "That's what we're trying to find out."

"Well, if he's not, and he's not already in town, I think I know where he is, because it's past time for him to feed his precious cows."

"Where would that be, son?"

"He's been seein' that rancher widow," Troy said, not masking the anger in his face and voice. "That MacAtee lady. But please don't call him down here. Please, at least not yet." Coal had never imagined this kind of pleading in Troy's voice.

Stepping close to Troy, the doctor, and Annie, easily within striking distance if Troy decided to go berserk, Coal said, "It'll be okay, Troy. I promise it'll be okay." He was trying to keep his voice steady, trying not to let anyone see how gut-punched he felt to know that the worst he feared for Kathy was true, and she was still seeing Gunn Westerlind. The very thought of them together made him feel almost ill. Kathy was his best friend's wife!

"It won't be okay," Troy said quietly. His voice and his eyes had gone dull. "He'll always win. He always wins."

"You're seventeen," Coal said, stepping closer still, to put a hand on Troy's arm. "I have to have your father here if he's able to be. You have to try and understand. Please go back in your room with the doctor, all right? And Annie. You know, Troy, this woman's a close friend of mine. Treat her good for me."

Troy turned to Annie, almost mechanically, and he almost smiled. Then he turned for his room. Coal could describe his pace going back into the room as nothing more than a shuffle.

Returning to the receptionist's desk, Coal dialed up Flo, asking her to have Grant Fairbourne try Kathy's ranch if they couldn't find Gunn Westerlind elsewhere. Then he hung up the phone, feeling almost numb, and turned to walk back down to Dale Moore's room. He imagined his own plodding pace probably didn't look much better than a shuffle, too, to anyone who might be watching.

Reaching Dale's room, Coal steadied himself, then turned the handle and pushed the door open. Dale was sitting nearly upright in the bed now, and once more Dawn was sitting next to him. Coal realized as Dawn jerked away that they had been holding hands. She started swiping angrily at her cheeks, which were wet with tears.

Coal stood there as long as he could stand the silence and the fear. "We were suspecting an Indian man of the killings," he said. "I guess I can tell you that now. His name is Joe Teton, and he has two little boys at home, with only him to take care of them."

Dale and Dawn whipped their faces back toward each other, and she reached a shaking hand out once more to take Dale's left hand in a stranglehold.

"Do we talk to you together?" Dawn asked. "Or do we have to be alone?"

"Alone is best," said Coal. "I'll explain why afterward."

They both nodded. Dale tried to clear his throat, then gave out with a weak-sounding, high-pitched cough. It made Coal cringe to think of how close the boy had come to leaving this world, when he might have so much good ahead of him if he stayed.

"Do you need anything?" Coal asked, now stalling for time until Bob arrived. They both said no, and then the waiting game was on.

Seeing no great reason to remain standing, since Dawn had given up her chair to be on the bed with Dale, Coal went over and pulled the chair a few feet away from the kids, sinking down onto it. He had thought about trying to comfort these two again, but to judge by the current air in the room, they were past needing, or wanting, comfort from a man wearing a badge.

Out at the MacAtee ranch, Kathy was shoveling scrambled eggs out of a cast iron frying pan onto a waiting plate she had warmed up. Gunnar Westerlind, his hat hanging from his chair, his hair combed perfectly to one side, stared out the window at the beautiful, slightly overcast morning.

Turning to smile at Kathy, he said, "That smells mighty good."

"Thank you. I—"

The ringing of the phone cut off what she was going to say. "Oh, my. That figures," she said with a light laugh.

She set down the frying pan, wiped her fingers on a towel, and answered the phone. The voice of Flo Hawkins was on the other end. *Hi, Kathy! I'm sorry to bother you. This could sound like a really bizarre question, but would Gunnar Westerlind happen to be out at your house?*

Momentarily confused, Kathy looked over at Westerlind. "Why . . . yes, he is, Flo! How did you know that?"

Coal suggested it, said Flo. *I have a message for Mr. Westerlind.*

Still feeling confused, Kathy took the phone from her ear and held it out to the rancher. “Weird,” she said. “It’s our dispatcher. It’s for you.”

Brow furrowing, Westerlind picked up the phone and answered. As he listened silently, his expression changed and began to grow darker and darker. He was about to say something, but he looked over at Kathy and cut his words short. “Okay, ma’am. Thank you for the call, and I’ll head in to the hospital right now.”

“What is it?” asked Kathy as he hung up. “Something about a fight. That boy of mine!” he said, trying unsuccessfully to hide his anger. “And this time it had something to do with that Savage kid.”

“Virgil?” asked Kathy, snapping fully erect.

“Yeah, I guess.”

Reaching out to flip the stove off, she said, “Wait! I’m going with you.”

“I’d rather you didn’t, frankly,” said Westerlind, then quickly followed up on that. “I don’t want to make you feel bad, but darn, I hate to have you see my son in his element.”

Kathy gave a little frown, wiping her hands on a towel and laying it aside with measured movements. “Well, if this is something to do with Virgil, I want to go. That boy has been like a part of our family since the day he was born.”

Westerlind measured her with his eyes. He wanted to insist she not come. She could see it in his eyes.

“It’s fine if you’d rather go alone. I understand. I’ll take my own car.”

At this, Westerlind frowned. “All right, Kathy. No, it’s fine. You might as well ride with me as waste gas on two vehicles.”

Kathy grabbed her coat, fighting back a growing sense of worry. She prayed shy Virgil wasn’t going down that same dark path Katie Leigh had been traveling when the Savages first arrived back in Salmon. Coal had already suffered so much.

Coal cleared his throat, after five minutes had passed—or it might have been ten. He looked at Dawn and Dale, wanting someone to help them, but knowing that like everyone else they would have to deal with their own judgment.

"Just so you know, before this is all over, we'll have to have you both come up to the jail, or down to City Hall, so we can record your statements. I just want to do this initial one short and neat. We'll fill in the detail later, on tape."

Neither of the kids showed any reaction beyond the worry that was already in their faces. Both of them had resigned themselves to whatever was to come. Coal guessed they both had seen more than their share of disciplinary action by authorities. Maybe by now they were desensitized to it—even though this time it would probably be far, far harsher than any justice they had ever known in the past.

There was a sudden knock on the door, the knock of someone who brooked no nonsense. "Come in, Bob," said Coal.

The door opened, and Bob Wilson gave Coal a grim little smile. "You know my code."

"I just know your style, my friend," Coal said. Looking back at Dawn and Dale, he said, "Which of you wants to get this out of the way?"

The kids looked at each other, and Coal almost smiled. He kept thinking of them as kids, but both were nearly adults, in the legal sense. He could only hope their juvenile status would earn them some kind of leniency, and that somehow his influence might sway the judge in that direction.

"I guess . . . me," said Dawn quietly. "And maybe we could get Dale some water? And something soft for his throat."

"Sure," said Coal with a smile. "I'll get one of the nurses to bring something."

He stood up, wanting to reach his hand out to Dawn to help her up, but he didn't know how it would look to Bob, and he didn't even know if the girl would take it now. She was still acting polite, but all the former warmth had fled her.

They got up and started for the door, but before Bob could reach for the handle, it flew open, almost hitting him. There stood Gunnar Westerlind, and in the claws of his left hand was gripped his son's upper arm. Troy's teeth were clenched, in anger, pain, or some of both.

"What do you think you're doing?" Westerlind asked. "Talking to these kids without their parents? Or a lawyer?"

"I'd advise you to stand down," said Bob Wilson, straightening up. "This is none of your affair."

"None of my affair?" Westerlind growled the question. "You're about to grill two innocent little kids, without any adult representation present, and they're going to drag my family's name through the fire. That's none of my affair?"

"Step away from the door, Westerlind," Coal spoke evenly. "I won't tell you again."

"Or what? You'll shoot me?" This time the rancher almost spat the words. "You are *not* going to try and pin something on my family's name. Not in *this* state. You kids—get up out of there, Dale. Dawn? Come with us. I'll get you out of here. This clown has no right to—"

"Hey!" the word coming from Troy Westerlind was almost an animalistic snarl.

With an expression of livid anger, he ripped his arm out of his father's grasp and took several steps out into the hall. Stunned to motionlessness only for a second, Westerlind charged after him, reaching. Troy angrily slapped his father's hands away as Coal and Bob barreled into the hall together. Coal was remotely conscious of a dark-haired woman in a blue plaid shirt standing close by on his left, but mentally he was beyond the point of her presence fully registering on him.

Westerlind got close to his son. He raised his right fist up high, set to bring it down hard on his son's face.

"Westerlind!" Coal barked, at the exact same time that Bob's voice rang out with, *"Hold it!"*

The rancher's right hand, still in a fist, lowered a little, but the left reached out and clawed into the boy's shirt, jerking him closer. The fist came up again slightly higher, but by then Coal and Bob had both reached the rancher, and while Coal got his right arm, Bob grabbed the left, and they dragged him backward. For a few seconds, the furious rancher pulled his son with him, but finally his grip gave out, and Coal and Bob whirled him around, throwing him face first against the wall.

"Settle down!" growled Coal.

"Get your hands off me!" Westerlind roared. "I'll have both your jobs—*today!"*

"You do that," said Bob, sounding much cooler than Coal felt.

Coal's tone grew deeper, but certainly not quieter. He knew it was loud, but he almost didn't hear himself speak, past his rage. "I said settle down, Westerlind, or I'll break your arm. And my job be damned. Dealing with people like you every day, I'm getting tired of it anyway."

Westerlind began to struggle, pulling hard against both strong men who held him. He fought and cursed and snarled, until Coal kicked hard against the inside of the right foot, making the rancher's stance splay out wide. Keeping his lower leg locked to the inside of the rancher's, he yanked him backward sharply, leaning a little lower as he felt something give way and heard a gruesome grinding noise, like the sound a drumstick makes when torn from a raw chicken. Westerlind cried out in pain and would have gone to the floor on his back if Bob Wilson hadn't been holding him up.

As swiftly as he had grabbed hold of it, Coal let go of the rancher's arm and put his left hand on his back, shoring him up and helping Bob push him all the way back erect. As Bob relaxed his hold, Westerlind whirled on them, his face purple. He reached across his body with his left hand, grabbing his other arm. "You tore my shoulder out!" Westerlind snarled. "You'll go to jail for this!"

"We'll see about that," Bob said. He turned around, searching for someone, and that made Coal turn too. He knew Bob was seeking out medical personnel.

Coal's searching gaze was stopped long before he could focus on the doctor and nurses he knew were standing by. His eyes zeroed in on the horror-struck face of Kathy MacAtee.

The first thought that raced through Coal's mind was to apologize to his friend for what she had seen, and how he had acted, but he stopped himself short. It wasn't the time. Anyway, Kathy reeled back several steps from the scene of the tussle, and when Coal turned his apologetic eyes away from her she seemed physically fifteen feet away, and in emotional space she could have been on the moon.

Breathing hard, Gunnar Westerlind spun back and forth, still holding tight to his arm. "You'll pay for this! Both of you," he snapped. "Come on, Troy. They're not going to pin anything on any kid of mine!"

Without any warning, Troy Westerlind lunged forward. "Would you just shut up!" He was almost screaming into his father's face. "Shut your damn mouth! For once in your horrible life!"

The father gaped at the son, his mouth hanging open. By now, both Dale and Dawn had gathered at the doorway to the boy's room as well. Both their faces were white.

Coal was conscious of Grant Fairbourne striding down the hall, looking ready for trouble. Coal didn't look at him directly because his eyes were pinned on Gunn and Troy Westerlind.

"You're so pathetic," Troy spat at his father, probably completely unaware of the tears staining his cheeks. "You're so worried about your *family name.* WHAT family name? No one likes you. No one *needs* you. You wanna talk about family name? I'll tell you about family name. You're so worried about keepin' out of the paper. Well, I'm gonna tell the whole world who the Westerlind family is!"

Troy whirled back and forth, his eyes passing over everyone, but not seeming to see any of them. His father stood speechless.

"You wanna know why I was out the night of those killings? You all wanna know? Okay. I'll tell you! I was out drivin' my old man's all-important truck, using his gas, so I could drag the only friends I got in this world down to some Indian dude's house, go in and steal a lance off his wall. Why? 'Cause it was funny! 'Cause it was ripe for the pickin'!

"Stop, Troy!" yelled Gunnar. "Just stop now! Don't say another word!"

"YOU STOP!" roared Troy, his face turning dark red. *"STOP!* Stop and shut your stupid—damn—mouth! It's *my* turn . . . *Daddy. Mine!* Get it?"

The boy pivoted around again on his heels, staring blindly at the speechless crowd. "Know what I did with that lance? You really wanna know what I did?" The boy's gaze sped across the other faces, all the way from one side of the hall to the other, faltering only a moment on the frightened white faces of his friends, Dale and Dawn. His dark, crazy eyes settled at last once more on the face of his father.

"All you ever cared about is your name. You never cared one bit about me—old man! Well, I don't care about *you!* Remember your great big, fancy bull? Yeah, Prince what's-his-name?" He roared with laughter. "Well, it turns out you threw all that money away, because he's dead! *Dead!* Lyin' down in the trees up at the ranch, just waitin' for you to go pick him up and haul him home in the spring. You ain't gonna have nothin' left to haul but maybe some old hide, and some bones. Eight hundred bucks, old man! And it's *gone!* Gone—just like me."

CHAPTER FIFTY

The echoes of the explosion in the hall of Steele Memorial Hospital had faded into non-existence, and the medical personnel, all but Annie Price, had returned to their jobs, one of those jobs being that of examining Gunnar Westerlind's shoulder, and trying to see what kind of damage it had sustained.

Of course Coal couldn't help wondering if that move was going to come back to haunt him. He really didn't know what people in what high-up places in Idaho the rancher actually might know who could make Coal's life miserable. But thinking back, considering the way Westerlind had been acting, and how he had been about to batter his son with his fist, there really wasn't much he could say he wouldn't do the same, all over again. Anyway, he had more important things to think about right now—three teenagers he had to figure out what to do with, and a good friend who needed at the very least a minute of his time.

Asking Annie, who still stood there watching, to take the three teenagers and try to sort things out with them—everything short of officially discharging them, Coal turned to Kathy. The woman was badly shaken, her face pale even underneath her always carefully applied makeup. But beyond the paleness, her eyes told Coal the story. Dodging this way and that, unable to rest on his face for long, they left him wondering how much real, physical violence Kathy had ever had to confront face to face.

He stepped slowly to her, saying the first words that came to his mind. "I'm sorry, Kathy. I'm really sorry you had to see that."

Kathy responded by coming to him to throw her arms around him, squeezing hard. A tremor went through her body, which was hard and firm from years of throwing hay, and throwing calves. Finally, when someone walked past them and made the extended embrace feel awkward, she stepped back, but reached out to maintain physical contact by grabbing his hand.

"I'm not sorry, Coal. Please don't you be. I just saw a side of Gunn Westerlind I never could have believed existed, and I'm not sorry. I'm glad I was here to see that—before it was too late."

That comment wrenched at Coal's heart. *Too late?* Had whatever relationship was developing between Kathy and Westerlind actually gone that far?

"Well, I'm sorry you had to see me like that."

She shook her head adamantly, her eyes misting over, and taking his other hand, she squeezed them both hard. "Sorry for standing up for three helpless kids, Coal? I'm sure not. I'll never forget seeing that kind of passion in you. If you had acted any different, I might be disappointed."

He laughed. "Okay, well if me losing my temper over people being bullied is a turn-on for you, then I guess we'll keep getting along great."

She laughed with him, and hugged him again. To heck with anyone who happened to see. Neither of them realized that the only person who did see, this time, was Annie, when she started to come back around the corner of the hallway where she had left the three teenagers.

"I really want to take you out for a bite, Kathy," Coal said.

"Well, I, uh . . ."

"It's okay," he said, stopping her because she seemed so hesitant. "I'm sure you're busy, and I've got a mountain of things I have to do anyway. Maybe some other time?"

She stared at him for a few seconds, then went for the understanding smile approach. "Sure, Coal. You bet! Maybe some other time. Maybe we can get the Camaro out and take a ride—burn off some of that leftover summer gas."

The suggestion made him smile. She was willing to share Larry's Camaro with him again? Maybe she wasn't as disappointed in his bad behavior as he had feared.

After Kathy left, Coal walked around the hospital until almost by accident he ran into Annie. For some reason, her demeanor was a little cool. "Hey. Those kids treat you all right?"

She shot him a smile. "Oh, sure. I'm sorry they're in trouble. They seem like decent kids."

"They might be," Coal said. "I don't know what to believe anymore."

"No. Me either," Annie agreed.

The woman left Coal with that cryptic comment, and he found the three kids in the room where she had left them. Letting them know he was going up to the jail to get his tape recording machine so they could record all three of their interviews right there at the hospital, Coal took off. He found Bob Wilson eating a genuine Wally's to-go burger up at the jailhouse, and Grant was there with him.

Around a mouthful of burger, Bob waved from Coal's desk. He tried to say something while Coal stood looking at him with a half-smile on his face. Finally, Bob choked down his bite. "Sorry about that."

"You were always a pig," said Coal.

Bob gave an almost-smile. "So hey. I wanted to let you know I remembered getting a call from Curt Dykus, up past the cemetery at the Swinging V ranch. You know the place?"

"Vaguely," Coal said. "Remember, it's been a while since I spent a lot of time in this valley."

"Yeah, yeah." Bob looked back down at his burger, contemplating whether or not to take another bite. He relaxed his hand full of burger back on the desk and said, "Well, anyway, I remembered the call about a missing bull. Dykus thought it either wandered off or might even have got stolen. It just stopped coming in when it was feeding time."

"Okay?"

"So I called him, and he said he was getting ready to call me too."

"And?"

"And he found the bull. Dead down in the trees below his place—just like the kid said."

Coal gave a slow nod. "Stabbed, I guess?"

"He couldn't tell for sure, but he said we can come up and look it over. Coyotes and eagles have been at it already—and some ravens and magpies."

"I guess we'll look at it," Coal agreed. "But it seems pretty cut and dried."

"You sure?"

"Yeah. I think so. I didn't see how those kids could be part of a murder anyway. Troy? Maybe. But not Dawn and Dale."

"Seems like you might've got kind of attached to those two," Bob observed.

"That obvious, huh? I guess my poker face is a pile of . . . something."

Bob almost smiled. "Yep. Sure is."

Coal took his recording machine back down off the Bar to the hospital, where he met with each of the kids individually—first Dawn, then Dale, who made his best attempt at telling the story, even with his injured windpipe, and last of all Troy. All of their stories were almost exact, with the exception of minor, unimportant details that any kid who was upset, in a stressful situation, could have perceived differently from another.

One part of the story Coal made a point of jotting down specifically in his notes, and marked with a big star, a point made by all three of the kids, was that they didn't actually break into Hunter Jack's house, because the doorframe around the knob was already broken, and all they had to do was turn the knob and walk in.

Troy's fingerprints on the murder weapon were explained exactly as Coal already knew they would be, because Troy, like all the younger Boy Scouts who had been with him at Jack's house, hand handled that lance.

"Did you see anyone else when you were up there?" Coal asked Troy. He had already asked the same question of the other two, and gotten the same answer back.

"Yeah. Some old Indian guy."

"Can you describe him? Or identify him if I were to show you a photograph?"

"Sure, I guess—except we weren't really super close."

"Did he say anything to you?"

"No. We saw him running to a pickup that was parked up in the middle of the graves."

Coal got Troy's description of the man's clothing, which fit pretty close with what Dawn and Dale had said, with allowances for the fact that citizens untrained in careful observation often miss small details.

Everything Troy said fit every detail Coal would have used to describe Joseph Teton, if he had never seen him any closer than twenty feet away.

"Okay, Troy," Coal finally said. He held up his hand to keep the boy from speaking, while he stated the date and time clearly into the microphone of his recorder, then reached out and shut it off.

For half a minute, the two of them sat in contemplative silence. Coal finally asked Troy if he could get him a pop or anything. Troy didn't directly reply.

"Sheriff?"

"Yeah."

"I don't get all this."

"Get what?"

"All this . . . with you and Dale—and Dawn. And me. You just bein' nice to me because of that thing with your son?"

Coal studied Troy Westerlind for several seconds. "Troy, let me ask you something before I reply to that. What about you? Why did you step in and help Virgil? You know you could've walked away, and stayed out of more trouble. I mean you already knew this whole thing with the bull was hanging over your head."

"I . . . They were pickin' on him. Four to one, and he's a sophomore. They're all in my grade. I let it go at first."

Coal raised an eyebrow. "And then?"

"And then your son started fightin' back—and two of them hit him."

"And that's when you came in." Troy nodded. "Troy? Did you know Virgil was my son?"

The boy met his gaze, thinking. Finally, he nodded. "Yeah."

"And you still helped him."

"That's why, I guess."

"That's why?"

"Yeah. Because you stood up for me to my old man."

"Thank you for that, Troy. It won't be forgotten."

Troy waved that comment off. "It's all right. I don't expect nothin' in return. I didn't do it for that."

Coal stood up. "It won't be forgotten," he said again.

"But you didn't answer my question," Troy reminded him. "Why are you bein' like this to us, after everything we did? The way we are?"

"Because. I was a young man once too, Troy. I've talked to all three of you, and I can see good in every one of you. A lot of good. And that's why we are where we are. If I give up on you three kids, I give up on myself, my own kids—and all humanity. And that would be an awfully dark and ugly place to go, wouldn't it?"

He held out his hand, and Troy looked down at it for several seconds. Finally, he reached out, slowly, and gave Coal his hand. Coal had never seen Troy Westerlind smile until that moment.

Before leaving the hospital, Coal met with all three of the kids. No one knew from that point what was going to happen with them, but Coal made sure they all knew he was there if they needed to talk to anyone. Dawn looked nervously over at Troy, then came and wrapped her arms around Coal's waist, holding on tight for ten or fifteen seconds. Dale came and gave him a quick hug too. Troy stood back during the exchanges. Of course he couldn't let his friends see him interact in any friendly manner with a man who wore a badge.

As Coal sat down in the pickup, he jotted a note down in his notepad, putting a number one in front of it, and circling the one:

Look into new living arrangements for the kids

Free of all his duties at the hospital in any way but emotionally, Coal drove back to the courthouse and put away the recording machine, storing the recording of the interviews with all the other evidence from the murder investigation.

He was down to one suspect in this case now—the one he had suspected most from the start: Joe Teton.

Typing up an affidavit of application for a warrant to bring Joe Teton to the station for fingerprinting, Coal ripped the single sheet of paper out of his Smith-Corona typewriter, and leaving the typewriter on his desk, he headed upstairs, hoping Judge Sinclair would be up there, and available.

He was in luck.

Wiley Sinclair invited Coal into his office with a warm smile, reaching for his cigar box. He paused with his fingers on the lid of the box, then looked up at Coal with a sheepish grin. "Oh, yeah! Well damn it. You need to take up cigar smoking, Coal—so I'll quit making a fool of myself."

Coal laughed. "You go ahead. I'll just breathe yours."

Smiling, Sinclair finished flipping back the lid on the wooden cigar box, spent a second looking them over, as if any of them were different from, or better than, its neighbors, then pulled one out.

"I hope you're not that judgmental when it comes to people," said Coal, then instantly realized how insulting that might have sounded. Before he could apologize, the judge broke into a quick fit of laughter.

"You're right," admitted Sinclair. "And I have absolutely no idea why I even do that! So what can I help you with this afternoon, my friend?"

Coal still couldn't help a little jolt of surprise whenever this man acted so friendly toward him. It certainly had not always been that way.

"Well, two things, Wiley. And I already know one of them is a stretch."

"So give me the easy one first," said the judge, taking several puffs of his stinky cigar.

Coal set his carefully typed affidavit up on the smooth wooden top of the desk and slid it all the way across in front of the judge. "I think we've got the murder case almost nailed down. We only need one more thing, and that's a warrant to bring Joe Teton in for fingerprinting."

"Okay, let's see here," said Sinclair, and he picked up his reading glasses and shook the stems open, adjusting them on his face.

He carefully read down through Coal's type, glanced at his signature, and set the paper back down. "Perfectly written, as usual." He picked up his phone and called Wilma Frank, and she popped in, took the affidavit, and left.

"Now for the hard one," said the judge. "If it's a raise, I have no power over that."

They laughed together, and Coal said, "Not a worry. I used to be a soldier. I'm independently wealthy. Seriously, though, what I'd like to find out is if I can do something to get Hunter Jack back out of my jail. Not only is he smelling the place up, but . . . Well, I just don't feel like jail is the place for him."

"No? Now let me refresh my own memory here really quick. He got out on bail once already, for stabbing an officer, correct? You vouched for him, and then the next time officers approached him he attacked them violently, put up a rip-roaring fight, even to the point of his front door being torn off, and . . . Am I missing anything?"

Coal felt sheepish. "No, you nailed it all pretty well."

"And now you want him back out. Does he even have anything left with which to make bail?"

"Well, that car of his is worth more than the last bail, actually. The bond agency would probably be happy to get their hands on it—worst case."

Sinclair smiled patiently. "Or, worst case, he is out on bail and next time someone tries to question or arrest them, he puts a knife in their belly."

Coal nodded his understanding. What could he even say?

"Tell me, Coal—why does this thing mean so much to you anyway? I mean his trial is set for next Tuesday, right? We moved it along really fast on your recommendation. If he is found innocent, he's free. Even if he is found guilty, he'll be sentenced to some jail time, maybe in Bonneville County, and possibly a fine. But he'll be out soon enough—right? I'm not sure I understand your deep interest in this. Why put your neck out?"

"I've never told you this, Wiley, but I was held in jail once too—in North Korea. Not as nice a jail as this one, but still jail. And there are some men who weren't made to stand being behind bars. It's kind of like caging an eagle. In my opinion."

The judge studied Coal's face for a long time, his expression as compassionate as any judge he could remember. "No, I never knew that about you, Coal. I'm sorry. Really sorry to hear that."

Coal shrugged, trying to smile even though the memories were still harsh, and sometimes so fresh it seemed like only yesterday. "That was another life," he said.

"And now we're dealing with a new life—Hunter Jack, an eagle in a cage."

"Yes, sir."

"Coal? It's irregular, of course, but . . . you trust Mr. Jack completely, don't you? Do you?"

"I think so."

"You have complete control over him?"

Coal chuckled. "That's a loaded question. No man actually has complete control over another one, do they? Especially if one is an eagle."

"A reasonable amount of control then, let's say."

"Enough control that he won't try to kill you, Wiley. And we won't even get blood on your floor trying to stop him if he does."

The judge nodded. "I guess . . . Do me a favor, would you? Give me a call at the end of the day, and if I'm not busy, I'll have you bring him up here for a visit."

With a smile, Coal stood up. "Thank you. I'll call."

"I leave here at five, by the way," Sinclair added. "Promptly."

"Noted."

The judge held out his hand, and Coal took it. "Thank you, Wiley."

"You're most welcome. Make sure to pick up your warrant from Wilma on the way out."

Coal went to Joe Teton's place all alone. Maybe it was foolish. He couldn't claim he had never made a foolish move before. Joe was an old soldier, and Coal had no reason to doubt he still had firearms in his possession. Teton might be starting to feel like he was backed into a corner, although he knew nothing about the status of the investigation. He was about to, however.

Coal knew he should have brought Grant along, or Jordan. Even Bob Wilson, or the chief. And yet here he was.

He knocked on the door of the run-down house. Then he knocked again. The pickup, its tires full of air again, was parked in the only semblance of a parking spot Teton had, and Coal had never seen any other vehicle here.

At last, a light came on inside, and the door creaked open, revealing the seamed, tired-looking face of Joe Teton.

"How."

"How yourself, Mr. Teton."

"I s'pose you wanna come in."

"That'd be mighty white of you," Coal said, suppressing a smile.

The comment almost got a grin out of the older man. "Come in. You're here anyway. Don't be lookin' for me to be white enough to offer you anything to eat, though. Want a beer?"

Coal allowed himself to smile. "It's against my code."

Teton looked at the two boys who sat back on their splayed-out legs in front of the television. "Boys. Go read a book or somethin'. Or make a bow an' arrows. I gotta talk to the fuzz."

Without argument, the older of the two boys got up, then held a hand down to his brother, helped him up, and they marched off silently down the hall.

Joe Teton turned back to Coal. "Gettin' down to it, uh?"

"What's that?"

"Makin' an arrest."

"Do you need arresting?" asked Coal.

"I knew you'd be comin' for me, so . . ."

"Do you have something to say, Mr. Teton?"

Teton shrugged. "Not really so much."

Coal watched him for a long time, trying to gauge him. But there was no gauging a man with a poker face like Teton's. "I'm only here to bring you over to the jail for some fingerprints, Mr. Teton."

"Yeah?"

"Yeah. You aren't under arrest—as long as you come peaceful."

"Been a long time since I was a fightin' man, Savage," said Teton. "I'll come peaceful."

"You're going to drive my pickup," said Coal.

"Why is that?"

"So you can't fight me."

"You ain't seen me drive, I guess."

Coal laughed. "You got me there."

Teton drove them to the jail, while Coal's pistol sat on his far hip, against the passenger door—safe. The drive went smoothly, as did the walk down into the jail. It was on the cool side down there, and dimly lit, because the day remained overcast, the sky gloomy. Coal solved half of that by flipping on the light switch.

"You're only here to be printed, Mr. Teton. I'll get you home to your kids as quick as we can get this done—unless you'd like to sit for an interview while you're here."

"A interview? I ain't needin' no job."

Coal grinned. "We can do the interview next time if you'd rather. Do you have a lawyer?"

"Do I look like a fool?"

"Nope. I don't trust them either, my friend. But I think . . . I'm going to advise you to get busy looking for one, all right?"

"Why is that?"

"Just take my advice."

"Yep. We are to that point."

"We're to that point."

Joe Teton was quiet throughout the process of fingerprinting. After each finger was printed, he would raise his hand, studying the black on the ends of his fingers. After his right hand was completely done, he looked at the whole stained collection, where an obvious scar streaked across the exact middle of "finger number three". "Won't be hard to spot that one. Makes your fingers look dirty, uh?"

"We have soap."

"Ah, what the hell, right? Gonna get a lot dirtier in the pen."

"Are you making a confession?" asked Coal.

"Finger's dirty," said Teton, lifting only his middle finger and raising it so to him it probably appeared squarely between Coal's eyes.

Coal couldn't help a grin. "Next hand, Teton."

So Joe Teton flipped him the bird with his left hand too.

After Coal dropped Joe Teton back off at his house, he drove straight to the jail again and went downstairs. Pulling out the fingerprint sheets Tony Nwanzé had sent him from the Bureau, he sat down at his desk and flipped the lamp on, swearing when it hit him in the eyes. "Hell. I'll never get used to that."

He set Teton's shiny, brand-new fingerprints side by side with the latent ones pulled off the lance handle. He started to scan the sheets of adult-size fingerprints.

It took no time at all. There in the center of the sheet it was, labeled "PRINT #13"—a good luck number. Right in the center of print 13 was a big horizontal scar. Coal didn't even need to look at the rest of the print.

CHAPTER FIFTY-ONE

Home. Family. Misguided children. Wrong pathways taken in anger. All these things ran circles in and flew loops around Coal's mind after he ordered Hunter Jack's nighttime meal, then sat at his desk and waited to go downtown and pick it up, pretending he didn't smell the last of the burned coffee he had left all day on the burner. He wanted to sit up all night and drink coffee—not the trash you bought at the grocery store, but good beans you bought, roasted, and ground yourself, then instantly turned into strong black nectar of the gods. He wanted to wrap his teeth around a pound of ribeye steak, or a dozen lightly fried eggs sprinkled with cayenne pepper, just the way his father, old Prince Colt Savage used to fix them.

Or, and preferably, he wanted to wrap himself up with all his kids, his dogs, his mom, and all his memories that were pleasant, and stay in a cocoon with them until hell froze over. In short, he was tired of death, destruction, and wrecked families.

He had thought about Kathy off and on since they parted ways earlier, and he wondered how she was feeling. He wondered how close she had really gotten to Gunnar Westerlind, and if he had any right to know, or even to ask.

Coal's best friend, Larry, had won Kathy's hand, all those years ago, and they had been so good for each other. Kathy couldn't have found a kinder, more giving man, a tougher one, a more protective one, not if she had had time to search the whole world over. Larry was a good-looking man, maybe more because of his personality and his winning smile than because he was any Robert Conrad or Clark Gable. Maybe he didn't have the looks of a Gunn Westerlind, and maybe not the money, but in every other way Larry could have run circles around Gunn Westerlind. And if Larry had been able to see his widow with that man . . . Coal gritted his teeth. The idea was crushing to his heart.

With a trembling hand, he reached out and dragged the heavy black telephone closer to him and pulled the handset off the base. He slowly turned the dial for each of the five numbers that would send his voice down the highway to the MacAtee ranch.

The phone rang. Once. Two times. Almost in a panic, he reached out and pushed down on the white disconnect button in the cradle, then held it down until his hand stopped shaking.

Kathy was a grown woman. She was doing a good job raising three daughters, and running a good-sized ranch most likely with help from all the neighbors Larry had always been there for. Who was Coal to suggest who Kathy could or could not see, anyway? He was a ne'er-do-well whose marriage had crashed in the flames of drug use and neglect. Kathy didn't need his kind around.

Taking a deep breath, he stood up and went to the cellblock door, opening it and startling Hunter Jack into sitting up on his cot. There was no way to escape the assault of the air in this room, a smell like socks that hadn't been washed in weeks, mixed with body odor, mixed with other things too unpleasant to think about. "Man. It smells like a bear's den in here, Badger."

"Good thing I like bears."

"Right. I'm going down early to get your food. You want any treats or anything? Maybe a brick of soap?"

"Naw. Whatever they have for food is good, but I don't like the taste of soap. Savage?"

"Yeah?"

"I'm goin' crazy in here."

"I'm working on that, my friend. I talked to the judge today. I was supposed to take you up to talk to him, but I'm not taking you when you smell like this."

He hadn't planned on letting Jack know about that meeting until he found out either way, but it was out there now. Feeling hopeful yet wary, he drove down off the Bar.

After feeding Hunter Jack, and wondering how the man could have an appetite when the whole cellblock smelled like it did, Coal sat down at his desk again and picked up the phone. He meant to call Judge Sinclair, but instead he dialed most of the digits of Kathy MacAtee's number, then disconnected the line again before the last digit. He grunted at himself. What was wrong with Coal Savage?

Dialing the judge's number, he listened to it ring, and soon Wilma Frank's voice was on the other end.

"Wilma, is the judge in? And is he busy? This is Coal."

Hello, dear. Just one minute, all right? I'll go check. Out of habit, Coal looked at the second hand on the clock. It was exactly twenty-two seconds when he heard Wilma's voice again. *He's in, Coal, and he says to come up.*

"Great. By the way, Wilma, that was only twenty-two seconds. You are not only a beautiful specimen of womanhood, but efficient as a whole farm of ants."

Wilma Frank hung up still laughing.

Coal was grinning when he got to Wilma's desk, and she was there waiting, and already shaking her finger at him. "You know I'm already married, Coal Savage, or you would be in such trouble." They laughed. "Go on in, dear. He's waiting for you."

Stepping into the judge's office, he was met by a smile, but it was the kind of smile that didn't lend itself to a whole lot of optimism. The judge looked past Coal. "If your friend is here, I am either losing my eyesight, or he is invisible."

Coal chuckled. "Yeah, sorry about that. The way he smells, I just couldn't bring myself to have him up here smelling up your office."

"Then I suppose I have to go down to the jail and see him? Actually, it's not a bad idea anyway. It would be nice for me to stay on top of conditions for our incarcerated people in this county."

"You're welcome any time, Wiley—but you had better off a good constitution."

Judge Sinclair smiled. "Have a seat, Coal?"

"Sure. It's pushing five, though."

"No matter. We go into overtime then I go into friend mode, and out of magistrate mode."

Coal sat down in front of the desk, and the judge took his plush seat again as well. Coal looked at him expectantly.

"You inspire great confidence in me, Coal Savage. You always have, almost from the start. As long as you can keep from running me off the road, that is."

Coal blushed, then laughed. That wasn't a memory he liked to relive. "I'll apologize for that until the day I die."

"You don't have to. It's a story I have told many times at dinner parties, much to the delight of listeners. Coal? Since I don't get to see our prisoner anyway, I would like the weekend. Please?"

"Sir?"

"The weekend, to talk with my wife—not necessarily about Hunter Jack, mind you. Simply about life. The weekend to watch a movie. To go for a drive down the river. To go to church, listen to lessons about God. To meditate. Eat good food. I'd like you to do the same. *All* of the same. Good?"

"Sure, Wiley. And then?"

"Let's talk. Monday morning. This time I'll call and come down to your domain. Visit with this man myself. I can't promise you I'll decide to let Hunter Jack bail out, but at least by then I will have made a well-thought-out judgment."

"That sounds good. I think Badger can hold out at least that long."

"I think so too. And Coal? Be kind to yourself this weekend, all right? This valley needs you."

It was four fifty-five when Coal stepped back into the office, clicking the metal door shut behind him. The smell of new but not spectacular coffee was in the room, which meant Jordan Peterson had already come to work, and now was probably somewhere out on the road. He had taken half the pot of coffee with him.

Steeling himself, Coal went back to see Hunter Jack.

The big Shoshone was standing up within seconds after Coal came through the door. He moved to the bars and wrapped his paws around them. They both looked at each other.

"I just came down from seeing the judge."

Jack stared at Coal, now and then making contact with his eyes. It wasn't Shoshone-like, but he had gotten that from his time in the Marines. "I'm not gettin' out, huh?"

"Monday, my friend. He said he'll think about it over the weekend, and Monday he'll come down here for a visit with you, then make a decision."

Jack's face remained neutral, except that Coal could see the change in his eyes. "So . . . that means unless you tell your deputies to feed me, you gotta come in here at least four more times. When you should be having time off with your family."

"It comes with the territory, Badger. I'll be all right."

"Well, maybe just bring food one time a day. Most times I don't eat more than once anyway."

"Are you being serious?"

"I am most always bein' serious."

"All right. You're on. One big meal, once a day."

"Uh," replied Badger. "Savage, who you got for fam'ly? Got a wife? Some kids?"

"My wife died. I have a wonderful, beautiful daughter and three great sons. Two girls we took in. And my mother. She takes care of everything when I'm gone."

"Sure would like to meet your fam'ly, Savage. I ain't got one. Nobody out there anywhere waits for Dark Badger."

"I'm sorry about that," said Coal, and right then he felt it deeply.

Jack shrugged. "My fault. I chose. When I went to the Marines, the girl I thought I would marry left. Moved to Fort Hall and married one o' them Edmos. Never had no use for them Edmos since then."

Coal had heard the Edmo family name, apparently a big, important one on the Sho-Ban reservation. "Sorry to hear that too."

"Life," said Badger.

"You want to shower before you eat?" Coal asked.

"Do I stink?"

"It is getting a little ripe back here," Coal said. "Actually, the truth is it smells like someone turned a pack of apes and a herd of cows on green feed loose in a fish factory."

For the first time in a day or more, Hunter Jack grinned. "I am doin' myself proud then. Smells like a old time Injun camp."

"Right. More like an old dead Injun," Coal quipped. "Well, I'll give you your food, and then I'll stay till you finish it—out in my office, that is. If you decide you don't want to smell yourself anymore, just holler. Either way, I'll come let you out after, and you can use the restroom. Then we'll go walk out in the yard for a while and send some of that zoo smell downwind. How does that sound?"

"Judge says I can't get out till Monday," Jack reminded him.

"Getting out is when you get to go home, my friend. We're just doing school recess."

Coal drove down off the Bar later, satisfied that Hunter Jack had at least been able to smell some fresh air, and exercise his legs. He meant to drive straight home. He even made it past Annie's, although he would have liked to stop and say hi and thank her for her help with the kids that morning.

But he didn't go home. Instead, he drove to Kathy's. After all, she was the one to whom he truly owed a visit.

When he parked in front of the door, he left his pickup lights on, the engine running. He hadn't called ahead, so the lights were his only calling card. Kathy met him at the door, before he could knock. She was just shrugging into a denim jacket, which seemed fine right then because it was still over thirty degrees.

"Hi," she greeted him with an uncertain smile, looking around as if she might find someone else out here with him. "Everything okay?"

"Yeah. Sure. You?"

"It's all right. I've . . . I've been missing you all day, Coal."

Without waiting for an invitation, he grabbed her and hugged her tight, his voice muffled in her mass of dark hair. "Me too. Me too. I've been feeling sick about today. I tried to call a couple times, but . . . Kathy, I had to see you face to face."

When he released his death hold on her, she pulled away. "I'm glad. Some things phone calls just won't work for, huh? Can you come in for a while?"

"If you'll let me, I'd love that. But . . . would you mind sitting in the truck with me for a few minutes first?"

"Of course not! Let me just tell the girls." She stepped inside, then came back out and shut the door behind herself.

He followed her to the driver's side of the pickup, feeling the pound of his heart. He opened the door and helped her up inside the warm cab, then climbed in and sat next to her. She had left him only enough room not to sit on her lap.

The radio was playing Glen Campbell's "Galveston", a song that always stirred Coal's heart, and his last big hit, from sixty-nine. Both huge fans of Glen Campbell, they sat and listened to it, saying nothing, until Kathy fumblingly reached over and took his hand.

He thought back to the day he had come to see her, the first time he laid eyes on Gunnar Westerlind. It was the birthday of her long lost son, who had died in a car wreck. "I'm sorry I didn't say anything to you on Luke's birthday, Kathy."

"Oh, Coal. It's all right. That was . . . That was the day you came out and Gunn was here. Wasn't it?"

"Yeah."

"Coal? I didn't mean to send you packing. I would gladly have kept you here the whole day instead of him if you would just have stayed."

"I didn't know," he said. "I wanted to stay. I thought that day might be hard for you. But it seemed like you were doing all right."

She gave his hand a harder squeeze. "Don't beat yourself up for it. You tried. That's what's important."

He shifted gears. "I miss Larry, Kathy. I miss that guy every day."

"Me too. It never goes away. It never gets easier."

Pulling his hand away from hers, he put his right arm around her, then reached with his left hand and took hers, gripping it like he couldn't risk her pulling away. "Will this pain ever go away?" he asked into the fragrance of her hair.

She only shook her head, and they both fell silent, while Glen Campbell faded away and Jerry Wallace began slow-crooning, "Don't Give Up On Me," whose timing was so perfect it almost made Coal laugh. Entertaining their own thoughts about the lyrics of the song, they sat silent all the way through.

Finally, when the deejay started talking, Kathy pulled away from his embrace so she could look into his face. "How are you doing, Coal? Is everything okay in your life?"

"Right now? I won't lie. It's kind of a mess," he said.

"Why?"

"Well, you know about Maura. I can't imagine you haven't heard."

She nodded. "Word gets around. Sometimes too much, in a town this size. I'm sorry she hurt you like that."

He shrugged, still trying to salvage a little pride. "It sure killed the kids."

"I imagine so. It was sure a rough way to go. They thought a lot of her, huh?"

"Yeah. She had become a big part of the family."

Kathy leaned closer and took his hand again. "You'll find somebody new, Coal. I know you will, when the time is right."

He breathed deeply. "I'm not so sure anymore. Sometimes I'm not even sure I want to find anyone new. I'm really not sure I wasn't supposed to live my life alone."

She laughed, but it was a sad sound. "I know exactly how that feels. But at least we have some beautiful kids, right? That counts for something."

He smiled. "Yeah, it does. It counts for a lot."

The local news commentator was on, and then the sports and weather reports. All of it was unimportant. Coal hardly heard any of the words, but Kathy did.

"It seems like it's never going to get warm again, huh?"

"Someday it will. Someday we'll see the sun again."

CHAPTER FIFTY-TWO

Over the weekend, Coal tried to scrub his mind of the murder investigation, just as Judge Sinclair had wished him to do. The valley's call volume, except for the every-week Friday and Saturday night fights, helped immensely. The weekend was quiet, and it was lovely.

The things Coal learned about his own children, and the girls he had happily agreed to care for, amazed him. First off, he found out that Cynthia Batterton had a very nice, polite boy at school whom she liked to consider her boyfriend. It sounded like he was nothing like the last one, the one Coal had rescued her from.

Second, he found out Katie Leigh *didn't* have a boyfriend, and that made him even happier. It did, however, sound like she had gotten in with a pretty nice group of God-fearing girls, which made him miss Broad Run, Virginia, their last home, all the less. He still wondered where she would be today had they stayed.

The twins were starting to get interested in horses, and with Cynthia having been raised around a ranch their chances of getting a good education around stock animals were excellent.

Virgil, in his quiet way, finally got Coal's attention Friday night after supper was over by hovering around his chair while they were watching a movie, with Sissy and Morgan each on one of Coal's legs. Coal gave the kids over to his mother, insisting he would be back, while he and Virgil went out in the ever-cooling air to visit near the horses, while Shadow and Dobe frolicked around the yard and at their feet.

"What's up, Virg? Seems like you must have something big on your mind."

"Well . . . Dad, do you think it would be weird to go visit Troy Westerlind?"

Coal hid his surprise. "Visit him? Well, no, Son. I don't think it would be weird at all, if that's what you want. At the hospital, you mean?"

"Yeah. I wouldn't want to go to his house."

"Well, we may not have to go to his house *or* the hospital."

"How come?"

"Because I've been working with the judge, and with a couple of my friends from town, and I might have found some places that would take those three kids in. You know, give them a better chance to grow up right, with a decent family."

"Wow. Who would they go with?"

"I have several folks I've talked to. Mostly business owners in town."

Virgil smiled, then stood there as if deep in thought for quite a while without speaking.

"What're you thinking?" Coal finally asked him.

"Well . . . Troy speared that big bull to death, right?"

"I guess he did."

"And you still think he's safe?"

"What he did wasn't right, Son, and I'll never stick up for him for that. But I think he was just desperate to lash out. I think his father has been abusing him for a long time, maybe as far back as that boy can remember. Killing his dad's bull was the only thing he could come up with to take a good chunk out of him—to strike back."

"Troy never did or said anything bad to me," revealed Virgil. "He was always quiet around me in school. I think he finally stood up for me only because of you."

"You think so?"

"Yeah. I think everybody likes you, Dad. And everybody's glad you're the sheriff."

Coal laughed, reaching out to squeeze his son's shoulder. "I'm not sure about that, but thank you. I'm pretty sure Gunnar Westerlind isn't my biggest fan, though."

"Nope," said Virgil, looking down at his feet and mumbling something else Coal couldn't hear.

"I didn't catch that, Virg."

Virgil looked up, trying to appear tough. "I said *I'm* your biggest fan." And then Virgil gave his dad a bearhug, the kind of hug that melts old men's hearts.

Saturday night Coal asked his mother if she could cook enough food for Kathy and the girls, and of course Connie was only happy to do so. Both families made up a huge, warm group in the house, a group that had to scatter around widely for all of them to find places to sit and eat the delicious meal of egg noodle and chicken casserole Connie fixed them. Later, they played board games and card games, both of which Coal had to grit his teeth to do because neither were on his list of favorite things. After that, he was pressed into playing the guitar and singing, something he used to do with Larry backing him up on harmony.

The whole troop of them took a walk down Savage Lane to the highway later and then back, and Kathy took Coal's elbow without asking. He didn't mind a bit.

"Coal, did you feel Larry there tonight?"

He blinked back the tears her words brought to his eyes. "I was going to ask you the same thing. He was there, all right. Sometimes I feel like that old boy is everywhere I go."

She smiled, leaning into him. "Me too. Everywhere I go."

On Sunday, after church, Coal made some phone calls and learned that both boys had been released from the hospital, and Dale Moore had gone to stay with Coal's friend Jay Castillo.

Dale's placement was especially important, considering how he had ended up in the hospital. They couldn't have found a nicer couple for the boy to stay with than Jay and Carrie.

Troy, under Judge Sinclair's order, was staying temporarily with auto mechanic Ken Parks and his wife and sons. Troy had revealed an interest in automotive work, and both Ken and Coal had high hopes the boy would immerse himself in helping Ken at the shop, learning a skill that might serve him throughout his life.

As for Dawn Kelly, she was the sad case, as far as Coal was concerned, for she had insisted on returning home, and there wasn't enough evidence against either of her parents to justify forcibly removing her from the home. So Dawn was the one Coal would have to keep in closest contact with, because he refused to see her in further danger if he could help it.

Sunday evening, just after dark, Coal and Virgil made the trip to the Ken Parks home to see Troy Westerlind.

Ken answered the knock at his door, already expecting the visit, for he had been warned with a phone call. "Hey, guys. Come on in."

Coal and Virgil stepped inside, and Ken shut the door behind them, then called to Troy. Soon, the boy's quiet footsteps could be heard coming down the carpeted hall, and he appeared in the opening.

"Hi, Troy," Coal said.

"Hi, Sheriff." The boy looked beyond uncomfortable.

"Hey, did Ken tell you why we came over?"

"Yeah, he did." Troy's eyes flickered over toward Virgil, and he nodded.

"Well then we're going to leave you two to talk in your room or whatever, and we'll just be out here when you're done."

"Sure," replied Troy. Looking at the younger boy, he said, "You can come back here, if you want."

Without a word, which was normal for him, Virgil followed Troy stiffly down the hall.

They stepped through an open doorway, and Troy closed it softly, turning to glance at Virgil. “Hey. You like music?”

Virgil, hands in his pockets, gave a shrug. “Sure.”

“What kind in particular?”

“Country, I guess?”

Troy gave a little laugh, nodding. He seemed to realize only then that Virgil was serious. “Yeah? Country? I like some too, actually—but don’t tell anybody at school.” He laughed again. “Like me and Dawn Kelly used to get down with Kris Kristofferson a lot. And Merle Haggard. I like Johnny Cash, too. How about you?”

“I like all those guys. My new favorite is a guy named Johnny Rodriguez, or at least one of his songs.”

“‘Ridin’ My Thumb to Mexico’!” exclaimed Troy, his eyes lighting up. “That one?”

“Yeah.”

“Man, that’s a killer song. It sure makes me wanna hit eighteen, you know. Bug outta this town. Hit the highway. ‘With my thumb up in the air’, huh? Just like in the song. Never look back here. How about you, man?”

“I’m not sure. I’m starting to like it here, I guess.”

Troy stuffed his hands in his pockets, looking like he was mimicking Virgil. “Yeah. Sure, I understand. With a dad like yours? Sure. I’d wanna hang out here too.”

After ten seconds or so of silence, Virgil indicated the bandages wrapped around Troy’s head like a hat. “Does that hurt a lot?”

“Nah. That’s nothin’ at all. You kiddin’? I been hit a lot harder than that in a dozen football games.”

Silently, Virgil nodded. “Hey, man . . .”

“Here!” Troy stopped him. “Let me throw some Man in Black on the phonograph, huh?”

"Sure," said Virgil, rescued for the moment from having to speak of uncomfortable things.

Troy slid Cash's record *Orange Blossom Special* down the phonograph spindle, and the title song started jamming right out of the chute, as soon as he set the needle down and it got through its nest of static. "Man!" Troy smiled. "Now that's some kinda music, huh?"

"Sure is," Virgil agreed. "Hey, Troy?"

The much larger boy turned. "Yeah?"

"I really wanted to thank you—for Friday."

"Aw, hell, kid. It's nothin'. Your dad . . . Well, he went to bat for me against my old man. You know? How does a guy ever forget somethin' like that, right?"

"Sure. I guess you can't."

"Nope. Not me anyway. Your dad, that's the kinda guy I wanna be like someday, when I get out of this stupid town. When I get past all this trouble I'm in. You know what would be funny? If I went off and became a cop somewhere too. That would make everybody that ever remembered me from this town have a good laugh."

Smiling, Virgil gave Troy Westerlind a big nod. He sure felt proud of Sheriff Coal Savage about then, and someday he hoped he would be brave enough to tell him, face to face, how he felt.

"Listen up, kid," said Troy, squaring himself with Virgil. "Virgil, right? Listen. You got a good, square deal bein' born into a family like yours. I sure hope you make the most of it, 'cause most people never had it so good."

Troy held out his big, scarred hand, and Virgil, filled with pride, reached out and took it.

Coal awoke with a start. He lay there staring up at the dark ceiling for a bit, trying to get his bearings. He had been dreaming about the murder scene, specifically about a man in a light-colored cowboy hat, cowboy boots, and a heavy jacket with a sheepskin collar, running up the hill from the scene, toward the cemetery.

Sleep had fled from Coal, and he lay there for a while after flipping on his flashlight to look at the clock and see it was two in the morning, the time of night he seemed to be awake a lot lately. In his head, without the benefit of having all the reports from the various officers in front of him, he picked the case apart, bit by bit. There was something bothering him, and it had to do with that man who had run from the scene—the most obvious suspect in the case and who had been from the first moment.

Something kept coming back to Coal with a surge of urgency, but he kept praying it wasn't true, because he couldn't accept that neither he, nor Grant, nor any of the other officers had followed up that night on one of the biggest clues in the case. Yet try as he might, and he had scoured the reports, front and back, he could not remember one single note about anyone tracing the fleeing trail of the man who ran.

With an idea like that clawing through and screaming in his brain now, there would be no more sleep tonight. No amount of self-hypnosis, or any other method, would change that. Whose report would something like that be in? He himself had gone down to Hunter Jack's place, and then he had the incident with Joe Teton and his pickup. Grant had been finalizing everything at the murder scene, while Jordan and Bob had been with Curlie Burks and Melissa Talty. State bull Lyle Gentry had gone out to contact Gunnar Westerlind about the whereabouts of his truck that night, and of his son. Chief Dan George? Try as he might, Coal couldn't even remember seeing a report from his hand.

The reports of Horace Teal and William Verret, once he finally got to read them, were very succinct, and neither of them had anything of import to say other than the one item of *highest* importance: that they had stopped Joe Teton driving down from the cemetery, from the exact direction in which the one suspect anyone had actually seen had disappeared. And the plate they had written down proved it to be Joe Teton, if his description already hadn't.

Coal must have actually fallen asleep, perhaps for half an hour, and he wasn't happy to wake up when it was yet dark on Monday morning. But Dobe, his big male Doberman pinscher, wanted out, and Shadow the German shepherd was waiting patiently at the door as well, although not the whining noise machine Dobe was when he couldn't hold his water much longer.

Coal rolled over and sat on the edge of the bed to pull on his brown Dickey's jeans and a blue plaid shirt over a cotton tee shirt. Yawning, he grabbed a pair of socks out of his drawer and stumbled out of the room, watching the dogs fly down the hall and listening to the thunder of them descending the stairs.

It was way too early to make any phone calls or do any tracking, so he made his standard quarter pot of coffee and then headed down into the basement to throw weights around for a while. He had come to love his new program, a very short, high intensity full body workout with lighter weights and very little rest. Even if it only saved him a half hour, that would be something, but there had been times before when he had wiled away two, sometimes three hours in a weight room. With this job, those days were gone forever.

Connie had gone outside by the time he came upstairs and wiped himself down with a washcloth and cold water, skipping a shower, but soaping his face and shaving closely because he had started seeing some white crop up among his dark beard lately, and the thought of looking old at forty-two flat ticked him off.

Coal was frying eggs when Connie came back in, and reaching over every so often to pick up his mug of coffee and sip it. "Are you running late for work, Son?" Connie asked.

"No, Mom. I have time. You want me to cook for the kids, too?"

"Oh, heavens no! Go on. Read the paper or a magazine. Go through your reports. I don't know—pet the dog. But don't deprive me the right to cook for my babies."

Coal grinned and hugged her shoulders from behind. "All right, Mom. You win." He slid the ten eggs he had fried for himself onto a flowered plastic plate, one of those his mother set such great store by, then grabbed the front-most gallon of raw milk from the top shelf of the fridge and carried it, a glass, and the plate of eggs to the table. Pulling out the fork he had stowed in his shirt pocket, he mounted the bar stool and ate quietly. He would be reading enough throughout the day. He didn't need to read now too.

By the time the kids' breakfast was done, they were starting to stumble from their rooms and get ready. Katie Leigh came right to him and gave him a huge, long hug. He thought of the girl she had been last November, less than three short months earlier, and he felt stunned at the change in his girl. He guessed he would always feel stunned, and always blessed of God.

Sissy wandered in and wanted up on his lap. He couldn't remember turning her down yet. Hoisting her up, he gave her a little bite of his eggs now and then. She sat there on his left leg for a long while before turning a little and wrapping both her arms around his upper arm and leaning into him. She didn't look up toward him when she spoke. "Pop Coal? Gramma Con has a picture of Maur'."

He looked down at the top of the girl's head. "She— She does? Really?" He raised his eyes to his mother, who had heard Sissy's comment and cranked around at the torso to meet his look she knew would be coming.

"I do," Connie said. "I picked up my film at Rexall's when I was in town yesterday. I didn't even remember taking the photographs until I saw them. Want to see?"

Coal froze. It had only been a short, harsh time since Maura's terrible departure, but he felt like he had come so far toward healing. Now, almost in one breath, all that was being stolen from him.

"Not now, Ma. Maybe tonight," he replied after a pause, dropping his eyes away.

His mother turned back to her work at the stove, addressing the eggs in her pan: "I understand how you feel."

Sissy still didn't look up at Coal, but she squeezed his arm harder. "Maur' is holdin' onto me. Holdin' on Pop Coal too."

Out of the mouths of babes . . . Those were the words that ran through Coal's mind. The innocent words of a child could send a man soaring to the moon, but they could also drop him from the greatest heights into the depths of despair.

Coal struggled as best he could through goodbyes with all the children, then this time left them to catch the bus. It wouldn't do to make the bus driver unhappy about trying to pick them up and never having anyone there to meet him.

Grant still had the Thunderbird, and Jordan had Coal's old truck, so without a police radio he drove into town with no chance of having his morning dose of radio KSRA disrupted. Charley Pride, Lynn Anderson, and Tom T. Hall serenaded Coal all the way in to town, and by the time he hit downtown, "Old Dogs, Children, and Watermelon Wine" had put Dawn Kelly so strong on Coal's mind that he veered off at her street and went to knock on her door. Much to his disappointment, nobody was home. Or, at least, no one answered his knock.

Driving on up to the courthouse, he went in and found Grant getting ready for the day. Coal held up the keys to the pickup. "I want my car back."

"Oh, man! I was hoping to get out of here before you came in. That's a sweet ride."

"Thanks. I got it in a trade with a real live Sioux Indian. You wouldn't believe the burned-out wreck I gave him for it."

Grant grinned, digging the Thunderbird keys out of his pocket and handing them to Coal in exchange for the truck keys. He had heard the story of the Pine Ridge reservation and the blown-up LTD one too many times.

"Hey, Grant," said Coal.

"Yeah?"

"Two things. Damn you for not making coffee, and . . . please tell me somebody went and followed the tracks of the man who ran away from the murder scene."

Grant Fairbourne stared a long time at Coal, the wheels of his mind churning like a wildfire behind his eyes. Suddenly, he swore, a sound that coming from Coal wouldn't have sounded like much more than a drip of water from a long-time leaky faucet. But from Grant, it sounded flat and ugly like a semi-truck running into a brick outhouse.

CHAPTER FIFTY-THREE

After a mutual self-flagellation period where two officers of the law, one of them a highly trained crime scene investigator, tried to figure how they could have missed such a detail, Coal plopped down at his desk and pulled out his Rolodex. Thumbing through, he found the local tracker, Eric Hansen, whose friends called him "Trax", and dialed up his number. This time of day, Coal wasn't hoping for much success, and that's what he had. He called Flo Hawkins to see if she would telephone Trax throughout the day, and then radio in to him if she had any success, and then he turned to Grant.

"Well, I guess it's time for you and me to go up there and see what we can salvage, huh?"

Grant nodded sheepishly. "Sure. I didn't have any concrete plans anyway."

"That's what I'm hoping that guy's tracks turned into after he went through the snow that night," replied Coal. "Concrete!"

They drove together up past the rundown camp trailer, where today, just to look at it, no one would know anything evil had ever taken place. Up above, where Cemetery Lane turned, they pulled over and got out. It took no time at all on the downhill side of the road to pick up a man's tracks. A lot of the snow had melted, so the prints were no longer clear, but they appeared to be cowboy boot tracks, as Curlie and Melissa had claimed.

Stepping over to the other side of the road, Coal found the matching trail. The man who fled had continued straight up into the cemetery where there was no road.

Soon, the tracks began to veer off to the left, where eventually they reached a road, and on that road was a double line of tire tracks which to Coal and Grant looked to have been made around the same time period as the boot tracks. After nearly a full week of melting and refreezing, even Trax Hansen wasn't going to be able to tell for sure.

Walking along the double line made by the tire tracks, Coal and Grant could see a partial boot track now and then, and sometimes a full one, but most of them had been run over and obliterated. It wasn't until they reached the place where the vehicle making the tracks had been parked that they saw foot tracks make a wider swing, like a person would do in skirting a vehicle, then come around to a point some six or seven feet from the last tire mark, turn sideways, and disappear. Here was where the man had climbed back in his vehicle—presumably the pickup Horace Teal and William Verret had seen Joe Teton driving—and driven back out of the cemetery.

"Teton said he was up here looking at his wife's grave," Coal told Grant.

"Yeah, I read that in Verret and Teal's reports," said Grant.

"I don't know about you, but doesn't it seem like a guy who came up to look at his wife's grave would do it in the daylight? And make some kind of tracks that weren't straight up from the road to where this truck was parked? Without veering off one way or another to look at any graves?"

"Which he would have had to do with a flashlight," added Grant. "Yeah. Agreed. Joe Teton is lying through his teeth."

"Let's go down to the Indian village," Coal said. "I'd like to have a chat with our friend Joe about his wife's grave."

They drove down Cemetery Lane, back to the Indian village, and pulled up in front of Joe Teton's house. Coal frowned when he didn't see Joe's truck parked outside. He got out anyway and met Grant at Teton's door, where Grant gave a four-beat rap with his knuckles. Nobody answered the door, and Coal knew it was Teton.

"Well, thanks anyway. We'll find him later, I guess. Just keep an eye out for his truck today, all right? And if you see him, pull him over. That's your main job today. We have the prints. It's time to bring him in."

"An actual arrest, or bring him in for questioning?" asked Grant.

"I think it's pretty clear who our man is," said Coal. "If you find him, make the arrest."

Since Grant didn't have a radio in his truck, Coal told him to try to keep in touch as much as he could by stopping to use people's phones and check in with Flo. He also swore in his next budget there was going to be a third radio, and if the County wouldn't spring for it he was going to pay for it out of his own pocket—or at least out of the petty cash fund.

Coal watched Grant drive off, and then he got back in the Thunderbird and re-parked it across the street, in front of where old Buck Darnell lived with his daughter, Renée and her family. He went up and knocked on the door, and Renée answered. Her eyes looked even more closed over by her copper-colored cheeks this early in the morning.

"Good mornin', Coal Savage."

He smiled back at her. "Good morning, Renée. Can I come in for a bit?"

"Oh, sure. My father is already up, watchin' TV."

Coal looked to the left and waved at old Buck, who waved back.

"Savage! Good mornin'. Come. Sit."

"Did you want me too?" asked the woman.

"It would be nice. I won't take long. I just have a question or two."

Renée followed Coal over to where her father was sitting. She sat down next to him on the couch after shutting off whatever game show he had been staring mindlessly at. Coal took a brown fabric chair that had seen better days—apparently a whole lot of them.

"What I wanted to ask about is Joe Teton's wife. You said she died of cirrhosis of the liver?"

"If that's what it's called," said Renée. "I can't ever remember them fancy names."

"Cirrhosis," repeated Coal. "Yes, it's a little presumptuous sounding."

"So is that one," said Buck, his face straight.

"What's that?"

"That word you said—presumshus."

Coal laughed. "Yes, I guess it is."

"You want to know about Lily?" Renée kindly got them back on topic.

"Yes, if that was the name of Joe's wife."

"Lily Teton," said Buck, with a nod. "A mighty kind woman. Made the best fry bread I ever had."

"My question is, is she buried up here at the cemetery?"

Buck instantly shook his head. "No, no. We don't bury our people up there. Least not many of us."

"Where's she buried then?"

"Out along the river in a cave, like most of our dead. We put 'em in caves, then cover the hole over with rocks. Indian burial."

"So . . . you couldn't be mistaken?"

Buck shook his head adamantly. "I could still walk okay when she went on. I was there for the ceremony, with Joe."

Coal drew a deep breath. "Okay. That's all I needed to know."

Buck Darnell stared at Coal, his eyes like black beads within his thatch of wrinkles. "I reckon I prob'ly made Joe get caught tellin' you a lie, Savage. I hope he don't get in trouble over it. But it wouldn't take long to find out Lily ain't up at the white cemetery, would it?"

"No. It wouldn't take long."

Joe Teton was driving. His two boys were asleep. The road going beyond Challis was windy, but whenever he hit a straight spot he looked down at Pete, and Nathan. They were such good boys. Never caused him any trouble. He wondered what kind of a future they had ahead of them.

Joe knew he was in trouble. But if he could just get to the Rez, he could find some of Lily's people, who lived out toward the river bottoms on the Rez, and he knew they would take the boys in, at least until whatever was going to happen with Joe was over.

He drew a deep breath, looking at the scoped hunting rifle leaning up against the seat, between his leg and Nate. He guessed maybe he wouldn't use it, not even if the cops pulled him over. He didn't want to spend time in any cage, but it was better than being dead. Better than never seeing these two boys again.

He should not have done what he did. There was no doubt of that now. He had thought it would be easy, a simple thing to get away with. After all, people got away with crimes all the time, especially in a remote place like Salmon.

One thing was sure. Everett Sherman had needed to die, before he killed somebody else. He was sorry about the Bannock girl, Irene Boyer, but she shouldn't have taken up with Sherman anyway. That was her own downfall.

But Everett Sherman was a bad man, a man who cared about no one else and lived his life a scourge to others. He had deserved to die, and Joe Teton was glad he was gone.

He simply had not been prepared to burn for the killing. But sometimes some things had to be, and ever since being stopped sneaking off the hill by the two cops, he had known his time was coming.

The only thing he cared about now was his boys.

Bringing breakfast for Hunter Jack, Coal returned to his office, called Flo, and had her put a county-wide attempt-to-locate out on Joe Teton's pickup, along with an order to arrest him for the murders of Everett Sherman and Irene Boyer.

Even as he was still on the phone with Flo, a strange, uneasy feeling came over him. Maybe it was simply the tragedy of putting away a man with two little boys he loved dearly, a man whose neighbors seemed to adore him, and all over a waste of skin like Everett Sherman. The truth was, had Joe Teton only been patient, someone, or something, would have been the death of Everett Sherman. Then maybe Irene Boyer, if she didn't die in a fiery wreck somewhere with Sherman, could have moved on to something better in life, or at least something less destructive.

But it hadn't happened that way. Teton had lost his cool, taken the law into his own hands, and Coal could not simply look past it. His only hope now was that he would be the one arresting Teton, and not men like Horace Teal and William Verret. He feared what would happen if the Shoshone happened to be found first by them.

After hanging up the phone, Coal picked up the breakfast tray and stepped to the cellblock door, cringing inside. Every time he went in here it smelled worse, and today was the day he was going to see if Judge Sinclair would let the big Shoshone out. The smell was shameful, not only for Jack, but for the whole sheriff's department, if that was how they took care of prisoners. Then again, perhaps the stench would be the thing that convinced the judge to set Badger free—just to get his stink out of the courthouse, before it somehow got up through the lower floors and into Sinclair's office on the second floor.

Coal didn't even want to breathe through his nose back here anymore, but when he chose to breathe through his mouth instead he was pretty sure he could taste the odor. He was almost positive that if he squinted his eyes he could see a brownish green fog misting and swirling around the entire cell block, and if anyone else were to be arrested in this county before this smell was gone, they would get their actual punishment, right in this jail, long before they were proven guilty of any crime.

Coal leaned down and slid the food tray under the bottom bar. "Here you go, Badger. The judge is going to come visit you soon. Are you sure you don't want to shower?"

"I'm sure."

Coal grunted. "Yeah. It's too late to clear this air out now anyway, I guess. I'm not sure how you can even taste your food anymore."

Turning, he walked out, shut the door soundly, and sucked in a big, lung-filling breath. The air in the office was a little stale, but stale was preferable to the cloud behind the door.

Coal had no way of knowing if Sinclair might already have been trying to call him, as he had said he would, so he took the initiative and made the call upstairs himself. Wilma Frank put him right in to the judge.

Well, good morning, Coal. Sorry I didn't catch you earlier.

"That's my fault. I had to step out to do an errand."

No harm done. Are you ready for a visit down there?

Coal chuckled. "I think the question is are you? When you smell this cellblock, you might lose your breakfast."

Well, fortunately I only had coffee. I'll be right down.

True to his word, within two minutes Coal saw the judge, in a nicely pressed black suit and tie, come down the outside stairs, give a little rap on the door, and push inside. He scanned the room with a judge's eye, then at last came to Coal and shook his hand.

"It's nice and clean in here, and smells like good coffee," he said. "Maybe you could use some brighter new paint, though."

"Maybe," agreed Coal. "It hasn't been high on my priority list."

The judge sniffed the air. "Besides the coffee, I detect . . ." He stopped and gave a mild look of alarm to Coal. "Is that the prisoner?"

Coal felt instantly mortified. "You smell it already?"

The judge laughed, something Coal had only seen him do a few times. "No, I'm just playing around with you. I don't smell anything but the coffee. Let's go see this friend of yours, shall we?"

Shaking his head and grinning, Coal picked the keys out of his open desk drawer and walked to the big metal cellblock door. "All right, Wiley, this is where they separate the men from the boys. I get that you were only joking, but when I open this door you're going to see what I'm talking about. I tried to get him to shower, but he seems pretty proud of what he has accomplished back here."

The judge looked at Coal, trying to gauge him. "All right, well you are starting to worry me a little bit, but let's proceed."

Coal opened the door, stepping in before Wiley Sinclair. The judge followed him in, and Coal couldn't help grinning when he heard a quiet, "Oh, my" behind him.

However, undaunted, the judge stepped around Coal and strolled to the only occupied cell, watching the monstrous-looking

Hunter Jack rise up off his cot. "Your honor," said the big man with a nod.

"Good morning, Mr. Jack. How are they treating you in here?"

"Good. Savage is always good to me."

"That's great. Good to hear. So I hear you're getting tired of being in here."

"Yes, sir."

"Tell me, Mr. Jack, what can you offer me in the way of convincing me that you'll behave if I let you bail out? After all, I am told you are a little rough on my local officers, and I can't afford to lose any more of them, even temporarily."

"I am sorry," said Jack. "I won't let my temper get me again."

"I'm happy to hear that," said the judge, glancing around at the surroundings, and at the network of metal bars. "But of course you understand that it's always easy to make such a claim, until the moment that anger takes us over again."

"I do," said Jack. "I understand. I . . ." His voice faded out, and he looked over at Coal with a look as near pleading as Coal could imagine his normally noncommittal face ever showing.

"This is all you, Badger," Coal said with a shrug. "You worked yourself into here. Now you'll have to talk yourself out."

When Hunter Jack returned his eyes to the judge, a worried look had come over him. Perhaps a desperate look.

"I'll do anything you ask if you let me get out, your honor. My soul is dying in here. I'll even leave Salmon forever if you want me to."

"I wouldn't ask you to leave your ancestral home, Mr. Jack," said the judge. "I'm not that kind of white man. And yes, I will let you bail out. Also, I will be kind; I know you don't have much."

Coal looked at the relief on Hunter Jack's face and thought he was going to pass out.

He thought he was going to pass out himself if he didn't get some fresh air.

CHAPTER FIFTY-FOUR

Things could be done differently in Salmon from how they would be done in a larger municipality, and because they could, they often were. It wasn't uncommon for lawmen in Salmon, on busy days, simply to let a prisoner out, "on his or her own recognizance", to go downtown and buy themselves a meal or have a beer, as long as it was agreed they would come back to jail and turn themselves in when their errand was over. It was this kind of informality that let Judge Sinclair set bail for Hunter Jack right there in the jail, without having to sit in a courtroom and proclaim it from the bench.

Coal brought Jack out into the office for the procedure, and had him sit on the wooden chair across from the desk. He would have it fumigated or burn it later. Judge Sinclair sat on Coal's chair behind the desk.

"I'm going to set the price of your beautiful car as your bail," said the judge. "The entire value, understand? But we'll pretend the entire car is only worth one thousand dollars. That way you don't have to come up with a tremendous sum up front, but Cherry Bales still has something worthwhile if by chance you vanish from the county. Does this make sense?"

Hunter Jack's face had taken on its normal, impassive look once more, and he glanced over at Coal after the judge spoke. Coal knew Jack well enough to know he was pleading with him to help, asking Coal in the way of a proud Shoshone if this sounded like a good deal.

"You can trust the judge," said Coal. "He wouldn't do anything to steer you wrong."

Hunter Jack nodded his voiceless thanks and looked back at Sinclair. "I understand."

"And let me add," said the judge, "that the only reason I'm listing the car as a lump sum to pay for your bail is that I think it will be a really good incentive for you to come to court when your date is set."

Hunter Jack nodded once more. "Thank you, your honor." Coal was proud of the Shoshone. He had obviously been practicing up on his etiquette, getting ready to impress the magistrate, at least with everything besides his horrendous body odor.

"Okay," said the judge, smacking the top of Coal's desk with the flat of his fist, as if using a gavel. "If you can get Miz Bales to post one thousand dollars, you need only come up with one hundred—for your ten percent."

"Thank you, sir," said Hunter Jack.

And Judge Sinclair was gone. Coal watched him walk all the way up the three concrete steps and out into the parking lot without vomiting one single time. Now there was a man who could have licked the sewer walls of hell.

Coal put Hunter Jack back in his cell while he made a call to Cherry Bales. Technically, it was Jack's place to make that call, but Coal couldn't stand having him out here one minute longer, and he sure as dogs sniff each other's butts wasn't going to let Jack's hand touch his phone.

The handset on the other end of Coal's call clattered off the hook, and he heard a woman swearing, in a strong northeast accent.

You've reached Cherry Bale Bonds. This is Cherry speaking.

"Good morning, Miz Bales. This is Sheriff Savage."

I'm not sure what's good about the morning, Coal, but thank you. I suspect you must have a customer for me, correct? Or were you calling for a date?

Coal would have cringed if he thought the wizened, hard little woman was serious. "Your first guess," he said. "Hunter Jack again."

Oh, Lord, have mercy. What has he done now?

"He's up to his usual. Just doesn't like many cops, I guess. But the good news is this time if he takes off you get that beautiful car of his—free and clear. Judge's orders."

Then I'm not complaining, Coal Savage. I'll be right down. Give me . . . five minutes?

"Whenever you get here," said Coal. "Always nice to see your bright, smiling face."

All right there, sweethaht, now I suspect you must be trying to build up points for latuh, when I have t' bail you *out fer something. Caio.*

Before he could reply or even laugh in her ear, the phone went dead. He was still chuckling about the little woman when he saw her curly dark hair and her awful red blazer, skirt, and matching pink blouse bobbing down the outer stairs. He had been hoping she only wore that around Valentine's Day.

Cherry Bales walked on into the office without knocking. She stopped, her eyes locked right on Coal, at his desk, and pushed the ugly, outdated glasses up all the way on her nose. "What in the name of New Yawk is that awful smell?"

"Must be my coffee," said Coal. "I think it's Folger's."

Cherry frowned, which was hard to detect because of the perpetual frown she always seemed to wear. "Ah, now listen, shoogah. Numbuh one, I happen t' drink Folguh's myself, an' I happen t' like it, an' it does *not* smell like this. Numbuh two, if this is you that smells this way, I can unduhstand why you want t' blame it on bad coffee."

Coal laughed. "Okay, I won't try to jerk your chain, Miz Bales. The smell is actually coming from your client."

"Oh, no. Sweethaht, you have t' tell me that isn't true. Well, I can sure see why you would want him outta your jail, huh? By the way—if you call me Miz Bales one more time, I am going to take my business elsewhere, see? My name is Cherry."

"All right, Cherry, it's a deal. And hey—if you want to do yourself a favor, maybe you should go up to see the court clerk and post bond for Hunter Jack, then come down and let me know. I'll let him out, and you won't even have to get close to him."

"Au contraire," she said. "Sure, I'll go up an' post his bond, but I am *not* gonna miss out on a close-up view of the kind of animal that puts off a smell like this. It's history in the making."

It was only ten minutes later, at the longest, when Cherry Bales came back down, her glaring red and pink costume a harsh announcement of her arrival. Walking into the jail, even though Coal got up and picked up his keys when he saw her coming, she stepped over and sat down on the chair Hunter Jack had sat in earlier. She sat there only a second before voicing one vulgar curse word.

"Oh please don't you tell me he was sitting in this cheh." She tipped her chin down and glared at Coal over the top of her glasses.

"I wish I could say no, Cherry."

"Heavens to Manhattan," she said. "What have I got myself into?"

"If you want to sit, there's another chair over there," he said, pointing. "I'll get it for you."

"And transfer this aroma off my nice clothes onto anothuh chair? Don't bothuh. So . . . what is the story with Dahk Badguh anyway? Not that I'm changin' mah mind, you know."

"He's had a rough spell, Cherry. He can't seem to make any good choices. Somebody broke the front doorframe on his house the night of the Sherman-Boyer murders, stole some of his Indian weapons, and used one of his lances, and maybe a knife, to do the murders."

"Dreadful!" she exclaimed. "Poor sap. Do you know who did the killing?"

"Pretty sure. We'll pick him up today, good Lord willing."

They chatted for another ten minutes, with Cherry Bales sharing some of her dry humor with Coal now and then, before she stood abruptly up. "Well, befaw you think I'm hittin' on ya, I guess I should go."

"Still want to see the prisoner?" By now, Coal really had to strive not to say his words in Cherry's accent.

"No, I changed my mind, sweethaht. You jus' make sure he knows I'll eat him alive if he tries to run. Remember t' tell 'im my 'Jump, Bales, an' Dye' story. See you around, Coal—an' don't say 'not if I see you first'. You know how easy it is t' hurt my feelings."

Without smiling or even winking, she turned and strode out, her too-high heels clicking on the floor like distant gun shouts all the way out.

Coal waited until Cherry Bales was good and gone before going into the cellblock with his handful of keys to empty the zoo of animals.

The only animal in the Lemhi County zoo was Dark Badger, who had made the place smell like a hundred unkempt badgers lived, and voided, in a hole in the back of the cell.

"Grab all your stuff, Badger," said Coal as he turned the key in the lock. "And go use the john before you leave, so you don't have to squat in the bushes."

"Guess you don't want no hug before I go," mused Jack.

"Uh, yeah . . . Your guesser is right on track, my friend."

Jack let out one of his rare laughs and lumbered back to the restroom, then came out to find Coal had blocked open the metal door. He had also opened the door leading outside, and it already felt icy inside the room, but Coal could think of—and smell—worse things.

"You didn't bring anything in but this little frog sticker," said Coal, handing Jack an Old Timer pocketknife. "Do me a favor and don't poke anything but frogs with it."

The man nodded at Coal. "Thank you, Savage. Maybe before I show up for court I'll take a shower, uh?"

"Good idea, my friend. If you went in every store in town and did a poll, I'm betting you'd get a hundred of the same answer."

Coal agreed to shake the big paw of Dark Badger, wondering how fast he would have to run for the soap and water before anything he got on his hand could crawl up his arm and into his mouth. He watched the man lumber out, up the stairs, and then out of the parking lot, realizing that "lumber" wasn't really an accurate word, because for a man who looked so big and powerful, Jack actually moved very gracefully.

After scouring the skin off his hands in the sink, Coal went to pour himself a cup of coffee, then decided against it and dumped it out. He didn't like to think what might be swimming around in it by now.

He went down to the Salmon River Coffee Shop, where he was greeted by the happy faces of Jodi and Tammy, the waitresses on duty, and of course Jay Castillo. After a brief conversation with the three of them, Coal dined on a pound of half-cooked Hereford beef, left a generous tip, and headed out on the road.

Coal was happy to hear from Jay that things were going well with Dale Moore. The boy was settling in well, and already seemed like a happy part of their family. Hearing about Dale made him think of Troy Westerlind, so he also stopped in at Ken's Automotive and got an earful of listening to Ken brag about what a big help Troy already was in the shop. The news about Dale was pleasing, but to hear that the ringleader of the trio was actually doing so well warmed Coal's heart deeply.

That left only one of the Three Musketeers to check on, but Coal was too nervous to stop at the Kelly home. He already knew too much about Amber Kelly to want to interrupt any of her *extra-curricular activities* at the house while hopefully Dawn was in school today with the boys.

Coal ended up spending the better part of the day paying visits around the county, as far out in one direction as Leadore, and the other direction clear to the North Fork store. When he wasn't hob-nobbing, seeing how things were running in the outlying areas of his county, he was pulled over on the side of the road, and in a yellow legal pad he jotted down items and figures, getting a start on this year's budget, his least favorite part of this job or any other supervisory position.

He drove back into town toward the end of the day, stopped at the jail to see if the air there had improved any, which it had, and made a call to Flo Hawkins.

Hi, Coal! How is your day?

"Good, Flo, and I hope yours has been too. Say, have we heard anything about Joe Teton? I've been away from my radio quite a few times."

Not a word, she said. *Now don't cuss, Coal. I'm sure somebody will pick him up.*

Shocked, Coal said, "Flo! Why would you even think to tell me not to cuss?"

Flo laughed gleefully on the other end of the line. *Oh, stop! You're getting pretty well known for your colorful vocabulary, you know. Remember, it's a small town!*

"You're kidding me, right?" Coal was pretty sure he actually felt himself getting warm around the collar.

I would never kid you! Oh, don't worry about it. It's all in fun, honey.

After Coal hung up, he sat at his desk brooding. Was his language really as bad as all that? He thought he was pretty good at keeping it mostly to himself. The funniest comment, but the biggest blow to Coal's ego, was when Flo told him people in the county were starting to refer to him as "Sheriff Savage Language".

Well, hell. Maybe it really *was* time to clean up his damn language.

One of the perks of being boss is that you get to tell your underlings to do the menial janitorial work, but Coal couldn't do that. After all, he was the one who had told his deputies not to open Dark Badger's cell under any circumstances. So the very last part of his shift he spent with a bottle of Pine-Sol, a rag, a mop and bucket, and he cleaned out the entire area of Badger's cell and the restroom as best he could, then left the door propped open to air out, ran a mop around the office area, and a Pine-Sol-soaked rag over the chair Badger had used. By the time all fragrant reminders of the Shoshone's visit were removed, Coal was feeling pretty proud of himself, and his last act of the day was to take a blank piece of white paper and write on it, in huge black letters,

THESE PREMISES FUMIGATED AND SEALED

He left the sign taped to the window, for his deputies to get a chuckle out of, then headed home.

It wasn't until he was on his way down Twenty-Eight that he allowed himself any time to contemplate the thought that had kept pecking at his broken heart all day: At home, in Connie's loving, caring hands, waited photographs of Maura PlentyWounds, the cruel woman who by now he was supposed to have banished forever from his memory.

CHAPTER FIFTY-FIVE

The happy faces of children and dogs, the hugs, the licks, the smiles, the wagging tails, all of that will go far in the healing of a man or a woman from the most traumatic of events. When Coal got home, that was almost true.

But no amount of the bliss of happy greetings could make up for the pounding of Coal's heart, after a long day of images of Maura insisting on clawing their way into his brain.

Coal gave plenty of time that evening, to *all* his children, including the two girls that were not of his blood, and to the four-legged children that weren't even of his species. When the explosion of smiles and tail wagging, and the colorful stew of stories about everyone's day, were over, Shadow lay at Coal's feet shedding like she was ten dogs instead of one, the way German shepherds do, and Dobe sprawled out to the left of his chair. Coal drew in a deep breath, smelling the fragrance of Sissy's newly washed hair, as she sat high on his lap, her arms around his neck, her cheek on his chest.

Softly stroking the little girl's back, Coal waited. He knew this girl didn't give up, and once she had an idea in her head, it was going to keep coming back. He looked across the top of Sissy's head at Connie, who sat on the sofa, having given up her chair to him. She too was waiting for Sissy, but she had not been able to hide from his sight the big white envelope she held down along her leg.

At last, Sissy looked up at him. "Pop Coal? Time to see pictures now?"

Coal's eyes darted to his mother. Her understanding smile looked so warm toward him, and her eyes had filled with tears. She held up the envelope whose contents Coal grasped all too well, and shook it meaningfully. Even through her tears, Connie seemed excited to share with him. He wondered how much of that excitement came from Sissy.

Coal looked at the little girl, whose hopeful smile was so bright. "You ready, Sis?"

She gave him a huge nod.

"Then I guess we should look at them."

Connie stood up and walked over to her chair, kneeling on the right side of it, the only place besides the back that wasn't occupied by a smelly canine sea. Sissy turned around and wiggled down into position on Coal's lap, and then she held out her little hands, and Connie placed a photograph in front of her. Sissy took the photo between both thumbs and index fingers as delicately as if it were broken glass. She cranked around, looking at Coal, and held it up.

Coal's heart leaped. It was a photo of Maura, with the twins playing back behind her. The smile on her face was like a piece of heaven, her teeth so bright, her eyes like sapphires. "See Maur'?" Sissy said. He fought back tears, blinking hard.

"I sure do, Sis. Look at that smile, huh? I think she's probably smiling that way because of you."

That made the big smile on Maura's face transfer to Sissy's lips. Coal fought back harder against his emotion.

Gently, Sissy passed the photo back to Connie, who took it the same way, and to Sissy's, "one more?" she handed over another shot. This one was of Maura holding Sissy in front of her, with Katie Leigh to one side. Connie had caught Maura off-guard this time, so her mouth was open in surprise, and her eyes wide as well, making them seem all the more bright and blue.

"Maur' holdin' me," Sissy said, beaming.

"Yep, that's Maura holding you, all right. I think she likes you!"

Connie reached out and squeezed Coal's knee, giving it a little shake. When he looked at her, she wasn't watching him, but Sissy. "You think Maura likes Papa Coal too, honey?"

Sissy gave her a huge nod, straight-arming her hand out in front of her so fast it made Connie give out a little squeal. "Careful, Sissy! You might poke my eye out!" That made Sissy giggle, but she immediately straightened her arm out again, undaunted.

Connie took the second photo from Sissy's fingers and gave her the third. Sissy held it up for Coal either to look at or to take, and when he started to reach for it he realized all of a sudden that his fingers were shaking.

The photograph was like gold, a piece of heaven . . . or a bullet straight to Coal's heart. It was a picture of Coal with one arm wrapped around Maura's shoulders, his left hand pulling her tight into him, and Maura hugging him hard with both arms around his middle. Everything about her face in the photograph was perfect, her golden hair tumbling down around her face, and there was a light in his own eyes that he couldn't try to deny. It wasn't too long ago, talking to Jordan Peterson, that he had bemoaned the fact that he didn't have any such photographs of himself and Maura. Now that he was looking at this one which was such a surprise, he didn't know if it was worse having one, or not having one.

Overwhelming emotion swept over Coal, and tears filled his eyes. Connie had yet to let go of his knee, and now he knew why. She had been preparing to comfort him, in the way that only a lover, a best friend, or a mother can do.

It was all Coal could do to choke out the words, "Hey, Sis, Papa Coal needs to use the bathroom, okay?"

Sizing up the situation like an old pro, Connie took the photograph and put it in the envelope, then put out her arms to Sissy.

"Come on, Sis, let's let Papa Coal up, okay? And he'll be right back."

With a beaming face, Sissy let Connie take her, and Coal lunged up off the chair and made his getaway down the hall, to the sounds of dead silence behind him from the entire family. They had all been watching him close, and he didn't guess any of them had missed his reaction to the last photo.

Coal stood in the bathroom doorway with the door partway open. Upon coming home, he had dressed down to jeans and a thin, tight tee shirt of deep blood red that accentuated his muscular build. A jolting memory reminded him that Maura PlentyWounds had given him this shirt as a gift.

Looking in the mirror, he saw all that, but he saw much more. The way the mirrors reflected each other, with the vanity mirror right over the sink, a much larger one next to it over the toilet, to dress by, and the one behind him, on the back of the door, it struck him that his images went on and on, as if they would continue, successively smaller, clear into eternity.

He remembered his mother presenting that idea to him as a young boy, talking about how the mirrors reflected the way life continues forever, and so the people we love never truly die. It was the day they held the funeral for his granddad on his father's side, and she had been trying late that night to comfort him from the loss.

Now, as he stared at those red-shirted men in the mirror, those men who went on and on, at the heavily whiskered face that he suddenly realized had not been shaved in several days, with shaggy hair he had neglected to have barbered into a civilized hair-do in a month, perhaps two, he saw only that something was missing.

He saw that, even if he, Coal Savage, did indeed go on and on like this, into eternity, he had been meant to have Maura Plenty-Wounds standing there, passing into eternity beside him. And she wasn't. Maura had left him, and Sissy, and the whole family.

Maura had left him with only this blood-red shirt that matched the color of his broken heart.

It was after all the kids had gone to bed, when Coal and Connie were sitting watching the news, with the dogs strewn around the floor, that the ringing phone sent its typical jolt through Coal. He proudly managed not to swear, and before Connie could get up to answer it, he stopped her.

"Phones that ring this late are most likely emergency garbage, Mom. I'll get it."

He got up and picked up the hallway phone. "Savages."

Hi, Coal! This is Nadine. Yes, sorry to bother you, hon, but I just took a call from a Lieutenant Horst, with the Pocatello Police, and he said they have located Joseph Teton and have him in custody.

Coal tried to catch up to this surprising turn of events. "Wait, Nadine—did he say how he knew we were after him?"

Oh, I'm sorry—I just figured you had heard. One of the times when you were busy today, Deputy Fairbourne called down here and had me put an ATL out statewide. He said everyone had been looking for Mr. Teton most of the day, and by now he was probably well on his way out of the state.

Good boy, Grant! thought Coal. To Nadine, he said, "Oh, that's good. I should already have done that myself. So did this Horst say what he wants me to do?"

He only said to have you call him.

Nadine gave Coal the number to the Pocatello PD, and after she hung up, feeling weary, Coal dialed the number. Lieutenant Horst sounded like a decent sort of fellow. He told Coal if he wanted to, he or a deputy could start heading their way in the morning, someone from Pocatello could drive their way, and they could meet somewhere in the middle to pick up the prisoner. To Coal's biggest question, Lieutenant Horst said, *No, there are no kids. It was just Joseph Teton, heading south down Fourth Street when our officer recognized the pickup from your APB and nabbed him.*

Coal told Horst goodbye, settling the phone down gravely on its hook. He hung his head and took a deep breath. Tomorrow was going to be a long, long day.

In the night, Coal dreamed, and he could only wonder what his sleeping body had been doing, for when he awoke, in the proverbial cold sweat, both dogs were up and moving around, and Shadow was whining, almost the way Dobe did whenever he needed to go out.

For a long several minutes, Coal lay there staring at the ceiling, listening to the dogs pace. He raised a hand and scrubbed at his weary eyes, and slowly his heart returned to its normal pace.

The dream was ugly. As ugly as almost anything he had faced in real life. He had dreamed that he went looking for Dawn Kelly again, knocking on her door. There still was no car parked outside, but he had been to the school already, and someone in the dream he didn't recognize from real life had told him Dawn had not come in that day.

He knocked on the door as long as he could stand, then almost in a panic kicked open the front door. The gruesome sight that was there to greet him hung in his fevered mind even now, long after he had realized it was only a dream.

There, in the center of the living room in the Kelly home, pretty young Dawn Kelly was hanging by a rope from the living room chandelier, a chair tipped over on the ground at her feet.

Coal couldn't get the image of Dawn's swollen, purple face out of his head. It seemed so real he had to fight back a feeling of panic. Rolling over, he sat up on the side of the bed, and the dogs came over to start their tongue lashing of his exposed legs. Shadow seemed to grasp how badly the dream had shaken him, so finally she jumped up on the bed and started to rub against him, not unlike a cat. He hugged her neck and spoke to her soothingly. She had always been as sensitive to his moods as any person might have been, even his mother.

At last, he stumbled all over the dogs getting out of the room, went downstairs, and drank a tall glass of creamy raw milk, letting the dogs run outside. He finally let the dogs back in and returned to his room to fall into a miraculous, but still restless sleep that continued that way until his alarm startled him awake.

Coal went over to the radio and flipped it on, still trying to get the nightmare about Dawn Kelly to clear his head. A song he hardly heard on the radio ended, and the news came on. They were still talking about how the day before, February twenty-sixth, was exactly one month since the governments finally called an end to the Vietnam War. But the bad news was that North Vietnam and the Viet Cong had announced they were done releasing any more American prisoners, because they said the United States government had acted in bad faith in getting troops out of the country in a timely manner.

The news made Coal feel more sick than he already had. He couldn't help but think of all those boys still over there, suffering. Boys that had wanted no more to do with that damned war than he had, but whose lives, health, and futures, would probably be wrecked forever, and all because of the money-grubbing, fumbling politicians in every government who had had anything to do with that war, without whom there would never have been such a war to begin with. He thought of men like Slugger Janx, whose only peace, before or after the war, was found in death.

Where was the fairness in a world where sheltered, grossly overfed bureaucrats created wars, and scared boys had to go out and learn to kill to fight those wars for the men who would never willingly raise a bloody finger?

Though it all made him sick, Coal listened all the way through the news, sports, and weather, and then while John Denver was singing "Take Me Home, Country Roads", he got up and started his workout, then gave himself an actual shave, which felt strange after so many days. He dressed in new blue jeans, cowboy boots, and a plain gray shirt, a uniform fit for a backwoods sheriff to go to the city in and pick up a prisoner.

Coal went outside to help Connie feed the horses, although to her it was an old routine, a routine she actually enjoyed, and she had never asked for or even seemed to want help.

They stood out there afterward, watching steam rise from the trough and watching Maura's horses, Brusher, Hilly, Sarah, and Homer, and Cody and Bolt, his mother's dark bay, munch on the fragrant hay they had flaked out on the ground in front of them. It gave Coal a strange sense of satisfaction that his father's old horse, Cody, had long since put the black horse, Homer, in his place. Homer had been the bully of the pasture when the four of them had been at Maura's. Here at the Savage Ranch, he now had to play second fiddle.

"Son? Are you doing okay?" Connie's voice broke into Coal's reverie, with that question that came completely out of the blue.

"Sure. What makes you ask?"

She was silent for a time, a long enough time that he knew she was on to him. Try as he might, there were few times he had actually been able to get things past this woman.

"Because I know you pretty well, Son. For, let's see—maybe forty-two years now? What is it? Still thinking about Maura?"

He realized the easy way out right now could be to agree that he was only thinking about Maura. After all, she already knew Maura was on his mind. But maybe this once he really did need to talk, and if he was going to open up, this was his chance.

"It's probably nothing. I just had a really bad dream—about Dawn Kelly."

"Really? I'm sorry. Do you want to talk about it?"

"That's a loaded question," he replied. "Hey—want to go back in the house where it's warm?"

She smiled at him and put her arm around his waist. "Sure, as long as you promise not to clam up once we get in there."

They walked with their arms around each other to the house and hung their coats by the door, where Connie also threw off her boots. Then they settled onto the sofa in the living room.

Not waiting for her too often taciturn son, Connie said, "Tell me about your dream, Coal. I know for me it helps to get it out."

He agreed. "You're right. It will. But . . . Wow, it really shook me up." He went on and told her in as much detail as he dared about the dream, and she listened attentively, stroking Dobe's narrow, intelligent head throughout the time Coal was speaking.

When he finished, she said, "Coal? I think that's one of those dreams you need to take seriously."

He stared at her, letting her words soak in. He had actually hoped she would give him some other advice. "So . . . you don't think it was just a dream?"

"I don't. I used to have dreams like that, sweetheart. And if I ignored them, I almost always regretted it. Go check on her today. I think you need to—maybe for both of you."

"I'm kind of afraid to. What if . . ." He stopped his words there, but his mother had too much intuition not to know already what he had been about to say.

"What if, Son? What if? Don't let yourself have to keep asking that question the rest of your life. I'm sure you've been thinking the same thing I am, that a lot of times when somebody takes his own life, or even just tries to, it gets the people he knows thinking too much about their own lives, and they often do the same thing."

Coal nodded, feeling sick at the thought. "Copycat suicides," he said quietly.

His mother only nodded, reaching over to give his leg a squeeze. “Yes. Go see her, Coal. We’ll both be worried now until you do.”

From that moment on, Coal’s heart was pounding harder than he wanted it to, and even when he was telling the dogs and the kids goodbye, he couldn’t get Dawn Kelly’s face, or his horrible dream, out of his head.

He had to go to the Kellys’ house before he headed toward Pocatello. It was the thing he wanted to do least, and the thing he needed to most.

Throughout the long drive into Salmon, the image of Dawn’s face from his nightmare would not leave him, except when he thought of one other thing: the last time she came to him and threw her arms around him, in an embrace almost savage in its intensity.

CHAPTER FIFTY-SIX

Coal had left the house early enough to be at Dawn’s before she could leave for school. He sat in front of the little gray house now. As if the color of the siding itself weren’t enough, the cold blue shadows made the place seem even less hospitable. There still was no car parked in front. Had Dawn and her mother left town? Had Amber Kelly spent the night at some man’s house, as the rumors said she was prone to do?

He could ask himself questions all morning, but there was only one way to find out if Dawn was here. Coal stared out through the passenger window at the front door. It looked so rigid and impenetrable from where he was, but the gut-wrenching question remained: Did he really want to know what was on the other side?

Steeling himself, he got out, straightening his gun on his hip. He walked up the sidewalk, which shot like an arrow from the parking to the front steps. It was fifteen feet long. It seemed like fifteen hundred.

He raised his hand, paused, then knocked, softly at first. Then more insistent. No one came. No lights came on. He looked down at the flimsy door handle and doorframe, the cheap door. It would be an easy in, if he wanted it. Exigent circumstances rule, he told himself—checking on the welfare of a citizen. The problem was if his dream were true, he didn't want to be inside.

He could not stop thinking about Laura, his little Laura, hanging from the rafter in the big barn in Broad Run, Virginia. He had never actually seen her. It was poor little Katie who had found her—Katie, who was surely scarred for life. But Coal had seen other people hanging dead, so he couldn't help seeing Laura that way, even though he had been spared the actuality.

Please, Dawn, he kept telling himself silently. *Please don't do this.*

He started around the house, peering into any window he passed, even if it was only through a crack in the curtains. He felt like some whacked out peeping tom, but it was better than breaking in a door unnecessarily.

Finally, at the back of the house, he found a window that, although streaked and water-stained, he could see through. In the dim light inside, he thought he could see legs stretched out on a bed, but he couldn't get the right angle to see the whole person, and he could see no movement at all.

He tapped on the window. Nothing. He pounded on it. The feet jerked up suddenly, and the owner of those feet spun and sat up on the bed. It was Dawn!

A huge wash of emotion flooded over Coal as he saw the girl grab a set of headphones and jerk them down off her head, leaning closer to look out the window. He waved at her, and suddenly she put both her hands to her mouth, and he heard her let out a little squeal through the glass.

Rather than run right for the bedroom door, the girl walked over to a stereo and pushed the power button in, then went, almost nonchalantly, to the door. She vanished from sight, but soon a window to his left, after some obvious sounds of someone inside struggling with it, slid up a crack.

"Can you come around to the front door?"

Of course he could, and he did. But the whole time around, he couldn't help thinking something really was wrong. The voice he had just heard wasn't the Dawn Kelly he had come to know.

Before he could knock on the front door, it opened. The look in Dawn's face was drawn, emotion-dead. "Did you come to see why I wasn't going to school?"

"I don't care about school right now, Dawn," he said. "I came to see how you're doing."

She offered a listless shrug. "Fine, I guess."

She allowed her head to turn a little bit too far in one direction, far enough that he could see a discolored place there. Had her mother hit her? Or was it only the lighting?

Words were out of his mouth before he could think about them. "Do you want to go on a day trip with me, Dawn? Go for a drive?"

It was the first time her eyes actually met his. "A drive? Where?" There was no light in her eyes. No joy. The only thing he could see was suspicion.

"I have to go to Rexburg. To pick up a prisoner."

She let his words register for a few seconds. "You got him? The killer guy in the hat?"

"We got him. The Pocatello police picked him up."

Still her face was emotionless, but he had to push on. If he had wondered before, now he knew that something was very wrong.

"Come with me, Dawn. Please? That's a long way without any company."

"But why me?" she asked after several seconds.

"Because I enjoy your company."

Her eyes filled with tears before she could stop them, and she turned her head quickly the other way. When she could speak again, without looking at him, she said, "I guess I could come. Can I bring some music? I saw you have a tape deck in your car."

"Of course. I'd love to hear your music."

"Okay. I'll get my coat too."

She walked off, and when she returned she carried a brown paper bag, which he assumed was full of tapes. She was wearing a ratty-looking brown coat with a faux fur collar, and when she saw him looking at it she said, "It's the only thing I have that's warm enough for this kind of day."

"I didn't say anything. I think it has character."

She rolled her eyes and shut the door.

"You're not going to lock it?"

She shrugged. "Who cares? I don't care if somebody comes and burns it down while I'm gone."

Aching inside that he couldn't seem to melt the ice with Dawn anymore, they went to the car, and he opened her door and got her settled, then went to the trunk and got out a blanket he kept there for emergencies. He took it and set it on the back seat.

"Do you want to stop and grab a bite before we head out?" he asked as he pulled away from the grass parking into the street.

"Naw. Er . . . Well, I guess. Somethin', maybe. But I won't have to go in, will I?"

"Of course not. I can grab you a pop and a candy bar if that's all you want. Maybe some chips?"

"Sure."

B & B Foods, on Main, was where Coal planned to go, but as he turned right onto the street, he saw the A & W down on the right. When Dawn didn't object, he stopped, went in, and bought them fries and root beer floats. It wasn't even remotely his normal diet, but then again it wasn't normal for him to drive hundreds of miles with a teenage girl he hardly knew, either.

With the hot fries aromatizing the inside of the Thunderbird, Coal headed east on Highway 28, slipping the first 8-track tape Dawn handed him into the deck. It was Kris Kristofferson—*Border Lord.*

As Kristofferson's one of a kind voice poured out of the Thunderbird speakers, Coal tried to plan ahead, envisioning how it would be seeing Joe Teton again, how it would be handcuffing him and putting him in his backseat. Would Joe make a full confession right away, in the car, or would they have to come home and get him an attorney? And how much did he want to let Dawn hear anyway, when she seemed already to have had such a hard life?

Coal had never listened to Kristofferson's *Border Lord* album, so he had no idea what to expect. But when they began to play a track titled "Little Girl Lost", and right where the lyrics said, "she's a little girl lost, pleading silently for help", he looked over at Dawn Kelly. They hadn't even made it to Leadore yet, her fries were hardly gone, and already her body was shaking, and tears streamed down her face.

Whipping the car to the side of the road, Coal threw it in park and turned to Dawn. "Hey. Dawn. Come here."

She practically flew over the console and fell into his arms, wailing out loud in her pain. She couldn't speak, and Coal didn't try either. He held her, rubbing her back, and she poured her soul out on him as Kris Kristofferson, oblivious to the pain he had just released, sang on.

When Dawn stopped crying, and *Border Lord* had played all the way around and was starting again, Coal reached into the back seat and pulled the blanket up, using it as a cushion on the console. Dawn leaned against him and the console, and with one arm he cradled her as he pulled back out on the highway. Dawn squeezed his arm with both of hers, hanging on for all she was worth.

When Coal felt Dawn could listen, after they had gone another forty miles and were passing through rolling sagebrush hills, with the Lemhi Range looming on their right, he got up enough strength to tell her his story. He told her how Laura had died, and how it was the children who found her. He told her how for so long it had torn him to pieces, and how sometimes late at night when he was alone, and all was still, it still did.

Then he told her what he had dreamed last night. And Dawn Kelly sat still, feeling warm against him, but barely breathing.

Peter, Paul, and Mary's *A Song Will Rise* album lulled them, the tires hummed on the highway, and a bright sun poured through the windshield and warmed them to the bone.

Twenty minutes passed after Coal finished telling her his dream, and for a while he thought maybe she had fallen asleep and heard nothing of it. But then she drew in a deep breath, and her lips parted, as the haunting song, "Jimmy Whalen" played to the trio's perfect, beautiful harmony.

"Everything seems hopeless," she said softly. Even while the words sounded dark, her tone sounded dreamy.

"Why, Dawn?"

"I don't even have a life."

"Sure you do. You're a beautiful girl with a huge heart. Everybody around you loves you."

She sat silent for a long time after that before finally saying, "How do you know that?"

"That everybody loves you?"

"Uh-huh."

"It's just a guess. Because of how I feel."

Another long while of silence before she said, "You love me?"

"I do, Dawn."

Coal chanced a glance down at the girl after another five minutes' silence, and her cheeks were stained with tears. She must have been crying the whole time, but she was a pro at keeping it quiet.

A shuddering sigh finally left the girl, and she said, "I don't know why anyone would love me. There's nothing I've ever done good—for anyone."

Coal's heart was breaking for this girl. He wondered how many other millions of children felt like this. And how many adults. There was so much pain in the world. He wished he could take it all away. He wondered about himself. He wondered how the Corps hadn't stolen all these feelings from him. Yet they had, at least for a while. Part of him felt like it was only in the past few months that he was growing his soul back again, even after all the human emotion and natural love the military had attempted to train out of him.

"What am I going to do if you're ever gone, Coal?" Dawn suddenly asked. He was surprised to hear his name spoken in her voice.

"I'm nobody special," he said. "There are plenty of other people who will love you."

"But not people like you."

"You'll see. But the first person who has to love you is you. Don't ever forget that. You have to truly love yourself before anyone else can love you." It was advice he knew was true, and advice it had taken him years to learn—and that sometimes he still had to fight to apply

"I only want to be a good person," Dawn said after another long spell of silence.

"Then be that. Your smile has already come a long way to warming my heart. Bring that to the table, and you're halfway home."

"Coal?"

"Yeah?"

"If I took my life, it would hurt you . . . wouldn't it?"

"It would break my heart, Dawn."

Tires humming. Peter, Paul, and Mary singing "Motherless Child". Dawn suddenly squeezed Coal's arm tightly.

"Today you saved my life. I wish someday I could save yours too. I'll never break your heart."

Dawn snuggled tighter against him, letting out a long sigh. A few minutes later, by the sound of her breathing, he knew she had gone to sleep.

A while later, disappointed that Dawn couldn't have slept longer, Coal pulled over in Rexburg and stopped at the Sinclair, where he had arranged for Flo to have the Pocatello police officer meet him to pick up the prisoner.

As he was scanning the parking lot, he saw a black and white squad car appear from the other side of the service station. It pulled up and stopped ten feet away from his car.

A tall, slender man with high and tight dark hair got out of the car and smiled at him. "I guess you're Sheriff Savage, judging from the T-Bird description."

Coal grinned back. He had been about to say something about his suicide doors, but as Dawn climbed out the passenger side, the word struck him hard, and he managed to stop himself mid-swing.

"Can't drive around in a car just like everybody else's right?"

"Well, heck no," said the officer. "And if you have to be different, well, I can only say that is one sweet chariot to pick!"

"Thanks. How is the prisoner?" asked Coal.

"Polite. And quiet. Not much for conversation."

As the policeman spoke, he opened the back door, reaching in to grab Joe Teton's elbow and help him struggle out and stand up. Teton stared at Coal's chest and nodded.

"Savage. I guess I get to go back home."

“Hi there, Mr. Teton. Yes, I guess you do. It would have been much easier if you had stayed there in the first place.”

“Life ain’t easy though,” replied Teton. “And where would my little boys be then?”

“Where are they now?” asked Coal.

“Someplace where white man can’t go get ’em.”

CHAPTER FIFTY-SEVEN

Speaking of caged eagles, Coal hated seeing Joe Teton in handcuffs. He hated the moment when the Pocatello officer took his handcuffs off the Shoshone, and Coal had to turn right around and apply his own. He couldn’t help but think much more highly of this proud Indian than he would have of Everett Sherman, from everything he had heard about that peach of a human being. Joe Teton had fought for a country that had driven his ancestors to the ground. He didn’t have to go to Korea, but go he did.

Teton had returned to his native home, started to raise a family, and cirrhosis had taken his wife from him, leaving this eagle spirit to raise two little boys alone. Now one bad choice had forced Teton to give his boys to someone else to raise, and he had to know his boys would be changed drastically before he could ever be with them again. Yet even still, he didn’t fight Coal’s handcuffs. He knew he had done wrong, he quietly accepted it, and now he made ready to pay the price—another eagle in a cage.

As Coal drove quietly home, half the time with some of Dawn’s music playing, the rest of the time with only the singing of the tires, he kept trading his glances between Joe Teton, in the rearview mirror, and Dawn Kelly, beside him. They were two lost spirits—the one losing his children, and his freedom, the other not even having a clear vision of what her future might hold, but with too many memories of her rocky past.

Sometimes Dawn dozed, but Joe Teton never did. The entire ride he spent studying the sagebrush hills and the mountains. Coal could only imagine the crushing weight that was closing in on this man's heart.

Dawn woke up once, crying again. She wanted to talk about the Angus bull, about the sleepless nights she had spent after Troy made her put her hands on the lance that was taking the animal's life. "Do you think animals go to heaven?" she asked.

Coal nodded. "I have no doubt about it. They're a lot more pure than people are. How could they go anywhere else?"

"Do you think they have souls?"

"Of course."

"Do you think he'd be able to forgive me?"

The question made a lump rise in Coal's throat that he had to choke down. "I don't think he ever held anything against you. I think he knew he was feeling pain, and weakness. That's all he knew. And then he was just gone."

She looked down at her hands, which were folded in her lap, and tears tumbled down her cheeks. "I could never put a blade into another living thing again. I can't get it out of my head."

"It will get easier over time," he assured her. "That's one thing I do promise."

At last, they neared Savage Lane, and Coal had never felt a greater urge to drive to his house, run in and give his mother and little Sissy Miley a huge hug, and tell them how much he loved them. But of course he would have to wait until an appropriate time. He rolled past without looking up the lane.

They reached Salmon not too long before school was out, and Coal got on the radio and asked Flo to call the city police and ask them to meet him in the back parking lot of city hall. He was tired of having eagles caged in his jail, of having to look into the eyes of men who needed to be free. Besides, he had the excuse that his cells were still airing out, so this time he was putting his prisoner in the City's jail.

Bob Wilson drove from the other side of town, a trip of two minutes, and met Coal in the back lot. Coal got Joe Teton out of his car, and he and Bob walked the Shoshone down the back stairs as Dawn followed along behind.

There was one other prisoner in the city jail, a short, obese man with a balding head but greasy, stringy blond hair some six inches long growing off the back of his skull. He was white as vanilla pudding and bare-chested, with a straggling of long blond hairs on his chest—in short, pretty hard to look at for very long. They put Teton on the far end of the jail from the other man, just shy of the cage the city used to house female or juvenile prisoners.

Coal removed the handcuffs from Teton's wrists while the man stood quietly. Teton had only one request: "Can I keep my hat and boots in here?"

"Of course," Bob said. "You need anything else?"

"Quiet. And the smell of sagebrush."

Bob and Coal looked at each other, and each could read the sadness that request put in the other's mind. "I can't help you with the sagebrush," said Bob. "But I hope it will be quiet."

The other prisoner had stood up and shuffled to the bars. He gripped them and erupted with a throaty giggle, looking out at Coal and Bob, and down through the corridor of bars at Joe Teton. "Quiet? You want quiet, Injun? You ain't a gonna get much in here. No quiet, no quiet—*no quiet!*" He started giggling again until Bob stared him down for a few seconds.

"Will you shut up? Please shut your mouth, or I'll let Joe sew it up for you."

The strange, squatty prisoner stared at Bob, then started cackling and shaking his bars. He seemed suddenly to notice Dawn standing there at the entrance to the cellblock. "Hey, little girl! Little girrrr-leeee. What're you doin' here, little girl? They puttin' you in prison too? I sure hope so."

Eyes simmering, Bob turned and stepped to the cellblock door, putting a hand on Dawn's shoulder and easing her out. "You might want to wait out here, just for a little bit," he advised her. Reaching over, he picked a can of mace up off a shelf and stepped back into the jail, shaking it ominously.

"You want to shut your trap now?" He glared at the obese prisoner, who stopped talking on the instant. "One more noise out of you, and I'm emptying this can."

The man stared at Bob, shifted his eyes over to Coal, then returned them to Bob. "Fine."

Bob looked down the way at Joe Teton. "I'm sorry about that, Joe. If we get any more noise in this place, I'll give you a towel to put over your head, and we'll see how this joker likes a can of mace for breakfast."

Coal and Bob left the cellblock, and Bob locked the door. Coal asked, "What in the world is that guy in here for?"

"Protective custody! What else? I caught him walking down the street the other night just like that—no shirt, talking to himself. It was after we all got done up at the cemetery, in fact. Crazy as a hoot owl."

The outer door opened suddenly, and Horace Teal walked in. He saw Coal and nodded. "Hey. They caught the guy, huh?"

"They did. Over in Pocatello."

"Huh. Well hey, I want to just say I'm sorry if I acted like an idiot. We thought for sure it was Hunter Jack. You know?"

Coal shrugged. "Forget about it. Everybody makes mistakes."

"Sure, sure. Well, I'll tell Bill when I see him," Teal said. "He don't wanna get it outta his head that other Injun's the real killer."

"I guess it doesn't matter," Coal said. "Everything works out in the long run." And yet really, did it? Joe Teton had done all of Salmon a favor, in many ways, and now he would spend years behind bars for it.

"Hey, Bob, I'll probably be back later. I'll bring you some of our petty cash—to feed Teton. Is that all right?"

"Sure. I'll see how the Chief wants to work everything out. You know, really we should consolidate these jails anyway—yours and ours. It would make a lot more sense if the city and the county could chip in together and pay one or two full-time guards than have it the way it is now."

Coal and Dawn left the dark, depressing city jail and went back up to Coal's car. It was all Coal could do to push Joe Teton out of his mind. The Shoshone had never pleaded for mercy. He had hardly spoken at all, in fact, just taken his incarceration in stride. Yet that image of another golden eagle rotting away behind bars would not leave Coal's mind.

"You hungry?" Coal asked Dawn. "It's been a while since we ate."

"I am, but you don't have to buy me anything." She smiled at him.

"Well, what if I want to?"

She smiled bigger. "Okay. If you want to."

They went to have a sit-down meal at the Coffee Shop, and both of them were surprised when their meal was almost finished and they saw Dale Moore come in from the back. When he recognized them, he practically came running. As they stood up, Dale and Dawn took each other in a crushing embrace.

It turned out Dale was working here now as a busboy and dishwasher. This would be his first day on the job, working for his temporary guardian, Jay Castillo. Coal was delighted, listening to the boy, to hear that his voice was recovering nicely, but even more importantly that he seemed so happy.

After Dale hugged Coal, then hugged Dawn once more, he left them and went into the back to start work. Coal and Dawn finished their meal, and Coal was delighted to see Dawn smiling so much. Maybe she was thinking life was all right after all.

Finally, it was time to go, and Coal took Dawn back to her house. Her mom's beat-up Buick was parked in the driveway. Coal looked over in time to see Dawn's entire countenance change. Her eyes seemed to take on a dullness again, and if it was possible for a girl of her age, the skin of her face seemed actually to sag.

"You'll be all right, Dawn," he said. "And if things get hard, you call the operator and have them send me to your house, okay? I promise I'll leave anything I'm in the middle of and come running. Cross my heart."

She took a deep breath and tightened her jaw, turning to look at him. She nodded, and he saw the strength in her eyes. "You know what you told me today? I love you too."

With that, she threw open her door and jumped out before he could think to come around and open it for her. She marched up the sidewalk, pushed through the front door, and started to shut it. But at the last second, the door opened wider again, and she smiled out and gave him a little wave.

And then Dawn vanished into her gray house, in her little gray world.

In the morning, Coal got two phone calls, almost back-to-back. The first was from Flo Hawkins, who sounded like she had just woken up. Apparently during the night William Verret and Horace Teal had gone to a bar fight at the Owl Club, and in the process of sorting out suspects after the fight, one of them ended up having a warrant for his arrest out of Hamilton, Montana. Verret and Teal let the police in Hamilton know they had a prisoner for them, but that morning the police chief had called dispatch to say he had two officers out on sick leave, and he didn't have anyone he could send to pick up the prisoner. He wanted to talk to someone he could work arrangements out with, and of course that would be Coal.

Coal called the Hamilton police chief back, and it was decided that the City of Hamilton would pay mileage, plus fifty dollars and any meal costs, if Lemhi County could send someone to deliver the prisoner to Hamilton, rather than having to leave him in jail in Salmon.

The second call was from Dawn Kelly. Her voice was plaintive.

Sheriff Savage? I'm sorry for calling you at home. It's Dawn.

Coal pushed back a jolt of panic. "Hi. Are you okay?"

Yes, but . . . Is there any way I could spend the day with you today again? I'll do anything.

Coal started to come up with any reason she couldn't—the biggest reason being that she should be in school. But her voice sounded so delicate, almost wounded. He couldn't turn her down. That was also when he decided to take the transport to Hamilton himself.

"Sure, Dawn," he said. "We'll make another day trip of it, because I have to go to Hamilton with a prisoner anyway. But only on one condition."

What is it?

"Two conditions, actually. The first is you have to go to school tomorrow. The second is you might as well start calling me Coal full time. Deal?"

The voice on the other end of the line was full of warmth and gratitude. *Deal . . . Coal.*

Coal picked Dawn up at her house again. This time her mother was back in her room asleep—with or without company, Dawn didn't bother to find out—and she came running out of the house when Coal pulled up. They drove down to the jail, and this time it was Chief Dan George who let Coal in when he knocked at the basement door.

"You don't go anywhere for weeks, and then it all hits at once, right?" said George, chuckling. "Let's go back and get your prisoner."

The prisoner, a man named Craig Luger, was a scrawny blond man with a red beard, wanted for burglarizing a gun store in Hamilton, then robbing two stores with the gun he stole. He wasn't smiley or talkative, but at least he seemed complacent, as if he knew he had already enjoyed more freedom than he deserved.

As Coal was leading Luger out in handcuffs, he happened to look over at Joe Teton. The light was bad in the cell block, but if Coal's eyes weren't playing tricks on him, Teton's face seemed to be wreathed in bruises.

Glancing over at the far cell, Coal saw the crazy fat man sleeping on his cot, so he didn't say anything until they got back out into the lobby. The last thing he wanted to do was wake that strange man.

"What the hell happened to Teton?"

Dan George stared at Coal. "What's that?"

"Teton. He looks like he got in a bar fight."

"I'm not sure what you mean. That's not how he looked when you brought him?"

"No," said Coal, a dark cloud growing inside him. "It isn't. He was fine when I brought him. There wasn't a mark on him, in fact."

"Well, shoot, Coal! I don't know then. Nobody said one word to me. There's not a note around, report—anything."

"Please do some checking into it," Coal said. "Maybe I should take him up to the courthouse if he's going to get that kind of treatment here." He didn't want to sound angry, but he couldn't help it. He hadn't known Joe Teton long, but from what he had seen, he seriously doubted the man would have done anything to invite someone to beat him—and beat him they sure enough had.

"I'll be stopping back in here when I get back from Hamilton," said Coal. "I'll expect some answers."

"Sure thing—Sheriff." The chief's entire tone had changed. Apparently, he didn't like other officers sounding threatening toward him. But Coal didn't like having his prisoners beaten for no reason. So they were even.

Coal turned with his prisoner and headed up the stairs, and Chief George didn't attempt to follow him up and give him any help loading the man, as was the usual custom.

When Coal sat back down in his seat, he looked over at Dawn. He wanted to growl about what he had seen, but the girl had enough on her plate.

Craig Luger's scratchy, almost whiny-sounding voice came suddenly from the back seat. "You really wanna know what happened to that Injun? I was there for the whole thing."

Coal backed out of his spot, swung around in the lot, and pulled out onto the street. He wanted to be out of Salmon before he heard this story.

They were passing the Shady Nook Inn, heading out on Highway 93, when Coal finally looked at Craig Luger again in the rearview mirror.

"Sorry to make you wait, Luger, but I'm ready now. What happened to Joe Teton?"

Craig gave Coal a broken-toothed smile. "Well, apparently, that's how the cops in Salmon get guys to sign confessions when they don't like to cooperate."

CHAPTER FIFTY-EIGHT

Coal had been wise to wait until he was almost out of the city limits to hear Craig Luger begin his story. As the story unfolded, at least the story according to a man who didn't seem to have a thing to gain by lying, *or* by speaking the truth, after William Verret and Horace Teal brought Luger to the jail and booked him, Verret went over and began harassing Teton verbally. He kept telling him what a lowlife he was for being willing to let someone else take the blame for his crime, and saying how if he had his way he would get every detail of the murders from him and not spend one dime on any attorney the taxpayers would be required to pay for.

Teton stayed silent, refusing even to look at the two reserve officers. Coal knew from his experience with the Shoshone that was exactly how he would deal with them. Unfortunately, William Verret got louder and louder, and seemed to take great offense at Teton's "haughty Injun attitude", as he called it.

Finally, he went into Teton's cell and began pushing him around. Even a peaceable man can be pushed too far, and apparently Teton was, for according to Luger's story, Teton threw the first punch, sending William Verret sprawling.

After that, the gloves were off. Horace Teal came raging into the cell with his club, and he and Verret "took care of business", as they called it later when telling Luger and the other inmate to keep their mouths shut about what had happened. When it was all said and done, the two men decided since they had already "softened the Injun up" that they should also try to get him to sign a confession. According to Luger, that was another "smashing success".

As soon as they had their signed confession, the two reserves left the jail, and that was the last time Luger saw them.

Coal's chest felt like it was on fire. He was plowing along the river road, bearing down on the turn-off going up Lost Trail Pass, when Dawn Kelly's cool head reined him in.

"Coal? Do you know you're going that fast?"

He looked down at his speedometer, to see they were going seventy-five, along a road he normally wouldn't take at that speed even when the pavement was clear.

Letting off the gas, he reached over and gave Dawn's hand a squeeze, then patted it. "Thanks, Dawn. Dang. You might really have to keep an eye on me today, all right? As long as you're riding shotgun on this coach." He tried to grin, hoping to relieve some of the tension in the car.

"It's okay. I don't blame you for being upset. I can tell you like Mr. Teton."

That comment put a surprising lump in Coal's throat. Dawn was right—he actually did like that Shoshone. One of the hardest things he would do in this job would be getting on the stand to testify against him. And one of the most pleasurable would be trying to get Horace Teal and William Verret brought up on charges.

It was another idyllic day, as far as weather around the area went in February. It actually climbed clear up into the fifties, an almost unheard-of feat. Coal, Dawn, and Craig Luger had the music of James Taylor, Simon and Garfunkel, Karen Carpenter, and Creedence Clearwater Revival to listen to as they went up over the pass, then down the other side into Montana, watching the snowbanks that had been plowed to the sides of the road melt and run down the asphalt in rivulets and tiny little rivers.

They dropped the prisoner off at the Hamilton jail, where the chief of police paid Coal a bigger amount than Coal had been expecting, mostly because the man said as long as Coal had a shotgun guard, they had to make sure and feed her well. Afterward, Coal and Dawn ended up eating at a nice little roadside café, and the burgers and fries were as good as Coal had eaten anywhere. Finally, they started back toward Salmon, and Dawn Kelly leaned over and fell asleep almost instantly against Coal's shoulder.

They were passing North Fork when the emergency call came in for a wreck out on Highway 93, toward Challis. Coal heard Jordan tell dispatch he copied the call and that he had Deputy Fairbourne with him. He also heard the state officer, Gentry, respond from west of Tendoy and head that way.

As Coal heard the ambulance go out he decided to keep the speed limit all the way back into town, partly not to endanger Dawn, and partly because he was flat-out worn out and figured three cops and an ambulance could handle whatever they were going to find at the wreck down the river.

Then the radio crackled open again, and he heard Jordan Peterson's voice. *Deputy Peterson to Sheriff. Sheriff, you out there?*

Coal reached down and grabbed the mic. Dawn had come awake during all the radio traffic, so he didn't have to disturb her while he was moving around. "This is the sheriff. Go ahead, Jordan."

Hey, Coal, check your desk when you get in. There's a bunch of paperwork on there that you should read through right away.

"Will do. What's it in reference to, Jordan?"

Umm . . . Better not say over the air, boss, came back Jordan's reply. *But we'll get back there as soon as we can and meet with you. Road's getting pretty windy. I'd better clear. Peterson out.*

Feeling antsy, Coal pushed down a little harder on the gas pedal, then waited to see if Dawn would mention it. This time he was only going ten over the speed limit, and she said nothing.

They were almost back to town when the radio airwaves opened up again, and this time it was Flo's voice. *Salmon to sheriff's car. Sheriff, do you copy me?*

Dawn reached down and took the mic off the hook, handing it to Coal, who thanked her. "This is the sheriff."

Coal, I just took a call from a gentleman down in the Sho-Ban village who said he's a friend of yours? A Mr. Darnell?

"Yes, Flo. We're friends."

Well, he needs you to go to his house directly when you get back in town, if you're able. He said he has some very important information for you.

Coal grunted. It seemed like suddenly just about *everything* was important. "Flo? He didn't say what it was about, I take it."

No, sir. He said he would only speak to you.

"Copy," said Coal with a sigh. "I'll head that way. Sheriff out."

Coal turned to Dawn, with a half grin. "Well, you wanted to have a ride with the sheriff. I guess you get the whole tamale today."

"It's okay," she said. "It's kind of fun."

Smiling at the innocence of a girl who thought things like this were fun and exciting, Coal pulled up to the stop sign, waited for a string of cars to pass, then turned left onto Main. Within three minutes after that, they were pulling up in front of the Darnell shack. There was a long, faded blue Cadillac parked in front that Coal hadn't seen here before.

When Coal knocked, the chunky-faced Renée answered the door, but a mid-thirties Indian man came up behind her. "I'm Henry," he said. "Renée's husband. Heard a lot about you, Savage."

Coal shook the man's outstretched hand, waving as if on an afterthought at Buck Darnell, who was at his usual station on the couch.

"Good to meet you, Henry. So . . . what's up?"

"You got the wrong man for the murder." Statements don't come much more succinct than that.

"What?" said Coal. "How's that again?"

"Joe Teton. He ain't the guy."

"I'm sorry, but every bit of evidence points to him, and he admitted to the killings. Besides, he took off and ran with his two boys. He had to be chased down in Pocatello."

"No, I'm sorry, Savage, but I think you gotta listen. The man you want is a guy named Rowdy Yates."

Coal stared at Henry, trying to decide if he should laugh. Was this guy pulling his leg? Rowdy Yates was a well-known name to anyone who had ever spent any amount of time watching TV Westerns. A young actor by the name of Clint Eastwood played the part, on a series called *Rawhide*.

From off to the side, Buck Darnell said loudly, "Just like on the TV, huh, Savage?"

Coal smiled over at Buck. "Just like that." He looked back at Henry and Renée. "So what's the catch? You're kidding me, right?"

"No. Hey, I know it sounds nuts, man, but I'm talkin' about some crazy dude. I don't know what the guy's real name is, but he calls himself Rowdy Yates. Right? I know the city cops know him."

Finally realizing that Henry was being straight with him, or at least believed he was, Coal said, "Okay. Well, what else can you tell me? How do you know any of this?"

"How? 'Cause he's been goin' around tellin' everybody. I guess that Sherman dude shot his dog one day, right in front of him, and he yelled he was gonna kill him."

"That's it?" said Coal. "A lot of people claim they're going to kill somebody, but most of them are just talking in anger."

"No, man, but that's just it—he's been tellin' everybody he actually went and did it! Says he was up there that night by the cemetery, followed those two home an' everything. Said he's just been bidin' his time, and that night the time was right. I'm sorry, man, but that's his story! I heard about it all day at work. You got the wrong guy if you think Teton did it."

"Tell me more about this Yates guy," said Coal. Of course he couldn't believe any of this, but Henry was so adamant, how did he simply shrug him off? And besides, in spite of everything, he really wished somebody could give him something to convince him that Joe Teton really wasn't guilty.

"He lives not too far that way from the village," said Henry, pointing toward town. "I'm not sure exactly where, but that Wilson cop knows him. I seen him talkin' to him before." Henry lifted both his hands to the sides in an expansive shrug. "I'm just tellin' ya, Savage, this dude is braggin' everywhere that he did that killin', an' he seems like he's got an awful lot of details about it."

"All right, Henry. Thanks for the tip," said Coal. He waved over at Buck Darnell. "Good to see you again, Buck. Renée." He touched his hat brim and stepped to the door. "If I need anything else, I'll stop back by."

Expecting absolutely nothing from this bizarre tip, Coal got back in his car and looked at Dawn. "Okay, we've got a weird one, Dawn. If I get a chance later, I'll tell you the whole story." Picking up the mic, he called, "Officer Wilson, Lemhi Sheriff. Bob, are you on the air?"

He called one more time, and then Bob's voice came over the line. "Hey, Bob—you anywhere near the office?"

Pretty near it, replied Bob. *I'm* in *it.*

"Stay there. I need to talk to you about something. I'll be there in two."

Coal sped over to City Hall, and Dawn didn't try to stop him from breaking the law this time. She seemed to be in her glory, getting more out of this day than she had likely planned for. Coal took Dawn and went down the basement stairs, where Bob Wilson opened the door and let them in.

"Bob, I smell coffee," said Coal. "I am in dire need of a good cup of coffee."

"Well, sorry, Coal. I guess you'll just have to settle for ours instead. You won't call it good."

Coal laughed. "I don't care. Just give me something hot."

"Hey! Let me outta here, fuzz!" came a screaming voice from the cell block.

Bob turned from pouring coffee and glared at Coal, his jaw hardening. "Coal, I swear I'm going to take that guy down to the river and baptize him three times and bring him up twice."

Coal laughed. "What's his deal?"

"Hey! Hey! *Hey!* I'm gonna kill you all if you don't unlock this door!" This time the man's proclamation was punctuated by a bunch of fearsome curse words that would make a county sheriff proud.

"Rowdy! Shut the hell up, or I *will* come let you out."

Coal stared at Bob. "What? Did you just call him Rowdy?"

Bob shook his head in disgust. "That kook thinks he's Rowdy Yates, Coal. Straight off a cattle drive. Heaven help me, I'm gonna shoot him if this keeps up."

"So . . . that's the guy who thinks he's Rowdy Yates?" repeated Coal. "Bob, that's exactly the guy I came here to talk to you about. Do you know he's going around claiming he's the one who killed Sherman and the girl?"

It was Bob Wilson's turn to stare. When he found his tongue again, his almost black eyes shot toward the cellblock, then returned to Coal. "Who the heck told you that?"

"Some friends in the Sho-Ban village. Buck Darnell's son-in-law, Henry."

"Huh? Henry Tendoy?"

"I guess, if that's his last name. His wife's Renée?"

"Sure! Yeah, Henry Tendoy. He told you Rowdy Yates is claiming he did the murders? Hold on—*not* Rowdy Yates. His real name is Shea Irvine."

"Okay—Rowdy Yates, Shea Irvine—whatever. Yes, that's what Henry said."

"Come on," said Bob, and he turned and went to the cellblock door, pulled out his keys, and opened it. He threw the door wide and let Coal in in front of him, seeming to completely forget Dawn. To the girl, that oversight seemed as good as permission, so she slipped in behind them.

"Rowdy," growled Bob. "Did you kill those two people up by the cemetery?" Nothing like a direct question.

Shea Irvine, a.k.a Rowdy Yates, stared Bob Wilson down, then suddenly started to laugh maniacally. "You finally figured it out!" His voice was now almost a shrill scream. "You finally figured it out! I killed 'em! I'd kill 'em again! He shot my dog!" Irvine screamed again. "Killed 'im, right in front of me! Shot my dog! Shot 'im! *Shot 'im!*"

"Rowdy, stop!"

"He shot my dog, an' nobody else would do NOTHIN'! He killed my *dog!*" By now, Shea Irvine had hold of the jail bars, and he was leaping up and down like a gorilla on PCP.

Coal glanced around and saw Dawn Kelly. She looked like a volcano had erupted in the middle of Main Street, right before her eyes.

"Dawn, maybe you should go out," Coal said. "I'll be out in a bit."

"He killed my dog! He killed him!" Shea Irvine started screaming again.

Bob turned around and left the holding area, returning with his can of mace. He raised it up and pointed it straight at Irvine's face. "Shut up, Rowdy, or I'm going to empty this entire can on you."

Shea Irvine froze, staring at Bob and shaking all over. "You can spray me, you can beat me, you can shoot me," he said in a subdued voice, the muscles of his bare torso quivering. "But you'll never take back from me what I did. What I had the *right* to do!"

CHAPTER FIFTY-NINE

As Coal stared at Shea Irvine, almost mesmerized by the man's psychotic display, he heard a sound off to his left, and looked over to see Joe Teton standing there staring out. Teton was completely quiet, standing with bruises all over his face, a badly swollen lip, and one eye closed almost all the way over.

"Don't listen to him, Savage," said Teton in his normal soft voice, except it was hard to understand him when he had to speak with a lip so badly swollen. "He's nuts. He didn't do it. He has no idea what he's talkin' about."

Shea Irvine drew in a huge lungful of air, obviously preparing to start screaming again. He halted mid-blow when Bob Wilson's arm came out straight again, the spray nozzle aimed right at his face.

"Rowdy," said Bob in a low, menacing voice. "Don't you dare make one more sound."

Coal turned and walked over to Joe Teton, looking him up and down. "Look at you, Teton! You're a mess. Did anybody take you to the hospital to have the doctor check you out?"

"I don't need no doctor, Savage. I'm a warrior."

"Yeah, you look it, too. Listen, Teton, you don't have to say anything more. And I would suggest you don't."

"No matter. I signed a confession with them other two deputies already."

"You did *what?* Did they offer you to have an attorney here? Did they—" Coal stopped mid-sentence. He was so furious he knew he shouldn't say another word.

"Did you hear this, Bob?"

"I did." Bob's voice was noncommittal, but that didn't mean a whole lot, because Bob Wilson had always been expert at not letting people know exactly what was on his mind.

After trying to decipher Bob's code for a few seconds, Coal spun back to Joe Teton. "You said you signed a confession. Where is it?"

"They took it when they left."

"Did you fight them? Why did they do this?"

"I guess I got mad. I hit one of 'em."

"Aw, Teton! Damn it! Why?"

"Sometimes a warrior has to fight."

"But a warrior doesn't have to stand up for some nut he doesn't even know. Do you know this guy down here? Shea Irvine?"

"I have seen him around."

"That's all? Seen him around? Teton, he's telling us he killed those two people. Why would he say that if he didn't do it?"

"Because he is crazy. Just let it go. Let it go, Savage. You don't need to work so hard."

Frustrated beyond any further ability to speak to Joe Teton, Coal turned back on Bob. "You know something? With how Joe looks right now, and when I testify and the Pocatello PD testifies how he looked when he came in here, it's not going to take even half a lawyer to get his confession thrown out. You know that, right? Those two rented cops of yours might have thrown this entire case in the toilet, no matter which one of these guys did it."

Bob shrugged. He always looked a little on the angry side. That's how his face was made. But right now it looked to Coal like

Bob really was working up to being angry, if only out of pure frustration. Seeing that, Coal threw up the white flag, and his hands.

"I'm going, Bob. I'll take Teton with me—just in case."

"In case of what?"

It was Coal's turn to start feeling angry again. "You're joking, right? As long as you have those two clowns for reserve officers, *nobody* is safe in this jail."

Without another word from Bob, Coal walked over and plucked the keys out of his hand, went to Joe Teton's cell, and opened it. He threw the keys back to Bob, then put his cuffs on Teton without any struggle and led him back out into the main office. Her face still looking drained of blood, Dawn Kelly stood against the far wall, staring at the cellblock door. Coal was a little surprised she was still here.

"Come on, Dawn. I have to go up to our own jail, okay? I'll get you back home as soon as I can. I promise."

Nodding, she came to him, and they went out, up the stairs and got loaded in the still-running Thunderbird. Coal drove back to the courthouse, all the while trying to calm his heart back to normal.

"I'm sorry about all this garbage, Dawn," he told the girl when he was parked at the jail. "It really isn't like this very often. This is just a bad case. You can stay out here if you don't feel like going in the jail with me."

"It's okay," she replied. "I'd rather be with you."

So the three of them marched down into the jail, and Coal put Joe Teton in a cell. He locked the door, but before walking away, he said, "As soon as I drop the girl off back home, I'll come back and get you and we'll go have a doctor look you over."

"No, Savage. No doctor."

"You look like hell, Teton."

"So? I've looked a whole lot worse than this before."

Coal stepped out, and as he did he saw the outer door open, and William Verret and Horace Teal stepped inside. Teal hung back a little, but Verret swaggered right up to Coal, holding out a piece of paper.

"I got a present for you, Sheriff."

"What is it?"

"Signed confession from your prisoner. To both murders."

Coal was near a boiling point. "And it took you both to walk it down here? Well, then again, I guess it took you both to beat the hell out of that old soldier too."

Verret's face was always hard-looking, but when Coal's tone and words registered on him, the officer's eyes narrowed, and he stopped chewing his gum, or whatever was in his mouth.

"You ain't man enough to say anything like that to me when you aren't on duty."

"Try me." Reaching up, Coal slowly unpinned his badge. "Dawn? Go out to my car."

Dawn didn't move, and Coal looked over at her. "Dawn?"

"I'm not going to go. I'm sorry. What if you need a witness?"

William Verret suddenly laughed, but it was a forced sound. "He just needs a nursemaid," he said. "He don't want to fight me in the first place."

"The fight isn't just with you, Verret." Coal's gaze was cold. "I fight you both together, or neither one."

Teal grunted off to the side. "Hey, man! No, I didn't say I wanted any part of this."

"It sounds like you wanted a part when you had a club, and you both had an old man in a jail cell."

"I'm not losin' my job over a squabble," Teal replied. "You ever want a fight with me, you're gonna have to go somewhere way out in the county. I'm not fightin' you right here in the jail. No, sir."

Coal looked back at Verret. "It looks like the fight's already over."

"Damn lucky for you."

Coal almost wanted to laugh. Verret and Teal had no idea what they had just avoided. He reached out his hand, snapping his fingers. Verret handed the signed confession to Coal, who looked down on it and saw that it was the original. Looking up at Verret, he tore the paper into four pieces, then leaned over to let them flutter down into the garbage can.

Verret's face went red, and he started to take a step closer, balling a fist. "Oh, real smart, Sheriff. Real smart. Now somebody's gonna have to do it all over again."

"Maybe next time it will even be admissible in court," Coal replied. "Now get out of this office, and don't dare set a foot in here again."

"I'll be lookin' for you when you ain't on duty," said Verret, backing away. "Just you, an' me."

"I wouldn't waste energy on just one of you. Get!"

Coal looked over at Dawn. She was shaking. He walked to her and wrapped her in his arms. "I'm really sorry, Dawn. Most cops usually like each other. It usually isn't like this, but those guys are a couple of real bad eggs, especially the one with the big mustache. I just wish you didn't have to see that."

The door swung suddenly open. Coal looked over to see none other than Hunter Jack standing there.

"Badger! What in the world are you doing back here?" He let go of Dawn Kelly. "As bad as you hate this place, I thought you'd be long gone."

"Uh." Dark Badger almost smiled at him. "Well, I owe you, Savage. So I brought you a gift. Some jerky I made from a big elk."

The Shoshone walked close, holding out a paper bag. Coal reached out and accepted the gift and looked inside. "That looks really good, Badger. Thank you. I sure thought you'd be down the river on your traps by now."

"No. I'm headin' down there, but I wanted to give you that first."

"Hey, I have to take Dawn home pretty soon," said Coal. "You interested in going downtown for a drink later? And I'm not joking, either. I won't drink a lot, but I could use at least one stiff one after a day like this."

"Uh. If you're serious, then yes."

Coal nodded. "Then you're on. Let me look over some stuff my deputy set out here for me real quick, all right? There are some magazines over there, if you like to read. Dawn?" He looked over at the girl. "I'll make this super fast."

Sitting down, he flipped on the lamp and started sliding the papers around that Grant or Jordan had stacked in the middle of his desk.

The first thing he noticed was a piece of notepad paper that had been scotch-taped to the top of a page. The note said simply:

Coal, make sure you look at this stuff and see what you think. We can hash it out when I get back
— Grant

That was pretty much what Jordan had told him by radio, so as Coal had suspected, Jordan was only relaying a message from Grant because he was the one with the radio.

Reaching out, almost absent-mindedly, Coal took a piece of jerky from the bag Badger had given him and chewed off a piece. This stuff was good! He lifted the remainder up to Badger in a little salute of gratitude. "Good stuff, my friend."

Badger nodded, making a satisfied face. "Glad you like it. For what you did for me, I will make you more any time."

Coal returned his attention to the papers, carefully peeling away the scotch tape and starting to read.

Coal, I hope these notes make sense. I'm just trying to gather my wits and put all of this in order.

Got some strange leads today. Don't know if they mean anything, but I'll list it all in order so we can go over it.

1- *Cherry Bales called—the bail bonds lady—and said she thought of something weird after she was here. She said she went to H. Jack's house to take him some paperwork, and she saw his doorframe was all busted up, and H.J. said he locked himself out quite a while ago and had to break in. But he called in a break-in later, didn't he? Maybe I'm confusing my facts.*
2- *Bocek came by from the Fish and Game to see if H.J. was still here in jail because he has to talk to him, possibly with a citation? He said H.J. isn't checking his traps? Or at least not all of them. Bocek says that's part of the permit—to check the traps periodically? Some guy had to shoot a bobcat a few days ago in one of H.J.'s traps way down the river. Said it had been in the trap for a few days before that. I thought H.J. said after he bailed out that he went downriver and worked all his traps. Weird, right?*

By this point in the narrative, Coal was beyond the head-scratching stage. The notes were actually making him start to feel nervous. Those two discrepancies seemed hard to explain. But until he finished reading everything, he wasn't going to bring it up to Badger. There had to be some simple explanation. He moved on to the next number on the list.

3- *This next one is pretty alarming. Not sure I can make a whole lot of sense out of it, but I guess I'll wait to get your take on it. So Wilson took a call from that guy Burt Landry? The one that had his car stolen and run into the river? I guess B.L. was picking up a sheet of plywood that got blown over in a windstorm out by the side of his house, and he found a way clearer track that hadn't been disturbed. Wilson called me over, and we called in some friend of yours—Trax Hansen? He did a lot of looking around, and it sounds like the car thief came up from down along the river, not from the street like we thought. That track was really pretty small, and made by somebody either in moccasins or their socks. Didn't you tell me H.J. only ever wears moccasins? Anyway, Hansen wanted to go down to where the car went in the river, so we took a drive down there, and he located some more of what could be the same tracks, walking back toward town from where the car went in the river. I took pictures. Looks like maybe he was walking the road but had to step off into the snow when cars passed him or something? Just a guess, but me and Hansen thought the same thing.*

Coal's mind was racing. He looked back over everything one more time, hating the feeling of being distracted when he had Badger and Dawn Kelly right there. He thought about Joe Teton. Every little piece of evidence and testimony pointed to him as the murderer—didn't it? And although he had signed his statement about committing the murders only under duress, he still had signed it. And he hadn't gone back on the statement, even when he was away from Verret and Teal, and should have felt protected. In fact, during the entire time he had been under investigation, he never once had tried to defend himself or present any kind of alibi.

Coal stared at Grant's notes until they started to blur. Finally, he looked over at Dark Badger. He was slumped into a chair, looking quite relaxed as his bulk dwarfed the chair, his fingers laced together in his lap, his ankles crossed out in front of him. His dark eyes were zeroed in on Coal, and his lips were curved up in what almost could have been called a smile, beneath his thin, downward-bowed mustache.

Their eyes held for several seconds. Suddenly, Badger's narrowed, almost imperceptibly except Coal was looking too closely to miss it. The big Shoshone drew his feet back a little, and his laced fingers started to separate. Furrowing his brow, Coal looked over at Dawn. She was quiet, leafing through some hunting or shooting sports magazine, probably bored out of her mind.

Coal got up. "Hey, guys, I'll be right back. I have to go say something to Teton really quick."

Taking the keys, and Grant's notes, he went back into the cellblock, opened Teton's cell as he sat on his bunk eyeing him, and stopped in front of him. He was easily within striking distance of Teton, but he felt no danger from him.

"Can I just call you Joe?" Coal asked.

Teton shrugged. "Sure, I guess. Don't much matter."

"All right. Joe. You know you're allowed to have a lawyer—right?"

"Yes."

"You know you don't have to say a word about anything, but if you do I can record it and use it in court—right?"

"Yes."

"Do you want a lawyer?"

"Uh-uh."

"You're positive."

"Yes, sir, Savage. Positive."

"Okay, then I want to ask you something. I've never really heard you come right out and admit you killed those people. So . . . did you put a spear in Everett Sherman and a knife or another spear in Irene Boyer?"

Joe Teton kept trying to meet Coal's gaze. Finally, he shrugged, but it was several seconds after the question. "You have all the evidence, Savage. And everything people said they saw."

"I'm asking you a yes or no question. Did you kill them?"

Teton stared him down until Coal caught a little flicker in his eyes. "Savage. I told you what I told you."

Coal was frozen in place. It felt like electricity was running all up and down his body, and everything in his brain started to become ultra-clear, ultra-sensitive, as if he were on some kind of strange drug. He felt his mouth twitch underneath his mustache before he spoke.

"Joe, you didn't kill those two people at all, did you? You're just a loyal friend—taking the fall."

Joe Teton's lips started to move, as if he was going to speak. Then they closed softly. Coal wondered if Joe even realized he was slowly, almost imperceptibly, nodding his head.

"Son of a—" Coal stopped mid-curse. He felt numb all over. He didn't bother to re-lock Joe Teton's cell door when he turned around, rolled Grant's notes, and put them in his back pocket.

Walking to the cellblock door, he looked out the window. Hunter Jack was gone. And so was Dawn Kelly.

CHAPTER SIXTY

Coal had no time to tell himself how stupid he had been. He had no time for anything but to act. Pushing back his panic, he shoved through the door and headed for the rifle rack.

He was two steps from the rack when it hit him that the chain was hanging free, and one of the rifles was gone. Had it been that way when he came in? Had Grant or Jordan taken a rifle and forgot to lock the chain again?

"Everything good, Savage?"

At the sound of the voice, Coal whirled, his hand going instinctively to his gun. There, standing against the wall where he had been hidden by the cellblock door, stood Dark Badger. He had an arm locked around the upper chest of Dawn Kelly, who stood in front of him with a panicked face, and tears rolling down her cheeks.

"Badger! Let her go!" Coal barked.

"Damn," said Badger, scoffing softly. "I was sure hopin' I was wrong. Hopin' I was wrong readin' that look in your face. You white men. Too easy to read you. What was in them papers, anyhow?"

Coal straightened out of his crouch. "Notes from my investigator. You lied about somebody breaking in your house."

"They didn't have to break in, but somebody still stole one of my lances."

"Right. I figured that out." Coal purposely forced himself not to look at Dawn. He couldn't bear to see the panic in her face. But still he spoke to her. "It'll be okay, Dawn. I promise. Badger wouldn't hurt you."

The girl didn't reply, and Badger's eyes didn't flicker. Coal pushed the thought of Irene Boyer out of his mind—Irene Boyer, who had died simply because she was "there".

"You didn't get to all your traps after you left here," Coal said. "You stayed in Salmon long enough to kill Everett Sherman, and then you stole a car to get you downriver fast so it looked like you had left right away. But you didn't get to the end of your trapline, did you? Because the biggest hole in the river was this side of the end of your line, and you had to have a place to sink that car. Then you hoofed it back for town."

Badger had started edging toward the door, inches at a time. Coal tried to ignore the shiny blade of the knife the big Shoshone had pressed to Dawn's throat, while the rifle was slung over his shoulder by its sling.

"That car was a pile of junk," said Badger.

"Sure is now," agreed Coal. "So let me ask you something: I guess it was okay for you to let your friend take the fall for you, huh?"

"Joe? He chose that."

"Chose how?"

"He's the one that followed me up there. I never asked him to."

"He followed you up there and what?"

"He told me to run. He thought I was too drunk to be no good to him. He said he would cover everything up for me so nobody could tell I was there. Said he could get away before anybody knew. So I let him. And I left."

"You mean you ran. You were all right to let your friend take all the chances."

Coal was aware that the cellblock door was opening, and he knew without turning around that Joe Teton was now standing there beyond his right shoulder.

"He took chances because he chose to. No white man could understand how a Injun feels." His eyes moved off behind Coal. "Hey—Joe. Put his cuffs on him."

Badger was nearly to the door, his arm still around Dawn's upper chest, and the blade of his knife pushing against her throat. Coal half expected at any moment to see blood start flowing.

"Where are the cuffs?" Teton asked, his voice noncommittal.

Coal let out a long breath. "In the bottom right drawer, Joe. But you can still get free of this. Don't let him take you any farther down with him."

"I already made my choices," said Joe Teton.

Walking to the desk, he opened the drawer. He stared into it for a long time, while Coal didn't dare look at him. Leaning way low, Joe fidgeted around in the drawer, then leaned farther down to straighten the bottom of a pant leg that seemed to have ridden up over the top of his boot. He stood up straight, turning with the handcuffs in his hand.

He walked around behind Coal. "Give me your hands."

Coal put his hands around behind him. He felt the first cuff close around his left wrist, and he cringed. He had felt handcuffs before, in practice and training. He had never worn them as a prisoner.

Joe Teton took Coal's right hand and raised it toward the left one. Coal heard the sound of the cuff as the teeth on one side engaged with the pawl on the other—closing, but not over his wrist! Teton placed the closed cuff into Coal's half-open fist.

Coal saw movement in the parking lot and looked up to see a brown pickup pull in, and then his green GMC behind it. He could tell Teton was looking too.

"You got company, Badger," said Joe Teton, his voice level.

Dark Badger's eyes sharpened. "Who?"

"Looks like them deputies, Grant and Jordan."

Dark Badger's eyes didn't change, but his face seemed to harden. "Take Savage's gun, then come open the door and tell them we got the girl," he told Teton. "Tell them to put down their guns and come in here."

After some hesitation, Teton slipped Coal's Smith and Wesson from the holster and walked across the room. As Badger side-stepped away from the door, tugging Dawn along with him, the other Shoshone opened the door.

"Hey. Don't come no closer," he said. "Put down your guns, because if you don't, Jack's gonna kill this girl—and Savage."

Coal could only see the lower legs of his deputies, but he could see that both men froze. Teton looked over at Badger. "They stopped, but they ain't puttin' their guns down."

"Open the door bigger. Let Savage tell them."

Teton did as told, opening the door, then looking back toward Coal. Coal yelled out. "Grant! Jordan! Get back in your rigs and go!"

"No!" barked Dark Badger, raising his voice for the first time. "Tell 'em put down their guns!"

"Wait!" Coal yelled. "Boys, you need to put your guns on the ground first."

Coal saw the faces of his deputies for the first time as they both bent low to set their pistols on the asphalt.

"Now tell them to back over by them trucks. But don't get in. I want to see them when I go out."

Coal passed on the instruction to Grant and Jordan, then let his eyes fall to Dawn's face for the first time. "Please don't worry, Dawn. Badger wouldn't hurt you," he said again.

But he didn't even believe it himself. Badger would do anything Badger had to do to stay out of a cage, including letting his best friend be thrown into a pit—or murdering an innocent girl.

Coal had free hands now, but he had nothing else. And he was fifteen feet away from Dark Badger. He had seen Teton slip the hideaway pistol out that he kept in the drawer with his spare cuffs, and Teton had put it down in his boot. That was exactly as he hoped, because he was banking everything on Joe Teton being on his side, if only to help Dawn Kelly. When Teton failed to put the right handcuff on him, it proved his trust in the man. But at the last second Badger took his hope away when he told Teton to take the pistol from his holster. Now Teton had both guns. That meant everything from here to the end was in his hands.

And Joe Teton had a friendship riding on this outcome—a friendship he had already proven willing to throw his own freedom away for.

On a whim, Coal started to move closer to Badger, hoping to close the gap before the Shoshone thought much about the distance between them. Outside, he could see his deputies had backed away, and both of them stood against the green GMC.

Everything now rested on the shoulders of Joe Teton, a man who had taken his boys and given them up to someone else to raise. A man, as the Bible spoke of, had been willing to lay down his life for his friend.

"Give me the gun," said Badger to Teton, as he lowered his knife hand to put the knife back in the sheath at his waist. Teton hesitated, apparently too long. "Give it to me!" Badger growled.

Slowly, Teton raised the .44, placing it into Badger's open hand. The man's entire body looked tense. He was doing Badger's bidding, but his body language said it was all against his will.

Badger looked over at Savage.

"Savage? You been good to me. Very good. I wish none of this was this way."

This part, Coal believed. At least he could have that much satisfaction—Dark Badger actually had been grateful for how Coal had treated him. If new evidence hadn't come to light, he was sure the two of them would have remained friends, all while Joe Teton rotted his life away in the pen and never said one word.

Here was Joe Teton, who never had to help his friend in the first place. Could have let Badger take his own fall from the start. Then had a second chance at freedom when he could have let a total stranger, a crazy man who meant nothing to society, go to the pen for Badger on his own confession to the murders. Joe Teton, with two young boys he adored to raise, and yet he had been willing to give all that up, for the fear of seeing his fellow eagle spend perhaps a decade or more in a cage.

And then there was the friend, Dark Badger, willing to let his best friend take the fall for him and not say one word.

That man would kill Dawn Kelly. He would kill Coal Savage. He would do anything, kill anyone, if it meant staying out of prison.

Without warning, Joe Teton reached out and grabbed Dark Badger's wrist, shoving it skyward. Dawn, feeling herself released, threw herself to one side. With the reflexes of a rattlesnake, Badger brought that giant fist, the deadly fist that had killed a man before, down against the side of Joe Teton's head, as Coal was charging across the room, hands pumping.

Coal had hold of Badger's wrist now, and he slammed it back against the door. He stumbled over Joe Teton's prone body, but in going down he made Badger fold over with him. Desperately, unable to catch his balance because his feet were slipping around on Teton, who was trying to rise, Coal pulled Badger's wrist down, clamping his teeth over it and biting down hard.

Badger roared out, and Coal felt the revolver hit him on the bent thigh, then go clattering away across the floor. Again, he felt a wooden club to the side of his head, a wooden club he knew was only Badger's fist. His head reeled. He couldn't get his bearings. He went to both knees.

Badger hit him again, and Coal fell back. As he tried to open his eyes, he saw Teton curled up on the floor. Teton was out of the fight!

Coal saw Badger's legs as he started past him, making his way to where the .44 had fallen. Head still spinning, he managed to grab Badger's legs, and the man fell forward before he could reach the revolver. Coal heard the rifle strike the floor. Badger was struggling up, and he struck Coal again, making him release the hold he had on his legs.

Coal couldn't take another hit like that. But he couldn't let Badger get hold of Dawn again either, and the big Shoshone was in front of the door. Dawn had no escape!

With all his will, Coal drove upward, his legs feeling shaky. He and Badger came up as one, and Coal struck out. His fist landed square on Badger's nose, knocking him back against the door. He stepped back, trying to buy himself time while his head stopped whirling. He had to get his bearings, or he was no good in this fight!

Leaning back, Coal let loose with a side kick. It struck home, and Badger fell against the door again, but this time he had hold of Coal's lower leg with one arm, and he drove a fist into his knee.

Cringing, Coal fell back. He was trying to keep his eyes open against the pain, and he saw Dawn streak past Badger, toward the door. Oblivious of the girl, Badger staggered forward. Coal was on the ground, and the Shoshone was going to make the most of it. But so would Coal.

Using the leverage of his back against the floor, Coal drove both feet into Badger's midsection, hurling him backward. He was rolling over to push back up when he realized what he had done. Badger slammed against the door again, only this time Dawn Kelly was behind him, and the Indian's weight drove the air from her lungs, crushing her against the metal door.

Badger straightened up as Coal, short of breath and still dizzy, stood and waited for the Indian's next onslaught. Then, like a flash, Dawn stepped forward, and Coal dropped his eyes in time to see her whip the knife out of Badger's sheath. Badger felt it come out, and he whirled on the girl, but it was just as Coal lurched forward and landed his fist as hard as he could between Badger's shoulder blades.

Whirling and striking out with a roundhouse punch at the same time, Badger hit Coal in the side of his already damaged head. Coal was fighting a losing battle. He had been weakened from the start, he couldn't get his bearings, and the fight that should have been so easy for him was ending before it began.

Suddenly, Coal heard Badger let out a blood-curdling scream, and the Indian whirled around, toward the door. Cringing, crouched half over against the door, was Dawn Kelly, and as Coal's eyes came to focus he saw Badger's knife, protruding from his back.

"Badger!" Coal roared. "Leave the girl!"

Badger wasn't obeying any white man's order. He was only trying to defend himself when he whirled at the sound of Coal's voice. "You ain't got nothin' left, Savage," said the big man, and he was right. He lurched toward Coal.

The crash of the shot was deafening in the room, apparently to everyone but Badger. He kept coming for Coal, who backed up, blinking rapidly, trying to make his world stop spinning. Another shot thundered against the concrete of the floor and ceiling, against the cinder block walls.

This time Badger stopped, looking around, confused. His eyes fell toward the floor, where Joe Teton lay with both arms locked in front of him, Coal's hideaway gun in his hands.

Dark Badger, brother of the eagle, would never spend another day inside a cage.

Teton squeezed the trigger again, and Badger grunted loudly and looked down at his chest, then back at Joe Teton, his best friend. Perhaps his only friend.

Badger went to his knees. Joe Teton struggled up, holding the pistol in one hand now. Dawn, seeing her chance, scrambled around the edge of the room and made it to Coal, throwing her arms around him as she broke down sobbing.

The door burst open. Grant and Jordan came shoving inside, guns out. "Nobody move!" Grant yelled, his voice sounding more authoritative than Coal had ever heard it before.

But Badger moved. He moved only to slump forward onto his face, at the feet of Joe Teton, the man who had given his all to save Dark Badger from a cage.

CHAPTER SIXTY-ONE

After the coroner came and went from the jail, carting off the body of Dark Badger, Grant Fairbourne drove Coal, Dawn, and Joe Teton down to Steele Memorial in the Thunderbird, while Jordan followed them, so he could take Grant back to the courthouse.

Coal's head still didn't feel quite right. Dawn Kelly and Joe Teton were only there for him.

Annie Price was not on duty, but she came in because Dr. Levi Bent asked them to call her when he saw who his incoming patient was.

While Dawn and Joe Teton sat in the waiting room, as the light grew dim outside with the sun having sunk behind the mountains, Annie came hurrying down the hall to the room number they had given her, finding Coal inside, alone.

"Coal! What happened?" Annie's concern was etched over every fiber of her face. She rushed to him and grabbed his hand in both of hers.

Lying on the cot, Coal smiled up at her slightly blurred image. "Aw, hell, Annie. You won't believe me when I tell you."

"Do you want a bet? Try me."

He smiled again. "By the way—hi, good looking."

She grinned back at him, blinking at tears that came into her eyes. "Well, hi yourself."

Coal lay there silently praying for his head and his vision to return to normal and told Annie as much as he could recall of the scene at the jail. Throughout the story, her grip kept getting tighter and tighter, until he had to look down to see if his hand was in a vise.

"I never had a clue you had such a grip," he said.

She let off the pressure. "Sorry!"

He smiled again. "It's okay. I've been a little tense too."

"I'm sure you have! Hey—do you think Dawn will be all right? Or is she going to need to talk to somebody?" Coal had told Annie the story of Dawn's involvement in the killing of Westerlind's bull, and how she had only recently told him she would never be able to put a blade into another living thing again.

"I'm betting she'll need some counseling. That girl has been right through the mill," he said. "I doubt she'll ever want to go riding with a cop again. At least not *this* cop."

"Right! If she wants to ride with *any* cop, of course it will still be you." She stood there holding his hand, staring down at him, and he gazed back. It felt like his vision was slowly beginning to clear. "I'm glad Dr. Bent called me, Coal."

"Me too. I didn't even know he did."

She looked surprised. "Oh. I assumed you asked him to. I guess he knows me too well."

"I'm glad he does."

"Well, I'm going to go tell your two fans out there that you're able to talk, all right? And I'm going to go make you and me a cup of really black coffee—since I'm guessing you don't want me to run home and get that old bottle of Wild Turkey."

He laughed at that, thinking about her bottle, which would probably evaporate before anyone ever finished the last of it. "It's almost bedtime," he pointed out.

"I know, but I don't think you're going to sleep any time soon."

After Annie left the room, the door opened again within two minutes, and Joe Teton and Dawn filed in together. Dawn's face was drawn with worry. She stared at him for a few seconds until he raised his arm to her, his hand out. Then she went to him and took his hand. "Hey. You doing okay?"

She nodded. From her looks, the fear on her face, and the film of tears in her eyes, he guessed she was afraid to speak.

"I'll be all right," he said. "Thanks to you and Joe."

The girl turned and looked up at the Indian, who was watching Coal, but turned and gave her a little nod, and a blink of his eyes.

"I hope you'll go back to wherever you hid your boys, Joe. And bring them back here to Salmon. This place can't afford to lose a citizen like you."

"I'll be here, Savage. If you're gonna let me. But what about what I done?"

"It's over now. There was never any paperwork started on you with a charge of aiding and abetting anybody. Let's just let it go, shall we?"

"You sure? I know I made a bad choice."

"You were protecting a friend. You almost gave up your own freedom for that. I'm not going to punish you for being loyal."

Teton nodded. "Well . . . I guess I'll walk home."

"If you wait, I'll drive you."

"No. Thank you. I think I need to see what free air feels like."

After Joe had gone, Dawn crawled up on the bed beside Coal and put her arm across him. "I guess I can't come riding with you anymore, huh?" He could tell she was trying to sound brave, but her voice didn't support her.

"Oh, sure you can. But I want you back in school first. All right? At least for a few weeks."

She nodded, keeping her face down against his chest. "Thank you, Coal."

"Thank you. I know tonight was really hard on you."

"Yeah. I was scared to death."

"You did good. Better than most people would have."

"I couldn't stand to let you get hurt."

"I'll always count my lucky stars you were there."

Coal drove himself home after dropping Dawn Kelly off at that sad, lonely little house, where a big semi-truck tractor was parked out in front. It was Dawn's father, home at last from his latest over-the-road trip.

Nobody back home knew what Coal had been through today, and maybe they wouldn't, at least for a while. He wasn't sure he wanted to tell the story again. Somebody would ask about his cauliflower ear. Of that, he was sure. And he would tell them, simply, "Just another day at the office."

Coal got on his knees inside the front door, to make his greetings with Shadow, Dobe, the twins, and Sissy the proper kind—face to face. When he stood and met the onslaught of embraces from Katie, Cynthia, his mother, and even Virgil, that was when he knew someone had called ahead of his arrival. The story he had meant to hide, they already knew. He smiled.

Thanks, Annie. Always got me covered.

Before Coal could even sit down, the phone rang, and Connie went to the corner of the hallway to answer it. Coal watched her, breathless. If they were calling him back to work, he had a special place in mind to tell them they could go.

"Hello?" Connie was staring off across the room when she answered the phone. She gasped, and her eyes jumped over to Coal. "Oh, my. My. I sure was not expecting . . ." Connie looked at Coal again, then turned and paced down the hall, speaking in a lower voice.

At the farthest reach of the telephone cord, she stopped, said something quiet into the receiver, then dropped the phone to her side, turned, and walked back to Coal. She stared at him for several seconds, and the look on her face made his heart begin to race.

She raised the phone up between them.

"It's Maura."

THE END

Look next for ***BOOK 8: MORGAN ROSE***

Author's note

My only real "note" here is a thank you to retired detective Paul Newbold, for his very kind assistance in the arts of the criminal investigation. For obvious reasons, in a book that is meant first and foremost to entertain, I didn't delve too deeply into everything Paul does. And truthfully, as this series takes place in the 1970's, a lot of techniques used in criminal investigation now did not pertain to anything that was developed then. Also, I am always a little hesitant to give away too much of the criminal investigator's craft, for fear that something I use might help some reader, somewhere, become better at covering his or her tracks. Therefore, I always use "just enough" without tipping the hand of law enforcement and hampering their ability to solve crimes.

When all is said and done, this book, like most of the *Savage Law* series, is basically what I will call a crime drama with heavy undertones of romance, family drama, and good old-fashioned Western, where for the most part the good guys are good, and the bad guys are often painted in varied shades of black, gray, and sometimes even a little white.

I hope you have enjoyed meeting the characters who peopled this book: Dark Badger, Joe Teton, Troy Westerlind and his father, Gunnar, Dale Moore, Dawn Kelly, Cherry Bales, and any I have forgotten. This time around, other than characters who have been introduced in other books in the series, none of those in this book are based on any real person, and as always, the ones who are were used in a completely fictitious manner that may or may not have a thing to do with anything they would or wouldn't do in real life.

About the Author

Kirby Frank Jonas was born in 1965 in Bozeman, Montana. His earliest memories are of living seven miles outside of town in a wide crack in the mountains known as Bear Canyon. At that time it was a remote and lonely place, but a place where a boy with an imagination could grow and nurture his mind, body and soul.

From Montana, the Jonas family moved almost as far across the country as they could go, to Broad Run, Virginia, to a place that, although not as deep in the timbered mountains as Bear Canyon was every bit as remote—Roland Farm. Once again, young Jonas spent his time mostly alone, or with his older brother, if he was not in school. Jonas learned to hike with his mother, fish with his father, and to dodge an unruly horse.

Jonas moved to Shelley, Idaho, in 1971, and from that time forth, with the exception of a few sojourns elsewhere, he became an Idahoan. Jonas attended all twelve years of school in Shelley, graduating in 1983. In the sixth grade, he penned his first novel, *The Tumbleweed,* and in high school he wrote his second, *The Vigilante.* It was also during this time that he first became acquainted with Salmon, Idaho, staying toward the end of the road at the Golden Boulder Orchard and taking his first steps to manhood.

Jonas has lived in six cities in France, in Mesa, Arizona, and explored the United States extensively. He has fought fires for the Bureau of Land Management in five western states and carried a gun on his hip in three different jobs.

In 1987, Jonas met his wife-to-be, Debbie Chatterton, and in 1989 took her to the altar. Over some rough and rocky roads they have traveled, and across some raging rivers that have at times threatened to draw them under, but they survived, and with four beautiful children to show for it: Cheyenne, Jacob, Clay and Matthew.

Jonas has been employed as a Wells Fargo armored guard, a wildland firefighter, a security guard for California Plant Protection and Inter-Con, and police officer. He is now retired after almost twenty-four years of proud employment as a municipal firefighter for the city of Pocatello, Idaho, and works full-time job as a private security officer guarding the federal courthouse under contract with the security company Paragon.

One of Jonas's greatest joys in life is watching his second son, Clay, become a recognized writer of much talent in his own chosen field, that of fantasy and science fiction, with his current series *The Descendants of Light*. There is no greater compliment a son could give to his father than to follow in his footsteps.

Books by Kirby Jonas

Season of the Vigilante, Book One: The Bloody Season
Season of the Vigilante, Book Two: Season's End
The Dansing Star
Legend of the Tumbleweed
Lady Winchester
The Devil's Blood
The Secret of Two Hawks
Knight of the Ribbons
Drygulch to Destiny
Samuel's Angel
The Night of My Hanging (And Other Short Stories)
Russet

***Savage Law* series**

1. *Law of the Lemhi, part 1*
   Law of the Lemhi, part 2
2. *River of Death*
3. *Lockdown for Lockwood*
4. *Like a Man Without a Country*
5. *Thunderbird* (forthcoming)
6. *Savage Alliance* (forthcoming)

***The Badlands* series**

1. *Yaqui Gold* (co-author Clint Walker)
2. *Canyon of the Haunted Shadows* (Kindle only)

***Legends West* series**

1. *Disciples of the Wind* (co-author Jamie Jonas)
2. *Reapers of the Wind* (co-author Jamie Jonas)

***Lehi's Dream* series**

1. *Nephi Was My Friend*
2. *The Faith of a Man*
3. *A Land Called Bountiful*
4. *Shores of Promise* (forthcoming)

Gray Eagle series (e-book format only—forthcoming in print)

1. *The Fledgling*
2. *Flight of the Fledgling*
3. *Wings on the Wind*

Death of an Eagle (e-book and large format softbound)

Books on audio

The Dansing Star, narrated by James Drury, *"The Virginian"*
Death of an Eagle, narrated by James Drury
Legend of the Tumbleweed, narrated by James Drury
Lady Winchester, narrated by James Drury
Yaqui Gold, narrated by Gene Engene
The Secret of Two Hawks, narrated by Kevin Foley
Knight of the Ribbons, narrated by Rusty Nelson
Drygulch to Destiny, narrated by Kirby Jonas

Available through the author at www.kirbyjonas.com

Email the author at: kirby@kirbyjonas.com or write to:

Howling Wolf Publishing
1611 City Creek Road
Pocatello ID 83204

Made in the USA
Monee, IL
02 November 2023

45652354R00298